IS

SHE

ME?

LAUREN GRACE

CRANTHORPE
MILLNER
PUBLISHERS

First published by Cranthorpe Millner Publishers (2025)

ISBN 978-1-80378-279-9 (Paperback)

www.cranthorpemillner.com

Cranthorpe Millner Publishers

Printed and bound by CPI Group (UK) Ltd
Croydon, CR0 4YY

MIX
Paper | Supporting
responsible forestry
FSC® C013604

Listen along with the *Is She Me?* Spotify playlist

Dream – Imagine Dragons

Iris – The Goo Goo Dolls

Falling Slowly – Glen Hansard and Markéta Irglová

Lover, Please Stay – Nothing But Thieves

This Year's Love – David Gray

You Say – Lauren Daigle

All I Want – Kodaline

Stars Are on Your Side – Ross Copperman

Where's My Love – SYML

Amen – John Adams

Ho Hey – The Lumineers

Lose Control – Teddy Swims

Heal – Tom Odell

Stone – Jaymes Young

The Only Exception – Paramore

Deserving better is a choice we make about ourselves,
for ourselves.

1

Escaping Henworth?

I could have blown out the spark creeping up the fuse in my mind. I could have poured the same excuses over it – extinguished it with familiar lies or stamped it out with more well-rehearsed denial – but I didn't.

Not this time.

This time, I packed up the shreds of my pathetic life into my worn holdall.

Now that I wasn't desperately clasping the pieces of myself together, they flew apart like bullets. Piercing and tearing.

Finding that photo in their caravan had felt like waking bolt upright in bed after a nightmare. I couldn't deny what I'd seen.

Her. *Maeve White.*

My fingertip bobbed as I ran it over the photo's creases. They looked like ugly veins sprawled across her angelically plump cheeks. The pigment of the picture had faded, her name on the back barely visible, yet her blonde hair was still a sharp contrast to her dark, round eyes.

I had blonde hair. Well, not now, it had been box dyed – shade 'Mocha 32'. A strict condition of the fracturing façade.

"Is *this* what you wanted?" Mum had yelled at Dad after I'd stormed out of their caravan earlier that day.

It was silly, really; pathetic that a boy had pushed me so far over the edge I thought I could stand-up to them, having barely survived past repercussions of doing so. But something about what had happened with Sam was too much, even for me.

Their caravan had shaken on its foundations, my parents whirling around each other, animated with fury. Her garish blue eyeshadow smeared; his beer belly rippling as she had tossed the tin at him. The worn little tin that had no place; that held a photograph they had no good reason to possess.

A photograph of five-year-old Maeve White, who went missing nineteen years ago.

I lunged for the holdall as it slipped off my bed. I'd crammed in faded t-shirts and unintentionally ripped jeans; worn boots and mismatched underwear. What do you pack when you're running away from your entire life? *Is it even running away when you're an adult?*

I hauled it back onto my bed, glancing out of the green-tinged plastic window over the muddy site. No one was coming; no one had noticed yet.

I pushed my feet into my trainers, my toes curling at the dampness lingering from that morning. Even a warm August could be cold and dank living in a mouldy caravan. I ran my fingertip over the photograph again before tucking it into the bag's side pocket and pulling the zip closed, the metallic buzz loud in my ears. It was getting dark outside, the light creeping over the tips of the trees surrounding Henworth.

My caravan was at the edge of park, the obvious outcast – apt that their ostracism of me had become my advantage. I would still have to make it to the metal gate separating the imposing wire fences, then up the gravel path before anyone saw me. Before anyone saw what I'd become, saw what had snapped inside of me. I could taste it, the adrenaline. I could feel the heat in my bones. I could see the blue Ford I'd swiped the key for.

I hitched my bag on my shoulder, grabbing my black waterproof. My body pulsed when my hand hesitated on the flimsy door handle. It wasn't just a door, it was destruction. Destruction of my entire life. There would be no going back.

Last week, I'd been with Sam. We'd laughed and kissed and stayed up watching some stupid old film on Channel 5. He was going to help me get out; he was just biding his time. Two years we'd been together, near enough. It was the only relationship I'd dared to extend past mutually beneficial sex. Sam was harmless and they knew it, so they

2

had allowed it. I was a moth to a flame, fixated on the light that his little bit of love gave me in the darkness. We'd kept it low-key. I only stayed round his two or three times a month, and never when I was needed.

It was my fault, what had happened. I knew it was. I'd mentioned, stupidly, that one of the new cousins could take my van when I moved out.

My knuckles went white as my grip on the door handle tightened, but my wrist wouldn't turn. I rolled my shoulders and tipped my head from one side to the other, attempting to stir up more anger. The storm had been brewing for a while now; I'd felt it growing inside of me, churning. I hadn't stopped to think as I'd quietly crept back into their caravan after my parents' fight was over, looking for the tin; taking the car key and the photograph.

After a quick internet search, I'd found the missing persons appeal for Maeve, and a home address for her parents. They were still searching. Nineteen years later and this perfect family, who looked like they had jumped straight out of a colourful Christmas TV advert, were still looking for their daughter.

I knew Henworth residents lived by their own rules – I'd seen darkness in all of them.

But would they really take a child?

Sam had been the one thing I'd asked for, for myself. Losing him, having him taken, then finding the photograph... it was like someone had knocked off my rose-tinted glasses. I couldn't do it anymore, I wouldn't. Spent was the mild mannered, submissive Chantelle. The Chantelle who had studied so she could forge her parents dodgy accounts; who had cared for the horses and tutored the kids whose parents were too drunk; who had kept those police officers happy in the hopes her parents would thank her, appreciate her, *see her*? I refused to be that Chantelle anymore.

As my hand finally pulled down the door handle, the lock clicked, reverberating through the plastic walls. I turned around one last time, taking in the worn red carpet, the unmade bed, the decaying kitchen.

No one remembers being five, do they?

The thought was intrusive and intimidating; it felt too big, especially for that moment. So, I pushed it out and packed it neatly away for later. Anyone with my upbringing would dream of being the child of those perfect people; of growing up in that beautiful house; of having a whole website dedicated to finding her and bringing her home.

Stop.

I would reach out to Maeve's parents, tell them what I'd found, do the right thing, whatever the cost. They deserved closure. This wasn't about me.

I flung open the door.

Panting to catch my breath after running to the car, I fell into the worn seat and twisted the key in the ignition. Everything was going too fast, yet the world around me seemed to slow, as if time itself was aiding me. My eyes focused on the fuel gauge, not blinking, as the needle moved painfully slowly.

I exhaled. It was past the first mark, that was enough to get me out.

My foot pressed down forcefully on the accelerator, sending the car lurching forwards, gravel spitting behind me. I was doing it. I was really doing it. The gate was open. The road was right there.

I can do this.

My heart couldn't take any more beatings, my soul any more weight after being forced to look the other way, time and again. I wasn't cut out for this life. I couldn't let things go or turn a blind eye anymore. All I could see in my mind was little Maeve clutching that teddy.

I heard yelling as I neared the gate, but Marcus was too late. I swerved violently onto the road, clinging to the steering wheel like my life depended on it. Because, for the first time, it felt worth the risk.

2

Grudging chivalry

My little blue saviour eventually stuttered to a halt down a narrow country road, just past a bend. The fuel had drained from the car like my rage, slowly depleting as we drove until we were both cold and empty. I'd been aiming for the layby, realising I was in a precarious position as the last fume of petrol evaporated and the engine cut-out. I pulled up the handbrake, taking a second to stretch my fingers from the position they'd become fixed in. I'd have to push the car the last few meters.

The air was soggy as I walked around the back.

"Thanks for trying," I whispered to the corroded boot as I bent my knees and pressed my palms down.

The road was surrounded by ominous-looking woodland. I wasn't sure which option would be *less* like a scene from a horror film: girl walks alone through darkening woods, or girl sleeps in rusty car at the side of the road. I wasn't scared of the dark, but one thing I'd never been was on my own. I'd always had people waiting for me to do something, or a horse to speak to. Mum always said I was weak; I wasn't strong or smart. She told me I needed them, to keep me safe. Looking around, maybe she was right?

Gritting my teeth, I pushed again. My thighs shook as my wrists pinched, but I kept going, the wheels slowly edging forwards.

Until they hit a patch of mud.

The car careered off to the side, pulling away from me, heading towards the trees. I ran around to slam my hands on the front, pain surging through my tired joints.

"No, no, no!"

The mud squelched around my trainers as I fought to find grip, the bonnet slowing just in time to avoid crashing into a giant oak tree. I locked my elbows and winced, the sound of something rustling in the greenery ahead prompting me to spin around. My eyes scanned the dense branches and blanket of weeds. They would be looking for me, and they would be pissed.

I need to move.

Lifting my hands from the cold metal bonnet, I zipped my jacket up to my neck.

"You can do this," I told myself, shaking my fingers out.

I walked back around the car and started pushing again, this time against the right-hand taillight. My wrists bent backwards, my toes dug harder into the ground, soaking my socks, and my legs throbbed as I pushed through the drizzle. It wasn't enough though, and as the wind whipped through the trees, I could have sworn they were laughing at me.

"I'm doing this!" I shouted back at them.

When the wheel gave an inch, the force threw me to the ground, the splat so blatant I flinched as my hands flew down to break my fall, skidding away from me instantly. On my hands and knees, I stared down at the mud; an exhausted, lost, miserable pile of person in the earth I'd freshly churned. I couldn't help but fold – emotionally and physically – turning to sit on my backside and pulling my knees into my chest. Thumping my head back against the bumper, I raked my hands through my hair, first frustrated, then devastated.

A shrill screech of tyres filled the air as headlights tore around the corner and a car veered across the road, the tunnel of light incising the darkness. I buried my face in the crease of my elbow, instinctually hugging my knees tighter. A door slammed before I could think; before I could run.

The car had stopped.

Was this them? Was it over already? I glanced at the muddy tracks on the road. *What was I thinking?* A sinking feeling of acceptance fell like lead into my stomach as I turned and clambered to my feet, ready to face my fate.

But then I felt it again – that fresh splinter of hurt; another wave of anger within my reach.

"What the bloody hell are you doing?" came a deep, well-spoken voice. "Are you trying to get yourself killed?"

Rage was written across his strikingly handsome face, dark eyebrows furrowed behind black-framed glasses; neatly swept brown hair threatening to muss. This was a businessman in a smart navy suit – *not their usual type* – but I was beyond second guessing. He stopped a few steps before me, between the passenger door and the darkening treeline.

"Sorry, I—"

"*You* might have a death wish, but what about other people?" he shouted, fresh creases appearing in his otherwise spotless appearance. "My family are coming through here and you're just sat in the road! Are you stupid?"

"I—"

"What are you even doing out here?"

Shame was a painfully familiar emotion, but it was also the ignition I needed. I felt a renewed pounding of my heart; a surge of rage.

My voice came deep from my gut as I shouted back at him. "If you would let me finish, I'd tell you, or are you just planning to yell some more?"

I stepped towards the disgruntled stranger. He was taller, sure; stronger no doubt if it came to it, but the adrenaline in my blood was convincing me it didn't matter. Or maybe I just didn't care anymore.

He pointed aggressively. "You were sat in the road!"

"I fell!" I spat. "Trying to move the car *out* of the road so that no angry arseholes would pull over and yell at me!" My voice sounded strong, yet I couldn't deny the flinch of fear at what might follow.

We stood for a second in silence as rain collected on his glasses, the brown eyes behind them staring at me, meeting the challenge in mine.

"Hold this," he remarked with disdain, extending it to me.

I flinched as his movement broke our stand-off. "Why?"

"So I can push this car out of the road before you cause an

accident."

"I don't need your help," I snapped, still riding on my rage trip.

I could've sworn he smirked.

"You don't need my help?"

He didn't retract his arm, insinuating I would be the one backing down. Not today. Not anymore. It was a small rebellion, but it meant something. If I could stand up to him, maybe I could stand up to them.

I shook my head and folded my arms, pressing dampness into my chest. "No, thank you. Not from you."

"From who, then? Because as far as I can see, you've already nearly hit the tree, and soon it'll be pitch black. You may have a death wish, but I have a meeting to get to."

I glanced over his shoulder, noticing his polished, silver Audi parked in the layby ahead. "So get back in your fancy car and go."

He looked back at the car, considering it, before fixing me with a disapproving glare. "What the hell is your problem?"

I stepped forwards, looking up at him. "Clearly, many things. For one, I'm sick of being yelled at, so either you calm down and help me, I thank you, and you go to your meeting. Or, you piss off."

"Great," he replied quickly.

"Super."

He didn't look away though. He just stared at me, unmoving. The mist from his breath drifted over my head.

After a few more slow seconds, during which my brain quickly kicked into overdrive, he lurched forwards, grabbed the door handle and dropped his jacket onto the Ford's back seat. Rolling up his sleeves, he walked straight past me, expensive shoes squelching in the mud as he lined himself up at the rear of the car.

I took a step towards him, preparing myself to push again. "Thank you."

"What're you doing?" He gestured to the car. "Get in there and steer."

"What? Why don't you steer, save your suit?" I meant it genuinely –I was already filthy – but it came out snarky and I was too fed up to correct it. This whole exchange needed to be over with.

He pointed to the open door. "Get in the front, or I'll push this tin can into the goddamn trees."

Nope, snarky it is then.

I relented, muttering 'arsehole' loudly under my breath.

Infuriatingly, as soon as my legs were in, the car lurched forwards as if it weighed nothing. It slid as I fought to steer it towards the layby and finally off the road. When I heard him shout, I pulled back on the handbrake, trying to hide my relief. The back door clicked open and he retrieved his jacket, before slamming it shut, shaking the whole car. I swung my legs out to face him, noticing the new splattering of mud up his trousers.

"Thanks," I mumbled.

He nodded brusquely. "You've called it in, at least?" he asked, staring at his own muddy hands as if he was unsure what to do with them.

"Of course," I lied, wondering if I had a cloth in the car or something to help him clean up. He was looking increasingly uncomfortable.

Definitely not a country boy.

He glanced at his watch and rolled his eyes. "I'll wait," he insisted, the notion clearly as unpleasant to him as it was to me.

"Not necessary," I blurted out. "My boyfriend's on his way." *Why did I say that?*

He scowled. "I can't just leave you here in the dark."

"I'm fine, really."

"You were sat in the road."

"I fell." I felt silly sitting in the seat looking up at him, but he was stood too close; I didn't want to risk any contact by standing.

He looked back down at his watch. "How long will he be?"

"Five minutes."

He glared down at the mud on his arms once more, then at the road, looking left and right. "Fine, just stay in the car and lock the door; that corner is treacherous. If he doesn't get here soon, there's a garage in town you can call."

"I got it," I asserted, digging my nails into the thin material of the car seat.

He paused, taking a breath, before evidently deciding against whatever he was about to say. He stepped away and I stood, watching his bright headlights flash as he pulled the key from his pocket.

"Thank you," I called as he paced off, suddenly not wanting him to leave.

Wanting to stand and argue with him a little longer.

He turned to look back, standing by his door, light reflecting off the rain between us as if the very air was electric. My clothes felt heavy; strands of wet hair blew across my face.

Nodding, the stranger lowered himself into the car, and before I could shout after him, he drove off into the night.

3

Powerful kindness

Nature was loud as I waited for my imaginary boyfriend. A deer bolted across the road, stopping to give me a curious look before bounding off, barely visible in the drizzle. The dark grew thicker, the noise of the rain on the windscreen my music, its gentle pitter patter beginning to match my shivers as the chill of evening set in. I pictured Sam pulling up in his Corsa, coming to whisk me away to his warm house and make me beans on toast – smug, like he was a Michelin Star chef. I wondered if he would've leant me his coat. I imagined the feel of the car heaters blazing. It was pathetic, but it was all I had.

After an hour, I realised the difficult truth; I couldn't sleep here. The car would be the first thing they'd look for. It had felt good standing up to that man; like fighting for myself, even if I felt sort of guilty about it. I leant over, pulling open the glove box to find a map. The worn paper crinkled under my fingers as I shoved it into my holdall. The car battery had died about twenty minutes ago – my only option was to walk. The direction would have to just be 'away' for now, until I could find a road sign.

Hoping there might be a torch or something more useful than everything I'd packed, I walked out and around to the boot.

Bright yellow lights glowed once more – an exposing spotlight – as another car came humming around the bend. I winced at the glare, blinking away the white circles. When I lowered my arm, I saw it. A grey VW pulled up in front of the old Ford.

I swallowed, a fresh wave of fear rushing through my bloodstream. At least the adrenaline might stop me from freezing to death. My damp clothes were heavy and I could feel the cold tightening its grip on me.

"Are you okay?"

Shit. Shit. Shit.

"Yes, thank you," I replied, trying to sound confident as pure panic took hold. Something about the voice's soft tone felt more threatening than the yelling man.

A woman appeared, her features mostly invisible in the night, but I could make out a long camel coat as she pulled it more tightly around herself.

"Oh... sorry, I thought you might be lost. Are you local? Can I help you with directions?" she asked, staring right at me, thick hair blowing in the wind.

I pulled the empty boot shut as the breeze whistled through the nearby trees. I could sense she saw right through my cheery façade. "Um, I'm on my way to Hampshire, do you know where the station is, please?"

She tilted her head, as if considering her answer. *Should I tell her the truth?* Would she believe me? The last hour had been an uncomfortable reality check, and even though every cell in my brain was telling me that trusting her was a bad idea, I couldn't help the seed of hope that took root. I had no phone or light to see the map. Who knew how many people had been sent after me this time. This woman... she was only a few years older than me. Surely she was safe?

The silence dragged before she tentatively spoke. "The station is too far to walk, maybe we could give you a lift?"

I looked back towards the blue Ford, covered in mud and lifeless, as if it were screaming its own fate. Her unquestioning kindness stung. I felt my throat dry – why would she help me?

"I couldn't ask you to do that, but thank you. If you could just point me in the right direction—"

"I insist," she interrupted, remaining a respectful distance. "You look like you've had quite the day."

"They're, um, picking it up tomorrow. I just need to find a train, or a bus or something."

Her shoulders hunched. "I can't leave you here on your own. I'd never forgive myself."

There was a commotion from the open door behind her.

"Mum, what are you doing? Can I get out?"

My heart sank. "I couldn't bother you like that, but thank you." I hooked my bag back over my shoulder.

"Come on," the woman said, her tone tempting, inviting. "I'll feel terrible if I drive away and leave you here walking all evening. Please? You can't walk through the woods alone. Is there someone I can call for you? I can wait."

I shook my head, trying not to hear the voice in my head saying, *nobody, I'm totally alone.*

I noticed her round eyes as she tentatively stepped closer, kind and curious. Then I noticed the darkness of the surrounding woodland, the expanse of black, of rustling trees. A thousand thoughts wrestled each other in my mind as she looked at me, willing me to step towards the comfort.

I glanced once more down the road; not even the bend of the tarmac was visible without the beam of a headlight.

It's just to the station; just a lift.

Low on options and resistance, I allowed myself the small mercy of taking the chance, desperately hoping I wouldn't regret it.

In the back of the car were a boy and a girl of primary school age, still wearing red school uniforms. The interior was warm and smelt like cookies, with wipes and trinkets tucked into every pocket.

"We're going to stay in our cottage," the boy said.

"What's wrong with your car?" the girl asked.

"Kids, we're just giving her a lift to the station and I'm sure she doesn't want to answer a hundred questions before we get there." She shot me an apologetic glance. I noticed her neat, small hands and short, French tipped nails as they slid over the steering wheel.

"It's okay. My car has a broken battery," I explained as we pulled away. Guilt for abandoning the Ford struck me, amongst a cascade of other emotions. The simple joy of the children's questions was a welcome distraction. "Lucky you, going on holiday. What are your names?"

"I'm Sophie and this is Isac. I am seven and Isac is ten. Uncle Ben is coming tomorrow. I made him promise on my birthday last week. Where do you live? Why is your makeup so messy?"

"Sophie!" the woman exclaimed.

"It's alright," I assured her, laughing softly. Glancing over, I admired the glints of well-placed silver jewellery. No wedding ring. "Sorry, what was your name?"

"Lucy," she answered, with a gentle smile. "There are some wipes in the side of the door if you'd like one. Not that I'm agreeing, you know, each to their own."

I nodded and gratefully reached for a packet. "Thank you. I'm Chantelle, Elle, for short."

Lucy drove on for about fifteen minutes as I chatted with the kids in an attempt to keep my mind busy. Seeing the station sign, I tensed, realising I'd let my body relax into the soft seat. For some reason, the sight of my destination made my stomach twist. I couldn't remember the last time I'd felt such simple warmth and kindness.

When the VW pulled up into the tiny, empty car park, Lucy looked at me as she had in the lay-by, like she was thinking deeply.

She opened her mouth and the words fell out. "You could stay with us, for the night. The cottage is split into two, we have room. It doesn't look like the trains are even running and your clothes are damp. It makes more sense to try tomorrow, with a good night's rest. I mean, if this isn't just sounding horribly rude and imposing."

The confusion must have been written all over my face because she kept babbling.

"It's two sublets, so completely separate. You can have a warm shower and get some rest. Ben isn't coming back until tomorrow afternoon. I can drive you back here in the morning."

"I... that's... Lucy, that's such a kind offer, really. Like, you don't know how kind. But I can't. It'd be really unfair of me—"

"I'm offering, you're not asking. In fact, I'm insisting – so no, it wouldn't be unfair. Just one night, honestly, we'll be back here tomorrow morning, first thing."

I swallowed, only just realising how narrow my throat had become. "Why... why would you offer that?"

"Stay, Elle!" Sophie chanted. "Please!"

Lucy pressed her lip between her knuckle and thumb, pausing before carefully replying. "I'm a nurse. I... I know the signs of someone who might be... getting away from a difficult situation."

My gaze flew down to my knees as I pulled my sleeves over my hands, tugging on the coat material. The shame ached. It was suffocating.

I reached for the door handle.

Lucy gently rested her hand on my damp knee.

"I'm sorry. You don't need to tell me, I just... let me help. One night. Please."

I knew I had to decline.

But the wrong words came out.

We pulled up to a beautiful, secluded country cottage with roses clinging to the bricks, grey against the evening sky. I could smell the sweet blooms in the wrap-around garden as the kids poured out of the car. Sophie grabbed my hand, dragging me to the white wooden door.

"This is our cottage. It's called Rose Cottage after our gran. She planted the roses. Grandad used to take Mum fishing in the river at the end of the garden when she was little. Once they found a crayfish, which is like a lobster, but me and Isac have never seen one."

I could see her better in the light emanating from the house. She had curly hair, like her mum, tumbling out of a loose ponytail, pink-framed glasses sitting on a dainty nose; big, shiny eyes full of excitement.

"Mum, make sure you order enough pizza," yelled Isac. "I want pineapple still."

"I hate pineapple on pizza!" Sophie whined.

"It's not all about you, Sophie!" he bit back.

Isac had darker hair than his sister. His red jumper was smeared with what looked like glue, his eyes not as bright.

"What about broccoli pizza, that's the best, isn't it?" I teased. "You grate carrots for the sauce and, instead of cheese, you sprinkle on tuna, and then, of course, add the brussels sprouts."

They both giggled, making gagging noises and sticking out their tongues.

"Alright, go unpack your bags. I'll order lots of pizza," Lucy assured them, smiling.

Something about her was like melted butter on warm toast – easy, comfortable, harmless.

I squeezed her hand as we crossed the threshold. "Thank you. I'll be no trouble, I swear; this is so incredibly kind. I'll be gone as soon as I get up. I can walk to the station."

"Don't be silly. I'll drive you, it's fine. If you head around that little path to the right there's a door key under the third pot. You can sleep in there, have the place to yourself. There's an adjoining door that's locked, but you can knock if you need anything. Ben, my brother, stayed last night, but he's away at a conference. There are fresh sheets and towels in the wardrobe. If you don't mind, though," she winked, "we'll stick with standard pizzas tonight."

I laughed in response, holding tight to my duffle bag as I made my way around to the other entrance.

It wasn't until I was alone in the quaint, characterful cottage by the main house that I felt an unwelcome rush of reality. The feeling forced its way through my body, taking hold and turning my muscles to steel.

"One night," I chanted to a fox-shaped draught excluder. "One night, what's the harm? It was cold and dark, and even the deer gave me side-eye." I raised my eyes to the vaulted ceiling. "Oh god."

Shaking myself out of my frozen panic, I looked around the space. The cottage was filled with sturdy wooden furniture; the main room an open area with chunky stone floors and a metal staircase leading to a mezzanine with a big, inviting bed. Removing my sodden trainers and socks, I plodded up, wincing at the loud clang of metal, until I reached the carpet at the top. The dense pile felt luxurious against my aching feet.

There was a lingering scent of an expensive aftershave, and what I assumed must be Ben's black suitcase open by the wardrobe. I dropped my bag and leant over the wooden banister, looking down onto the kitchen. On the wall was a large canvas print of a pebbled beach, the moonlight through the window mottled by rose branches.

I walked through the bedroom tentatively. There was a small dresser with a mirror, where I caught a glance of my sorry, exhausted state. I rubbed at the black smudges around my eyes, feeling the brittle shell of the mud encasing my hair as I tucked it back behind my ears. I hated bruises. They were a cruel reminder of pain that you had to wear for days, sometimes weeks.

I swiftly turned towards the shower, before the reality of the choices I'd made could sink in any further.

The adjoining, main cottage was bigger, but still homely. Sophie proudly showed me a collection of beach stones she had painted whilst we all ate around the solid oak table. The siblings couldn't be more different from one another. Sophie was pretty, spirited, but sensitive, and Isac wasn't a typical boisterous boy; he was quiet and studious, and asked great questions.

"Why aren't you in your house?" Sophie asked, delaying brushing her teeth.

"I..." Voices shouted crude responses in my mind. "I decided to move away. I'm looking for a new place to live, but I need to speak to some people in Hampshire first, so I'm going to visit them." The words tasted bitter, stinging my tongue in protest.

"Do you have a dog?"

"Um, I've had dogs before. I was always closest to the horses, though."

"Woah! You have *horses*? How many? Can you ride? Do you jump?" she exclaimed, twitching in her seat.

I laughed, folding the pizza boxes shut as I helped Lucy to clear up. "I can jump and ride, but my favourite part was caring for them, actually. The more you look after your horse, the more you bond as a team. I used to love hacking in the morning with Ebony; he was a gorgeous black stallion with a white smudge on the end of his nose." I felt awful for leaving the animals, abandoning them in that place. "Do you ride?" I asked, trying to distract myself.

"Not yet, but Ben's bought me a lesson. I want to go down to the local stables. The lesson lady told me sometimes you can scoop the poo and they let you ride, but I was too little. Which was rubbish, because it's only poo, and anyone could have done it," Sophie rattled on, licking tomato sauce from her fingers.

"Well, maybe one day I can help you learn? To repay you all for letting me have a sleepover." I smiled at Lucy.

"Yes please, oh, please! Lisa, in my class, told everyone that the stable said I was too rubbish. Mum said she was jealous, but—"

"Come on, Sophie," Lucy urged, gathering the plates and heading for the dishwasher. "I'm sure Elle doesn't want to hear about all of that. Maybe we can take her up on her offer once she's settled."

"Will you read us a story, Elle?" Sophie asked with a toothy grin.

"We don't have books here, dummy," Isac cut in. "Unless you want her to read you Gran's cookbook and dream about vegetables."

I bit my lip, stifling a smile. He was a boy of few words, but when he offered them, his comebacks were always quick-witted.

"Well..." I hesitated. "I don't mind making one up, as long as it's okay with your mum?"

Lucy raised an eyebrow. "You don't have to do that."

"I don't mind, really, as long as you don't?"

She smiled at me and waved her hands towards the stairs in approval.

Once the kids were asleep, I found Lucy holding two glasses of wine, sitting in one of the comfy-looking tweed armchairs. She'd changed into an oversized cream turtleneck and tartan pyjama bottoms. There was a small heater wafting dry warmth and an orange glow through the homely room. A Persian rug broke up the cool stone floor, offering comfort to my aching feet.

"I didn't know whether you drank," Lucy commented, looking tired all of a sudden, "but then I figured it was an excuse for me to have two if you didn't. Win win."

"Thanks," I replied, taking the glass from her hand and curling up on the red two-seater. I had a complicated relationship with alcohol, but it had been a complicated kind of day. "Sorry to disappoint."

She smiled, raising her drink.

The red wine felt soothing as it lined my throat.

Lucy swirled her glass. "So, what happened that left you stranded?"

Something about her easy tone made me want to tell her everything. I knew I couldn't, though; I hadn't even wholly acknowledged it myself.

"A few different things, I guess. I'm travelling to Hampshire to find some people. The car ran out of fuel on the way; I should've stopped but I was just... in a rush." My jaw tightened.

She raised an eyebrow. "And your family couldn't come and get you?"

"Well, it's not like that. I don't—"

She looked at me as I hesitated, willing me to continue.

I took a breath. "It's a long story. My parents weren't supportive of me leaving."

"You ran away?"

"I suppose."

"I'm sure they'll be worried, whatever it was you fought about. If you need to borrow a phone or something, just let me know."

If only.

"Thank you, but I need to do this on my own."

"Why?" she asked boldly.

I flinched, but her gaze didn't falter.

"It was getting hard to stay on the site, lots of different problems over the years. Lots of fights."

"The 'site'?"

"Yeah, Henworth. It's a big caravan park."

"So, you just drove into the night on your own?"

She looked into my eyes again with that searching gaze, drawing mine up. I winced. It did sound pretty stupid.

"None of it was ideal. I don't want to burden you with it, but I think they'll be looking for me, so I need to get straight out of here tomorrow."

"Surely your parents realise you're, what, in your early twenties? What is it, some sort of cult?" she joked, swinging one leg over the top of the other and relaxing back.

I rolled my shoulders awkwardly.

Her eyes widened. "Oh shit. Is it a cult?"

"No... no, it's not like that. They're an old-school community. They live by their own rules, on their own land." I'd said too much; the words hung in the air.

"Where?"

"About an hour away, towards Bristol."

There was a pause, and I was unsure what she might ask next. Unsure whether I should answer.

Taking another sip, she looped a curl around her finger. "What made you leave so suddenly?"

I bit my tongue hard, feeling the sharpness of my teeth in the soft muscle. The pain was a circuit break from the tempting spiral, from opening the doors to the storm; the storm of pain I was fighting so hard to deny. I couldn't fall apart here; I couldn't open that door fully. What if it wouldn't shut? What if I cried and cried and couldn't stop?

"Sorry to be so blunt," Lucy said, interrupting my mental frenzy. "I don't mean to pry."

She swept the hair from her face with her fingers. Almost immediately, two strands flopped back across her rosy cheeks. I still couldn't find any words.

"I needed the break, coming here," she continued, glancing around the room. "I got divorced from the kids' father, Steven, four years ago, and his shiny new family are a fucking nightmare. I left him because he didn't want to take any responsibility for anything: for the marriage, the kids, the house, his temper. Then he goes and finds a family of teenagers!"

I kept quiet, happy to listen and not talk myself into any more of a hole. Maybe this is why we were drawn to each other? Maybe we both needed an evening where we could talk to a stranger? This was certainly healthier than shouting at trees. After all, I'd be on a train tomorrow, what did it matter?

"That sounds... man-like," I offered, circling my finger around the rim of my glass.

"I love my kids, but it's been an adjustment doing it all on my own. My colleagues at the hospital pushed and pushed me to leave him, but when I did, they didn't want to flex-up shifts. They moan every time I finish earlier than them on a Thursday to do the school run." She grimaced. "Isac, he's just not been himself lately. He was sad, sure, then he seemed better. But it's like this new family Steven has... it's just made him close himself off. I used to think I was a good mum – well, an okay mum – but now I just can't seem to connect with him at all."

We both processed the words, sipping wine.

I adjusted on the sofa; the cushions were worn and bouncy, so I tucked both my legs up, pulling at my jeans. "You were brave to get a divorce, your family is beautiful. Isac is bright, I can tell." I pushed my damp hair behind my ear. "Not many people would've stopped their car."

"I shouldn't have, let's be real! I mean, if I was on my own, maybe, but not with the kids. You could've been a serial killer – I mean, no one would have had sympathy for me in *that* Netflix documentary."

"I can go, I can get a taxi or something."

"No, no, you're here now, and I've enjoyed your company. It's quite nice talking to a stranger about all this. It feels easier."

I felt myself smile and lifted my glass to her. "To strangers."

She tilted hers back.

"This place is stunning, even in the dark," I murmured, looking around the room, noticing even more details: photo albums, cross stitched cushions, chipped skirting boards. "Do your parents ever come here with the kids?"

"They died," she answered quickly. "When me and Ben were young."

My eyes darted to hers. "I'm so sorry."

"It's alright, it was a long time ago. I wish they'd met the children... they would've hated Steve though. My mum could always see through people."

"Some people are good at putting on a show."

The words felt a bit harsh as they came out, aimed too much at my own situation. My resentment had built up over the years I'd spent in that pokey caravan, following my parents' rules only to end up bruised and alone, time after time. It always felt like I was the one who lost something, like my happiness was always expendable, but then they would draw me back in, convince me I was better off with them. I'd always hated myself for it.

"Totally. I loved Steve too easily. He was handsome, fun, but he was good at making promises and charming people, and not much else. Ben's always been there for me, but when Steve wanted to be my everything, it was too tempting. I think I was always conscious my family was small, so I jumped at the chance of growing it. Which is ridiculous, because now I feel more alone than ever." Lucy reached for the bottle of wine on the coffee table, pouring us both another glass. She didn't look up.

"It's not ridiculous. You seem like you have it together despite him."

She smiled ingenuously at me, placing the bottle back down. "Thanks. I guess I thought he would fight me on it; it was like an extra stab in the gut when he seemed pleased. He was so weak that he needed to drive me to it, rather than pluck up the courage himself."

I took a deep breath and tucked my legs in tighter. "Sounds like you're better off without him, however hard it is."

I hoped they were wrong, Frank and Ruby. All of them. I hoped I was better without them.

"I miss him sometimes, despite everything. It makes me so angry."

"I'm sure that's how most people would feel in your situation."

She narrowed her eyes at me. "I just wish I could hate him."

"I get that. I miss Sam, and I really shouldn't."

"Sam?"

I swallowed. I couldn't tell her.

Except... I wanted to.

I stared at my glass, checking how much I'd had to drink – not enough to blame for the words collecting on my tongue.

"We were together, but he left me. Then I found out my dad had paid him to leave."

Lucy swept her hair back again, trying to politely hide her confusion. "Why?"

I sighed and took another sip, before attempting to carefully colour the picture just enough to relieve the weight on my chest, but not so much as to be... well... too much.

"We were talking about moving out. I made a comment about it. They didn't want change; they never liked me going off the site for a reason that didn't suit them. A few other things happened and I just snapped. I know it was reckless. That this" – I gestured around the room – "is reckless, but I had to get out. I knew they were controlling; I tolerated it because they were my parents. I never thought they would do something like that – it felt so extreme, what happened with Sam. I realised I needed space to think. " I looked up. "You must think that all sounds so stupid."

"No, it sounds like a good reason to leave. They have no right to control your life like that. Did you speak to them about how you feel, before you left?"

"There isn't any talking to them. It rarely ends well. If they don't like something, they deal with it their way. I just can't believe Sam took their money."

"Men are such idiots. I'm sorry, Elle, that sounds awful." She smiled comfortingly at me before a frown creased her forehead. "Haven't they been calling you? Aren't they worried?"

I thought about it for a second. *They won't be worried, they'll be mad. Really, really mad.* "We didn't really have a relationship like that, and I left my phone, on purpose."

I pressed my lips shut, painfully aware that this was the most candid conversation I'd had with anyone in years; even filled with so many half-truths. Telling Lucy part of the story... it felt liberating, especially as she was yet to jump from her seat and chase me out of the door.

"Well, I hope you find what you're looking for."

The rest of the evening passed far more easily than it should have. Lucy continued talking about Steven, and her kids, and I happily listened. It was as if we both knew we could get a certain amount out before we had to swap emotional wounds, taking it in turns to talk. When the wine bottle was empty, we hugged, and somehow, she felt like a friend. It was as jarring as it was soothing – how had this stranger made me feel comfort, made me feel heard?

Realising how it actually felt to be listened to and not demeaned, or belittled, made my chest ache.

My life suddenly seemed utterly hopeless.

4

Misplaced magnetism

I slept so deeply I dreamt of Maeve. She was strolling through a crowded supermarket aisle. People pushed past her as she stared at all the colourful tins and shiny bottles.

I replayed the details in my mind as I tucked my hairbrush into my holdall, checking that the worn little photo was still safely in the side pocket. Sliding open the thick taupe curtains, the sunlight instantly warmed the room. Pink roses lining thick, spiky branches interrupted the shaft of yellow light. I'd left the covers on the bed last night – the subtle smell of aftershave had been strangely comforting – so I stripped them off, wondering what Ben was like as I pulled on new ones. Lucy was so warm and kind, and the kids had been so excited to see him.

When I was content that I'd left the place tidy, I carried my bag out to find Lucy waiting on the patio table with a cup of tea. Conversation was again too easy as we watched the kids kick a ball around, but putting down my empty mug, I knew we needed to make a move. The picturesque garden and rolling hills beyond would be a perfectly peaceful memory for me to treasure. I scanned the scenery carefully, taking in the thick flowerbeds filled with pinks and purples, the distant sound of a stream, and the sweet-smelling lilac decorated with butterflies. I wanted to remember this.

A few minutes later, Lucy was pulling on her camel jacket.

"Sophie!" she called, for the second time.

Isac appeared in the doorway. "She's hiding again," he announced, unamused.

Lucy clapped, reaching for her keys. "Well go find her in the trunk then, Isac, come on."

"Why do I have to go?" He tilted his head back and dragged out the words.

"Come on, don't start. The sooner we go, the sooner we can get to the beach later."

He groaned, turning to plod loudly back up the stairs. "Sophie, I know you're in the trunk."

Lucy rolled her eyes, tucking two of the chairs back under the table.

"How can I thank you for this?" I hoped the words carried the gravity of emotion I felt as I said them.

For all the years I had considered a fresh start, I couldn't have imagined such luck. It was like the fast-charge I'd needed to brave the next steps. There *were* good people out there. I might just be okay after all. *They* might have been wrong.

"Easy. You bring the wine next time."

I grinned; she wanted to see me again. "I can bring the wine."

Lucy grabbed a piece of pink paper from a notepad and scribbled her number on it with one of Sophie's fluffy pens.

"Text me," she said, handing it to me.

We were interrupted by Isac's annoyed shout. "She's not up here!"

Lucy blew a sigh through her lips. "Alright, alright, I'm coming." She walked towards the stairs, stopping to look back. "Can you go check the bedroom while I go upstairs and look in the trunk?"

I nodded, placing the folded paper carefully into the pocket of my jeans.

I couldn't find Sophie under the bed in the downstairs bedroom, or in the wardrobe, but as I peered into the bathroom, I heard a noise come from the kitchen. I tip-toed back across the stone floor of the hall, stopping just outside the door to the lounge. I could see the sofa and chairs, but not all the way round to the kitchen. I heard the lid of what I assumed was the cookie tin pop open, so I quieted my breath. I considered delaying for a second, letting Sophie have the victory of stashing her cookies for later, but Isac was shouting upstairs. When I heard the tin slide across the worktop, I made my move. I leant my weight back, bent my legs and sprung through the doorway.

"Put the biscuits down!"

I blinked, slowly straightening my legs from where I'd landed.

It wasn't Sophie.

It wasn't Sophie I'd just shouted at, springing through the door like some ridiculous pantomime kangaroo.

It was a man.

That man.

I steadied myself as I stared at him.

He slowly lowered the biscuit from his lips, licking a stray crumb. I saw the reality dawn on him as his face grew tense, his brow furrowing.

"*You.*"

His dark eyes, framed by his black glasses, met mine, his tousled hair looking almost too soft compared to his icy demeanour and harsh jawline. I wondered if I could bolt for the patio doors. Standing on opposite sides of the room, neither of us spoke for a few slow seconds as the silent hostility built.

"Sorry, I—" I stammered as he glared at me, his mouth twitching against his clean-shaven cheeks.

I took a step back, sensing footsteps behind me.

"Now I feel awful. She was in the airing cupboard with a towel over her head. She always..." Lucy stopped as she saw the man. "Ben?" She walked past me. "I thought you weren't coming until later?"

He was her brother? That rude, obnoxious man was *her* brother? How?

Oh god... I just yelled at him. Again.

He didn't look at Lucy. He just kept staring at me, glaring at me. It sent heat straight to my cheeks. I searched myself for that sassy girl he'd met yesterday, but of course, she was gone. Apparently, dry clothes and good sleep made me soft. God, why was I so weak?

Lucy paused just past me. She looked at him, then back at me. I looked down at the floor.

Pulling his eyes from me, he fixed his pointed stare onto Lucy. "What exactly is going on? Tell me you two know each other or I swear to god, Lucy..."

"I thought you weren't coming—"

"Tell me you did not pick her up from the side of the road and bring her home."

Not just rude to strangers, then.

Lucy looked at me, but he spoke again before I could explain.

"Tell me right now, Lucy."

"He helped me," I blurted, finding some voice at last. "Last night, he pushed the car out of the road. I didn't know he was your brother."

"Wait, you saw her there yesterday in the dark and *left* her? You left a woman alone and clearly upset at the side of the road? *Out there?*"

"No," I stuttered. "I... I insisted."

Lucy put her hand up, a signal for me to be quiet, as she glowered at her brother like she was about to hurdle the breakfast bar.

Out of nowhere, Ben's expression shifted, and he glanced at me with round, soft eyes. "Were you out there all night?"

"No," Lucy answered for me. "God, Ben, that's a dick move, even by your standards. What were you thinking?"

His eyes lingered for an unnerving second before turning to scowl at Lucy. "What were you thinking bringing her here? With the children?"

Frantic feet thundered past me.

"Ben!" Sophie squealed, running to throw her arms around him.

He scooped her up and swung her around, lighting up as he hugged her. He was fire and ice, like I had never seen before. Lucy strolled over and snatched the biscuit from his hand, shoving it in her mouth and managing to chew it in a threatening way, goading him. He stared back at her and raised both his eyebrows. She winked.

"I was in the cupboard, no one could find me for ages," Sophie told Ben excitedly.

I wondered how it would feel to melt into a puddle on the floor.

"We're just heading to the station," Lucy explained. "So your timing is perfect. You can watch the kids."

"The station?" he asked with forced calm, lowering Sophie back down as Isac appeared and walked over more sedately to hug him from the other side.

"Yeah," Sophie said. "Elle needs to get to the station."

I felt my jaw tense. *Damn mouthy kids.*

"I thought your boyfriend was picking you up?"

Shit.

Sophie shook her head at him. "Nuh-uh, last night—"

My stomach churned. I needed to get going. I needed to get out.

Thankfully, Lucy jumped in. "Alright, Sophie, I'm sure Ben is tired and Elle wants to get going." She looked at me, understanding in her eyes.

"A word, Lucy?" Ben requested.

She rolled her eyes. "I'll fill you in when I'm back."

"Now."

"Don't talk to me like a child, Ben."

He raised his eyebrows and they entered some sort of covert eyebrow conversation. Lucy evidently lost, huffing and following him down the hall, still holding my bag.

Great. I couldn't even skulk off.

Trying not to listen to the rumbling, hushed words, I said my goodbyes to Sophie and Isac, stepping back onto the patio to wait. A robin landed on a rose branch, fluffing its gorgeous orange tummy. I watched as its preening ceased in response to the thundering footsteps behind me.

"Let's go," Ben commanded through gritted teeth, suddenly appearing next to me, not making eye contact.

With you? No thanks.

He thrust my bag at my feet and headed towards the car, leaving the zip ajar.

"Hang on—"

He glared at me, halting at the edge of the lawn. "That's what you want, isn't it?"

"Well..." I stuttered, taken aback.

Lucy burst out of the doors. "Don't you dare!" she shouted after him as I stood there, shrinking further into myself. "Sorry, Elle, he lives on a fucking power trip."

"Have you lost your mind?" he growled back at her.

My stomach lurched. "It's okay, really, I'll—"

Lucy looked at me and pointed aggressively. "No, don't you go anywhere."

I raised my hands in surrender, stumbling back a step towards the grass. The robin stayed on its rose stem, taking it all in.

"Why are you fighting?" Sophie asked, peering into the garden around the open door.

Lucy and Ben looked towards her, then stared at each other, speaking again with aggressive eyebrow movements. They must have communicated something as Ben reluctantly followed her back inside.

I took a deep breath. This was it. My bag was on the slabs; I could slip away. I could stop causing Lucy's family all this hassle.

"Sophie, tell your mum I'll text her as soon as I can. I'm going to sneak out before I cause any more trouble, okay?"

Sophie's eyes glossed over instantly. "No, don't go. Please stay, we're going to the beach, you have to see the beach."

I bent down to her level, silently screaming at myself to hurry up. "Sophie, sweetheart, your mummy has been super kind to me, but I need to go get my train. You can't be late for trains, you know that, right? If I sneak off now, you can all head to the beach. That's what you want, isn't it?"

She threw her arms around me. "I'd rather stay with you. You can teach me about horses. Can I at least come to the station?"

"Sophie, I need to go now before anyone gets more frustrated, okay?" I stood up, gently unhooking her little arms. "Now, go and give Isac another hug from me, and as soon as I've sorted myself out, I'll give you a call and we'll go riding. I promise."

"You swear?"

"I swear. Look," I pointed to the rose bush, "why don't you see if there are some crusts for that little robin. He looks hungry."

She folded her arms in protest, a little mirror of Lucy. I winced, tearing myself away.

I strode down the side of the quaint cottage, gravel crunching underfoot. It felt like walking away from something warm and safe; walking into darkness again, even though the sun was shining warmer that morning. God, I'd messed it all up. I'd found this amazingly kind stranger, crashed her holiday, and now she'd fallen out with her brother.

There was a verge that lined the narrow road, so I walked through the grass, the moist blades licking at my ankles and dampening my jeans. I'd find my way to the station. My feet paced, faster and faster – I didn't want Lucy to come running out of the house. I'd message her, of course, and thank her again, but I didn't want to have to leave twice. I didn't have the strength.

My bag weighed heavy on my shoulder. I felt vulnerable without the car, but I could make out a sign at the top of the road. All of this would be easier if I still had my phone, but they'd tracked me on it before. I couldn't risk it. One of the boys who worked in the library had asked me to the cinema once, and our date had been ruined by my family physically dragging me from the ticket line. Needless to say, he didn't chase me for another. I'd ended up with a split ear after losing my rag and throwing a punch in protest.

"Hey."

My thoughts were once again interrupted by that annoyingly sensual, masculine voice.

"Hey!" Ben repeated, louder this time.

I took a deep breath and turned around. He was powering along the verge, his smart shoes looking out of place as they trampled through the wet grass. I considered just running, but by the look on his face he might have made chase. I figured it would be easier to hear him out, let him rant about my intrusion as I'm sure was his plan. Then I could apologise and go on my way.

He came to an abrupt stop, the wind dragging that woody, zesty cologne towards me as he squinted in the sun.

We both just... stood.

His body was stiff, but his eyes had softened since he'd discovered me at the cottage. He used his knuckle to press his glasses up his nose, silver cufflinks glinting in the light

"I'm—" I started impatiently, wanting to get the apology over with. I understood why he was mad, but I was tired.

"It's a—" he said at the exact same time.

I clamped my lips shut.

"Lucy is... kind," he explained, standing straighter. "Too kind. People have taken advantage of her in the past."

He was significantly taller than me; older too, maybe thirty? They looked marginally alike, he and his sister. Similarly curved noses and thick eyebrows. But, unlike Lucy, Ben hadn't waited to ask questions of me.

"Look, I'm going to the station. Tell Lucy I'll text her when I have a phone. I'm sorry I lied last night, I just didn't want to cause anyone any trouble. Lucy insisted on helping, but I know I should have said no."

I had no interest in explaining myself any further to him. I turned back in the direction of the distant sign.

"You don't have a phone?"

I twisted back to face him. "We don't have to do this, Ben. I genuinely am sorry for the trouble."

I couldn't understand why he was still standing there; why he'd followed me at all.

"I'll drive you to the station." His tone left no room for argument.

"Not necessary."

"You don't know where you're going."

Presumptuous arse. God, he was arrogant. "And how did you come to that conclusion?"

"You just said you don't have a phone."

I shrugged. "I'll figure it out."

I noticed his eye twitch as his lip curled slightly. "What's your game here?"

"My game?" My eyes widened as my voice rose in anger. "What's *your* game? I'm the one trying to leave, not that it's any of your business."

Ben looked over his glasses, folding his arms. "It's my business when you involve my family."

"Lucy stopped the car! I didn't ask her to. I told her to go, several times, in fact." I exhaled slowly, adjusting. "She should have left me. Don't you think I know that? But she didn't, and I'll always be grateful for that; I'll always be indebted to her."

"What do you gain from all this? You lied to me, clearly. Why?"

I should have run away for the conversation when I had the chance.

"Gain?" I exclaimed, shaking my head. "Clearly nothing you'd understand. Of course I lied, some prick burst out of his car and started yelling at me." I narrowed my eyes at him, remembering that my bag had been unzipped at the cottage. "You searched my bag, didn't you?"

I tucked it higher on my shoulder.

He looked marginally embarrassed.

"Did you find what you were looking for?" I asked spitefully, spinning on my heels and gritting my teeth as I made to walk away.

A warm hand took mine as my arm swung backwards, stopping me.

"Wait."

This time, I kept my body facing away.

He let go of my hand.

"Look, I get it," I offered, my rage calming, "I really do. But please, just let me go. You clearly don't want to be here, and—"

"I'm protective of my family," he interrupted, a whisper of softness nestled amidst his otherwise stern tone.

I don't know why – whether it was because of the shiver that shot up my spine when he reached for my hand, or something else – but the words just fell out. "Well, I'm running away from mine."

I took another step away.

We both drew in a few heavy breaths.

"Wait," he almost pleaded.

I hesitated, still facing the distant sign as a breeze pulled at my loose brown hair.

"Lucy wouldn't forgive me for leaving you here. Let me drive you to the station."

Mud squelched as I pressed my foot down.

"Please," he added.

I stared ahead as my heart started racing, the strain in his voice dangerously enticing.

"Tell her I'd rather walk."

He grunted, stepping beside me. "Why are you so stubborn?"

"Why are *you* so rude?"

He raised an eyebrow as I allowed myself a glance at his face, folding my arms to emphasise my point.

He adjusted his jaw, as if he was biting his tongue. "It's a long walk with no pavements. I can drive you there in twenty minutes. A safer journey for you and less of an earache for me. Let's just put an end to this so we can both move on with our lives."

I squinted at him, digging my fingers into my arms.

He drew a deep breath. "I'm sorry for searching your bag."

I was surprised he didn't choke on the word.

With another sideways glance, I conceded. "I'm sorry for freaking you out."

"If it makes you feel better, Lucy can take you."

My lip ached before I realised how hard I was pressing my teeth into it. I was fed up of standing here. I needed to move. Maybe he was right.

The realisation was infuriating.

"And if I do decide to walk?"

"For the sake of a quiet life, I'll probably have to slowly follow you in the car." There was a hint of a smile on his face as he spoke.

"That would be really annoying."

"It would, and creepy."

My body relaxed as he smiled a little more. The heat seemed to fizzle out in place of something else. There was a glint of Lucy's kindness in him, buried deep down. I felt myself getting drawn in. Just the tiniest bit.

"You said it yourself, I'm stubborn."

"You be less stubborn and I'll be less rude, how about that?"

A laugh slipped out; the last twenty-four hours had been so entirely unpredictable that even my body had given up fighting now. "That's probably a good place to start."

Awkwardly, we walked back to the cottage, keeping to opposing edges of the verge.

I was content in the uncomfortable silence until he asked, "Why are you running from your family?"

The air between us iced over. Even the birds seemed to have gone quiet.

"What did Lucy tell you?" I figured she must have said something to send him chasing after me. It was a sad realisation that my story was apparently tragic enough to turn such a hostile man on his heels.

"She said you were running away." He paused. "That you have bruises on your arms. I would have driven you to the station last night, you realise, if you hadn't lied."

The words were cold. My chest tightened. I pulled the sleeves of my grey hoodie down further. I hadn't even thought about what Lucy would think of the bruises – heck, I'd forgotten those ones were there. It explained her kindness. I suddenly felt stupid for assuming she had simply wanted to be my friend.

"Because you came across *so* helpful," I snapped, not wanting to talk about it. I bit my tongue again, the familiar sting of pain pushing down the swelling that had built rapidly in my throat.

"Where are you going?" he asked more gently.

"I have an address for some people I need to talk to." As the words came out, I realised how odd they sounded.

"People?"

"Yes, it's a long story." I grimaced. The more I spoke, the more ridiculous it sounded.

Thankfully, we walked the last few meters in silence, but while it was still awkward and strangely tense, the atmosphere grew warmer between us – less like he wanted to perform a citizen's arrest, at least. The pretty cottage slowly came back into view. It felt bizarre going back, even though it had only been about ten minutes. When he'd taken my hand, the part of me that was trying to make decisions had malfunctioned completely; I suddenly felt that nothing was in my control.

I was admiring the peach rose growing by the white front door when my ankle twisted suddenly in the grass. My breath hitched as my weight lurched towards the ground, momentum working against me, my limbs toppling over one another. Strong arms snatched around my waist, swift and decisive, and I blushed such a vivid red my teeth hurt.

"Oh god, I'm so sorry." I winced as Ben effortlessly lifted me back onto my feet.

In the arms of this well-dressed stranger, I realised what a mess I was. I hadn't applied any make-up, and my hair was in a bun on top of my head, looking like a ramshackle hat. My hoodie had been on its last legs *before* I'd run through the rain the previous night.

Ben smirked, not helping my rosy cheeks. "It's fine."

I stepped away and tried not to look back, taking a second to compose myself. This day was going from bad to worse.

Ben nudged me gently and grinned. "You wouldn't have made it to the station if you can't even survive the verge."

My eyes darted to him as I brushed my hands down my legs. "I'd have been fine."

I'd rather have fallen.

"Your strong words are let down by your blushing, you know that, right?"

Oh god. Why did I have to trip?

"I'm getting you off the hook, remember?" I retorted.

As we walked around the corner, I saw relief light up Lucy's face.

She stepped forwards, hugging me tightly "I'm so sorry. Ben is a prick," she whispered in my ear.

I pulled away. "Maybe... maybe I can see where he's coming from."

I knew he'd heard me. I didn't care.

"Yay!" Sophie yelled. "Now you can come for lunch with us!" Her little arms were surprisingly strong as they squeezed my leg.

"I can't, Sophie. I have to go soon, but thanks for inviting me."

She stared up at me, her eyes pleading. "Please, please, please! Then we can go to the beach I was telling you about."

Lucy jangled her keys. "Elle, it might not be the worst idea. Maybe we can help. Maybe we should have a chat first, make some sort of plan? We can take you straight to the station after lunch."

Isac stepped out of the back door. "You said we could have a rematch of UNO."

Suddenly, the weight of many eyes landed on me. "I-I can't. You've all done enough, really. I'm sure someone else will play with you, Isac."

He looked down at his feet, hunching his shoulders. "Mum is rubbish and Ben always wins."

I couldn't help but shoot Ben a look. Of course he never let the kid win.

He stared right back. "You should come." His expression was almost sly, as though my discomfort amused him.

"I agree," Lucy said after a moment's pause. "We'll be an hour, tops."

I looked from one of them to the other as Sophie sneakily looped her hand in mine.

"I can't intrude on your holiday anymore."

Ben fixed me with a look. "Come on, Elle. The kids won't forgive me if you leave now. I can drop you off after lunch. Unless your boyfriend is on his way now, of course?"

There was trouble written on his face; shining in his eyes. What was *his* game here?

I quickly realised I was outnumbered. What harm could there be in lunch? *A lot.* It was another stupid decision, of course it was. I looked around; even my stomach growled, joining the fight. My mind cleared entirely as I searched for a polite excuse. I wasn't sure I had any fight left after yesterday, and any that was lingering seemed a waste on lunch. What was another hour or so?

I couldn't help but appreciate my own weakness because lunch was lovely. We sat outside a country pub by a river; ducks floating by, people chatting and bustling about, the smell of hearty food and chips filling my nose. Sophie grilled me about horses and I won a round of UNO, much to Ben's apparent shock. Lucy *was* terrible, to be fair to Isac, who wasn't even upset when he lost our game, reaching over to high-five me when I beat Ben. I'd always felt too alone, too unlucky to believe in fate before. But the too-easy lunch with this family began to thaw something inside of me, and I let it.

"Who taught you to ride?" Sophie asked.

"We all taught each other as kids. I enjoyed reading equestrian books and watching training videos. Sometimes they would bring in a cheap rogue horse from an auction and leave it with me to break in."

"Have you ever fallen off?" she asked, wide-eyed.

"Of course." I smiled. "That's part of learning. You just have to keep trying."

"Did you ever help give the horses new shoes?" Sophie asked, but the waiter carrying out hot plates of food interrupted her questioning.

I turned to Isac, wanting to include him in the conversation. "What do you like to do for fun, Isac?"

Hunger churned in my stomach as the waiter lowered the plates. It had been a long while since I'd made time for lunch.

"He's boring. He just plays on his PlayStation," Sophie answered through a mouthful of chips.

Lucy chimed in. "Sophie, why don't you share the talking? Not everyone wants to hear only your voice all day. Be kind to your brother."

Isac didn't even look up, so I turned to Lucy. "Did you ever ride?"

"Yeah, I did. I used to love it, but when I decided to apply to medical school, I stopped to focus on my studies."

"I thought you said you were a nurse?"

"Yes, well, medical school was the plan, but nursing fit better with these two."

"I keep telling her she should go back," Ben added. "Especially now she's divorced and has more head space."

She scoffed. "It's easy for you to say. I don't want you looking after the kids all the time and turning them into miniature accountants."

"Isac is great at maths, aren't you buddy?" Ben encouraged, nudging his nephew.

Isac remained silent.

Part of me felt drawn to his pain; the divorce must have been really hard for him, Lucy was right. As we ate, I listened happily to Sophie as she told vibrant stories, though I couldn't help but wonder which one Maeve would have been like: chirpy and full of life, or quieter and more reserved.

It wasn't until the kids began eagerly collecting their discarded bits of burger bun to feed the awaiting ducks that Lucy turned to me with a concerned expression on her face.

"So... what's the plan? Will you let us help you?"

"What do you mean?" I felt immediately exposed, my eyes flitting to the kids, who were steadily drawing closer to the riverbank.

"Well, you say you have an address for these people... but what happens if they aren't who you're looking for?"

"Honestly? I'm not sure. I left in such a rush that I haven't really thought anything through. I guess, if I had, I'd still be there."

Lucy looked concerned. "You won't go back, though?"

"I don't know if I could even if I wanted to." Hearing the words in the cold light of day was sobering.

Ben sucked in a breath. "The bruises—"

Lucy shot him a sharp look.

Ben ignored her. "You should report them to the police."

"It's... it's complicated," I mumbled, my eyes darting as I tried to avoid looking at him. "They're slippery."

That was putting it mildly.

He focused his gaze on me. God, he was so *intense*. When he looked at me it was like he was physically pinning me to the floor.

"Is that why you ran away?"

"Ben!" Lucy chided.

I shifted uncomfortably on the wooden seat, my gaze moving back to Sophie and Isac.

Shit.

Jumping up from the table, I unhooked my legs from the bench and stumbled clumsily to the ground. Pushing up from the mud, I ran for the river's edge. I'd been watching Sophie wander closer and closer to the soft bank when she'd careered in, the murky water aggressively swallowing her.

I ran as fast as I could, my trainers sliding in the wet grass. It was a deep, wide river but I could see her thrashing up and down, fighting the coursing current. Isac was screaming, edging nearer to the fast-flowing water. I skidded over to the edge and threw myself in.

The cold water shocked my muscles, making my body tense up immediately. I'd hoped my feet would hit the bottom, but it was too deep. The water gushed into my nose, choking me as I fought my way to the surface. My legs kicked as I finally made it, lunging forwards, fighting the bitter, swirling torrents. I rubbed my eyes to clear the muddy haze before stretching my arms towards Sophie, both of us spluttering and struggling. I managed to draw her into me, my head tipping back under as I thrust her up for air. My jeans were fighting my every motion. I felt her fear; her panic; her small body seizing, her breathing short and laboured, only interrupted by shrill, gurgled screams. Finally managing to make contact with the riverbed, I propelled the two of us towards the slick bank.

Ben and Lucy were at the edge, arms out and faces white. Their mouths were moving frantically, but I could only hear sloshing water. One more kick and I felt a pull as Ben grabbed Sophie, heaving her out and handing her back to a manic Lucy. Water was streaming off her as she slid over the mud. The change in weight sent my head crashing back beneath the freezing surface, but Ben immediately twisted round and grabbed my forearm. I gasped, springing up as my body was dragged out of the river.

My chest thudded as our bodies collided, the force of him pulling me out sending us both backwards in a tangle of limbs.

"Bloody hell, are you alright?" he asked breathlessly, lying beneath me.

Water poured from my nose as I steadied myself, swiping my face on my arm and gasping for air. I looked down at him, a droplet of water running off my nose and hitting his cheek.

"Yeah..." I gasped back.

We lay there for a moment, catching our breath, the murky water soaking between us as our bodies stayed pressed together. His ribs rose and fell gently underneath me as I regained my senses. I could feel his strong fingers pressing into the cold skin of my side.

"Where's Sophie?" I asked, suddenly snapping out of whatever moment we were having.

Reaching one hand down, Ben pushed us up, steadying me as my eyes found Sophie. She was shaking in a blanket while Lucy gripped her and cooed in her ear.

"We need to get her home," Lucy said.

I scrambled to my feet, and a glance of understanding flashed between me and Ben as Sophie broke out in fresh sobs.

After Ben had thanked the pub owner for the blankets, and Lucy had pulled away with the kids, he popped open the pristine boot of his shining silver Audi.

"Your car is so clean! I can't cover it in mud!"

He looked at me with straight lips like I'd said something ridiculous. "Well, you covered me in mud too, but we can't stay here."

"Oh god, I'm sorry."

Ben frowned. "No, that's not what I meant." He sighed, turning his back to me and stepping away. "Just take off some of your wet clothes."

My bones began to ache as I rested back against the open boot. The adrenaline was filtering from my blood and my teeth started to chatter. Fighting to pull off my hoodie, I was thankful I'd put on a vest top that morning. It dropped to the ground with a heavy plop and, when no one was looking, I unceremoniously squeezed water from the cups of my bra. Pulling over one of the blankets, I wriggled out of my jeans. Ben pushed the back door shut and rounded the corner holding *that* blue suit jacket. He leant forwards and tucked it over my bare shoulder, hesitating to close it around me.

"Did you injure anything?"

I shook my head. "I'm fine."

Ben looked at me doubtfully. "Let's go. Your lips are turning blue."

I stood up on shaky legs, shivering as cold water trickled down the back of my top. I clutched the blanket and made my way carefully to the open passenger door. Ben had already sat down and was starting the engine.

He turned the heating on full blast before looking at me. "What are you waiting for?"

I grimaced, looking down at the pristine leather. "The car, it's—"

"A car," he interrupted. "I will clean it." I didn't move, so he went on, "It'll be easier to deal with than hypothermia, trust me. Look, please stop arguing. You just threw yourself in a river after my niece, let me look after you."

❧

Back at the cottage, Lucy bought Sophie out of the bathroom wrapped in a big white towel, before throwing her arms around me, pulling me in for a hug so tight I could feel the pounding of her heart.

"Thank you," she choked. "You just... you just ran! She can barely swim, Elle. Thank you so much."

I fidgeted, trying to keep hold of the blanket around my waist. "It's okay. I'm just glad I saw it happen in time."

"Go get warm," she instructed, shaking off some of the lingering shock and pulling back. "Next door is on a different tank, so there'll be more water, and more towels, too. I'll go find some wine."

Sophie looked up at me through red, puffy eyes. "Thank you, Elle. I had all this water up my nose, it was making bubbles, and it was horrible. I tried to swim, but it was so cold. Mum said we could go to the shop and get some chocolate."

I reached a hand out and rubbed her back. "You did good, it was really hard to swim."

She sniffled and Lucy looked like she was about to start crying all over again.

The shower was warm and soothing against my icy skin. I let the water ease the sludge out of my hair, carrying it over my body and down the plughole in swirling stripes. It was a gorgeous, spacious shower, not like the one in my caravan; I could wash my hair without elbowing the walls here. I traced my fingers over the large porcelain tiles with my arm fully stretched, just because I could. The soap bottle was square and smelt of neroli and basil, with one of those fancy black and white labels.

Closing my eyes, I let the bubbles wash over my face, starting to feel clean on the outside, wishing the water could cleanse the rest of me too. I was so overwhelmed my mind was blank, but at least the quiet was peaceful.

Stepping onto the chilly tiles, I flinched and gripped the heated towel rail. My knees throbbed and I struggled to balance as I hopped onto the carpet in the adjacent bedroom. I was desperate to get dry and stay that way for a while. My body ached as I pulled on my spare set of jeans and a white t-shirt.

I hadn't given the clothes I'd packed enough thought: light shirts and dark bras.

"Great," I muttered to myself.

I heard Ben walk into the kitchen below, so I sat down to try and brush my hair, squeezing more water out. I rummaged through my bag – purse, clothes, charger for a phone I didn't have – then, still in the side pocket, I found the photograph. I picked it up to flatten it back out, before tucking Maeve safely away.

Grabbing my mascara, I went over to the small mirror and stared into the eyes of the new me. A free person, an independent person, a person suddenly making all of her own decisions, however questionable. I dragged the mascara through my eyelashes, running my hands through my wet hair. This was the face that Susan and Derek White would meet on their doorstep.

"I don't want to be accused of being rude again," Ben's low voice called as the metal stairs rang out with his footsteps, "but did you want to salvage the jeans and hoodie in the bag?"

I dropped my head into my hands. "God, sorry. I don't know. I didn't realise how little I'd thrown in my bag."

Ben stepped into the bedroom. "Alright, we'll try and wash them."

He headed straight for his suitcase, pulling a green knit jumper over his black t-shirt and clean jeans. I hoped there had been enough warm water for him to shower next door. He seemed more relaxed and he looked less stern in his more casual outfit.

I put my brush down, realising I'd been brushing the same section of hair over and over. "Is your car alright?"

"Why are you so concerned about the car?"

I shrugged, tightening the lid on my crusty mascara. "Don't want to cause you any more trouble."

He narrowed his eyes, pressing his lips together. "You don't need to worry. We cleaned most of the mud off the seats. You soaked me, too, don't forget."

He smiled, clearly trying to get a read on me. He was wrong to think I had the energy to put on a front – I was spent. Ever since the anger had hit me and I'd packed my bag, I'd been acting on raw impulse.

"I'm sor—"

"Stop apologising, Elle. What is it with you apologising for everything? You pulled Sophie out of a river." He paused as I opened my mouth again. "Don't apologise for apologising," he interrupted, reading my mind. "Or I'll take my bed back and make you sleep on the sofa."

My cheeks flushed hot, my body only now managing to generate some heat at the least convenient time. "I can't stay again. If you could just take me to the station—"

"No."

He took his glasses off and dried a patch of mist on the rim of his jumper, exposing a strip of abdominal muscles that I didn't allow myself to look at for long. Seeing the way his face changed without the harsh frames was distracting. He looked younger, softer. The word lingered. That confidence he spoke with... it was like everything he said had conviction.

"No," he repeated, more gently this time. "You've had a very stressful day, and it's getting dark. You'll have some dinner, which will hopefully be a drama-free meal, and I'll take you in the morning. I promise. I'm not taking you tonight, Elle. You look exhausted. I listened to you before, and look where that got us all."

My voice shook. "I... I can't. I can't stay. They'll be looking for me. I've already stayed too long."

"You're an adult, Elle. You don't have to do what they say. Besides, they won't find us here – it's a holiday cottage in the middle of nowhere."

He was so blasé. He had *no* idea.

I continued to sit there, my mind buzzing with emotions – none of which would come to the surface. I felt my throat tighten up. Why did it make things so much more painful when people were kind? Even broody Ben was now being nice to me. I'd made so many excuses for the beatings, the simple lack of humanity, it was painful to realise exactly how much of a conscious choice it had been for all of them.

"Who are you running from?" he asked eventually, filling the silence.

I pinged the hairband on my wrist against my skin, the sting of it grounding me. "My family... they're from a tight-knit community. They'll be really, *really* angry with me for leaving."

His brown eyes searched my face.

"Elle, we're back!"

The door had barely slammed shut as the metal of the stairs rang out like some sort of clunky xylophone.

"I got you a present!" Sophie yelled excitedly, running up to me with a carrier bag.

"Oh, thank you," I replied, grateful for the interruption.

"It's a new jumper. Mum didn't know what colour to get, so I chose pink. Do you like it?"

I noticed Lucy standing in the doorway, looking tiredly from me to Ben.

"Let's open the wine," she said.

5

Old Scars

Apparently, laying soaking wet on top of someone who pulled you from a river resets any previous awkwardness you may have had, because sitting quietly with Ben in the smaller cottage whilst Lucy put the kids to bed, I felt strangely content.

"Why did you stay? What happened to make you leave like that?" Ben asked.

I exhaled slowly, heavily, as I considered how to respond. "I guess, because they were my family. It's complicated. I always hoped things would get better; I suppose I had to. But, then, they didn't. They got worse. If I had waited, I would have changed my mind."

I sipped my wine, allowing the liquid to ease into my bloodstream, welcoming any relief it could offer. There was something about the smaller size of this property that made it whimsical; cosy. I'd finally warmed up, but Ben had still thrown a few logs onto the black wood burner in the corner, just in case.

"If you have family in Hampshire, why didn't you go there before?"

I looked down at my jeans. It wasn't that I didn't want to tell him, I just didn't want to say it out loud. If I said it out loud, it would be exposed for how ridiculous and big-headed it was – to dream of being someone so important.

Whether due to bravery or exhaustion, I tried anyway. "Do you remember Maeve White? She was on the news a bit, I think?"

He looked at me, his cool tone and impassive expression unchanging. "The girl who got abducted when she was little, you mean?"

"Yeah, her. Well... umm... I'm planning to visit her parents."

He raised an eyebrow in question. "Why?"

I sighed shakily. "Well, I found Maeve's photo."

Ben stilled.

"We had this fight, me and my parents. I found out they paid off my ex, Sam, to leave me and I guess I... snapped. I saw my mum throw something, and when I went back to look what it was, I found an old photo of Maeve."

I watched him, waiting for him to react. Instead, he just stared at me.

Shakily, I continued. "I discovered that the Whites are still searching and I guess... I felt compelled to tell them. And, well, maybe..." I paused again, the next words being the hardest to admit. "Well, then things started to feel odd. Like how I had no baby photos or memories of being young. How they were so strict with me staying on the site. I know this sounds crazy, I know you're probably thinking I'm totally delusional, but it's like the more I think about it, the more it could fit. Whenever I wanted to do something for myself, other than work on the site, they said I was a 'waste of effort' or a 'disappointment'. I was always the outsider no matter how hard I tried."

I stared down into my empty wine glass, swirling round the last drop. The glow of the small fire reflected off Ben's fixed expression.

"I have blonde hair, naturally. They always made me dye it. When I questioned why, they told me that blondes attract attention and that I wasn't pretty enough to pull it off; that I'd embarrass myself. I always had to blend in. I know this all sounds ridiculous but... if it's a stupid, childish notion that gets me out of that place, maybe it doesn't matter."

I felt my breath stretching my lungs to their limit, my pulse thumping in my throat, my toes curling.

"She had a scar," Ben stated, startling me.

He hadn't questioned me. He hadn't laughed. He'd just listened. Did he *believe* me?

"Maeve?" I asked. The crackling logs suddenly sounded very loud.

Ben nodded. "It was all over the news. She had a scar behind her shoulder, or maybe a birthmark? The picture was drilled into us all: a figure of eight shape. Small but noticeable."

My blood ran cold. I could feel it racing around my body.

Blinking at him, I stood up slowly, as if the silence would actually shatter if I moved too fast. I slipped my arm out of my new pink hoodie robotically. Calmly, Ben stood too, taking two steps towards me like we were speaking telepathically, acting out some sort of dangerous dance. Pressing past my t-shirt sleeve, I ran my fingers over the bumpy skin behind my left shoulder.

I hadn't read that part of the story.

Turning to face the kitchen window, I pulled the material so he could see, watching the reflection of us against the dark garden as he stepped closer.

Ben looked down at my shoulder, slowly moving his hand towards the patch of exposed skin. I watched his fingers flinch as they grazed the sensitive scar. His touch was gentle, cautious, as he brushed soft strokes over the mark.

"They told me I'd splashed hot tea on myself when I was a child, but when I was twelve or thirteen, the skin started to even out. Then Marcus burnt me on a hot pipe; he shoved me against it in a rage, shouting that I'd left the gate open and that the horses had gotten out. I hadn't, I wouldn't have done that."

I felt Ben's fingers, the pressure on my skin, my nerves firing the messages to my brain to remind me they were there, so gentle, and still moving across the ugly, raised scar. A memory of the searing pain as I'd ripped myself from the pipe shot through my mind. I scrunched my eyes shut, smelling the burning. My mind fled back to Ben's touch: it felt intimate, comforting.

I glanced back at the window, at the two of us standing there. His eyes met mine in the glass, his warm breath tickling the hairs on my neck. I savoured the moment, the seconds before everything was about to change. It was too dangerous to hope.

"I mean... it must just be a coincidence." My voice sounded loud after so much quiet as Ben continued to stare at me in the window. "It couldn't be, that would be..."

"Horrific."

"I'm sorry, I shouldn't have said anything." I twisted to reach for my hoodie, wanting to cover back up, moving away from him.

Ben grasped my arm gently, stopping me. "If you are her..." He struggled to find the words. "If you are her... then it would be—"

"Elle?" Lucy suddenly appeared in the doorway, fracturing the moment.

Ben's hand flew back to his side. "Show her."

Lucy sat beside Ben on the small sofa as I attempted to explain again, showing her the scar that I had always owned but never paid much attention to.

"What do we do?" she asked.

I shrugged. "I was just going to go knock on their door."

"Knock on their door?" Ben scoffed.

"I don't have a number to call. I wouldn't know what to say. I thought maybe if I saw them, I'd know. If I felt something then I could try and tell them? If it was just a stupid mistake then I could walk away and make a new plan, start fresh."

Lucy frowned. "All on your own?"

I thought it a strange question. My eyes darted to the wood burner as a log crashed down, sending sparks into the glass door.

"I had no one to tell before. Saying it out loud to you has made me feel even more ridiculous. I mean, everyone with shitty parents would want to be that little girl. It's a desperate dream."

"It's not desperate, Elle, it's brave," Lucy said softly.

Brave. I scoffed in my head. I wasn't brave. A brave person wouldn't have stayed for so many years.

"Are you saying no one questioned any of this? Didn't you have a boyfriend?"

Lucy shot her brother a look.

"Yeah, Sam, but that was all a huge mess." I needed a break from this conversation. Maybe to go and lie in a dark room for a while...

"We'll help, whatever happens," Lucy assured me. "You aren't alone anymore, Elle."

My mind rejected her sentiment. "You've already helped me. Enormously. I can't ask for anything else. I won't. I just... I need to see this through."

"What about the police? There must be someone you can call," Ben insisted, leaning forwards.

"The police aren't an option for me. It's something I need to do on my own. It truly is probably just a coincidence."

"What if it's not?" Lucy pressed.

"I don't think it's worth thinking that far ahead." I pulled down my sleeves, attempting to hide and shrink. "I can't."

A cry from Sophie interrupted us. Lucy looked at me apologetically, but selfishly I was glad for the break as she went to check on her.

Ben and I sat silently, both deep in thought.

"Elle," Lucy yawned, once she'd returned after soothing Sophie, "I need to turn in, I'm sorry. I need to be with Sophie for a bit, she's pretty shaken up, and I know if I lie down, I'm going to fall asleep. We'll talk in the morning. Get some rest. We will help. We'll try and... process everything. Ben, can you make sure she has what she needs?"

"Of course."

After saying a warm goodnight to Lucy, the two of us were left alone, suddenly unsure of what to do, or say. Small talk seemed inappropriate, but it was easier than discussing my past again, or the bed situation.

"So, what's your story?" I cringed as I said it out loud. *What do you expect him to say to that? 'Once upon a time'?*

Ben laughed. "What do you want to know?" He leant back into the sofa, as if there was nothing I could ask that would trouble him.

"What do you do for work?" I tried, keeping it simpler this time; attempting to match how relaxed he suddenly looked.

"I own a company, a finance consultancy."

"Oh wow, that sounds stressful. Did you move up through the ranks?"

"No, I started it. I was always good with numbers." His face lit up as he spoke. "I worked a few jobs, made a few contacts, but I always

51

thought I could do better."

I placed my empty glass on the table. "How did you know you could do it?"

"What do you mean? The numbers?"

"No, how did you know you could start a business, be good enough to be in charge?"

He shifted in his seat. "I just did, I suppose."

Draining the rest of his wine, Ben rose to take our glasses to the sink. I followed him, busying myself by picking up a stray mug.

"What do you do, Elle?"

"Well, I don't think I can say now."

"Why?" he asked quickly, eyebrows twitching.

I paused and looked at him, trying to read his expression. "I do – did – the accounts for the site, a few other local businesses, stuff with the horses, and some other domestic bits."

Ben smiled. "Well, that's not what I would have guessed."

"I dread to think what you would have guessed."

"I thought you were a fraudster."

"Thought? I've finally convinced you, have I?" I joked. "Or am I sleeping with one eye open tonight?"

"I guess we're both sleeping with an eye open."

We shared a laugh. It was half-hearted, but it was there. Why did it feel so easy to make eye contact?

Ben reached over the wooden countertop, "There's another bottle here, it would be a shame to waste it."

"I don't know if I can stomach much more talking about my life today. About anything else... serious." My body was exhausted from the unexpected swim; my brain from, well, everything else.

"What do you want to talk about?"

"I'm actually a bit sick of talking all together. Sorry, that sounds rude. The past few days have been so intense, and tomorrow will be... a day."

He tilted his head, giving me a quizzical look. "There's a bench at the bottom of the garden if you fancy getting some fresh air?"

I nodded gratefully, following him over the lawn to a beautiful little arbour that shone a chalky blue in the light from the kitchen window. The wooden bench overlooked a small stream and a collection of sweeping fields. Above them was a beautiful starry sky, and the waning moon lit up the grass, highlighting the dewdrops, making them look like fallen stars. We sat there for a while, looking out, sipping. It was the head space I was greedy for; I felt my battery filling by one percent, then two as I soaked in the fresh night air.

The sound of nature was soothing. I absorbed it all, focusing on the rustling of the wind, the hooting of owls, drowning out everything else. We sat beside each other in a uniquely peaceful silence.

"We loved it here as kids," Ben mused.

"It's a beautiful place," I replied softly. I sensed his energy change as he sunk down into the wooden seat. "What happened to your parents?" I asked, looking at the side of his face. The moonlight bounced off his dark glasses.

"I thought you wanted to be quiet?"

"Sorry, I do. Maybe. It's been a weird day. I'm trying not to think about myself."

He took a slow inhale of breath.

"You don't have to answer," I added.

"My dad died at work when I was young, and my mum couldn't live without him," he explained, as if he'd said it a thousand times. "It's always hard being back here, with Lucy so stressed. I wish she had more people."

"What was your dad's job? Don't you have more family?"

"He was a fireman. I always knew it would end badly. He couldn't stop himself from helping people. He cared for everyone unquestioningly. Time after time, fire after fire, he just ran in. He didn't care if it was a prison or a school, he never looked back. Then, one day, one fire, he didn't come out."

I held my breath in the silence, waiting for him to continue, swallowing my own sorrow at his story.

"My mum's parents are in a home together; they found it hard. My dad's died. I used to get so angry with him going out to work. I would stay up at night listening to Mum talk to him on the phone, just to comfort myself that he was alive still. I don't know why she let him do it. They were so in love. They would sit here together, holding hands, watching us play in the stream."

My eyes followed the rhythmic stirring of grass in the distance. Two deer danced and bounded away into the thick bushes. I wondered if they were the same ones from the side of the road the other night, coming to check on me. The breeze lifted a few strands of my hair as I searched my mind for a suitable response. Ben was hard to read; pity didn't seem appropriate.

"I'm sorry, that must have been awful, especially being so aware as a child." I paused. "What happened with your mum?"

"She lived a year for us, then she started drinking. She didn't know how to be on her own. One day she went out to the shops and didn't come back. They said she'd been drinking; said the tyre marks didn't make sense, like she'd tried to hit the lamppost head-on."

He didn't flinch. I tried to squash the feeling in my throat, my heart speeding up. I tried to calm it, to match his nonchalance.

"You seem so... together. So strong. You own a business, you're present for your family, you have a nice car... how did you do it? Recover like that and still go on?"

There was a long moment of silence as he considered his reply. "I saw the pain my mum had caused her parents, Dad's parents, her own children. Me and Lucy promised each other we would always be there for one another – we wouldn't quit, no matter what – so I just tried to fill my life with things to stay busy, hence the business. My father always said he wanted me to be a firefighter too, which made me so mad. I still don't understand how he could put other people before his family. Risk his life... our life. I think he did it for the ego trip. God, he was so selfish." His tone spiked a little and he glanced over at me, agitated by his own words. "I know how bad that sounds. How it makes people feel."

I looked back at him, avoiding giving him the sympathy he would resent, even though I felt it surging through me. Picturing that little boy, all alone, over-tired, waiting to hear his dad was alive night after night. My parents always seemed to hate me; I was a drain, an annoyance. But to have that warmth, that safety, that *love*, and lose it? To feel it was preventable? For his mother to choose to leave him and Lucy like that? I'm not sure what's worse.

"It makes me admire you."

His brow twitched in response. "That's a new one."

"I mean, what happened to you, to Lucy, it's awful. But to live through that like you have... I doubt I would have had that strength."

"Seems to me like you've lived through your fair share."

I realised we were sat fairly close, the gentle warmth from his body wafting towards mine through the night air.

"Well, yeah, I mean, there was this dick who yelled at me yesterday," I joked.

We locked eyes again, and I noticed our hands were resting on the bench a few centimetres from one another.

He grinned. "I bet you held your own."

I liked the sound of his voice; I liked the feeling of him looking into my eyes; focusing on me. I wasn't sure whether it was the wine, or the drama of the day, but I suddenly needed to move. I stretched my jaw into a yawn, dragging my eyes away and standing up slowly. Ben reciprocated as I took one long look out into the darkness.

"I'm really tired," I confessed, blinking away a tear, styling it out.

He tilted his head toward the kitchen and we walked in side by side.

Ben locked the door, leaving the peace of the night to the half-moon, and I went to brush my teeth and gather my stuff from the bed. I didn't have any pyjamas; I would just have to sleep like this on the sofa. The night before I'd slept in my knickers and shirt, but that didn't feel appropriate. Not that it should have mattered, not in the context of my life; I was sure Ben had seen more than his fair share of legs.

I headed down towards the lounge to find him waiting. Even *that* he did with purpose.

"You can't sleep on the sofa, or in jeans," he informed me with smooth confidence as he turned his back to me and climbed the steps.

"I don't have much else to wear, and you won't convince me to take your bed. There is a whole spare room next door."

He appeared at the top of the mezzanine, leaning over the banister, holding a pair of loose fit, checkered blue boxers and a white t-shirt.

"I don't sleep in the same bed I did as a kid." He extended his arm, offering me the neatly folded garments. "These will be a bit more comfortable, I imagine?"

I *was* low on clothes for tomorrow.

"I can't wear your clothes..."

"Yes, you can." He smiled – a face-altering, goosebump-initiating, swoon-worthy smile – tossing them down towards me.

I stepped back to catch them, fumbling: the wine had clearly confused my reflexes alongside everything else.

I shot the fox-shaped draught excluder a look, sensing silent judgement from its beady plastic eyes at the thoughts that were tempting me. I looked back up, but Ben had walked away from the edge.

"Are you sure?" I asked, repeating *you're better off alone* in my head.

I kept doing this, getting lonely and distracted by men, Sam having been the most disastrous.

Just as I was garnering an ounce of self-respect, Ben's words emptied my mind again.

"I am. Is there anything else you need?"

I was glad he was still out of sight, because I took a step back, faltering, gripping his soft clothes.

Is there anything I need?

At Henworth, I wasn't permitted anything as indulgent as needs for myself. I'd been in survival mode for so long that his simple question shook me to the core.

I was a human being. I was a person. In my own right.

"Elle?"

Ben appeared, leaning over in just his jeans, his toned pectorals casting shadows against his tanned chest. Why couldn't he have been gross? I would have settled for a poorly-inked tattoo, or patchy chest hair – anything to make walking away from him easier.

I cleared my throat. "Can you please just let me sleep on the sofa? You're stressing me out."

"Stressing you out?"

"You're bossy."

He laughed.

"Intimidating too. Like you have total confidence in your every move," I added.

I'd said too much, exposed a little part of that human inside me that was distracted by the thought of wearing his clothes.

"It's an illusion, I promise," he assured me, smiling warmly, seeming to have enjoyed my comment. "But you are going to sleep in the bed. I'll take the sofa."

"You can't sleep on the sofa—"

"You want me to sleep in the bed with you?" he interrupted, turning back into the bedroom and busying himself with searching for something, as if his comment was nothing.

I wondered if his words were intended as a deflection. They had certainly stopped me blabbering and over-thinking. I felt the corners of my mouth twitch.

Narrowing my eyes I walked halfway up the stairs, gripping the cool, metallic rail. "I want you to sleep in the bed."

"*You* will be sleeping in the bed," he replied. "I guess we'll just have to see who's more stubborn."

I walked up the rest of the stairs to object, but he stepped into the bathroom.

I stood there, feeling utterly flustered for a minute, before pulling on the clothes he'd lent me. They were even more luxurious than I'd thought, and the smell of him enveloping me? That aftershave...

I looked down as I walked towards the bed, watching as the material shifted, the fabric creasing as I moved. Of course he ironed his boxers.

Standing there, I suddenly realised exactly how much wine I'd had. The carpet felt plush, like wool that was still attached to a sheep; the wooden banister looked like it was moving, growing roots.

My feet separated as I fought to steady myself.

When Ben re-emerged, he stopped in his tracks, looking at me with amusement.

"What're you doing?" he asked casually, strolling past me to climb under the white cotton duvet.

My eyes followed him. This was ridiculous, was he drunk too? He must be, he was smiling too much. It was a decent amount of wine. I hoped he was drunk, otherwise this would be even more embarrassing.

He raised an eyebrow at me. "Just get in the bed."

I scowled at him to make my feelings clear as I eased myself onto the soft double bed. When I slipped under the fluffy duvet, I felt his heat drawing me in. My caravan had always been freezing; I would stay up late to avoid the lumpy bed, wrapping myself in an old duvet and unzipped sleeping bag, just to try and catch a few hours of rest.

Ben casually flicked off the light and it took a moment for my eyes to adjust to the darkness. I lay awkwardly on my back, not daring to move. The bed, at least, wasn't moving as much as the floor had been. Being in this bed, smelling of Ben, being warmed by his body... it was dizzying. We were silent for a few minutes as my mind raced.

I was just about to make my escape to the sofa, hoping he had fallen asleep, when he broke the impasse. "Your ex, Sam, did he give you the bruises?"

My breath caught. "No."

"Why won't you ask for help?" The mattress moved as he turned to look at me, a waft of his clean scent drifting over. "You didn't have to lie the other night. Why won't you speak to the police?"

I sucked on my top lip. "The police were part of the problem. It's complicated. I just need to do this on my own. Even telling you and Lucy feels wrong, like I'm some sort of crazed fantasist. Hell, I probably am." I rolled to face him. "Promise me you won't tell anyone. Please, Ben."

He hesitated as my eyes searched for him in the dark. "Okay, but that's another stupid decision, you realise that, right? I'm not sure what tops the list, actually. Breaking down in the dark, jumping into a river—"

"Stop," I whined, picturing his smug face. "Promise me?"

"What are you, five years old? Want to do the little finger thing?"

I scoffed and rolled the other way. "I really don't like you."

I fought my smile as he laughed, shaking the mattress.

"I know."

"You're wrong," I teased. "Getting into bed with you was the most stupid decision by far."

6

Someone's home

I woke up snuggled under Ben's duvet, the sun breaking through the curtains. Stretching gently, I opened my eyes, my toes meeting the cool air. I could hear raised voices from outside the window.

Ben wasn't in the bed.

Within less than a second, my emotions raced from disappointment to relief to immediate frustration. I grunted, allowing myself another blissful moment in the indulgent comfort, chalking last night down to a wine-fuelled dream.

Once I was dressed, I wandered over to the adjacent cottage and found Lucy sitting in the kitchen with the patio doors open.

"Good morning," I greeted, smiling softly at her.

"Morning, Elle. Kettle's just boiled."

I went to grab a mug from the cupboard.

"Ben's gone for a run," Lucy added. "You've wound him right up." She seemed highly entertained.

"Wound him up?"

"Ben doesn't usually play nicely with others. How he got himself engaged I'll never know. He was furious this morning. Wouldn't stop grumbling at me, in fact." She sipped her coffee nonchalantly. "He must like you."

"I didn't mean to upset him. I thought we'd cleared the air last night."

"I think that's the problem." She sighed. "You jumped in the river, didn't you? You jumped straight in and it's freaked him out. He finds things like that hard to understand."

"Because of your dad?"

I poured myself a tea, going to pick up the bag with my fingers before remembering the specific item of floral crockery holding the designated teabag spoon. I couldn't understand why anyone would want to rest their teabags in a dish before putting them in the bin, but each to their own.

Lucy paused with her nose in her mug. "He told you about Dad?"

"Yeah, last night. He told me he died trying to save someone."

Silence followed as Lucy continued to stare into her coffee.

"Now that doesn't sound like Ben," she finally responded. "No wonder he went for a run."

I walked towards her, resting my steaming mug on the breakfast bar. "I'm so sorry that happened to you. It must have been so hard for you both."

Lucy nodded. "It still is. Dad was a very brave man. He cared for people, everyone he met. I was angry, like Ben, for a time. But now? Now I'm proud of him."

As I was about to reply, Sophie burst into the room, excited as ever to see me, clutching a fluffy unicorn.

Lucy looked at her phone. "We're in the news!"

"What do you mean?"

"Someone took a picture, we're in the local news! It just came up." Lucy laughed. "Look, it's you in the river."

The blood drained from my face.

There was a photograph. Of me.

The ground melted under my feet as I stumbled back to lean against the wall.

"We need to go."

Lucy looked confused.

"We need to go. Now. *Please.*"

The kids got dressed in a rush, though we had tried not to startle them. I'd convinced Lucy it was best for us all to leave in case someone knew where they were staying. We left Ben a note and drove straight for the station.

I let myself slide down in the car seat as my heart pounded. I knew I shouldn't have stayed. I'd been so stupid. I'd put them all in danger.

I'd seen the community burn houses down for less. Every time a car went past, I flinched.

When we finally pulled into the station, I reached immediately for my seatbelt before throwing my arms around Lucy.

"Thank you, you have no idea what you've done for me," I whispered in her ear, fighting tears.

She squeezed me back. "I'm not going to say goodbye, we're friends now. Message me by the end of the day or I'll send a search party."

"I will," I agreed, choking on the words as her thick hair tickled my nose.

She pulled back to glare at me. "I mean it, I thought we'd have time this morning. This doesn't feel right, Elle."

"You've done more than you know. I promise. I just need to go now."

I said as cheerful a goodbye as I could muster to the kids and climbed out of the car before I could change my mind. I headed straight for the ticket machine, the wind grazing my cheekbones. Lucy drove straight off like I'd insisted and I didn't look back. I couldn't. I was alone again, scared again, and yet to fully convince myself that any of this was a good idea.

On the train, every clunk of the tracks allowed me to breathe a little slower. At every flash of fields through the window, I felt a muscle relax into the patterned seat. The carriage was quiet, thankfully. The next stop, just half an hour away, was only five miles from Maeve's home. I didn't let my mind process this morning; I just forced it forwards instead. Summoning some more gumption. Praying for it.

It was six p.m. by the time I managed to convince my legs to take me to Maeve's parents' house.

I loitered down the road, counting the house numbers carefully. It was a quiet road. Streetlights highlighted normal cars, a dog barked in a window, and televisions flickered through curtains. My legs slowed as their house entered my view. It looked like it had been a bungalow at some point. There were windows with little triangular roofs, red bricks, and warm colours pouring from inside. The path through the front garden was straight, but not neat; hedges and a small iron gate separated it from the pavement. Most terrifying of all, the light downstairs was on, gleaming boldly through some net curtains.

Susan and Derek White were home.

I stood in the cover of the hedge, my body refusing to move. My hand balled into a fist. I knew that once I did this, I was committed, I couldn't just pretend I was passing. I heard a noise behind me. This was it, I needed to make my move.

So I did.

I reached for the gate.

7

Broken bones

I thought about the little iron gate as the doctors put me under for my tibia surgery. I remembered how cool it felt under my fingers before I was dragged away. Thankfully, I didn't remember exactly how my leg had been broken, or much of that night before I was found.

It was too easy to deny that I knew my attackers and to lie about what happened – old habits die hard, and all that.

The clinical room faded away and the smell of chemicals lined my throat. I pictured the smirk that had been plastered on Marcus's face; his slicked back hair moving with the effort of the beating he enjoyed so obviously; the yellow of his teeth and the smell of old, cheap whisky.

My eyelids grew heavier.

I dragged my tongue around my dry mouth, tuning in to the voices around me amongst bleeping machines. My lungs attempted to expand for a deep breath, forgetting the bruising on my ribs.

"Elle?"

It was a woman's voice. A voice I knew.

Lucy.

My eyelids shot open, and I saw her leaning over the edge of the bed in her blue uniform, her thick hair tousled and her mascara slightly smudged.

"Lucy?" I croaked.

She immediately reached behind her and held up a plastic cup and straw. I drank, the water washing away the artificial taste in my mouth.

"What happened?" she asked desperately. "And don't give me that crap about being randomly mugged."

I coughed, groaning as the effort pulled on my bruises. Everything inside and out felt swollen and tender.

"I told you to text me, or call me," she continued in a rant.

"Sorry," I whispered hoarsely, not knowing what else to say. I wiggled my toes, feeling the new cast pressing against my ankle.

"Oh, shut up," she retorted, regret in her voice. "I'm so sorry, Elle. I knew I should never have left you. I knew something was wrong. The one time I listen to my stupid, ignorant brother... I'm going to kill him. The amount of shit I've put up with from him, Elle." She looked straight at me. "I'm officially over it. How's your pain?" She looked up at one of the drip bags.

I shrugged, trying to move as little as possible.

"I should never have let you get on that train. I'd seen the bruises, for god's sake. I knew you were vulnerable, knew something was going on. I've been a nurse for enough bloody years to know I shouldn't have just let you get on that train alone."

I reached over and placed my hand on her arm, my elbow creaking. "It's not your fault," I tried to say, as a tear slid down my cheek. I tilted my head to face her more. "You didn't tell them about the photo, did you?"

A nurse reading a nearby machine shot us a sideways look when Lucy didn't answer.

I shook my head against the overly springy pillow, wincing as I tried to move myself up the bed. "Please, no."

Lucy instinctively pulled the pillow for me, leaning closer to speak quietly. "I'm only letting you get away with this extremely poor decision making because you look like shit. I haven't said anything. Yet."

I nodded gratefully as she pulled away. The other nurse collected my notes before wheeling me towards the ward, away from the post-surgery bay. Lucy followed, busying herself with asking medical questions I let go over my head. I watched the ceiling tiles as they passed, one after the other. When I looked ahead to the nearing double doors, my breath caught and it hurt.

Ben was standing there.

I blinked, twice. His navy suit was crinkled, jacket slung over one arm as he clenched the collar. I rolled my head to look at Lucy.

She pouted. "I know. Look, I'm mad at him, but he was going crazy. I'll throw him out in a bit."

As pathetic as it was, I had thought about him, while I was cowering in that park. After a while, the pain had all merged together into a single, all-over ache. I'd thought about how it felt sitting in the arbour with him, looking up at the night sky. How, if this was really it, if this was the end, maybe it was worth it to have had one evening of peace.

The doors squeaked open.

"What happened?" he demanded across me to Lucy as the bed was wheeled into the corner by the window.

Curtain hooks clattered as Ben pulled them shut.

"She's awake, Ben," Lucy stated, picking up an empty plastic jug and heading out of the cubicle.

I looked at the strange stain on the ceiling tile above my head. It looked like tea. The legs of a chair creaked as Ben sat between the bed and the window.

"Elle?" he murmured.

I stared at the adjacent, stain-free ceiling tile, pulling my top lip between my teeth, the muscles in my cheek twitching as I tried desperately not to cry.

It was no use.

My body shook as I sobbed, the grey frames of the tiles quivering as my eyes blurred. The tears were warm against my cool cheeks as they streamed down, dampening the pillow. I heard hurried footsteps as Lucy burst back through the curtain and draped her arms around me. She smelt like disinfectant and vanilla, her hair tickling my face; the cannula pulling on my hand as I lifted it to her back.

"We've got you," she said into my ear as I cried.

It didn't even feel like crying; it felt like bleeding.

Lucy lay next to me in bed after she'd mopped at my face and given me another drink. Ben had sat silently through the whole thing; stiff and unreadable.

"What ha—"

"Shut up, Ben," Lucy interjected. She pushed herself up, moving to sit on the end of the bed so she could face me. "I spoke to the doctors, Elle. It was a displaced fracture, but the repair went well. There are no other broken bones and the worst of the concussion will have passed now. They'll send you home with some anti-sickness meds and wanted to book a follow-up. But..."

I blinked, looking at her as she hesitated, struggling to focus

"They need an address."

I nodded slowly. An address. Because technically I was now homeless. The word rung in my ears. I was without a home, without a place to go. Broken.

Lucy continued, reading my mind. "I know a couple of local refuges where you will be safe, but it's complicated medically. I—"

"She can stay with me."

My gaze darted to Ben's before I could stop myself. His dark eyes were bloodshot and his brow furrowed – he looked exhausted.

"Are you on crack?" Lucy blurted.

For a moment, he just stared into me, offered what was almost a sympathetic smile. Then he turned to her. "You're a nurse, Lucy, have some decency, for Christ's sake."

"Oh, I'm sorry. Are you on cocaine or any other illegal substances that may be making you act out of character, *Ben*? Seriously, you slate me for picking her up, you both act like you want to kill each other, then you invite her to move in with you? God, you two must have had really great sex last week."

My cheeks warmed as she glared at him.

He scoffed. "You're foul, you know that? Of course we didn't have sex. How is that even relevant?"

"Because she's vulnerable, Ben."

"She's awake!" he snapped, repeating her earlier words.

I swallowed. "I'm fine, really."

They both glared at me.

"You're joking." Lucy rubbed her forehead. "I need more wine.

You said you would bring the wine next time."

"Elle, I mean it," Ben insisted. "I have a spare bedroom. You need to recover somewhere safe. You can stay as long as you need."

"I was going to say she could stay with us. The kids would love it and I could keep an eye on her injuries."

"Right, between childcare and a full-time job?"

"Lucy, that's—" I tried to butt in, my voice barely a whisper.

Lucy pointed at Ben, ignoring me. "Oh, right, like you don't live at the office. You meant you'd set her up in the stationary cupboard, did you?"

"I can work from home."

Lucy laughed loudly, rolling her eyes. "Right. Of course. You? Work from home?"

"I'm serious." Ben looked at me, prompting Lucy to groan loudly. "What do you want to do, Elle?"

I looked between them, my head pounding. How was I supposed to have any of these answers? I had no bloody idea what I was doing, clearly. Mum was right; they had all been right. Maybe I should have stayed. I couldn't live like this. What was I doing?

"I can't cause you any more trouble. You've both done enough. I'm very grateful, but I never should've stayed with you. I never should've gone looking for Maeve's parents, and now I need to finally make a sensible choice, one where I'm alone. So, I can figure this out." I said the words I needed to say, but they didn't feel genuine. They were empty. So I tried again as they both looked at me doubtfully. "I was lucky, I convinced them." I coughed, pausing as Lucy passed me a tissue. "I convinced them that I was just asking about the photo. That I'd leave them alone... build a life."

"But why won't you speak to the police?" Lucy asked. "Help us understand."

I looked at Ben, who was leaning forwards in his chair.

"The police aren't interested in helping me."

"Why?" Lucy pushed.

"Because it's not in their interest to. Because they'd come to the site for whisky... for *perks*."

Lucy stilled, suddenly stiff. Thankfully, a doctor came in at that exact moment, stopping abruptly as if he sensed what he was walking into. He started talking to me and Ben, explained that they wanted to keep me in overnight to monitor for infection. I didn't mind; it gave me a night in a warm bed to think about what the hell I was going to do.

As he left again, Lucy turned to me, still on the end of the bed. "Elle," she said, quietly.

The pity in her voice stung. I saw it on her face, the judgement. *What must she think of me?*

"It's fine. I didn't think I could get away from Henworth, but maybe I can now, properly, not just running. They found me and they let me go."

"Let you go?" Ben rested his elbows on the bed. "This is them letting you go?"

I pushed my hands down, wincing as I tried to sit up further. He stood and grabbed the cushion, holding it back for me as I adjusted. My bones were like red-hot rods burning as I moved. Ben pulled the sheet back over me as I dragged my leg up. Lucy was rolling her head from side to side, deep in thought.

"I'll heal. It'll be fine. I'll be fine," I asserted, as much for myself as them. "Really, you guys can go, get on with your lives."

"I told them you and Ben were engaged," Lucy blurted out.

"What?"

Lucy grimaced nervously, averting her eyes from her brother's stare. "I didn't want it to look like I was taking advantage of my hospital privileges."

I looked at Ben, waiting for him to snap at her again.

He just rolled his eyes, massaging his forehead.

"Lucy," I said quietly.

"I know." She reached out and placed a hand on my knee. "I'm sorry." She looked at Ben. "Just break up, or something. I'm sorry I said it, I was in a flap."

"Well, that explains a few things." Ben sighed, seeming agitated, but not angry.

A distant voice called the end of visiting hours. Lucy looked at the upside-down watch on her scrubs. "I'll drop the kids off and come over tomorrow, sort all of this out."

My body felt like it was being pressed down into the sterile bed. "Lucy, no, please."

She shrugged. "Technically, this is a family emergency."

"For god's sake, Lucy, I'll come in tomorrow," Ben told her. "You go to work and stop making this more complicated."

Lucy objected, but we were interrupted by another nurse ushering the ward clear. Reluctantly, they left me. I hadn't bothered to listen to the doctor about what medication they'd given me, but it must have been potent because I managed to drift in and out of sleep.

The next morning, when I'd had my observations done and the nurse seemed pleased, Ben appeared with a pair of coffees, keeping his word.

"Ben, you really don't have to be here," I insisted, pleased to be able to sit up and face him this time; ready to give him the independence speech I'd been rehearsing.

He handed me a cup and tossed a brown bag onto my lap. "Don't start. I say what I mean, you told me that, and I do, so stop telling me I don't have to be here. It's irritating." He paused, giving me a stern look. "I really don't see what your other options are here, Elle. Frankly, you making decisions on your own has only made things a hell of a lot worse."

"But they're still mine, Ben, the decisions," I replied, peering into the paper bag to find a golden pastry. "Thank you," I added, not the least bit hungry.

He sighed. "And you have the right to make them. I'm just telling you that you don't have to. Okay? So, are you going to go to an ill-equipped refuge, or come and live in my spare room? Is there another option I'm missing?"

"It's not that simple."

He shook his head. He looked like he hadn't slept a wink. "What's not simple?"

"I can't just move in with you. Look at me." I directed my own eyes over my broken body. "These people are dangerous. You don't know me."

"We're getting married, don't forget," he remarked, his tone rich with sarcasm. "God, sometimes I wonder if we're even related, Lucy and I." Ben rolled his eyes. "Regardless, I have no problem with you moving in, if that's what you want. Do you even know what you want, Elle? Do you really *want* to go and face Maeve's parents, alone?"

I tipped my head back, exasperated, the word *want* repeating in my head. 'Wanting' wasn't something I did; wanting was dangerous. Wanting led to disappointment, or worse, you reached a point where you stopped wanting things, when your soul couldn't do anything but survive by protecting the last of its light.

I groaned, my hands covering my face.

"It's not a complicated question."

I deflected. "Getting married? Oh, I don't know, I can just imagine you making the flower girl cry, or yelling at me for stepping on your toes during our first dance."

"Elle, the doctor will be coming around soon to discharge you. The spare room is yours if you want it, as long as you need it, or until you figure out what you want to do. I live alone; no one will bother you."

That word again. What did I *want*? My mind was frustratingly blank. Didn't Lucy say he was engaged already? Either way, no option was a good option. I knew I couldn't go to see Susan and Derek White looking like this. I'd sworn to Marcus that I'd leave it alone – I wondered if I should. My body was screaming for Ben's unconventional type of comfort in a way that made staying with him feel like the worst idea of the lot.

"I can't," I muttered.

"You can."

"No, it's not right."

"None of this is right!" he exclaimed, pacing the room. "Nothing about this is right. You in here, them out there. Any of what happened. But, please, for Christ's sake, make a decent choice now. You are the most infuriating woman I've ever met and I swear to you I'm about to get up and walk through those doors and not look back."

"So go," I spat, except it didn't sound aggressive; it sounded pathetic.

Ben marched to the side of the bed, pointing his finger at me. "Tell me that's what you want. Tell me you want me to go and I'll go. Right now."

"Ben..."

"Say it," he hissed.

I licked my lips, willing them to move. They didn't. I felt my eyes start to round as the oncoming tears grew heavy.

"Tell me you have a better, safer option, because I'm looking at you right now and you don't look like someone who can take much more."

I took a shaky breath as he waited me out, not flinching, not retreating from the bedside, towering over me.

"Why? Why are you even offering? I don't understand."

He gritted his teeth, accentuating his strong jaw. "You jumped in that river, Elle. You saved Sophie." His voice softened, his shoulders lowering as he took a step back. "I have a spare room; I have the flexibility. It's the least I can do. God, just let me help you."

"It's not the 'least' of anything. You would've jumped in, if you'd been sat where I was—"

"I'm not dignifying that with a response."

8

Next moves

At least I had clothes on this time.

"Come on," Ben said, exhaustion in his voice as he climbed out of the car.

We'd pulled into a pristine underground car park. The white lines were so crisp they looked like strips of paper.

Reaching for my seatbelt, I winced as the twisting aggravated my healing ribs. I fought to catch my breath as the strap swung across my chest. Ben opened the door for me, ducking back to get the crutches from the rear seats. I sat forwards, tightening my stomach to lift my knees, but the pain was too much and I cried out.

"Shit." I grabbed my own forehead in frustration.

Bloody fancy car with its stupid bucket seats.

"What wrong?" Ben asked, leaning through the door.

I stared at my palm, pressing my temples. "Nothing, I've got it."

Sighing heavily, I gripped behind my knee, clenching my teeth through the pain to lift my leg and swing it out. Ben held out his hand as I wiggled awkwardly into position. I reached for the body of the car, preparing to heave myself up, but my arms just shook.

Ben frowned at me, carefully unhooking my fingers from the metal and pulling me silently to my feet.

I straightened up. "Thanks, it's just the seats, they're really low."

I'd been able to navigate myself through the hospital room to the bathroom, but the distant doors of the car park would be a test for sure. I fumbled to slip my arms into the handles of the crutches.

"You got it?" Ben asked cautiously, backing away.

"Absolutely," I replied shakily, gripping the plastic harder to distract me from the pain.

I managed three pathetic steps before I let out another wince. My leg twisted underneath me and there was nothing I could do. Ben lunged to sweep a hand under my knees, draping my arm around his shoulders, his dark hair brushing against my skin, soft and thick as he lifted me.

"One thing at a time, Bambi," he remarked

It wasn't a joke; he meant it, but for a second, I could breathe deeply again.

I looked at him and gently gripped his shirt, pulling my other hand to rest against his muscular shoulder. I let my head fall into the soft space between his neck and arm, unable to find words; mentally and physically exasperated. I should have fought harder, I should have objected, but I had nothing.

He carried me into the lift before gently putting me back on my feet, keeping a firm, safe grip around my waist this time. The lift, like the car park, looked pristine. I quickly became aware of all the mirrors. I hadn't seen myself properly for what felt like a long time. I flinched. My skin was dull and patchy, my cheekbone sporting a purple bruise. There was a cut on my dry lips that made me look all the more broken. I was wearing the pink hoodie Lucy had washed for me, but it hung off my hunched shoulders. My hair was slung up into a messy bun, and not a good one.

Ben was irritatingly perfect. His almost black hair was swept away from his face, his glasses framing those rich, dark eyes. Every time I thought I'd hit rock bottom, I outdid myself.

Ben supported me effortlessly to the swanky black front door. When he pushed it open, I gasped without meaning to. I hadn't thought about what his home would be like, but it was just like him – preened, and polished, and put-together. The door led straight into a glossy grey kitchen with a breakfast bar. On the other side of the worktop was an angular, black sofa and there was a big television in the open plan lounge. I assumed the rooms to the left were bedrooms and a bathroom.

Ben led me to the sofa before going back to get our bags and my crutches. I sat silently, taking it in. The windows to the right were huge, looking out onto the city where big clouds swept across a blue sky. It was a beautiful place; mature, but interesting and unique. The wooden floor warmed the space and a scattering of books lay nestled between spiky houseplants. I spotted some artwork on the fridge, probably Sophie's if the glitter was anything to go by.

Ben came back with a rustle of bags, taking them straight to the first bedroom.

"Coffee?" he asked simply, relaxing into his home.

"Tea, please. If that's alright?" I sat stiffly, feeling out of place – the most unkept thing in here. "Your apartment is stunning."

He raised an eyebrow at me. "Is it okay if I make you tea? Elle, I'm not going to force you to drink coffee. Seriously, if this is going to be survivable for both of us, you need to stop asking ridiculous questions."

I ran my tongue over my teeth, too tired for restraint and agitated by his harsh reply. "What if you had no teabags?"

It's not what I'd meant; on reflection, it *was* a silly question, but there was something about his attitude that made me want to poke him.

He stared me out. "I have teabags."

"Great," I replied, as he reached for a spoon. "How long have you lived here?"

I took in the white walls. It looked like a show home; there wasn't a single chip in any of the paintwork, no hint of a smear on the large windows.

"Four years. I saw the building go up and bought it off-plan. I liked the big windows, and it's close to work."

The kettle began to hum, but as the boiling subsided, a thick silence remained.

"Thank you," I mumbled. "For helping me up here and letting me stay, again. I'll sort the crutches."

"Stop thanking me, it's unnecessary. Not many people come here – apart from Vicky, who cleans twice a week – so it'll be quiet. There's a television in the bedroom and I can get anything else you need. My secretary is coming to bring some things from work tomorrow so I can be here for the next few days."

He's thought all of this through.

"Oh, okay."

He walked over with two uniform, black, gloss mugs and sat next to me, easing back into the sofa with a sigh. I sat back carefully, positioning my back in a specific way – pressing too much to one side hurt my rib; the other side felt hot and swollen.

"How's your pain?" he asked. "You can take another codeine in an hour. It's all in the bag over there. They gave me all the instructions, courtesy of Lucy, no doubt. Did you want me to draw you up a timetable?" He pointed back to the kitchen units behind us.

"I'll manage, thanks," I assured him, slightly curious about what he would have produced. *I bet it would have been black and white, no colour coding.*

The truth was, I probably wouldn't take the codeine anyway. Strong painkillers complicated injuries because you couldn't tell if you were aggravating them, in my experience. Plus, I hated the headaches they gave me, and I already had one brewing.

There was a long pause as I tried to figure out what I was supposed to do next. Then Ben reached for a box beside the sofa, handing it to me.

"What's this?" I asked, confused, looking at the iPhone box.

"You needed a phone, so I had one set up. I put mine and Lucy's numbers in it for now."

"Ben, I can't take this. These are—"

He shot me a glare over his glasses. "You need a phone."

I looked around. "This is all too much. All of it." I extended the phone back to him. "Please."

He pushed it back so that the box jutted up against my chest. "It's not a big deal. Don't make it one. I said you can stay. You can't work like this. I'm not an idiot. Let me do the basics for you until you're back on your feet without making every part of it so difficult."

I looked down at the shiny box. "I don't know when I'll be able to pay you back."

"I don't need you to. You know, you're really taking all the good out of a good deed. I know you think I'm an arsehole, but you can stay here, I really don't care, money isn't a problem, and even if you tread on my toes, I'm not going to yell at you." He turned his head to look at me, forcing a smile of sorts. It didn't seem genuine. Not like at Rose Cottage.

"Step on your toes?"

"Never mind. Can I get you anything else?" he asked as I held the phone rigidly against my thigh.

"Would you mind if I had a bath?"

"Of course not, make yourself at home."

Without warning, he stood and walked to the main bathroom. I heard water running a few moments later.

"Lucy dropped off some stuff; she's put some toiletries in here for you and a plastic stool," he called across the open plan lounge. "She said you can prop your cast up and use the plastic sleeve."

"Oh, wow. Can you please thank her for me?"

He stuck his head round the door, raising his eyebrows. "Like I said, her number is in the phone."

I bit my tongue, opening the box.

The bath wasn't relaxing, but it made me feel better; more human. Lucy was a life-saver. There was a giant bag full of body wash, shampoo and conditioner, razors, face wash, make-up wipes, moisturiser, and a luxurious smelling body cream. She'd even thought of tweezers. I sat in the shallow bath and took my time, fighting to shave my leg and ankle. I just needed to re-set myself; scrub off some of the shame.

Fortunately, the bath had a mixer shower, so the body parts that wouldn't fit in the shallow water could still be washed. It was exhausting, but good. I sat in the bath until the water drained, getting cold, but I wanted to heave myself out. I couldn't let Ben see me like this.

The next few days were strange, but better that the ones before. Ben was busy for the most part – on the phone or in meetings – so I indulged in the need to stay in bed. He brought me regular meals and I tried to force the food down. The day he ordered Chinese, we sat together and ended up watching a documentary. Lucy had come with more stuff, including pink fluffy slippers and deodorant. I tried to give her some of the money I'd saved, but she refused.

I didn't have any clothes that I could get around my cast, so I had to wear pyjamas. They made me feel like a slob, especially around Ben, but I had no choice. Lucy said she'd take me shopping next weekend.

On Saturday, Ben had gone to the gym. I woke up having slept well, feeling refreshed. Usually, I woke up to a flood of unfinished thoughts, but that morning was quieter.

I ran my hand through my dank, box-dyed hair, remembering the shame they had made me feel whenever I wanted to go back blonde. I poked softly at the bruise under my eye, grounding myself with the soreness.

Once I'd brushed my teeth and washed my face, I hobbled over to the kitchen to make some tea, sitting down and staring out at the grey clouds still roaming above the city. Ben strolled out moments later, wearing blue jeans and a loose branded t-shirt, still rigorously rubbing a towel over his wet hair. He smiled at me, sliding his glasses back over his face.

"Do you want a coffee?" I asked, enjoying that I was now able to move enough to be mildly useful. Being stagnant was torture – I needed to function and move and do things, certainly not be left alone to think.

"No, I'll get it, thanks," he replied from the sofa.

I tried not to let his response wind me up, nodding as I poured my tea, watching several raindrops crash against the huge window.

"What do you do for fun?" Ben asked unexpectedly.

"For fun?" I hesitated, poking at the tea bag with a spoon. "Ride,

I guess. I've always loved being outside… all of the things I can't do at the moment."

"Oh, well, we can go for a walk, if you'd like. Lucy said she could get you a wheelchair."

I spun to look at him. I'd assumed he'd been asking to know, not so we could do something together.

"It's not the same, but thanks for the offer." I assessed his unusually carefree expression suspiciously. "What do you normally do for fun?"

"Not a lot."

"What do you mean?"

"I like my own company and my work." He winced. "That's why I asked you first."

"Do you ride?" I asked, styling out my hobble and trying to hide the dribble of tea that splashed on my finger as I walked over to the sofa, sitting down next to him.

"No. Big unpredictable animals aren't my thing."

"You don't have to entertain me, you know. I won't be offended if you go out. I'm sure you have lots of friends." I could easily picture him in some pretentious bar with his fancy friends, laughing at tedious jokes.

"Why would you think that? Are you trying to get rid of me?"

"Because you seem like the type, and no, not at this exact moment."

"What type is that?"

"Oh god." I laughed, desperately filtering my thoughts. "You know, attractive, intelligent, well-off, successful… are you going to make me go on?"

"Well, I'm not going to stop you," he smirked, lazing back.

"Bossy, rude, grumpy…"

Then he laughed. "Alright, alright, touché. Do you play chess?"

"No. I don't know how."

Ben walked over to one of the cupboards and pulled out a fancy wooden chess set. "If you like strategy and numbers, you'll enjoy this – no legs required."

The pieces clattered inside the box as I tried to identify the strange emotion rising through me. "Ben, really. You don't have to."

He slid the wooden box over the polished coffee table, glancing up at me. "I know."

It was less of a scolding this time, more of a tease.

We played through the first game slowly, so I could learn the moves; it was complicated, but intriguing. Ben won the first actual game, of course.

"Interesting," I said, studiously, trying not to admit how much I'd liked it. The game, not his company. The little pieces were strangely exciting as they charged around on their own little missions.

"You like it?"

"Let's play again." I stared at the castles as we moved them back to their starting lines. It was fascinating how each piece had its own rules.

"I don't have lots of friends, by the way," Ben remarked, continuing our conversation from earlier.

"Oh?" I didn't really know what else to say, focusing on what piece to move first instead. I went with a knight.

"I find people irritating usually."

I laughed. "Thanks for adding 'usually'."

I looked at him as he looked at the board. He moved a piece instantly, dragging a pawn two paces.

"Your opinion of me is interesting," he murmured. "I'm not sure how I've given you that impression."

I paused, distracted as we played a few more moves.

"Nice," he offered, tapping his chin, taking an additional second to choose his next piece.

I glanced up from the board. "You seem so close with Lucy and the kids."

"They're my family. The friends I've had in the past have just been... boring."

"Boring?"

"Don't you find that, when you've been through a journey..." He considered his words carefully. "People just, don't fight? I guess I have different drives than most."

"Well, don't feel obliged to get bored with me."

"I don't find you boring. Frustrating, yes," he replied.

I felt the skin lining my eyes crinkle as I suppressed a grin.

"And unpredictable. I never know what you're going to say, or do. But you're not boring. Checkmate."

"Again?"

"Want me to go easy on you?"

"Never," I huffed.

"You have to think two moves ahead." He paused as I rearranged the pieces. "Did you have friends on the site?"

"Not really. Whenever I connected with someone, it exploded, in a variety of messes. The vet, for example, I liked him before the contract was pulled. Vets have good margins; it was interesting work."

We chatted more as we played, Ben beating me again. I leant back into the sofa with the carved pieces flashing through my mind, pulling my leg up as it began to ache. Aching was better than itching, at this point. Casts were torture. I'd already asked Lucy to get me a comb just so I could ram it down the inside.

"I just need to practice," I reasoned, rolling my aching shoulders.

"How are you feeling? Have you given any more thought to Maeve's parents?" he asked, getting up to make us sandwiches.

I ran a knight through my fingers, placing it down on the board and shifting my weight back. "Constantly, but the more I think about it the more knots I tie myself in. I have no idea what to do."

A knife clunked against the wooden chopping board.

I groaned. "Do not ask me what I *want* to do. Please, for god's sake."

"Am I that transparent?"

I twisted so my arm was resting on the back of the sofa and I could watch him. The cheese slices were unnervingly identical in size.

"When I think about it too much, it all feels like a mistake."

"All of what?"

I rested my chin on my forearm. "Leaving Henworth. It feels like all I did was cause problems."

He looked up as he pressed the bread together. "Don't say that." He bent down and lifted two plates onto the counter. "I meant what I said, you can stay here for as long as you need. Don't repeat this, because I'll deny it, but I haven't hated having company." He headed back over with the two plates of food. "I don't mean to go on, but without the police, or reaching out, what is the plan?"

"Thanks," I said cautiously as he handed me the plate and sat back down. "What if... what if I don't want to be Maeve? What if I just want to get a job, rent a crappy flat, and maybe just, you know, be standard?"

"You can't be standard carrying around Pandora's box. That's not how it works. The lid always comes off, whether you want it to or not"

"That's a wise sounding sentence."

He scowled at me. "I have my moments." He paused, taking a bite; chewing and swallowing. "I don't think you want standard, not really."

"What do you mean?"

"I think you're tired, Elle. I don't think you'll like 'standard' when things settle down."

"I can't imagine anything in my life settling down." I watched his hand as he picked up a scrap of cheese, placing it carefully in his mouth. "Does your fiancée mind me living here?" As soon as the words left my mouth, I flinched. It had played on my mind, but I immediately regretting asking.

"What?" Ben stared at me, utterly confused.

Oh god. "Um," I floundered. "Lucy said... she told me you were engaged. Sorry."

He nodded slowly, narrowing his eyes as he assessed my squirming. "Of course she did. When did you two have this conversation, exactly?"

I straightened my lips and pressed my teeth together. "At Rose Cottage. We weren't really discussing it, as such, she just made a comment, and I don't want to, like, get you in trouble."

Why does it matter? Why did I ask that? Why isn't he answering?

Ben placed his plate down, clearing his throat. "I'm not engaged. Well, only to you, I suppose."

He smirked at me and I hated it. I knew he could see straight through me. My cheeks were burning.

"Why are you blushing?"

I threw my hands to cover my face. "You're making me feel uncomfortable."

He folded his arms, leaning back. Watching me.

"Stop! Stop making it worse."

He raised an eyebrow. "What else did Lucy say?"

I pulled my hands into my lap, scratching a nail across the top of my cast. "She said you're an arsehole. I concur."

He laughed. I watched as his broad chest shook and his eyes glinted.

"You're not funny," I added, scowling hard.

"Alright. Alright." He took a deep breath, lowering his shoulders. "To clarify, I was engaged before, it didn't work out. Anything else you want to know? Or were you just interested in whether I'm single?"

"Oh, get over yourself."

9

Being blonde

Tights.

I held the box in my hand. It was nearly autumn; I had to get them on. This dress needed tights, and jeans were impossible right now.

The black material floated out of the packaging, three pairs unravelling onto the bed. I slid my good leg through one with only minor pain, rocking around on the mattress, trying to balance. When it came to the cast leg though, it went as badly as expected; my fingers slid straight through.

Fantastic.

I held up pair number two, but as I tipped forward, my rib immediately throbbed from the bending. I squeezed all of the air from my lungs so I could fold in half sideways and ease the material over the cast. I wiggled it halfway up, but some of the fibres snagged and an ugly ladder snaked up the material.

"Fuck!" I shouted through clenched teeth, flopping back onto the bed after yanking off the second pair of ruined tights.

I was exhausted with fighting my body on everything – standing to brush my teeth, shaving one leg without dipping the other one in the water, even carrying a bloody cup of tea.

"You okay in there?" Ben called cautiously from the other side of the door.

"Yep," I replied, staring at the ceiling, waiting for a burst of energy that would likely never come.

"Do you need some help with something?"

"Nothing you can help me with, but thank you."

I sighed again, his voice calming me slightly.

Until he nudged the door open.

I sat bolt upright. The t-shirt dress on loan from Lucy wasn't long, and my hopeless sprawling wasn't dignified. I certainly didn't want to be the butt of any more of his jokes. He looked down at the tights on the floor in the silently judgemental way he always did. *Disapproval is his default expression, I swear.*

"Why don't you just wear your trackies? Lucy won't mind."

My reply was harsher than intended. "But I'm a slob *all the time*. I want to feel like a human woman again, not a sick, beaten invalid everyone immediately pities."

He winced. "I mean, that's a lot of emotion over two pairs of tights. Want me to throw them out the window? Burn them? Sue the company who made them?"

He was evidently trying to make me laugh, but I glared at him instead.

"Ha ha."

"I can help."

"With my tights?"

"You're doing better, but you're still fresh out of hospital, no one expects you to suddenly look perfect."

He walked over as he spoke. My eyes followed him as he picked up the remaining pair, looking at me over the top of his glasses. It infuriated me; even in his gym gear he looked like he was about to prance up a sand dune in some fancy aftershave advert.

"It's the last pair," I explained, wondering if he realised what putting on tights involved. "I'll figure it out."

He stretched the material in his fingers, investigating. "High stakes... big risk on your own."

I looked out of the window at the cold, grey weather. "Well, maybe if I put them half on, you can help with the cast," I conceded, provoked by a fresh stab of pain in my chest. "I thought I could cut one leg short, but the elastic just rolled up."

I reached over and took the tights from him, attempting, in vain, to style it out as I thrust in my good leg again. Ben went to speak but stopped himself, pressing a finger into his lips.

"What?"

He pointed, moving the finger. "If you start with the cast, it'll be easier. Your good leg is easier to manoeuvre."

I paused. He was right.

"Of course you're running statistics."

He gave me a look. "Naturally." Smoothly, he took the tights from my hand. "Bambi."

"Do not start calling me that. Seriously."

He smirked. "Why not, it's a classic? Now, lean back."

My body obliged, resting back onto my elbows, like I was temporarily hypnotised, following his command. My own breathing suddenly felt loud as he knelt carefully between my legs, his nose level with the rim of my dress.

I clambered for words to break the silence. "So, what, if I'm a baby deer who's all helpless because his mum got shot, who does that make you? Thumper, the cheerful bunny?"

"Fair," he replied, though he sounded distracted.

I swallowed, my eyes taking in the image of him between my thighs as his gaze trailed up my leg. Without speaking, he took the bundled material and threaded it over my toes. His fingers pulled it easily up over the cast in one steady movement, looking at me, then back down.

Men's hands had always felt rough before – thick and clumsy – but Ben's felt like the perfect balance of sturdy and gentle; he was so precise with everything he did. I decided I liked his hands. Hands that had pulled me back on the verge, caught me when I fell, and dragged me from the river. Hands that were now creeping up my thigh. He knelt up, bending one leg, leaning slightly closer to me, gathering the other leg of the tights. His warm breath settled against my bare skin. I couldn't help but wonder if he was doing it on purpose, seeing how I would react. I had no idea how to, so I just lay there, trying to resist the urge to press my legs into him. That would be wholly inappropriate. *This* was wholly inappropriate.

"Thank you," I said quietly, chewing the inside of my lip.

My fingers curled into the soft duvet. Ben watched my grip crease the material before daring to look straight into my eyes. I tried to read what he was thinking, thankful he couldn't read my mind.

He grinned as he slid his fingers around my other ankle. "I've had worse problems to solve."

I could've stopped him there; I could sort that leg myself. A subtle quiver tickled through me, my neck tilting back in response. He stretched the elastic material over my ankle, over my calf. Slowly. Too slowly. His knuckles glided over my skin, causing something inside me to flicker. I could feel the gentle grooves of his fingers caressing my freshly shaven, moisturised leg. He was just about to reach my knee when he raised those dark eyes again, looking up at me from between my legs, a hint of something carnal in them. Both of his firm hands were wrapped around my thigh.

We paused.

We breathed.

Oh god.

"Thank you," I rasped out. "I can do the rest."

I was terrified that my body was about to surrender. Ridiculous. Crazy. Deluded. It would have been the most foolish thing I had done up until this point, and that was saying something.

"If you rip them again, I'll be pissed," Ben replied, with the hint of a growl in his tone. "Be careful."

Ben's steady hands paused for a second; longer, as our gazes held. Then, with one easy movement, he stood up, and we both snapped back to our senses.

As he walked out of the room, my soul almost pulled towards him, yearning for him to stay. I pushed the feeling down.

He was just helping me. Nothing more.

Taking a long, slow breath, I finished getting myself ready for a day shopping with Lucy and Sophie. I hadn't managed to save much money over the past few years, but it would be enough for some much-needed essentials.

It felt amazing having a girly day with the two of them. I found thicker tights that I could get on more easily, alone; some denim shorts

– jeans would remain out for a while; short floaty dresses cinched at the waist, and leggings. I was drawn to soft jumpers, pretty colours, and floral fabrics. I'd never spent time thinking about style before. I had never wanted to look feminine, desperate to avoid attention on the site. That day, though, I allowed myself the small pleasure of liking things.

Looking at myself in the long, imposing shop mirrors, I realised I was starting to look like a person – a pink, girly one. One with a life, with choices, perhaps with a future all to herself. Riding on the dizzying feeling and new independence, anything felt possible, and, for what felt like the first time in my life, I decided to go with my heart.

I took a deep breath and looked at Lucy. "Don't suppose we have time to go to the hairdressers?"

She lit up. "What do you reckon, Soph? Shall we go get our nails done too?"

Walking into the salon, we caught people's attention and I doubted myself all over again. But when the hairdresser offered us a private room and Sophie went giddy over all the shades of pink nail polish, I found the words I'd toyed with for years.

"Make me blonde."

After that, it was pretty much magic. I let Sophie choose a design for my nails as the hairdresser battled with stripping the cheap hair colour as best he could. We drank hot chocolate, we giggled, and as the foils came off and the glitter went on, I found something in myself entirely new.

"Ben is going to lose his mind," Lucy whispered as we rode the lift back to his apartment.

I turned to look at her.

She grinned.

"We're becoming friends," I defended. "I hope, anyway. This last week has been a blur."

"Well, I feel like I'm taking back a different person, Elle. I mean it – you look bloody amazing!"

I blushed. What *would* Ben think? Nothing, I was sure. However, as Lucy wheeled me towards the door, I felt nervous, expectant. It was silly, but I wanted him to like how I looked, to see me; see me as a girl, a woman, not bloody Bambi.

The door opened and excitable voices rang out from the lounge; Ben and Isac were still on the PlayStation. Ben turned around to greet us as Sophie tumbled inside and Lucy wheeled me over the threshold with a metallic clatter.

"Hiya," he called, distracted, but as he went to look back at the screen, he did a double take.

I watched his eyes fall to my new clothes and track slowly up, pausing on my pink lips, then my hair, before he turned back to the game.

"You two look like you're having a nice time," Lucy called out. "Look what we've been up to!" She waved her hands over me dramatically like some sort of magician.

Ben turned again, smiled awkwardly at me. "I can see."

"Isn't she gorgeous?" Lucy said, resting her hands on my shoulders.

I shot her a look, standing up unsteadily as Ben hummed, turning back to the TV again.

My heart sank. It was irrational to have expected a reaction; I'd gotten carried away with the excitement of the day. Having been surrounded by Lucy's warmth, I'd forgotten how different the siblings were. Why would Ben care if I had different hair?

I squeezed Lucy again as we said our goodbyes, thanking her. Sophie hugged me tightly and told me she'd had the best day ever, which nearly bought a tear to my eye.

"Me too," I whispered back.

I was leaning on the breakfast bar when the door closed behind them and I finally realised how tired I was. My neck crackled and my stomach muscles ached.

"You look... different," Ben commented, taking me in again,

blatantly unsure.

"Um, thanks?" I pursed my lips, feeling my body shrink. I knew I shouldn't care, but he could have at least been polite about it.

He looked at me cautiously, standing in the kitchen, the worktop between us. "Do you like it?"

"What? *Do I like it?*" Irritation sparked inside of me. I stood up, balancing on my leg, adding extra distance. "Why would you ask me that?"

"That's not what I— look, I've been trying to give you space, Elle, but it's like Lucy has gone and swapped you out for a completely different person."

His words knocked me straight out of my good mood. I knew he was simply repaying a favour, after what I did for Sophie. Yet we seemed to have this... draw to each other. We'd started sitting together, choosing to chat, especially after we started playing chess. *Was it all a lie? Something he did out of pity?*

"Elle?" he probed, seeming to sense my freak out. "You look nice, really, you do. It's not that."

"Thanks," I interrupted, before he could continue.

Nice.

That was the word you said when you were saving someone's feelings.

God, they'd been right. I'd made a total fool of myself. I couldn't be pink and blonde and feminine, of course I couldn't. I was scarred and flawed and plain. Ruby, Frank, Marcus, they'd all said it. I sucked on my lip, suddenly struggling to keep it together.

I turned and hobbled towards the bathroom. Ben didn't say anything else, confirming this was another error of judgement to add my list. I scrubbed my teeth until my gums hurt before staring at myself in the mirror. Looking at the feathered edges of my long blonde hair, the pink eyeshadow and lashings of mascara, I rubbed my hands together, covering them in soap, and started washing off the make-up, needing to find my real self again. I splashed water over my face and looked back up. The peppered bruising was back, as were the dark circles under my reddening eyes, but with the new golden blonde frame, they looked different. Ben was right. My forehead fell into my hands as I broke; as I sobbed and cried and shook. What was I thinking? How had I become so lost?

I filled the bowl with fresh cold water, my cheeks tightening as I pressed it into my skin, steadying my gasping breaths as I tried to calm down.

When I heard Ben in his ensuite, I made a break for the guest bedroom, reaching for my pyjamas, needing to just get into bed and close my eyes. My ribs throbbed from all the effort as I pulled my jumper over my head.

Ben knocked on the door, making me jump.

"I'm going to bed," I called out, pulling my jumper down.

"I want to talk," came the muffled reply.

I hesitated, stuck between worrying about my blotchy face and unsure what to say, long enough for him to stride inside.

"*I* told Lucy not to call or follow you that day. *I* told her not to," he declared bluntly, standing agitated at the foot of the bed.

My eyebrows twitched as I tried to make sense of what was happening, still holding my jumper down as if it would leap over my head by itself.

"It's my fault you're hurt."

"What? No," I replied defensively. "Look, I'm sorry about earlier. I just, I guess, my relationships have been weird, at best. Unconventional. Living here, it's been too easy; I thought maybe we were becoming friends. I've enjoyed your company, and earlier, I just read too much into it. I expected something different, but you've been so honest with me, you keep saying you have the space and I—"

"Stop." He ran his hands through his hair. "God, Elle, no. You don't get it. It's *my fault* you ended up in hospital." His voice cracked. "I told Lucy not to go after you. I left you at the side of the road. I kicked you out of Rose Cottage. At every step, I've put you at risk."

"You were protecting your family, Ben. Besides, what's that got to do with anything?" I let go of the hem of my jumper, wringing my hands.

He started pacing, roughly raking his hand through his hair. I could have sworn his face had paled.

"Everything! I'm waiting for you to hate me. I'm waiting for you to figure it all out, put it all together. It's driving me crazy."

"Lucy told me, Ben, that you told her not to go after me, but I get it," I explained as my eyes tracked his erratic movements. "I told you they were dangerous. I knew they'd come after me. I didn't expect you or Lucy to do anything about that. You couldn't have."

He pulled his hand down, stopping before me as I perched on the edge of the bed. "You should, though. You should expect that." He paused. "You just jumped straight into that river without a thought, didn't you?"

I saw pain in his scrunched-up expression and stood, taking a second to get my balance. "Yes, because I saw Sophie fall, that's all. You offering me this room, Lucy being Lucy, it's all saved my life. In ways I can't even tell you."

He turned away and headed for the door. "I need a minute."

"Ben, wait."

He ignored me, disappearing.

"Don't walk away."

I heard clattering as he locked up; everything was clumsy and loud, so unlike him. I finished getting into my pyjamas, running through his words and growing angry. Nothing made sense. Why was he mad at me?

Ten minutes later, he tapped more gently on the door and crept into the lamplight.

I sat up in bed with the television flickering. "For a grown man, your communication is erratic, at best. I'm sorry for whatever I've done to wind you up."

He dropped down heavily at the end of the bed, gathering himself. "Your hair suits you."

The compliment didn't make me feel any better. "Right, great. Thanks."

"I don't understand you," he admitted.

I laughed with disbelief. "The feeling is mutual."

"How can you not be mad at me? When we talk, you get this look in your eyes like you like me, like you want to get to know me, and I can't work out if it's the concussion or..." He stopped, struggling to find the words.

I bought my finger and thumb to my bottom lip, pinching it, waiting for him to continue. "Or?"

"Or if your life was so hard before that you actually enjoy spending time with someone like me."

I frowned. "You're the one who stayed in to teach me chess; you suggested we watch that film; you told me I could keep you company while you worked?"

"Because you're strangely addictive."

"God, Ben! Are you just winding me up? Really? You know what, we joke, but maybe you really are an arsehole."

He looked taken aback, shaking his head quickly. "I'm being deadly serious."

"I'm sure you are."

"Hey," he growled. "I thought you looked beautiful, okay? When we first met, you played on my fucking mind all evening at the conference, and now, well, you get the gist."

I grunted loudly and did the only sensible thing I could think of – pulled the duvet up over my head and groaned into the material. What was he talking about? When we met, I was sat in a pile of mud. I knew I wasn't beautiful; Sam had said I was pretty a handful of times, but that was only when I didn't have riding gear on.

The duvet was tugged out of my hands, lurching my body forwards.

"What is wrong with you?"

"What's wrong with *you*?" I shouted, letting go of the fabric to thrash my arms around.

"How exactly have I offended you with the word 'beautiful' now?"

My lip quivered, my heart pounding as he said it again. He watched me, letting go of the duvet, assessing what I had accidentally laid out for him to see. I bit down on my tongue.

"I'm not vain, Ben. I know what I am and what I'm not. Just go away."

He didn't. He sat there, looking directly at me as I wished the bed would swallow me up.

"I'm lost. You don't care that I didn't chase after you, protect you, but I compliment you and that upsets you? What I've been trying, poorly, apparently, to explain, is that I like you. In fact, when I make you blush and your cheeks go that red, rosy colour, I think it may just be my favourite feeling in the world, but that's my problem. I feel like I can't tell you these things, like I have no right to tell you how breathtaking you look, because I'm the arsehole who let you get the train; who left you."

I blushed, pulling the duvet up desperately in an attempt to hide as I felt the blood rush through my veins. Ben gripped his end, pulling so I had nowhere to hide; so he could watch me squirm. I hunched my shoulders up and buried my face behind my arms. He grinned at me, like he had at Rose Cottage, tilting his glasses. I pulled my hands up in a last-ditch attempt to cower, but he took them, shuffling closer and placing them back down, threading his fingers through mine.

"Don't," he said simply.

Ben was sat in bed with me, holding my hands. I looked at our palms, slowly allowing my fingers to grip around his. I should have recoiled; this should feel wrong. After all the touches I'd never wanted, I thought I would be content to never be close to a human again. I didn't know if it was Ben's confidence, the surety with which he moved, but he felt... safe. He felt made me feel safe, even when he was being infuriating.

"I don't blame you, for any of it," I said softly.

"How are you so good? After everything?" He stroked his thumb over mine, the feeling washing through my entire body as our anger evaporated.

"I'm not good, Ben. But hate... it drowns people, and I don't think I can stomach another drop."

"So, you know you *should* hate me?"

"I shouldn't and I don't, however much you press my buttons."

We stayed together for a minute, just breathing.

"I should let you rest," he said quietly, but didn't move, still stroking my thumb.

"Probably," I nodded.

The TV programme changed and he turned to see what was playing; Countdown had come on, the late-night comedy version.

Ben shrugged one shoulder. "Don't want to say anything nice and make you angry again."

"Unlikely," I replied, fighting my smile, "knowing you."

"I'm that bad?"

"I seem to remember you calling me stupid within two minutes of meeting me."

"You were sat in the road."

I took my hands from his and batted his knee.

He didn't move back, content to torment me further. "Then you broke into my house, slept in my bed, and shouted at me for eating a biscuit."

I grinned, shaking my head. "Yep, you should definitely go."

He pushed his hands down and went to stand. "Good night, then."

I pulled the covers back up, not hiding this time. "I doubt your big ego would like it if I beat you at all the number rounds," I mumbled, cocking my head towards the television.

He paused, smiling again. "Big talk, Bambi."

"Seriously?" I gritted my teeth and lobbed a pillow at him. "If you call me that one more time, I swear I'm going to—"

"Hide under the duvet?"

I threw myself back with a growl as he picked up the pillow and walked around to the empty side of the bed, climbing in. He unfolded my arms, firmly taking my hand and holding it between us as we got comfortable.

This was becoming even more dangerous than before.

10

Prosecco truths

I beat Ben. When I got the tie breaker correct before the host had even stopped speaking, I laughed at the face he made so hard my ribs hurt.

Target: 245
Numbers: 25, 50, 2, 1, 4, 8

It made me wonder if I was a competitive person, underneath it all. Life outside of Henworth involved figuring out what colours I was inside. I wondered if every part of my personality was a coping mechanism to survive; each new day away from that place and those people, I felt I could explore a bit further, even if it felt like a disservice to the pain.

Drifting awake, I reached down to scratch my leg. Finding plaster, I grunted, reaching for my scratching comb. I was so over this cast; I swore they would find a home of ants in there when they eventually took it off. I noticed steam dancing from a mug of fresh tea. I stared at it whilst immediately trying to deny last night's conversation. I ran my fingers through my hair, twirling it in front of my eyes. Still blonde.

When I ventured out of the bedroom, things were immediately strange between me and Ben. Too much smiling.

Conveniently, he got called away on business the next day. I heard him angrily insisting he couldn't go, but convinced him I'd be alright, needing to try and figure out what was happening. Apparently, him thinking I was a thief was at least one animosity we were past.

BEN
Good morning. How you feeling today?

ME

Enjoying the peace and quiet, actually. Polishing every
surface to make sure the place still looks unlived in –
found your stash of premium microfibre cloths. 😊
How's Scotland?

BEN

Good. Successful. We've been making progress with
the restructure. I told you I'm not home a lot usually.
You don't need to clean, Vicky will be in later, don't
forget.

ME

Get back to work already x

When the evening came, Lucy burst through the door, shaking
two bottles of Prosecco at me, looking relaxed in leggings and a cream
jumper.

"El la la la! I've had a shitty day. Let's get drunk in my brother's
bachelor pad."

I grinned at her, instantly feeling her energy lift mine.

"Hi Lucy." I smirked, rising to grab some glasses. They were on
the top shelf, so even at full stretch only my fingers grazed the crystal
bases. Kitchens should be accessible for all heights; I hated that Ben's
cupboards had entire shelves I couldn't reach. "What's up?"

Lucy grimaced. "Steven is still pushing the issue of having Isac
back at his house. Then Teresa started messaging me."

She proceeded to show me the texts between her and Steven's
partner as we went to sit down. Isac had finally opened up to Lucy
that his stepbrothers were bullies, so Lucy had stopped him visiting.
Teresa was trying to make out that the boys were really upset, saying
that Lucy was causing drama and punishing Steven for the sake of it.

"She's jealous because she's not as pretty as you," I said, enjoying
the cool bubbles as they fizzed on my tongue.

"Younger."

"Barely. I mean, she'll always be waiting for him to get *bored of her* too."

"Here's hoping." Lucy had already finished her first glass and was now ordering pizzas as we sat on the sofa.

"So, what have you decided to do with your life?"

I laughed. "That's deep for one glass, Lucy. Give me a chance."

She grabbed the frosted bottle from the silver cooler –which, naturally, Ben just had lying around. The ice cubes rattled as she poured me a fresh glass with a wink.

"Drink up, then. What's the big plan? I'm kind of jealous. You have, like, this total fresh start, you know. You can be whoever you want to be."

I loved and hated how upfront she was. "I liked doing accounts before, and caring for the horses."

"Good god, no! You can't, please!" She feigned collapsing back into the sofa, a drop of prosecco sloshing on her jumper.

I laughed. "What do you mean?"

"What sort of weird therapy has Ben pulled on you? You tell him that and he might propose, for real this time."

I scowled at her.

"You know what I mean, Elle. What are you doing about your potentially sought after DNA?"

I took a long drink. "I don't think it's the right time. Look at me." I wiggled my toes. "What would they think? I need to get myself well before I stroll up to two people and drag up their painful past to just inevitably disappoint them, embarrass myself and piss on the tentative peace Marcus brokered."

Lucy frowned. "Peace is not the word I'd use. Look." She tucked her legs up on the sofa so she could face me, making herself comfortable. "I did some reading about them."

"Lucy!"

"What? You're telling me you haven't? You're not curious?"

Certain emotions had always overpowered others for me, and fear always trumped curiosity. Looking would make everything harder.

"No."

"Well, lucky for you, I'm nosey enough for the both of us. They do indeed still live in that house, and every year the whole street put out tealights for you on your birthday."

"You can't say *my* birthday."

"On her birthday, then. The girl who has the same scar as you; who looks remarkably similar to you; who disappeared when she was five years old, which is the same age you were in your first memories of the caravan park."

"We don't know that the first one is true, Lucy. I showed you, it's all scarred," I objected. "And just because we have the same eye and hair colour doesn't mean anything."

"So? Do a DNA test and find out," she retorted.

I rested my head back and shut my eyes. Lucy was bursting my safe bubble of denial.

"Elle." Lucy placed a friendly hand on my knee. "I cannot imagine how I would live if that happened to Soph or Isac. When children go missing... Elle, finding a body is sometimes better for the parents than the relentless uncertainty – at least death brings closure. They never had any other children. They're still searching, year after year, doing all those news stories and stuff."

"Exactly." I lifted my head. "What if I get their hopes up and I'm not her?"

"Then you move on with your life, and you maybe give the police a lead with the photo."

My breath caught. "I don't have it anymore."

"What?"

I put my glass down on a coaster, regret heavy in my bones. "The photo, I've not had it since the attack. They took it."

Lucy tapped her glass against her lips. "But you know it was there. That's something. Look, we go round in circles and we never seem to actually have the conversation. What if you *are* her? What if you find your family? What if they get their daughter back?"

I cleared my throat and sniffed back a wave of emotion. "What if they do, and they realise they were better off not knowing?"

Lucy squeezed my knee again, putting her glass down. "What do you mean?"

"Nothing." I lifted her glass onto a coaster.

"Oh, come off it. Tell me or I'll... I don't know."

"Arrange another marriage for me?"

She laughed. I liked how she laughed; it was always free and loud and jiggly.

"I like you, Elle, you know that? I was looking forward to hanging out more this evening."

I sighed. "Isn't it worse if they find out it's me? What have I got for them to be proud of?" My voice cracked as I aired the words that had bubbled up from a deep, dark well in my mind.

Lucy flung her arms around me, her thick hair tickling my nose. "Elle, don't be an idiot. You're the strongest woman I know. You left *them*, by yourself."

I held my body stiff, keeping the fragile wall of control as she moulded to me. "When I was twenty-four, after all those years. And I didn't just stay, Lucy, I did things. Things that make me incredibly unworthy of all of this, let alone them."

She reached round and lifted my hands to her back, making me hug her. "You went to their house once, wanting to find out. What changed?"

I pressed my hands into her back, blinking away an unwelcome tear. I was always one thought away from blubbering and I was sick of it.

"Every day that I'm not there, I remember more. It's like I was coping before; keeping my head above water." I pulled away and grabbed a tissue from the stainless-steel box, mopping at my face. "But now... you and Ben have been so kind, I finally see how wrong it all was. How everything was an ugly lie and how I could've done better, should've done better."

Lucy took my hand. "Stop being so hard on yourself."

I caught a glimpse of myself in the glass of the coffee table, I was still bruised, and now blotchy too. I looked at her. How much further was there to fall?

"When I wouldn't lift money from the books of one of the clients, they shot Baloo, my dog..."

I let the words hang in the air, heavy. Waiting for Lucy to pale and run for the door.

To her credit, she adjusted her position and reached down, passing me my glass. "Okay."

I traced a stripe of condensation. "So, I did, once, but I couldn't handle it, so I told the client – they'd become my friend and I knew they couldn't afford it. I begged them not to go to the police, to just steer clear and get another accountant, but they did, and things... escalated."

"What happened?" Lucy asked, calmly.

"They ended up in hospital."

"And you?"

"I deserved what I got." I licked my lips and rested my shaking hand, steadying the glass on my knee and watching as the drink rippled. Remembering didn't just feel like I was seeing it, recalling it; I was living it, feeling it, tasting it.

"Jesus, Elle. That's awful."

I looked up at her. "It was all my fault, Lucy. Whenever I tried to do the right thing, someone always got hurt. The police did nothing, things only got darker, and to make up for me involving them, they... made me keep the officers... quiet... *appease* them."

"Bastards," Lucy muttered.

"This is what I'm saying, Lucy. My past, it's all grey. I'm not this innocent victim. I saw things... I didn't know what to do, so I did nothing. It wasn't like I had anyone I could tell. Then it got worse when I met Sam; I finally had a reason to keep the peace, so I stopped fighting all together. They knew not to ask me to get directly involved any more, but I knew the things they were doing."

Lucy just shook her head.

"Do you see? That's why I can't just speak to the police. Not only do they already know, but I'm complicit. They made me part of it,

Barnes and Dores. *He* made me part of it." My stomach turned as I remembered the taste of the whisky they'd plied him with. The smell of his sweaty boxers. The feeling of desperately trying to relax so at least it wouldn't hurt.

"What about your parents?"

I scoffed. "I was never good enough for them. Especially Ruby, she resented me no matter what I did. I spent years trying to please her, but it was like the harder I tried the more disgusted she was."

"What about school?"

I shook my head. "I was homeschooled."

"By who?"

"Myself, I guess. I told you, this is why you can't get involved with me. I shouldn't have even told you those things. You have kids; Ben has this life. I'm a poison. Don't you see? I'll destroy it all without even meaning to. I'll do that to them, too, to Susan and Derek. They won't want this. I think it's probably better they just don't know."

Lucy grabbed both my hands, sloshing my drink. "Abusers do this, Elle. They make you feel small, they're clever like that. None of what happened was your fault. You're a kind, sweet, genuine person despite everything you have been through, which makes you a saint. A hero. You need help, and we can find it for you. You deserve to choose how to live the rest of your life. Let me help you."

Fresh tears filled my eyes, blurring my vision. "Why? Why would you do that? Why aren't you *listening*?"

"I want to help you *because* I've been listening."

I sobbed. "You don't hate me?" It sounded so juvenile; a pathetic plea I had no right to make.

"Not at all."

We looked at each other for a long second; a few long seconds.

"What if they hate me? I don't think I can take anyone else being ashamed of me," I mumbled, my voice cracking as my throat closed up.

Lucy held my eye contact, showing me that she wouldn't falter. "Either way, they won't. I promise."

"You can't promise that."

"I can."

The bell buzzed, making me jump.

"That'll be the pizza," Lucy said, walking to the door. She took the boxes, kicking the door shut, before setting them down on the coffee table. "I'm a mother, Elle, and I'm yet to hear you say a single thing that makes me think less of you. Well, apart from liking my hugely obnoxious brother."

I winced. "I appreciate you being so kind, really, I do, but they're bad people, and—"

"And what?" she interrupted. "Regardless of biology, it doesn't sound like they were real parents to you. Are you forgetting that I saw you in the hospital? After what they did? You just told me that you told that client the truth, despite the consequences."

"I could've done more," I mumbled, the words falling out of me as my eyes looked at the floor.

"Like what, exactly? Indulge me," Lucy pushed, staring at the side of my face.

I looked at her. "Like anything."

"Like told the police? Oh wait, no. How about pack a bag and run away with nowhere to go? Sit at the side of the road, in the dark, alone. Knowing how fucking scary they were, because even that was better than staying?"

She flicked open a box of pizza, letting the soothing smell of warm cheese fill the air before grabbing a slice and biting the end.

"You weren't there," I insisted. "I should have done something."

She grabbed a tissue from the box and rubbed her fingers on it. "Look, I don't want to come in here and push you to talk about things you're not ready for, but I don't want you to think you have these big secrets to be ashamed of. I want you to know we can talk about this stuff, when you want to." She shut the box and slid it over, leaving her palm flat on the top. "Alright?"

I relented, nodding.

Lucy smiled, slapping a huge slice of pizza into my hand, pulling at the string of cheese and licking her fingers.

"Thank you," I added.

"You're welcome. Now, what shall we watch to distract me from the sheer number of calories I'm enjoying right now?"

I straightened my lips. "A film with a woman so disastrous that I feel better about myself?"

She topped up both our glasses before wiping her hands on her leggings and reaching for the remote control. "*Bridget Jones*?"

"Hm, she's just unlucky, isn't she? She ends up with two hot men chasing after her even though she wears huge knickers."

"*Black Swan*?"

I laughed.

"Ooh, no, we need *Kill Bill*!"

My phone vibrated on the table in front of us.

BEN

How's your evening? Tell me Lucy isn't making a mess of my apartment? x

ME

She did say she should have bought some of that pink glitter you put in drinks. Maybe next time x

Lucy leaned over the now empty boxes; the alcohol had got us both to the point where all movements were exaggerated, and we had indeed started watching *Bridget Jones*.

"Is my brother texting you?" she asked, tilting my phone. "Oh, tell him to do one. Is he checking on me?"

I laughed and read her his text.

"Tell him you set me up on one of those funny dating apps, the uniform one. No, the older men one!"

We both laughed, falling into each other affectionately.

BEN

Hard no. What exactly are you up to? xx

We're having a drink and making her some dating profiles. She wanted to try that app for older men xxx

That better be a joke.

We laughed again. When the film was over and the bottles empty, Lucy made her exit, having both broken me and built me back up all in one evening.

I couldn't argue with her any more about my DNA. I knew I'd never really be ready.

It was time to open another can of worms.

The next day passed quietly as I carefully considered Lucy's suggestion.

LUCY

So, I looked at the DNA thing. Previous girls have come forward, so I think it'll work. We can drop something at the station and get them to check, see if we can rule you in without letting them know who you are. No harm no foul, right? XX

ME

Okay. How was Sophie's ballet show? XX

LUCY

It was adorable, sickly, even. I felt kind of bad for not tearing up like the other mums. I'll find out what we need to take. It's probably a swab. You want me to see if I can sort it today – before you change your mind? XX

ME

No, thanks. I need a bit more time to prepare myself XX

I'll come tomorrow XXX

Ben was due back the next day so I gave the surfaces another quick wipe – it had taken me hours, but I'd made a lasagne for him – before putting on pyjamas.

As I was getting a lost in *Tangled*, there was a loud bang at the door I sat bolt upright on the sofa.

I wasn't expecting anyone.

I went over to the door clumsily with one crutch. Peering through the peephole, I saw a woman. A tall, beautiful brunette, dressed impeccably in a suit dress and *Chanel* belt. She clutched a perfectly matching *Gucci* bag and her hair flowed in crafted curls. Her brown eyes were framed by what were either amazing natural lashes, or perfect extensions. I tipped the handle slowly to peer out the door, steadying myself.

Her toned body stiffened immediately. "Oh, who are you?"

The question threw me. "Erm, Ben's not in at the moment. Can I take a message?" My reply was nervy and uncomfortable.

"I don't need you to take a message," she spat through her shiny doll teeth. "What are you doing in his apartment if he isn't here. You're not even dressed? Is he in there?"

My grip on the door handle tightened with every word that came out of her mouth. "No, he's not, he's away."

She looked me up and down, smirking. "You landed on your feet, didn't you? Well played."

I felt even smaller than usual. "I don't really know what you want me to say, but I think you'd better go." I was pleased to be able to force the words out, trying to hide my panic. No one had spoken to me like that in weeks; I could feel my body starting to shake. That feeling of someone hating me, being disgusted by me, triggered my heart to start pounding. I wished I'd changed out of my bloody pyjamas.

"Of course, darling, just tell Ben he owes Jessica lunch when he's back." She looked me up and down again before flicking her hair and stomping off.

I clicked the door shut, turning to lean against it. I listened as her shiny black stilettos clattered rhythmically down the hall and let myself fall to the floor in a cascade of emotions. If that was the type of woman Ben normally spent time with, what was I doing? We couldn't be friends. Why would anyone want to be my friend? That's what they had said, again and again.

I slid down further, hugging my knees.

Marcus had once yelled at me so intensely that I'd scrubbed the spit off my face three times, until my skin was raw. The scrubbing had made my face sting, but that was a comfort compared to his venom. He'd lost his temper because I'd let one of the clients off a few payments when I'd known they were struggling financially.

"Stupid whore!" he'd yelled.

They'd ransacked my caravan, throwing the bed upside down, tossing my pots and pans in the mud, telling everyone I didn't respect the business or need the money, so I didn't need any of my stuff. Frank, my dad, had walked past, swigging whisky from the bottle, and hadn't even flinched as they shoved me into the mud. When your parent doesn't protect you, it makes you feel like you got exactly what you deserved. If your own parents have a low opinion of you, you must be shit. A shitty, useless person.

My mind was a circus of memories breaking free. Once they were there, if I ignored them, they just became louder, more real, fighting to perform for my attention. I could taste the mud, smell the whisky. Thankfully, my phone distracted me from my spiral, but I must have been there a while because the door had become warm against my back. The thought of standing up felt impossible; I'd been imprisoned by anxiety.

BEN

Good night, I'll be back tomorrow lunchtime, let me know if you need anything on the way back xx

I considered texting him straight back about Jessica, but it would just make me look more pathetic. Lucy was right, I needed to stop hiding. It was the cold, hard slap around the face I'd needed, sitting alone on a stranger's floor, somewhere I so clearly didn't belong. *That* was the sort of woman Ben had at his beck and call, of course it was. I couldn't stay here and get drawn in.

Lucy was my friend, and that was more than I'd ever dared to want.

11

Found photographs

Fate had seemingly grown impatient. I gawked at Susan on the television screen, barely recovered from the swab Lucy had taken earlier. I'd been waiting for Ben to get back, watching the lasagne crisp up, when I'd seen it on the news; when she'd held the photo up. I twisted so hard I hurt my barely recovered rib, sending myself tumbling into a heap against the worktop, struggling to find my grip. I'd been used to having two legs for longer than one. I didn't even remember leaving the kitchen area, but I was sitting down when I heard the door open. My eyes were fixed on the screen.

"Hello, Bambi," Ben called from behind.

I stared at the repeating news story.

"I mean, I didn't expect you to have missed me exactly, but—"

"The photo must have fallen out of my bag. Susan found it." I turned to him, finally blinking. "Maeve's mum found the photo, and now they're investigating it." I clutched the damp flannel in my hand – I'd knocked my lip when I fell.

Without dropping the laptop bag from his shoulder, he paced over to me, sitting beside me and gently taking my jaw in his hand, angling it up to look at my lip.

"What happened?" he gasped, not letting go.

"I was looking at it outside their gate; I thought Marcus took it."

His thumb grazed over my chin. "No, what happened to you?" He lowered his hand and dropped his bag from his shoulder.

"Oh, I fell," I explained. "I'm fine. But..." I looked back at the newsreel. "Look. They'll know, Ben. They'll all know." I could hear the air rushing in and out of my lungs.

He looked at the screen long enough to read the appeal running along the ticker tape. "How will they know?"

I tried desperately to slow my breathing. "Lucy took a DNA swab this morning. We thought we could do it anonymously, so they didn't have to know, you know, unless they needed to know."

He shook his head, suddenly animated. "What? Why didn't you tell me?"

I clenched the flannel, staring down at the fleck of blood. "Oh god."

"Hey. Elle, look at me."

I turned slowly to face him.

"It's going to be okay. You're okay." He rested his warm palms on my knees. "You're alright, Elle, just breathe."

He was right, I felt like I'd been pretending to breathe. My phone rang and my eyes darted towards the screen. Lucy. I stood up, forgetting yet again that one leg was useless, and stumbled around the corner of the sofa.

My mind was racing. "I can't, I can't..."

I can't be her. I can't speak to them. I can't see him *again.*

I stepped back, reaching a hand towards the worktop. "I can't."

Ben appeared beside me instantly, pulling me into his chest without hesitation. It felt like he was holding the pieces of me together. My phone went silent before starting up again.

"She can wait a minute," he reassured me, tucking my head into his shoulder and gently rubbing my back.

The next few hours were a haze. Lucy had insisted on coming over when Ben picked up the phone. We all sat and watched the news together on the sofa. Lucy asked me to explain what I'd told her the night before whilst Ben insisted that we could scrape the burnt black layer on the top of the lasagne off. Lucy twitched every time her phone lit up. She'd given the police my number, and it wasn't long before they called.

Lucy gripped my hand. "Answer it. It'll be okay."

"What if it's *them*?" I asked in a whisper, the hairs on my neck standing on end.

I glanced down as the phone vibrated steadily across the table, the reverberating glass escalating my heart rate with every buzz.

Ben looked at us both and Lucy nodded. He answered the call. I tried to hear the words, but it was like my brain refused.

He looked at me, placing his hand over the microphone. "It's a DS Ernest. From the Maeve case department."

I focused on breathing. Focused on letting the air in and out as I stayed frozen. Ben paced off into his bedroom with the phone.

"It'll be alright," Lucy soothed. "Ben will make sure it's alright."

In what felt like no time at all, Ben was back, extending the phone to me. "The two officers you mentioned before, you don't need to worry about them."

Tentatively, I took the phone. It didn't feel like me talking as I answered their questions. It felt robotic. Lucy had to leave to get the kids from their after-school club, so Ben sat with me while I explained the basics down the phone, including how I'd found the photo. It didn't take much before they were knocking on the door.

It was like walking on glass, waiting for one fracture to bring everything down. I told them about Henworth, keeping the details vague, leaving their colleagues out of it. Ben sat beside me, an arm around my shoulders, encouraging me to keep going when I couldn't. After an hour of questions, they asked to see the mark on my shoulder. I looked at Ben, who held me whilst one of the officers rolled up my shirt and made some notes. I buried my head in Ben's shirt. The DNA results would take two or three days, so we had no choice but to wait. The officers agreed to keep things anonymous for now, at least until the results came through.

Ben ran me a bath when they'd gone, insisting I eat something, despite my protests. I tried to hide the fact that I was sick shortly afterwards. When I eventually made it to bed, the room was spinning.

"Do you need anything else?" Ben asked, appearing with a glass of water and placing it down as I gripped the sheet, feeling like I genuinely might fall out of the bed.

"I'm so sorry, Ben."

He sat down carefully by my legs. "I'm going to get a sorry jar. Please stop. You have nothing to be sorry for, we knew this would happen one way or the other. At least now you'll know."

"What if they come here? Looking for me."

"They won't get into the building, and besides, it doesn't seem like the police knew anything. You could've told them more, but I understand why you didn't. One thing at a time. The way I see it, you're safer now; they won't be so bold as to make a move amongst all this media attention. We just have to wait for the results."

"You haven't even had time to change," I whispered, noting his creased shirt and the smudge of black on his shoulder from my mascara.

"I know." He ran his hands down his thighs. "I'm going to go shower. Will you be alright?"

I nodded.

When Ben re-appeared in his boxers and t-shirt a short while later, I hadn't moved.

"Would you like some company?" he asked.

I nodded again and forced a smile. He eased into the double bed next to me.

He gently pulled me over to him so that my head rested on his warm chest. "How are you so freezing?"

Warmth was the last thing my body was concerned with; ever since I'd laid down, everything had gone painfully quiet. I let my eyes close briefly as Ben delicately stroked my hair away from my face.

I swallowed, trying to find my voice. "Thank you. For everything. You really don't have to let me ruin your evening as well."

"An evening spent with you has yet to be a bad one. Maybe I want to stay with you, Elle, have you considered that?"

I shook my head. "I just don't know what I'm going to do. If I'm not her, they'll investigate Henworth. Well, I guess they will either way." I sighed. "If I am her, I'll have to meet Susan and Derek."

He stroked my hair again, the long strands tickling my neck as he brushed them back. "Right now, you need to rest."

"How?" I asked desperately.

"Just lie there and shut your eyes. I'm not going anywhere."

He smelt like bergamot shower gel, his chest rising rhythmically with his heartbeat. It felt like, for the first time in hours, my muscles relaxed, and as soon as they did, I remembered; as soon as my body gave an inch, my mind took a fresh mile, instantly ready with the next thing to panic about.

"Jessica stopped by, she said you owe her lunch," I said suddenly, tilting my face up to his.

"What?"

"She knocked on the door yesterday evening. I told her I'd pass on the message. Sorry, with everything going on, I forgot to tell you."

I felt his body tense underneath me as his hand paused on the back on my neck. "What else did she say?"

I looked back down, tucking into him further. "Nothing. Sorry, I should've said earlier. You should probably go text her." I savoured the temporary comfort, waiting for him to get up.

"She didn't say anything else to you?"

"No."

His hand swept back through my hair. "Okay, I'll speak to her tomorrow."

I lay there for a minute, enjoying the feeling of my eyelids growing heavy.

"Ben?"

"Yeah?"

"I did miss you. You asked me earlier." I didn't know why I'd said it, maybe I was just too tired to stop myself. I thought I'd regret it as soon as the words left my lips, but I didn't. I couldn't understand why I had missed a man I barely knew so much, but I had.

"Good. I missed you too."

12

Different worlds

After waking up entangled with Ben, the last thing I wanted was to be on my own. It was a surprise and a relief when he insisted I go to the office with him, needing to attend a few meetings he'd been putting off.

The building was bigger than I'd expected, one of those tall, shiny offices with separate receptions.

"Good morning, Mr Carlson," people chorused as we walked through the building.

I'd intentionally only bought a single crutch to try and walk as normally as possible, and I'd worn my green dress – the smartest thing I owned.

In the lift, there were a few other people, but Ben placed a hand on the small of my back. "Catherine is my assistant; she'll be happy to help if you need anything when I'm in meetings."

I nodded, feeling insignificant compared to all the other heel-clad women as I stared down at my single black pump and pokey toes.

Catherine wasn't what I'd expected; she was more like a fun aunt than an assistant. We were sat at her desk with another tea when Ben returned from his meeting, looking rushed off his feet and visibly anxious.

"Sorry that took so long, are you alright?" he asked me, stopping Catherine mid-story.

His face relaxed when he saw the spread of papers and the numbers on the screen.

"I'm fine, I've been helping Catherine. I wanted to keep busy. I hope that's okay?"

Catherine interrupted. "Okay? She saved me half a day's work; we can make our weekly lunch after all."

"Oh, great," Ben replied. "Listen, I think we'd better get back, Catherine. I'm sure Elle's tired."

I looked between them. "I'm okay if you need to go for lunch."

Ben smiled down at me softly. "We have a catch up every Friday," he explained, "to set up the week." He turned to his assistant. "Let's do Monday, or I can just email you tomorrow?"

"Honestly, it's okay," I insisted, looking up at him, attempting to avoid facing the reality of leaving the office. The thought of going back to the apartment was suffocating.

"You could always come with us?" Catherine offered.

Checking with Ben, and noting his nod of agreement, I smiled at her, slowly easing myself up from the desk.

As we walked to the lift, a young man with round, tortoise-shell glasses and broad shoulders stopped us abruptly. "Hi, are you Elle? Are you who suggested the VAT reclaim for Brookes? Sorry to interrupt."

I noticed how well-groomed his chocolatey brown hair and neatly shaped beard was. His energy was different than the rest of them; easier.

"This is Charlie," Catherine explained.

"Um, yes?" I replied, looking to Ben. I doubted the words as they left my lips, but at the same time, in my gut, I wanted to be useful again. I had suggested the international VAT reclaim to Ben when he'd seemed stressed over a spreadsheet last week.

Ben rested his hand on my back. "Yes, she also taught Catherine a VLOOKUP this morning."

Charlie grinned and shook my hand. He had a loose, friendly grip.

"I know you're all busy," Charlie added, looking to Ben, "but I actually think I could apply some of the frameworks to three of my clients. I'd like to run the numbers, see if it's worth a conversation, and I was hoping for some guidance?"

Charlie's eyes met mine and we smiled at each other.

"I'd be happy to help, if that would be appropriate?" I said, as Ben opened his mouth.

"Really?" Charlie looked thrilled.

"I enjoy being useful. Ben's done a lot for me, so if it's okay with him, I'm honestly happy to help if I can. Although, I can't make any promises I'll be any good."

Ben was taken aback. "It's okay with me, but you don't have to." He met my gaze as I turned to him, making everyone else disappear around me. "Only if you feel up to it. Maybe you and Charlie could sit down next week? If you're sure?"

I nodded eagerly.

"I'll arrange it," Catherine added.

"Amazing. I look forward to it," Charlie replied energetically, pausing awkwardly before walking back to his desk.

I sat quietly at lunch while Ben and Catherine talked through the work week. Plenty of women had stared, and I swear a few had made remarks, but I'd been happy to throw myself into helping Catherine. It really was the least I could do.

Ben kept telling me how grateful he was, but all I could think was that I was the grateful one; grateful to have spent the day at his office, instead of alone with my thoughts.

Stumbling back to the guest bedroom, I reached for my tights, letting out a gasping wince. Pain speared through my side. I panted. My ribs had settled down, but my fall in the kitchen had made the pain flare up again, and I'd spent far too much time up and about today. It was infuriating: my mind liked being busy, but my body couldn't handle it. Awkwardly, I slipped on some new blue pyjama shorts and managed to slowly inch the dress off over my head, feeling my hair flutter down to rest against my bare back. Deeper breaths became easier and easier as my ribs relinquished some space.

Reaching my arm around to my bra strap, a groan slipped out of my mouth as my ribs burned. I tried again, but the pain was so bad I choked on the air I was inhaling. *Fuck it.* I'd just have to sleep in my bra, but I needed to get some ice first; I knew from experience that I had to calm the swelling before tomorrow.

As I attempted to stand, I immediately curled into the pain and fell against the wall. "Shit," I whispered under my breath. I was still in just my shorts and my lacy, dark-blue bra.

I turned to look back at the strappy top on the bed.

"Are you alright? Do you want a glass of water?" came Ben's voice from the living area.

"Yes, no. I mean, I'm fine," I replied, but my voice broke as I stood there by the door, not sure I could move any further.

His voice drifted through more gently. "Are you okay?"

I felt my chest rise with a pang of pain. "Okay, maybe some ice please."

"Some ice water?"

"No. For my ribs... I irritated them yesterday," I explained, sounding hoarse. My wrist had started to redden as it steadied my weight, the door creeping ajar. "Just leave it there, thank you."

He laughed. "Why, what are you up to?"

"Nothing. I just... I can't get my bra off."

"Oh."

I bit my bottom lip, feeling embarrassed again as I heard the freezer open and shut.

"I have the ice. Will you let me help? You can lie down, I won't look." His voice was kind, but there was an air of something being stifled in his tone.

I flinched, stranded. "I can't get back to the bed right now."

"Let me help you," he coaxed, nudging the door open a little further.

"I don't want you to see me like this."

"Will you let me come in?"

I tried to move, but winced too loudly – he was there instantly. He peeled my hand off the wall where I was leaning, looping it around his shoulders, and walking me carefully to the bed. We didn't speak; I blushed so hard my cheeks stung.

He was in his boxers – he must have been getting ready for bed himself. His skin on my mine felt warm and soft as his strong arms guided me down onto the duvet, my face resting against the fluffy pillow, finally allowing my core to relax.

"You have a nasty bruise, no wonder you're struggling. You've got to let us help you, Elle. You could've made it worse, or were you just planning to sleep by the door?"

I tensed as he leaned over to press the cold ice pack against the swelling. I flinched, but it felt good. A drip of water slowly slid down my bare back, leaving a trail of tingling cold. Two fingers effortlessly undid my bra strap, releasing the catch and bringing instant relief. I savoured a deep breath, relinquishing my last iota of control.

"Thanks... definitely adding this to my list of least sexy ways to get a man to take off my underwear," I grunted.

"How do you normally do it?" he asked, the annoyance gone.

"Ben!" I exclaimed, staring at the wall. "I swear to god, it feels like you're flirting with me. You're so confusing – cut it out."

I couldn't see his face, only feel his breath settling on my skin, his warm body propped against my side. The mattress shifted as he relaxed down further, leaning on an arm whilst still gently holding the ice.

"I am flirting with you."

"Why?" I blurted crassly.

"Why would I not? You're a beautiful woman living in my apartment."

"I'm not— Ben, be serious."

"It was one of the reasons I was so angry when I first saw you. I was immediately drawn to you. People are predictable and disappointing, but you? You baffle me, intrigue me. Mostly with your kindness."

Another droplet of ice-cold water broke free of the pack, dribbling over the ridges of my ribs. Ben's finger interrupted its path, sweeping a long stroke across my sensitive skin, taking it with him and patting it on the small towel.

"I thought you found me impossible and infuriating?" I replied softly, trying to keep my mind on the words and not on anticipating his touch.

He chuckled. "See, this is why I like you so much."

I hesitated. What was happening? Had I banged my head again?

"I like you too, Ben," I whispered. "But this is a bad idea, we both know it."

"Maybe. But who cares? We enjoy each other's company. We're adults, and I hope you know that if anything ever happens..."

Another droplet fell and he once again dragged his finger through it, sending goosebumps up my arms. The warmth of his fingertip following the cold set my nerves alight.

"... it won't change your place here. You make me feel like doing the right thing and looking after you is a pleasure I will always be willing to fulfil."

"Ben... I don't... I don't understand. You're so together, so sensible. How do *you* find *me* sexy? Especially like this."

"Such compliments," he joked, as I became acutely aware of how the front of my body felt, pressed against the soft material of the bed. "You're the only person who sees yourself like that, you know. I'm done with holding back, Elle. I don't want to pussyfoot around you. Go on a date with me next Friday." He paused. "Please?"

"You want to go on a date?"

"Yes."

"With me? Like this?"

"Topless? I mean, I figured that wasn't an option, but if you insist—"

I flicked my leg up, gently kicking him. "Stop being a smartass. Yes, I'll go on a date with you. No, I won't go topless."

The mattress shifted again and I felt his lips press gently into the peak of my shoulder, sending pulses of heat through my body. I wanted desperately to arch into him in response.

God, what had I just agreed to? My eyes closed briefly; I couldn't move away without exposing myself. Not that I had any desire to, but somehow that notion escalated the sensation. I couldn't believe I'd agreed that easily. I was not in control, and, for the first time in a long time, I didn't care. It felt right, it felt easy. The less sense it made, the simpler it was to agree.

"Good," he said, brushing his lips over my skin again. "I look forward to Friday."

"I don't have anything to wear," I murmured, still looking at the wall, cutting the building tension with practicality.

"I don't care what you wear."

I could feel his breath against my skin. My whole body was on edge, but for once, it wasn't because I was afraid.

"I think you'd better go, Ben. Being close to you like this is... it's too nice."

He moaned low in his throat, planting a slow kiss between my shoulder blades, then another near my neck. My nerves came alive – my skin extra sensitive to the soft, sensual feeling of him. Pain disappeared as parts of me started aching in an entirely different way. Our bodies nearly totally connected as he leaned into me.

I'd had partners when I lived at Henworth, used them as a distraction, and Sam hadn't exactly been bad in bed. But Ben made me feel a whole new dimension of physical feelings, and he wasn't even trying that hard.

I couldn't decide if it was exciting or terrifying.

"That doesn't make sense," he whispered.

I felt myself smile into the pillow. "You know what I mean."

Ben grunted, and with a swift movement, he withdrew from the bed, causing the mattress to bounce softly.

"I'll look forward to Friday, then," he repeated. "I hope you feel better, let me know if you need anything else. I mean it. Don't suffer in silence."

13

Programmed hatred

I was due to receive my test results today.

Ben and I were curled up on the sofa together, my head resting on his shoulder. I wasn't sure when being so close to him had become acceptable, but I certainly wasn't going to complain – he was becoming a dangerous drug.

I turned to him as my curiosity got the better of me. "That looks like some heavy numbers."

"Yeah. Diorise are one of our new clients. They supply packaging, and the team spent ages on all these reports for a deadline they had. They're going after new investors, but the meeting is this Monday, and the team managed to sort all the data wrong. Now it's all mixed up. Every time I think I've solved it, the figures are out by a stupidly small number, but—"

"That means something is wrong," I concluded.

"Exactly."

"Want another pair of eyes?" I offered. I'd do anything to stop me from flinching every time my phone lit up.

He looked at me with surprise. "Would you mind?"

"No, I told you, it makes me feel good to help. Once, I spent days trying to figure out an exchange rate error, except it wasn't the exchange rate at all, it was a typo."

"Nice," he commended, shifting his weight to pick up our empty mugs.

"What's the latest pivot table?"

"Tab two, the one where the names are merged," he explained, heading for the kettle.

I looked at the numbers, scanning them. It looked like a pattern to me. Numbers made sense, I enjoyed the predictability of them. They were either right or wrong, there was no grey area.

"I see it," I exclaimed as he came back, trying to stifle my pride as he pulled me into his side again.

"Where? I've been on this for an hour."

"That name, it's been entered two different ways. When you carried the data across, it's not been recognised as the same. Check it."

Ben corrected the error before re-running the pivot. It worked.

"Yes!" he exclaimed, throwing his arms in the air and resting back into the sofa just as my phone finally rang.

I stared at it as it slowly buzzed on the arm of the sofa.

"It'll be okay," Ben soothed, wrapping his arm around me.

I took a deep breath and answered it, jumbling my own name, trying to say hello. It was the police station, but it wasn't the results. I listened to the stern officer, Ben's eyes burning into my cheek as I hesitated to respond. After a brief exchange, I said goodbye, only then realising how closely I was pressing the phone into my cheek.

"So?" Ben asked, wide eyed.

"The test was inconclusive. They need another sample."

"What?" He shook his head.

I looked at him as my pulse started to slow back down. "I know. They don't know what happened. They're coming around in an hour to take another sample so they can verify it. Because it's the weekend, the results are probably going to be in on Wednesday at the earliest, maybe Thursday."

He pushed his laptop closed. "Are you alright?"

I let out a deep breath. "Is it bad that I'm relieved?"

Ben shook his head, pulling me into a hug and running soothing hands up and down my back as we waited for the police to arrive.

Once they'd taken a new sample, we headed over to Lucy's for a roast dinner with the kids. I'd ordered a book for Sophie on horses, and we enjoyed flicking through the pages together. I hadn't known what to get Isac – he was such a quiet kid, and clearly having a tough time – but in the end I'd decided on a photo album and a disposable camera.

Fortunately, he seemed pleased, and had taken a lot of care arranging us all on the sofa to take a picture. I'd insisted it be just a family photo, but Isac was having none of it.

Being around them all sparked something in me, a new set of feelings, deeply fulfilling somehow, like an answer to a question that I hadn't known to ask. Living away from the site made everything feel easier. It was easier to breathe, to think, to exist. I was finally allowing myself to start imagining what life would be like beyond surviving.

Eventually, we had to say our goodbyes so Lucy could get the kids to bed.

"You're so sweet with the kids," Ben commented as we drove back to the apartment.

"They're great kids."

He nodded. "Isac seems a bit more himself."

"Hopefully Steve will stop fighting Lucy so much soon; realise she's serious. She's such a great mum. It comes so naturally to her."

Ruby had not found it natural. Once, when I was little, I'd accidently whined when she'd brushed through a knot in my hair. She'd twisted the bristles, yanking out a clump of brown strands in response. I couldn't decide what had been more painful: the act, her coldness afterwards, or the daily reminder of what had happened as I tried to craft hairstyles around the ugly bald patch. I had never understood why she hated me so much.

Another time, I'd accidentally dropped a milk bottle on the floor of the caravan. As the white liquid splattered and dissipated into the thin red carpet, I'd gulped, instantly aware of how bad it was. I'd burst into tears as Ruby stalked over to me, dropping despairingly to my knees. With a sinister glint in her eye, she'd lifted her trainer, stamping the shattered bottle glass hard to into the carpet, before demanding I pick up all the shards with my bare hands. The sound of the harsh crunching still rang through my ears all these years later.

"Yeah, she's always had a maternal side. When we were kids, she always tried to look after me, much to my annoyance. She used to make hospitals for my action men," Ben laughed.

I forced the image of Lucy's doll hospital into my head, attempting to regain control.

"Do you want kids?" I asked him, before realising how loaded the question might sound to him.

"I don't, no." He seemed unfazed. "But I enjoy spending time with Isac and Sophie."

Strangely, part of me felt disappointed. The feeling shocked me.

That evening, once I was certain he'd fallen asleep, the tears flooded down my cheeks as I quietly cried. Sophie had shown me her colourful, girly bedroom, and it had forced another uncontrollable cascade of buried, misunderstood emotions to the surface. I wondered if that was what Maeve's bedroom had been like at Susan and Derek's.

When I was little, I had a tiny room in Ruby and Frank's caravan. They'd stay up late, drinking and arguing, other people always coming and going. I always had dark circles under my eyes, never quite learning how to tune the noise out. They were all too unpredictable; the walls too thin.

Why did I feel like this? Lucy and Ben were so kind; we'd had such a lovely day. It felt intensely selfish to be sad, and a powerful, consuming guilt overwhelmed me. The good feelings of the day had drained completely, leaving a raw wound. Happiness... security... it wasn't my reality. This was all just a dangerous dream.

It wouldn't last.

The following week, Ben had to make a long overdue trip to Ireland. He would only be away Monday night, but after the events of the weekend, a quiet day was welcome. I put on the saddest film I could find – *Up* – and cried my eyes out. It was ridiculous, but I was so sick of holding it in all the time. I wanted a guilt free bawl.

BEN

Missing me again? xx

ME

No, stay an extra night. How's the client? Did they go for the acquisition? xxx

BEN

I hear that's the secret to a strong marriage, time apart. Yes, they did, thanks. Did you doubt me?

ME

Ever the romantic. You messaged me first, I was making conversation.

BEN

I'm a realist. At least wait till after our date to judge me. And yes, I was actually thinking I message you first too often. It's not usually my style. I'll speak to you Friday.

ME

Okay x

I grinned at my phone as I brushed my teeth.

"Oh, so what?" I said to my giddy reflection. I gave it five minutes and messaged him again.

ME

Good evening, fiancé dearest, how's your night? xxx

BEN

Nice 😊 It's been a successful day. Thank you for asking. What you up to?

ME

I watched *Up* and cried, tried on my date outfit, and actually decided to write a CV. You know you won't have me as a little housewife forever, right?

BEN

Was it when the gran died? A CV, good for you, I'll take

a look tomorrow, although there's no rush. That's a shame, I'm getting used to the burnt dinners.

ME

The whole thing makes me cry. Yeah, yeah, charming as ever. I'm in bed now, shouldn't you be drinking a Guinness or something? xxx

BEN

We went for lunch instead luckily. Good night, sleep tight. Message me first in the morning xxx

There was a pause.

BEN

So you don't actually miss me this time? Usually you add it in way too late in the conversation. I'm asking simply for continuity here.

ME

You caught me, I'm hugging your pillow and weeping.

BEN

That's actually a really cute image.

ME

Jeez, I'm joking.

BEN

Sure. Good night, sweetheart xxx

ME

I'm not sure whether that's a term of endearment or a fiancé joke. Sorry, calculating my response.

BEN

Good night, beautiful (genuine) xxx

ME

🖤

I'd just fallen asleep when there was a jarring clang of metal, like a rattle at the door.

I sat up.

Had Ben come back early?

It couldn't be Vicky; it was too late. I hoped to god Jessica didn't have a key.

Except... it didn't sound like a key.

Swinging my legs out of bed, still drowsy and coming to terms with being awake, I walked out into the main living space, listening, my eyes adjusting to the dark. The sound was coming from where the lock was. In an instant, my fear snapped me awake.

I stumbled back into the bedroom, frantically jamming the buttons on my phone to call Lucy. The noise stopped.

"Does anyone else have a key to Ben's?" I whispered. "It's probably just me, but I swear someone's trying to get in."

I was expecting her to be half asleep. Instead, she yelled down the line.

"Call the police, Elle, now!"

"Huh?" I questioned, finding the light switch. That wasn't what I'd expected her to say.

"No one else has a key, Elle. I spoke to Ben earlier and he's still at his hotel."

My heart dropped. Someone kicked the door. I jolted, feeling my body seize, dropping the phone on the floor with a crash, Lucy's voice trailing away.

Thump.

The rattle started again. It sounded like the claws of a frantic animal. *This is ridiculous, it's probably a friend of Ben's, or someone who's got the wrong door.* I sucked air in hard and fast, grabbed my crutch, and walked towards the front door. My feet became fixed in their position as two bloodshot eyes glared through the letterbox.

"Hello, Chantelle. Open the door, now. Let's not cause a scene."

Marcus.

Late at night, in the quiet moments, I'd thought about what I'd say if I saw any of them again. What I'd do if they tried to touch me again. How it would feel to stand up for myself. I had people now; people believed in me. I had worth; people wanted me.

I could do it.

I reached for the rage, but it was gone. My eyes started to well, desperate. Where were my words?

"Alright then, the hard way it is, you stupid bitch," Marcus spat as he drew away from the letter box.

The snap of the metal slot closing reverberated through the apartment. I heard thick, Bristolian accents bouncing down the hall. I felt the power drain out of me as my posture drooped. They'd break the door down and kill me. It would be the end, the end of the last chapter, the best chapter; what I thought could have been the first. I wouldn't go with them, they'd have to kill me. I had to find that strength, at least.

There was a splintering metal clang from outside; a crowbar, or something equally sinister. My body started slowly backing away from the door as my mind emptied.

Marcus's harsh, gravelly voice continued invading the sanctity of Ben's apartment. "Come on now Chantelle, did you think you could speak to the pigs and get away with it?"

There was a clunk as another hinge was breached.

"You deserve this. Y'always did. Thought you were too good fer us, eh? With everything Ruby and Frank did for ya."

I felt the door frame of Ben's room behind me; it was cold, hard – a boundary. I leant into it, my eyes fixed on the front door. There was a huge crash as it flew violently into the apartment, clinging on by a single hinge. I blinked away a tear, fear gripping me entirely. Nothing would ever change. All I had done was bring this horror upon Ben and his family. I was a coward.

Marcus charged towards me with two of his greasy sidekicks, the usual smell of cheap whisky seeping from their pores. His pace didn't change and my body wouldn't move, until his fist hit my stomach, knocking me off my feet, along with the air from my lungs. My head rebounded, hitting the wooden floor hard as my nerves scrambled to find the right response. Light danced around the room; darkness threatened to cover my vision, but dissolved.

Marcus bent down, gripping my cheeks hard, digging his dirty nails into my already tear-soaked face. I could smell his musty sweat. My eyes struggled to focus on his face as I caught the light glinting in his feral eyes.

"I would've fucked you well, I would. Frank told me I could ave yer after yer went and ruined yourself."

His followers began to trash the apartment; I could hear crockery smashing, glass shattering, paper flying through the air. Noise suffocated me until Marcus's rough voice cut through it, laughing.

"But now, now yer go and do this. Diggin up shit you 'ave no right diggin' into." His fingernails pressed harder, willing my skin to rupture. "Yer really think that family would want yer back?"

Spit landed on my cheek as he stood up, wrenching me violently with him. I shut my eyes. Something inside me cracked. I waited for the dark to come, welcomed it. I pictured Ben's face; imagined him stroking my hair.

A hard, round boot crushed my stomach, sending nausea rippling through me as my gut recoiled. I didn't let out a sound, sealing my dry lips together furiously. I couldn't fight or speak, but the least I could do was not give them the satisfaction.

My scalp stung as individual hairs tore from their follicles. Instinctively, my hand reached for my head, feeling his cold, thick grip on my hair. My body hung uncontrollably, ruled by pain, as I realised that I was being dragged across the floor towards the door.

"No, no." I let out a whimper, a pathetic whimper. I choked it back down. "Kill me," I pleaded, forcing my eyes shut, releasing a fresh pool of tears. I heard maniacal laughter. "Kill me!"

Marcus grinned. "Can't have sweet Susan knowing them DNA results, can we? Fancy that, getting yer daughter back after all this time and findin' out she's a filthy whore."

I kicked my leg out with all my energy, but it barely lifted. My jaw seized and my mouth filled with blood. My ears were ringing from the impact, my vision coming in flashes. I was drowning in agony.

I *was* Maeve White. I *was* the girl in the photograph.

Breath hissed past my teeth as more blows to my stomach landed. Adrenaline urged me to fight as, once again, my body was dragged. Killing me here would be a mercy. I felt the sharpness of my teeth against my tongue as my head crashed down to the floor again. My hands scrambled to find something to grasp as I saw them all head for the door. One of them dragged their arm along the walls, causing maximum chaos as all the pictures toppled. Something sharp grazed my cheek as I realised they were leaving, the pulling finally easing. I lunged to get my bearings but the apartment kept going in and out of focus.

Were they were running?

My ears picked up the sound of wailing sirens just before the apartment filled with people.

Arms were on my arms, on my face, on my neck, pulling at me. I thrashed, wanting to regain my space; come back into my physical body. I was numb, cold, and violently shaking. The multitude of hands helped me to the sofa. I sat there, frozen, muscles seized up, blood slowly dribbling from my nose. My eyes followed a shiny droplet as it fell onto my knee. Paramedics, in a sea of green uniforms, were crouching in front of me, slipping things onto my arms. I let them. I moved as if I were a puppet, fixated on the blood against my knee as it disappeared into my pyjamas.

I didn't know how much time had passed, but eventually, they slowly raised me from the sofa, directing me towards the wheelchair.

"No!" I gasped. "No hospital."

I lowered my weight back down onto the sofa. I didn't want to move; be moved. Suddenly, my body lulled as Lucy appeared and threw her arms around me. I remained rigid; my muscles wouldn't let go.

She leaned away, grabbing my face and making me look at her.

"What happened? What happened?"

I looked into her eyes as the voices transformed around me, forming understandable words.

"Marcus broke down the door," I stuttered, noticing how full the apartment was. Two police officers stood in front of me; others with bags and gloves were moving around the apartment.

It looked awful.

"I'm so sorry."

Lucy gently brushed the tears from my cheeks with her thumb. "Sorry? For what?"

"They ruined it."

"Don't be ridiculous."

Her face was slowly coming into focus.

"Where are the kids?" I asked, suddenly panicking.

"In the car downstairs. Don't worry, Sophie is grilling a police officer and Isac is on his tablet." She stroked a wet strand of hair out of my face. "Where are the wipes and gauze?" she asked the paramedic. "Can I?" She gestured to me softly.

I nodded, allowing her to tentatively roll up my pyjama top and press against my stomach. I flinched. There was a flash of a camera.

"You take the kids home, I'll be okay."

Lucy shook her head, putting down a handful of bloodied dressing. "I'm not going anywhere."

Suddenly remembering Marcus' words, I looked at one of the uniformed officers. "Is it true, the results?"

She nodded. "They match. You're the Maeve White we've been looking for."

I squeezed Lucy's hand as she paled.

"Elle," she whispered. "It's true." She got up steadily as her phone buzzed. "One second," she assured me.

A police officer quickly sat down to interrogate me all over again, flicking through pages of notes and asking for details that seemed no more than a terrible nightmare. When Lucy returned, I was staring at the blood highlighting the indentations of my palms. Why didn't I recognise them, Susan and Derek?

Steadily, Lucy led me over to the ensuite, helping me peel off my pyjama bottoms and cover my cast. I lowered myself into the shower cubicle, leaving my top on and sitting, needing to be still. The water felt warm as it trickled over my skin, creating a dramatic pattern as it mixed with the red blood. I watched numbly, unable to move.

"Let me help you with your shirt," Lucy offered gently from behind the shower door.

I leant over so she could reach, the water splattering on her arms.

"Do you want me to leave?" she asked.

I shook my head, staring into the distance as the red and brown water spiralled around the drain. The image of Marcus spitting lurched into my mind; I yelped and reached for the soap, squirting it frantically into my hands, rubbing it all over my face. Lucy placed her hands over mine as I carried on scrubbing, circling my hands, forcing the bubbles deeper. My eyes starting to burn.

"Hey, hey, you're okay," she repeated.

I reluctantly let her peel my hands down.

Another blurred amount of time passed before Lucy helped me stand up, wrapping a clean towel around me and squeezing the water out of my hair. She became my arms, my brain, so that I could focus on breathing.

"The kids?" I asked again, lurching to face her.

"Shh," she soothed. "Steven has taken them to mine, I made him call from there," she explained softly, leading me to the dressing table stool in the guest room.

She gathered the wet hair from around my neck and started to brush it, pulling it easily into a plait. Only once I was fully dressed, thanks to Lucy, did she ask if I was ready to head back out.

We rejoined the sombre party in the living room and Lucy made me some tea. My blue tracksuit was softer against the growing bruising, and the smell of shampoo was much better than vomit.

A stern looking police officer had shown up, dressed in a suit. He was probably in his forties, a little burly, and balding.

"We're organising for you to come to a safe house, then we can arrange a meeting with Susan and Derek. You need to pack a bag; we need to go now. We have some CCTV footage, but we didn't catch them, and we have reason to believe they'll be back; we need to get you safe. Someone will stay with you."

I could tell he was attempting to be reassuring, but the words washed over me. I looked at Lucy. She was standing in the kitchen, taking it in.

"Go when?" Lucy asked for me.

"Now. You need to understand the gravity of this case, especially combined with the Henworth group. We've tied the community to a series of crimes, including burglaries, fraud, assault, and two rapes. With Maeve's statement, we can get a warrant. We now have physical evidence, so we need to protect it. We need to do everything right; we can't lose this opportunity."

I licked my dry lips, still tasting metal.

"Can you help her pack?" he asked Lucy.

She nodded, leading me back to the bedroom. The officer followed us, standing to the side as we packed my things into a bag. I moved rhythmically, mechanically, taking time to fold my clothes carefully, layering them into my old holdall.

"It's all going to be okay now," Lucy reassured me, taking my hand. "They'll help you. I'll come and see you tomorrow, once you're settled, yeah?"

"I'm afraid the safe house needs to remain secure," the officer interrupted coldly.

"What? You can't just take her away, she needs us!" Lucy argued. "How do we know she'll be safe, that we can trust your team?"

The officer didn't falter. "We'll get someone to stay with her and call to let you know all is well. We need to do everything to keep her safe; she's too valuable to be in this apartment on her own. This could have been a lot worse."

Lucy took a sharp breath. I was confused as I reached for the bed and there were no more clothes to fold. I looked up. Lucy was staring at me intently. Why were there no more clothes? There were clothes there a minute ago.

"What do you want, Elle?" she asked.

The officer stepped towards us as I fixated on the duvet.

"I don't think it's fair to leave this decision to her, given her current mindset," the officer stated as he looked to me before picking up my bag.

I pictured all the clothes tipping out of their neat piles... all that folding.

"Will you come with us, Elle?" he asked, clearly and slowly.

I nodded and started limping to the lounge.

Looking around, I realised there were less people here now, less photos being taken.

"I can't leave all this mess," I whispered, not knowing where to look in the chaos of colours and shapes.

The previously uncluttered coffee table was buried under papers and scattered earth. I spotted shards of a white ceramic on the floor by one of the table legs and instantly went to pick them up, collecting them in my palm.

I heard the increasingly firm voice of the officer pipe up again.

"You don't need to do that, it'll all be sorted. We need to get going."

I ignored him, reaching for another piece. Lucy came to kneel beside me.

"Let me," she coaxed, dabbing a grey tea towel into the beige puddle of spilled tea, already holding out a bin for the mug's remains.

I straightened back up. Everything was wrong.

The officer walked towards me, holding my crutches. "Elle, come on," he said, more delicately this time, reaching an arm towards mine.

I flew backwards, nearly falling, as I retreated from his grasp.

"What is going on?" Ben's voice boomed furiously through the chaos.

I heard Lucy gasp with relief as the officer headed towards him.

"Mr Carlson?" he asked.

Ben ignored him, striding straight for me and Lucy. I winced as his feet crunched over the broken decor. Lucy immediately stepped into him, throwing her arms around him. I remained rooted to the spot. As Ben hugged her, he looked over her shoulder at me.

"They broke in, Ben," Lucy stuttered. "The police barely got here in time. If Elle hadn't called... if she hadn't called..." She broke off, her fingers gripping his back. "She's Maeve, Ben. It's all true, the DNA results came back."

The officer in charge tightened his hold on my bag. "We'll get Maeve to a safe house tonight, but we need to go now."

"She's not going anywhere," Ben stated gruffly.

Lucy eased away from him, wiping clumsily at her face.

He moved to stand in front of me. I looked past him to the door, at the ugly crack in the wooden edging. Neither of us spoke.

The officer continued, becoming impatient again. "She needs to go, Mr Carlson. It's procedure. She won't be left on her own."

"She could've been killed, Ben," Lucy sniffed.

He twisted to look back at her, rage radiating from his face. "You would've let her go, on her own?"

Lucy started sobbing again. There was a trickle of tea running towards the edge of the breakfast bar.

"She goes nowhere without us," Ben demanded angrily, looking back at me, hesitating to touch me.

"With respect, Mr Carlson, it's not your decision. The safe house is ready, and we'll call you," the officer stated. "This is a long running investigation—"

"It's not your decision either," Ben interrupted. "You have no right to stand here, in my apartment, making decisions for Elle."

"She's in no fit state to fully understand—"

Ben threw his hands up. "Exactly!"

I felt my leg wobble underneath me, a warning from my body that I was about to fold. I'd been standing for a while. Before I thought to reach out, Ben's hands flew to my arms, the steadying force a relief as he gripped me.

"You don't have to go." He spoke quietly, tentatively, searching for eye contact.

"I'm sorry, they messed up your apartment. They made such a mess, I'll clean it," I muttered, staring at the blood splatter on the wall.

Ben paused, still supporting my weight. "I don't give a shit about the apartment." He turned to the others. "You all need to go; can't you see the state she's in? You need to go so she can rest. Now."

"Ben," Lucy rasped.

"Don't you start. You really think she wants to go with the police? So what if she's Maeve, she's also Elle!"

Lucy shook her head and fumbled. "I wasn't thinking..." Her eyes dropped to the floor.

The officer interjected abrasively. "Elle... Maeve... we need to leave now. Leave Ben and Lucy to sort out the apartment, we can go find you somewhere to rest, away from the press."

"Get the fuck out," Ben growled, twisting to face him.

"Be careful, son," the officer commanded, anger rising in the air.

"What are you going to do, arrest me? Try it." Somehow, he stood taller, still holding my arms but now practically holding me up as my strength drained. He looked at me again, his expression instantly softening. "Elle, what do you want to do? Let me help you. Do you want to go?"

I looked around the room and, finally, a tear rolled down my cheek. As it tracked down my skin, I felt it bring with it pain, sorrow, and pangs of absolute terror. Ben understood.

"You need to say it," he spoke in almost a whisper. "Stay with me," he almost pleaded, making the other faces fade into nothing.

I looked at him, and what the tear had started, his eyes finished. My legs buckled.

"Don't make me go," I sobbed.

He pulled me tightly into him, his hand running through my hair as he tucked my face into his warm shoulder. I shut my eyes, feeling the soft cotton and breathing in the familiar smell of him; diving into the darkness and away from the chaos.

"Everyone happy?" he said aggressively to the officer.

The officer sighed in response and walked towards the door, waving his arms and talking to one of his uniformed colleagues. "We'll station an officer outside for tonight and speak in the morning, when we've all had some rest. I invite you to take this time to see sense."

As the police and forensics team departed, Ben moved so he could sit me on the sofa. Once the apartment was quiet, he said goodbye to Lucy, making sure the door was secure as she left. I heard the kettle boiling while he made some phone calls. Reaching over the coffee table, I started picking up shards of glass from a broken candle. One of the pieces pricked my hand, but I didn't feel it.

"Hey, hey, stop," he murmured, jogging over, placing down a steaming drink as he crouched in front of me, bringing one hand underneath mine and using the other to uncurl my fingers from the glass.

He tipped my palm gently so the pieces fell to the table, sticky with blood, before taking a tissue and dabbing the fresh specs of red from my palm, inspecting for shards. He closed my fingers around the tissue, lifting my hand to his lips, kissing my knuckles.

"Vicky's on her way over, do you need anything for the pain?"

I shook my head, wincing. He leant over and gingerly rolled up my tracksuit top, failing to hide his flinch.

Taking the tea in one hand and supporting me with the other, Ben led me to his bedroom. I tucked my legs in as he pulled the cover up, gently kissing my head.

"Give me an hour to get everything safe and I'll be in. Just call me if you need anything."

I lay there, listening to him clattering around; Vicky arrived shortly after, swearing obscenely. The clinking of glass and rustle of bags filled the apartment.

Maeve.

Maeve White.

"Thank you so much, Vicky," I heard Ben say. "Here, take this, please."

"Don't be ridiculous, that's far too generous. I would've come regardless, and you know it. I like Elle, she doesn't deserve this. I mean, no one does."

"Take it, please, or I'll just transfer it to you."

I heard muttering after that, then the door closing. The sound rang through me, my mind flashing through images of Marcus bursting through, how his steps had thundered towards me. I heard Ben in his bathroom and tried to focus on the familiar sound of his toothbrush, forcing air in and out as my eyes fixated on a small spot of white wall.

Ben climbed into the bed, pulling me towards him, one arm under my waist, the other over the top, gripping my hands. He was so much taller and broader than me, it felt deeply soothing to be held by him.

"I'm so sorry, sweetheart. I'm so sorry I wasn't here." His voice drifted through the darkness.

He sounded exhausted.

I forced an overdue blink. "I should go. It's not going to stop. It won't ever stop."

I felt his firm hand squeeze mine. "Don't you dare say that."

I found his confident, familiar tone soothing.

He hesitated. "What did he do, Elle?"

My voice was devoid of emotion. "Kicked me – I think. It was hard to tell. I... they wanted to take me back."

There was a pause as I felt his shoulder stiffen. "I should've been here."

"I'm glad you're here now."

He tucked his chin into my shoulder.

"The apartment, is it okay?"

He tucked both my hands into one of his, using the free one to stroke a strand of loose hair from my face, kissing my cheek. "It's all clean and tidy, don't worry. Just shut your eyes and try to rest."

***

Daylight stung my eyes, the reality of the night before punching the air from my lungs. The horror in Lucy's eyes... Ben's pain... it made it so much harder – not being alone. My hands flew to my mouth as panic suffocated me.

Ben tightened his arms around me, still curled against my back.

"It's okay, we're safe. You're safe."

"How did you get here so fast?" I asked, suddenly confused, struggling to calm myself.

Ben ran his thumb over my knuckles and the panic loosened its grip on me, the sensation helping me draw another reviving breath.

"Lucy called me, when you rang her and I knew something was wrong. I went straight to the airport; my hotel was onsite. There was a flight within the hour that they managed to get me on. I came as fast as I could."

I nestled back into him even further. "What about your client?"

"They'll understand."

My throat felt like it was going to close up again. "I'm so sorry."

"You're sorry that people attacked you, in your own home?"

"My home?" I rolled over carefully to face him, wincing.

I rested my hand on his arm, taking in his face. I didn't often see him without his glasses; it made him look younger, more vulnerable. His dark eyes stared freely into mine.

"I'm glad that's what you decided to focus on." He paused, eyes roving my face. "You could have gone, Elle, to the safe house. I didn't think you would want to, but considering the news, maybe you should?"

It hit me then, how I could've been alone right now, left to face all of this by myself, not tucked up in bed with Ben.

I shook my head. I remembered the details now. Ben's angry exchange with the officer; Lucy helping me pick up the shards of ceramic from the floor.

"Lucy, oh god, is she okay? She... she plaited my hair." I bought my hand up to feel my soft braid.

He kissed my forehead tenderly. "Don't worry, I'll get up and call her in a minute."

I nuzzled into him, surrounding myself in his warmth.

"It's all going to change again. Isn't it?" I whispered.

Ben pulled me tighter. "Yes. It is."

The rest of the day was sore and bizarre. The police came back and Ben argued with them again. This time, I made my feelings clearer. I didn't want to go, no matter who I was. Ben told them if they wanted my help with putting the case together, the least they could do was offer protection until arrests were made. After much back-and-forth, it was agreed that residents would be spoken to and building security upgraded. We both spoke to Lucy; I thanked her for helping me, and Ben apologised to her, although I'm not sure he meant it.

The police told us they were in the process of talking to Maeve's family, and a case worker, Linda, would be around in the afternoon to organise the next steps.

Just as I'd found my feet, I was back at the peak of the rollercoaster track, waiting for another free fall.

14

Facing biology

It didn't feel like a reunion. They were strangers; strangers desperate to reunite with me, whoever *me* was.

"Can we just stay here another minute, please?" I asked Ben as he pulled on the hand break.

"Of course."

We'd pulled into the car park at the police station, so they knew we were here. I flipped down the visor and stared at myself, running my finger through the black smudge under my eye. I'd tied half my hair up; I tucked some fly-aways behind my ear, but quickly pulled them back, changing my mind.

Ben reached for my hand, lowering it into his lap. "Stop it, you look perfect."

"I already cried off half my mascara, so I know you're lying."

He scowled at me. "I'm not rising to that."

"I should've worn my shorts. Maybe a dress is too, I don't know, fancy?" I chewed on my fake nail – they were still unicorn themed, as chosen by Sophie.

He looked at me over the top of his glasses; I hated it when he did that. "Too fancy?"

"Does it look like I'm trying too hard?" I pulled at the pink material of the tea dress, smoothing the little cherry blossoms. "Too pink?"

He squinted his eyes. "You want me to tell you if your dress is too pink?"

I sighed. "Urgh, I knew I should've come with Lucy."

He took both my hands. "Listen, I know you're stressed out, but they've been looking for you for nineteen years – you're their child. I can guarantee everything else is irrelevant. You look beautiful; the dress is just the right amount of pink, it makes your eyes look browner and your hair look like honey." His fingers wrapped around my clammy hands. "This is the hard bit. After this, it's going to get easier. You can tell the police the whole truth about those officers, you can get to know the family you deserve. You did it, Elle. You got this far. Now you've just got to take the last few steps."

Ben opened the car door, walking briskly around the front to open mine, reaching down for my hand. "Come on."

My heart felt light; my stomach heavy. Everything felt wrong, like stepping out onto a battlefield. Every part of me wanted to stay in the car.

"I've got you," Ben added, pulling my hand gently towards his, ushering me to stand.

I took it, hardly moving as he pulled me to my feet and pushed the door shut behind me. I leant back against the silver metal whilst he went to get my crutch, handing it to me carefully.

"Thank you," I whispered, barely finding my voice. "For everything."

He faltered, hesitating. "Are you breaking off our engagement?"

I shook my head, an unexpected smile blossoming across my face. "No, you?" I asked, pushing forwards to walk.

He shook his head as he held open the station doors. "Nope. I'm looking forward to Friday."

Friday, I repeated mentally as he spoke to the woman at the desk.

There would be days after this.

The receptionist stared right at me as two non-uniformed officers appeared, one being DS Ernest. They ushered us up some stairs and into a side room. I paused before the door, but they assured me Susan and Derek weren't scheduled to arrive for another twenty minutes.

The police station was grey and eerie. The small room had a desk, mismatched floor tiles, and two blue plastic sofas inside. Linda, the psychologist who had been assigned to the case, was waiting for us. She was eclectically dressed, wearing a long red skirt made of several prints and a beaded glasses necklace. She told me she'd travelled to work on the case, and was very experienced. That just added to the intimidation – even the authorities knew this was intense.

"Mr Carlson, we have a room next door ready, would you like a coffee?"

Linda smiled at me warmly. I gripped Ben's hand.

"You'll be alright," he assured me, stroking his thumb over my knuckles.

I turned to look at him, and for a brief second, it was just the two of us... for a second, I could breathe.

"Do you want me to stay in here with you?"

"Yes, but I know I need to do this on my own."

"Alright." He let go of my hand, affectionately rubbing my shoulder. "I'll see you after."

Sitting with Linda, I couldn't even hear the words she was saying; I stared so intently at the door that my eyes watered. When it finally opened, I looked straight at the empty notice board, averting my gaze. Out of the corner of my eye, I saw DS Ernest holding it open as the couple entered. I'd already eyed up a wastepaper bin in case I was sick, desperately hoping that wasn't the first impression I was about to give. I dug my nails into my knees, keeping my eyes low as the couple were guided to sit on the opposite sofa. It was Susan's piercing cry that made my eyes dart up before I could stop myself. She was hunched over as Derek held her, folding inwards with grief.

The noise rattled the walls.

"I'm sorry," I said quietly.

I hadn't planned on saying it, or anything, really. I didn't know what I was apologising for: not running over and greeting them like in the movies? Forgetting them? Or maybe for looking at them like they were complete strangers. They looked old; fragile and worn out. Susan had a bob of grey hair and wore a lilac blouse over flared jeans; Derek a v-neck that bunched around his rounded shoulders, and a similarly peppered head of thinning hair. They were harmless, in the way you can instantly tell some people are. They were the sweet, good people about to meet their ruined daughter.

Linda cleared her throat and passed Derek a box of tissues from the desk.

"Well, like I said to you both, we're going to take this slowly. There are no expectations here. Susan and Derek, this is Elle. Elle, Susan and Derek White. This is a unique situation in how fortunate it is that we can all be sat in this room together. So, let's try and keep as calm as we can. If anyone needs to take a break, you can do so at any point, okay?" She looked at me.

I nodded.

Derek patted Susan on the back as she kept sobbing.

It hurt my chest; made my bones ache, but I was fixed to the seat. It felt horrific to see someone so devastated and be powerless, or worse, to be the reason.

Derek spoke next, the sound of his voice startling me. "How are you, Elle?" he asked, so, so carefully.

I nodded first, as if that would be answer enough, before forcing out some words. "I'm alright."

Susan stared up at me, tears running down her cheeks. Derek smiled, a gentle, reassuring smile.

"I'm nervous," I added, in the absence of anything else.

"Us too, dear," Derek replied. "But we're really, really thankful you met with us today."

The pain in his voice stung. I nodded again.

"After all this time," Susan cried. "We looked and looked, and you found us!" Derek thrust another tissue into her hand, but she didn't seem to care. "How, why?"

I coughed to clear the lump in my throat, forcing my hands to relax before my nails broke the skin. "I found the photograph... I didn't think it was me, exactly, but I found the website and felt like you should know. I've tried to tell the police as much as I can."

Linda nodded at me. "You've done fantastically, Elle. Everyone thinks so."

"What did they do, to your eye, your leg?" Susan asked directly. Her voice was sweet and her posture stooped, but her eyes were wild.

I looked at Linda, a cry for help, and she obliged.

"That's not going to be the easiest thing for Elle to speak about right now, Susan, but I spoke to her before you got here and can assure you, she's going to be absolutely fine."

"They hurt you," Susan sobbed, going to stand.

I hated myself for it, but I flinched, pushing back in my seat. Derek took her hand and encouraged her to sit back down. I hadn't meant to recoil; the image of the pain in her eyes became seared into my memory – a new, deep scar.

"Was that what they did?" she cried, desperately looking at Derek, then back at me, her pupils round and dark. "Did they hurt you?"

Linda interjected. "Susan, we talked about this. This is a lot for us all to process; we need to take our time. Elle will share details with you when she's ready, and although I can't imagine how frustrating that is, we need to be patient."

"Susan, love," Derek tried.

"I'm sorry." Susan sobbed frantically. "I'm sorry." She pulled on his arm. "She's just sat there, Derek, after nineteen years, she's sat there. What, after another ten minutes I have to wait again? I can't do it. I can't."

"We have to, dear," he coaxed. He looked at me, adjusting the thick neckline of his jumper whilst clutching onto Susan. "Sorry, Elle. We're trying our best. Is there anything you need? Anything we can get you? They said you're staying with your fiancé."

Oh god. "I'm staying with Ben, he's a... new friend. It's a long story, but it's not an official engagement."

Linda adjusted in her seat, smoothing her vibrant skirt.

"But you were attacked, that's where you were attacked on Monday," Susan stuttered. "It's not safe."

"Susan, dear," Derek tried again as she shifted.

She pushed his hand away this time. "No, if one more person says to me *it's been nineteen years, what is a few more days,* I'm going to lose it. I lost all those days and hours, god, all those minutes." Fresh tears streamed as her voice faltered. "I can't lose any more. I can't."

She looked up at me desperately through red eyes. "Do you even remember? Maeve, sweetheart?"

I looked at Linda again as Derek dropped his head.

"Elle? Maeve, darling?" Susan shouted. "Please!"

My heart felt like it was about to explode, my vision darkening at the edges as I felt my control start to slip. I wanted to answer her, but I couldn't. Everything seized up at the thought of giving this poor woman the truth – *no I've never seen you before*. I couldn't do it.

Swiftly, Linda ushered me from the room before I'd even registered that I was moving. Susan fought against Derek as my ears rang and I was pulled towards the door. Linda exchanged words with an officer, who held it open.

The next room was similar to the previous, with a desk and two small chairs. Linda pulled one out and handed me a bottle of water. It crinkled as I gripped it, placing it down on the plastic desk. Linda organised herself and her notebooks before taking a deep breath.

"Well, that went exactly as I feared it would. How are you doing?" she asked, not looking up from her notes as she scribbled.

I took the cap off the bottle and willed the cool water to take the edge off the panic that was coursing furiously through my veins – it didn't, it simply sloshed in my stomach.

Linda glanced up. "I'll speak to Susan again; as you can imagine, this is a fraught situation for all involved."

I nodded.

"Are you able to come back tomorrow and we can try again? I suggest we keep it like this for a few sessions, until things calm down. Step by step, like we talked about."

"Tomorrow?" I repeated. "I, erm, don't have a car or anything."

Linda gathered her papers, stacking them. "I wanted to talk to you about that." She paused. "The living arrangement? I think it would be best if I picked you up from now on. Keep things simple."

"Right," I said, chaos giving way to unease.

"Mr Carlson seems well-meaning, as does his sister, but I don't think your current living arrangement is ideal. I wonder if it would be better to set you up on your own somewhere short-term. We have officers you can stay with."

"No," I replied without thinking. "I mean, no, thank you." Acid built in my throat as my mind helpfully flashed up the last time someone tried to convince me to go to an officer's house.

Linda leant back in her chair. "I understand your hesitation. There's been a lot of change, but this is a high-profile case. The press alone are going to be hard to handle, and after Monday, we know Mr Carlson's apartment isn't secure." She looked at me. "I'm here to help you. That's my role, to assist you. I know it'll take some time to build trust, but that's my focus. Not the investigation, not even Susan and Derek. Just think on it for me. I was a counsellor for many years before my PhD; trauma bonds are very real. When you meet someone in such extreme circumstances, it's hard to get a clear view on it. On top of that, you've escaped from what, by most parameters, can be classified as a cult, meaning there will be an adjustment period. You've come from a harsh, violent environment, meaning any solace can seem tempting. You need to take care of yourself, think about decisions as openly as possible." Her words were said kindly, yet they felt hostile.

"Ben and Lucy have been so kind," I muttered. It felt like gripping the rug as it was being pulled out from under me.

"Of course, and they could well turn out to be long-term friends. I hope they do."

"The police officers... I told DS Ernest about Barnes and Dores."

Linda nodded slowly. "There's an investigation under way. You don't need to worry about them, you are safe here with this team now. It may not feel like it, but this is good, all of these things are positive. When you come in tomorrow the team would like to install an app on your phone. It will allow you to be tracked in an emergency and we will set-up scheduled check-ins. It's a standard tool used by the police and I would recommend you take them up on it, at least until we have arrests and presumably remands. If you don't check in, or you're in trouble you activate it, an alert will go off, making the team aware that something could be amiss."

I swallowed my scoff; nothing about that had felt good and I struggled to see how an app would help. Regardless, I agreed to Linda's demands. Ben could at least get back to work if Linda drove me to and from sessions; I wouldn't have to keep putting him out.

I wasn't expecting the flashes and shouts as an officer led me to the front door. When they told me they'd asked Ben to bring the car round, I thought it was because I was so tired, not because there was a swarm of reporters. The silver Audi was a few steps away as an officer looped an arm around my shoulder and led me to the passenger side.

"Maeve, where have you been all these years?"

"What happened to your leg?"

"How do you know Ben Carlson?"

It was a chorus of chaos and I couldn't even fall into the seat quickly because of my cast. The officer held the door open whilst Linda rushed over, taking my crutch and sliding it onto the back seat. As soon as he could, and before we even spoke, Ben pulled us away from the storm.

"Are you okay? What happened?" he asked quickly, not taking his eyes from the road, his grip overly firm on the steering wheel. "Fucking hell," he cursed. "Elle?" He looked at me. "Are you okay? Shall I pull over?"

My eyes followed the white road-lines disappearing under the car. "Can we just go back to the apartment?"

***

I was cradling a cup of tea on Ben's sofa, replaying all the conversations from the day in my head. We'd had to drive through another group of reporters just to get into the garage.

I'd poured petrol on Ben's life.

"I'm so sorry. Linda said she can find me somewhere else to stay. How do they even know your name?"

Ben sat next to me, putting his coffee down on a coaster, sighing and massaging his forehead. "The press has followed Maeve for years."

"So, what do we do?"

"Wait, Linda wants you to go where?"

I stared down at my tea. "To live with an officer, or in a place on my own, while I find my feet."

"Surely with what you told them they can't expect you to stay with police? Is that what you want?"

I knew exactly what I wanted, unlike before. Ironically, it was with that exact thought that I realised what Linda was trying to explain; I realised how deep I'd dived.

"The officers are under investigation." I dragged my fingers through my hair, tugging at my scalp. "I want to be with you, Ben, but maybe that isn't such a good idea. Maybe it's time I let you have your life back. Look how crazy it was outside, on day one."

Ben looked at me, his eyes warm. "You're not usually this direct."

I rubbed the tips of my nails together. "Linda said that... lots of people in my position cling to people." I couldn't look at him as I said the words, desperately needing him to dispel the dirty truth now rooted inside of me.

"Are you serious? She thinks I've Stockholm syndromed you?"

"What?"

"She thinks I've pulled a Beauty and the Beast on you, as if you're Belle falling in love with her captor."

"No. She thinks I'm likely to fall in love with the first person who doesn't, you know... Bear in mind I did have to explain that we weren't technically engaged."

"Oh, right."

I bit my lip, waiting for his response.

For a second, the silence was heavy, the weight of what had changed making the last couple of weeks seem like a sanctuary that had burnt to the ground.

"Come here," he said simply, leaning over and wrapping an arm around my shoulder.

I tucked my legs up and slid closer to him, explaining everything that had happened with Susan and Derek. My tea had gone cold by the time I'd finished; no part of me wanted to move.

"They were strangers. She was hurting... and everything I did or said just made it worse."

"Give her time. It's just the shock."

"But I didn't even comfort her, Ben. I wanted to but I couldn't."

"It sounds to me like this Linda was being too abrasive. I think I'd have reacted like Susan did; if that was my kid, you wouldn't have got me sitting on the other sofa talking things through calmly."

"She's just trying to help," I defended.

"Maybe, but your situation isn't standard; don't assume that experts always know best."

I tilted my head to look up at him, and as he looked down, the moment suddenly felt very intimate.

I should have looked away, but I didn't.

"Okay."

Ben looked down at my lips, blinking twice and moving slightly back. "You can leave the castle any time, of course, but you have to come back on Friday."

"You still want to go out?"

"Of course."

The next day, Ben went into the office and Linda took me to a different station to avoid the grappling media. Susan was a bit calmer, but it was still a fraught ordeal as I tried to answer their difficult questions about my life as carefully as possible. Afterwards, I had a meeting with the investigating team, where they installed the app on my phone.

The two experiences were entirely contradictory. My time with Linda was slow and steady, like she was handling my trauma with gloves and tongs. Though, she did make a confronting point about bodily autonomy, attempting to start an extremely uncomfortable conversation about sexual abuse survivors and future intimacy. Not something I was ready to think about on any level, let alone discuss. The way she talked about victims was so black and white, like I hadn't had other relationships. Sex was the least of my worries and my relationship with Ben was a complicated luxury I had no desire to label or analyse – least of all because I probably wouldn't like my own conclusions.

By contrast, the police interviews were harsh and rapid-fire. Each question exposing a wound to unpick in unscrupulous detail. It was like they wanted to me relive each painful memory in the most traumatic way possible. Every time we discussed a new subject – be it the book fiddling or some violent crime – it made everything feel worse, more real. Surviving had required moving on constantly, but this new life I was living involved looking back and realising just how long ago I should have run for my goddamn life.

Needless to say, I went to bed with a headache that day.

15

Shots fired

It wasn't remembering, it was revising. Susan shuffled towards the edge of her sofa, leaning over to show me their photo album and pointing out family members. She had a brother, and Derek a sister. It was strange looking at the rosy-cheeked, jolly Christmas photos. Derek's side of the family had stubby noses, and Susan's all seemed to have wide, rounded eyes.

I could see their features so clearly in the photos, yet in the mirror, I looked nothing like them.

Susan beamed telling me about Harry, her baby great-nephew living with her nephew and his husband. I watched her profile as she spoke, wondering how it felt for her to be in all these photos with her brother's children, but not her own daughter.

"You mentioned that you ride?" she added. "That's Mary, your aunt, she has a horse. They never were able to have children. Do you remember when we would go to the stables?"

I chewed on my bottom lip and shook my head. "No, sorry."

She shut the book. "Nothing? You really don't remember anything."

"I—"

Out of nowhere, Susan put her hand on my arm. I don't think she necessarily intended to break the physical barrier so brazenly, but it happened. We both looked at her hand.

"You can tell me, I can take it. You can tell me the truth," she said, gently moving back.

My heart clenched. She should be able to touch her daughter, I felt that pain for her, wanted her to have that solace.

"I only remember Henworth. I want to recognise the people in these photos more than anything, but... look, I'm trying, really, I am."

"We know, dear," Derek assured me softly.

Susan hugged the album. "Do you think you might feel up to coming home, see if that helps?"

I looked down at the patchy grey carpet tiles. "I hate coming to the police station, but I feel like the harder I try to remember, the further I reach. I don't want you to be disappointed if it's the same."

Linda looked up from her notebook. "I can send you my availability, if you like, for home visits. Later in the week is easier. Although, I agree with Elle, we don't want to rush things. It's such an adjustment. If she is going to remember anything, it is unlikely to be when she's under additional stress."

After a few pleasantries, we said our goodbyes. I left the room first, watching as Derek comforted Susan before they also entered the dingy hallway. A couple of officers walked past, awkwardly avoiding eye contact.

"I, um, have a mobile phone," I said, catching the couple off guard. I pulled it out of my pocket and handed it to Derek. "If you like, you can put your number in."

"Elle, I'm not sure that's wise," Linda warned. "Susan, I know you're finding this all very hard, but Elle needs to feel able to distance herself."

I looked at Susan and she looked at me, her eyes glossing over as Derek held the phone loosely.

"It's okay," I confirmed.

Susan let out a desperate smile, and it felt like something inside me fell out of place. Although it sliced through me, it was a pleasant feeling. I decided I liked it.

"We'll try the front door," Ben suggested as he turned the car away from the raucous crowd surrounding the garage.

I wiggled lower into the leather seat, grumbling. He parked up onto a side road, twisting around and shuffling behind us before tossing a hoodie onto my lap.

"For stealth."

"Stealth? Are you trying to be funny?" I scowled, getting a waft of aftershave from the black jumper.

"Look, they haven't got a good photo of you yet, this will buy us, what, thirty seconds?"

"Ben Carlson walking beside a girl with a crutch, wearing a hoodie? Really?"

He scoffed and opened the door. "Just put it on, sunshine."

I pulled it over my head and clambered out, staring down the quiet side road at the traffic whizzing past. "You're annoying when you're chirpy."

He stepped towards me, making me back up against the car. Running his hands past my neck, he pulled the hood up, sending a shiver down my spine.

"You're annoying most of the time. Now come on." He pushed off the car and gripped my waist, pulling me forwards. "I want to shower before my date later. We'll just walk straight in the door."

"I can't, not without my crutch."

"Trust me, I've got you."

I wrapped my arm around his back as he practically lifted me off my feet at his side.

"Maeve, Maeve, have you seen your parents again today?"

"Maeve, how do you know Ben?"

The chorus was quieter with Ben, and he was right, we'd nearly made it to the big glass doors before the media stampeded.

"Told you," he gloated as we walked towards one of the lifts.

"Well, yeah, you practically threw me through the door." I squeezed his side.

"Oh, forgive me, princess. Want us to go back and try again?" He let go to press the button.

I steadied my legs as my cast rested against the marble floor. "And Lucy says you don't have a sense of humour."

"Maybe you—" Ben was interrupted by someone calling my name.

"Chantelle?"

It wasn't the reporters; they knew they couldn't cross the boundary. No, this was someone who had been sitting on the bottom step, but was now getting up. Someone in plaid, with messy hair, in his early twenties.

Sam.

I knew it was him, only... he'd changed; it was like I was looking at him through a different pair of eyes. He looked thin and short, young and flimsy. My body stiffened as my breath hitched. Ben looked at me, then at Sam, stepping away from the button and putting himself between us. The security team responsible for the building had contacted all residents about door access after Marcus got in, but the press outside were creating chaos.

"Chantelle, thank god, I've been so worried about you. Running off like that, after how we ended things?"

I swallowed, feeling my throat narrow.

Sam stepped closer.

"Who the hell are you?" Ben asked aggressively, standing firm.

Sam chuckled. "Stand the old man down, Elle."

"What are you doing here?" I asked in a hushed, breathy voice as my stomach somersaulted. My body remembered Henworth; it remembered Sam walking away.

He craned around Ben, still keeping a couple of steps distance. "I've come to tell you I'm sorry. To beg you to come back to me. I miss you, so much. It was a stupid mistake."

"I know about the money, Sam," I murmured as my heart instantly drank in his words, like a fool.

Ben stepped slightly to my side, still poised to intervene.

"Jesus. Look, you know I needed a new car. I needed the money."

Ben looked at me; I felt the warmth of his gaze as my eyes stayed fixed on Sam. I willed myself to step forwards, to face Sam, to take control. I wanted to.

I was disappointingly empty.

"I love you, Elle, you know," Sam blundered on. "I've always loved you. We can fix this. I spoke to Frank; they just want to talk. They're your parents, you should give them the chance to explain."

I looked away to find Ben clenching his fists at his side. My toes curled in my shoe as my knees loosened, threatening to fold. The thought of Frank and Ruby, the thought of seeing them... the ingrained desire for their approval.

"Just go, Sam," I whispered, begging myself not to cry. Not in front of him, not again.

"You heard her," Ben hissed as the lift doors slid open and the bell pinged. He reached out a hand and gently nudged me in. I took a few tenuous steps.

Sam looked between us, his expression dissolving into something colder. He dragged his phone from his back pocket and there was a blinding flash as he took a picture, then another. I lost my footing and stumbled back. The light bounced off the mirrored walls of the lift. I scrambled to stand just as I saw Ben launch himself across the floor and the doors began to close, sealing me in. I reached forwards, thumping my palms on the moving metal. I turned and hammered the buttons as I heard shouting and clattering. Painful seconds passed as I heard the commotion, but I was trapped, unable to see.

The doors opened ridiculously slowly, taunting me as I desperately waited to see what scene would unveil itself. Diving through the gap and clinging onto the wall, I toppled back into the foyer. Sam's phone was smashed on the floor and the two of them were scuffling by the doors, much to the excitement of the press. Red glistened on Sam's lip as Ben dragged him, by his shirt, to the entrance, wrenching it open and tossing him onto the concrete step. The press swarmed hungrily as Ben straightened himself up, waiting for the door to click shut before stretching out his fingers and turning back to me; breezing over to where I remained frozen, suspended with shock.

"Ben, god, I'm so sorry, I can't believe he showed up here," I gasped as he reached me.

The doors on the lift began to close so he pressed a hand against them, keeping them open, waiting for me to enter. Frantically focused on him, I did, scanning him for injuries as he followed.

Ben leant forwards and pressed the button, the doors closing again on the foyer, which was still lighting up with flashes

"Don't be," he said with an exhale, gathering himself as if nothing had happened. "I'm not."

"What?" I mumbled, my mind frenzied.

He adjusted his glasses and looked at me. "He had it coming. He's smaller than I imagined."

I remained in stunned silence until we reached Ben's floor.

"You coming?" he asked as he casually exited the lift, extending a hand.

I limped out, trying desperately to process what had just happened.

"I'm going to call security. I pay enough bloody service charges and I made myself quite clear after Monday. I will find out who let him in."

Walking into the apartment, Ben went straight to the kitchen and grabbed two glasses, filling them both with water. He slid one across the work top to me as he answered a phone call, attempting to reassure a frantic Lucy who'd seen the news. I dropped my head into my hands.

"You okay?" I heard once he'd hung up.

I looked up from my hands, stretching my cheeks with my fingers. "I have no idea. I am so sorry."

"I already told you, it's fine. Don't start, I'm looking forward to going out."

"Ben, you punched him, in front of the press, because of me. He was in your building and all you do is make some joke about him being small?"

He shrugged, unclipping his cuff links and setting them in the glass bowl. "You think I'd let him talk to you like that, take your photo?" Ben loosened his tie. "Hm?"

"You don't have to defend me, Ben, you could've hurt yourself."

He laughed, walking past me towards his bedroom. "Now I'm offended."

"Wait," I flapped. "You still want to go out?"

Ben turned in his doorway as he unbuttoned his shirt. "It's the least you owe me now."

16

First dates

I scrubbed desperately at my skin as if it would rub my stress away, going through the motions of showering as my mind became overwhelmed with noise again. Sam had looked so different. I couldn't believe I'd been so naïve, talk about showing your true colours. I'd realised by now how pathetic he was, but to try and take a photo? To sell? I suppose I shouldn't have been surprised, but that just made it hurt more.

Climbing out of the shower, I let my hair down and started on my make-up, putting extra blush on my cheeks to hide the lack of colour, more concealer around the remaining bruises, and pink eyeshadow to match the cord miniskirt I'd ordered – I'd paired it with a cream camisole and pleather jacket. I tugged at the sleeves once dressed, staring into the mirror, running my fingers through my hair as it fell softly to my mid back. My cleavage was plumped in my new pale pink bra. I could pass for someone going on a date, but not with Ben.

I heard a knock on the door. "Ready to come apologise excessively to me over dinner?"

"Good one," I said, opening the door, trying to look confident even though my legs were shaking, although it could have been from any number of things that had happened.

He stared at me, his brown eyes moving slowly and purposefully.

I fidgeted awkwardly against his gaze. "What?"

He smiled. "Nothing"

I scowled. "You're grinning at me, it's unnerving."

Ben laughed, passing me the crutch. He looked amazing in his stone chinos and a smart, navy, long-sleeved shirt, the top two buttons undone.

"I'm not going to bombard you with compliments right now, I still remember last time, so just imagine me thinking them all instead. Or, you know…" He stepped closer, so our chests were barely separated, trailing two fingers up my arm and tilting up my chin. "I could tell you right now, whisper them all into your ear. Then, when I'm done watching your whole face flush from my words, I could run my fingers through your hair and kiss you until you moan my name?"

I had no words, no verbal response. The only responses I had were entirely physical, including the immediate, inevitable heat flooding my cheeks, and a few other places. I didn't feel like I was standing, or breathing. I was entirely his, totally captivated, completely under his spell.

I retreated fiercely, twisting and taking a deep breath, feigning looking for something by my bed. The dates I'd been on before had been achievable; I'd gone for easy wins, whether I'd needed some polite conversation or physical intimacy. Doubt spiked as I thought about how different I felt now as I thought about *him* kissing me.

At least the fear cooled me down.

"Your bag is on the worktop," he offered from behind.

I winced, looking away, improvising and grabbing the wrong shade of lipstick, waving it at him and heading straight past him to put it in my bag. "Thanks, good to go."

Or maybe we should just stay in? It had been a while, no, it had been a long time. My body knew it; it was mad at me, like it felt that it had to remind me what it wanted, blatantly. I focused on not looking at him, not trusting myself as I took the crutch from him.

Sitting in the leather seat of the Audi, my eyes went straight to the harsh cast against my skirt. I longed to simply be a girl in a car with a sexy man. That wasn't my life. I wondered if it ever would be, especially now. Had it all been too much to set my path straight? *Probably*, I thought, resenting the sudden surge of self-pity.

He said he was going to kiss me. I'd been so swept up in everything else I hadn't thought about what going on a date meant. Of course, I'd thought about it, kissing him, imagined it, but never about what it would be like after. In a short amount of time, Ben had come to mean many things to me, things I felt like I needed, things I suddenly wasn't sure would be the same.

He turned briefly to me as the steering wheel spun through his hands. "I'm glad you still chose to come, but if you're too tired, or you want to come back, you just say, alright?"

I licked my lips to disguise my expression as my heart thumped. "Thanks, although it feels backwards leaving your apartment together. Very un-date like."

"Want me to ask you twenty questions? Or you can sit at the table and I can come back in after a couple of minutes?"

I forced myself to relax. "Death row food? Super power? Favourite book?"

He tapped the steering wheel. "Lasagne, Bernard's Watch, *Fantastic Mr Fox*, you?"

"Interesting. Now I feel even worse for burning that lasagne I made. The time thing I get, because you're a workaholic, but Roald Dahl? I was expecting something non-fiction, if I'm honest." I tugged my skirt down, watching the streetlights flash past.

"My dad used to read it to us, and I respect the ingenuity of the fox. It's a classic. Why, what's yours?"

I licked my lips, thinking. "I really like Milkybar chocolate, flying seems like an obvious choice, and probably *The Hunger Games*. I, um, found the set at a charity shop and have read it too many times to admit."

"Better?"

I smiled. "Yep."

I looked around as he flicked the indicator on; I hadn't cared to ask where we were headed.

"We can talk about earlier, if you'd like, about anything," he offered.

"Not on a first date, please."

We pulled into a small car park in one of the neighbouring towns. "You sure?"

"Unquestionably. Honestly, I'd love to just feel like a normal human girl for a bit."

He nodded. "Nothing serious again, hey?"

I smiled, at first, before his words sunk in and I realised he was referencing that night at Rose Cottage. The butterflies in my stomach flexed their wings. I thought back to that night, how complicated I thought things were then – it was laughable.

The restaurant was a slick Italian that Ben had been to before. We walked in the door and were led to a perfectly tucked away booth by a smartly dressed waiter. Ben asked if he could order for us, which I welcomed – no decisions, just amazing, authentic food. The pasta was light, creamy, and perfectly seasoned; it was almost refreshing.

"How many girls have you taken here, exactly?" I asked, half joking, half probing.

He looked up, raising an eyebrow. "Why do you ask?"

He was such hard work sometimes, too often giving a question for a question.

"So I know how hard I have to try," I answered, twisting pasta on my fork.

"Try at what, exactly?"

"At flirting. To flatter you. First date stuff."

He grinned. "Do your worst. I haven't taken anyone else here: a couple of colleagues, Lucy once for her birthday, if that counts, but no dates."

I hid my relief, trying to stay coy. "So, Jessica? What exactly is your type? She seemed a bit... highly strung?"

"I don't have a type because I don't like dating. I find it tedious."

I nearly coughed out my pasta. "Okay, noted." I wondered if he knew how blunt he was, whether he did it on purpose.

He laughed. "You don't need to worry about that."

"How long were you guys together? Have you had many serious relationships?" I questioned, not letting it drop, pushing him for once.

"Jessica and I knew each other from university. We were on and off for a while, then tried to make it work, but it never did. I thought it was what I wanted at the time, but then I decided it was more effort than it was worth."

I exaggerated a grimace. "No wonder she was annoyed."

"I saw a girl before Jessica that I'd met in France. The long distance worked for me – fun weekends, lots of personal space – but when she wanted more, I didn't."

"Have you not lived with a partner?"

"No, for one reason or another. Jessica had a place in London, so it made more sense to share our time between houses. Why didn't you move in with Sam?"

I shrugged. "He kept putting it off. He lived with two of his friends in a house share and didn't want to commit."

"Have you had any other serious relationships?"

I wondered if he was just playing along with the ex-talk. "We don't have to talk about this if you don't want to."

"I had my turn, apparently we're doing this."

"Okay, well, not really. I've had boys I liked, I've had flings, but whenever it got serious, past a few dates, the site just made it very difficult. Men weren't usually welcome. Sam got away with it because he was so straight forward and we knew the vets where he worked. We were together properly for a year. I felt like he'd grown up, like maybe we could've taken the next step, like I could've gotten out, but I think they sensed that."

"Did you ever date anyone from the site?" Ben asked.

"No, they really didn't like me. They were crass drunks, most of them. For me, when I did see men, it was mostly escapism. They tried to set me up with a guy from a different community once – introduced us at a wedding. He had this greased-back hair that stuck to his face and was instantly crude. I made my feelings clear when he got drunk and tried to dance with me. It didn't go down well."

"What did they say?"

I looked at him, pausing, considering how much he wanted to know. "When we got back, they told me they were ashamed of me and it got a little... physical."

"Physical?" He tightened his fingers on the edge of the cushioned seat.

"They were drunk, embarrassed; said I thought I was too good for them. Frank got cross and slapped me so hard I fell over, which they thought was completely hilarious. He told all the boys around that they could have me because I was a waste of his time."

I saw the shock crease his face; guilt settled in my stomach.

His eyes intensified. "What did your mum say?"

"Ruby was worse than Frank, most of the time. Frank was just an idiot, but Ruby was purposefully mean. She ignored things like that. One of the men tried it on that night, but I managed to knee him in balls so hard he cried – it was a lucky shot. I told him to back off or I'd tell everyone."

There was another, more awkward, pause.

"Bloody hell," Ben cursed. "And Sam let them treat you like that? Have you told the police officers all of this?"

"Some of it, when it comes up. Sam found it easier to turn a blind eye; he knew if he picked a fight, he'd lose. He just wasn't the type, didn't really ask. Once, I went to his with a burn – Marcus stubbed a cigarette out on me when I was working late with the horses – and Sam believed me when I said it was an accident. I could've been more honest with him, I just didn't want to draw him into it... get him beaten up, or scare him off."

I'd been speaking casually; it was my life, it sounded normal to me, but when I met Ben's gaze, I saw his jaw tight with anger.

"They're scum. Let me deal with them all."

"What do you mean?" I asked, alarmed.

"Get the whole place closed down."

My eyes widened. "You can't. It would cause too many repercussions. It wouldn't change them." My body tensed at the thought, at the memories of the sleazy male police officers. How DS Dores had laughed when they would come to give details of complaints made, so the repulsive clan could serve their own justice. Details I hadn't yet had the courage to admit, even to myself.

"You deserve it, you deserve the justice."

Justice was an odd sentiment to me, a luxury reserved for others.

"Thank you." I meant it. I focused on grounding myself, touching the leather of the booth as Linda had suggested, noticing my own breathing. It did feel nice to hear him say that, even though it scared me. "Sadly, it wouldn't help. It's more complicated than you would think."

Thankfully, the waiter interrupted with the dessert menu.

I changed the subject. "Tell me about your dad."

"That's definitely verging on a serious question."

"A trauma for a trauma."

His voice was unusually unsteady as he answered. "What do you want to know?"

"What was he like?"

I was desperate to know. I wondered if Ben was more like his mother, or his father? Though I couldn't imagine him pulling someone from a burning building after what he'd told me.

Ben sighed. "He was a stereotypical 'dad'. He taught me to ride a bike, to swim, shouted from the sidelines at my football games. He treated my mum like she was the only woman alive – called her his treasure. We would sit around and cook breakfast together on a Sunday morning. He would make 'everything pancakes', topped with everything we had in the cupboards: marshmallows, chocolate, honey. He made me feel like I could do anything. I always liked numbers, and even though he didn't get it himself, he encouraged me."

Listening to him, I could see hairline cracks appearing in his otherwise consistent façade, like a buried truth that left its mark.

"And he loved his work?" I pressed, admiring the square of chocolate desert that had appeared in front of me; the smell of fresh coffee and the texture of smooth cream.

Ben shifted in his seat, looking at the food. "He was addicted to it. It was so dangerous, I don't think he could bring himself to do anything that wasn't as exciting or risky. He would come home covered in soot, bruises, even blood, occasionally. I'd run up to him and hug him, but the smell would make me feel sick. I'd sip water and read to keep myself awake, waiting for him at night. I was so tired in the day I fell asleep at school, much to the entertainment of the other kids.

"The day he didn't come home I watched every extra minute tick by until his colleagues came to the door. I cried for an hour in bed before my mum had even noticed I'd heard. I'd cried and begged him so many times to stop, he just never saw me. He thought he was bulletproof. He was so brave, far braver than I was... am."

He swallowed, his jaw tightening as his eyes remained fixed on the table. I reached across and took his hand, looking at him, trying to swallow my own emotion.

"That's why you didn't want to sleep in the main cottage, that night? Because those rooms remind you of it all?"

He uncharacteristically fidgeted with his cutlery. "We would travel down to Rose Cottage with mum; he would meet us after work. It was even harder to sleep when he was further away."

"He sounds like he tried his best to be an amazing dad," I offered, not sure they were the right words.

Ben squeezed my hand back gently, so I got up from my side of the booth and slid in beside him, needing to feel his body against mine.

He pulled over my half-eaten dessert so I could reach it still and dropped his arm around my shoulders. "A great dad wouldn't have left us."

My breath shortened with the insight. "You feel like he left you?"

"He did. He chose his work. I wish I'd been enough for him."

His words hung in the air between us before I could fumble a reply.

"You were enough, Ben. His choices, his death, they're not on you. If people went into those jobs accepting, truly understanding, the risks and the impact on others, they wouldn't do it. They wouldn't."

"But he did," he murmured, a jerk of emotion in his voice.

We were both quiet for a while.

Sensing I'd pushed him enough, I tried to steer the conversation towards something easier. "Thank you for such an amazing dinner. It was so good, so nice to get out."

His finger traced a circle on my shoulder. "You're welcome. I was surprised you agreed to come with me."

"No, you weren't."

"What do you mean?"

"You undid my bra with one hand and took way too long pulling my tights on, you know you had me interested."

He laughed, relaxing back into the booth. "I thought the one hand had gone unnoticed."

"Oh, I noticed."

"You were wearing a very nice bra. I hope you noticed how respectful I was."

"Very respectful."

After Ben paid the bill, we walked back to the car, two people completely engrossed in one another and nothing else for those few perfect hours. He helped me lower myself back into the seat more slowly than before, his hand lingering in mine.

"This is weird," I blurted out as we pulled back into the garage, the press thankfully having decided they had better places to be. "Not right. We've been on a date, a good date—"

"Good?" he interrupted.

I raised an eyebrow.

"Yes, good," I repeated, trying to hide the nervous energy bubbling inside me. "But now what? We just walk back in together? Like, you invite me in and I say yes automatically? You shouldn't go home with a man after a first date." *Well, not if actually you like the guy.*

He turned the ignition off. "That depends on the date, surely?"

"Men like the chase. You never go back; you draw it out, build the tension. In fact, I should probably ignore you for at least twenty-four hours."

He laughed, undoing his seatbelt whilst looking at me. "You're kidding?"

"No, it works every time, men are primitive. Nothing worth having, and all that. My opportunities have always been scarce, so I've learnt to make the most of them."

Ben climbed out of the car, walking round to open the door for me and reaching out his hand. I took it, nearly losing my footing as he pulled me out more quickly than I'd anticipated. Something in his eyes told me he did it on purpose, my hands falling to rest on his chest before I stepped back.

"I can help you, if you prefer?" he offered, hesitating as he steadied me by holding my lower back.

I shrugged, stepping back. "Thanks, but... first date, you know?"

"I see."

Allowing me to fall into the support of the crutch, he walked beside me towards the lift.

"So, you won't be coming home with me?" he teased.

I leant against the glass as he pressed the button. I noticed us in the mirror and it distracted me from the flow of our conversation. We looked like two people on a date – you couldn't see my cast, and my bruises had mostly all cleared. It made me stand just a little bit taller.

I looked back to him as he settled opposite me. "I can go elsewhere. Maybe you're right, I mean, if we are dating, it's very inappropriate. Linda would have a field day."

He shrugged. "She would. Tell you what, you can say goodbye to me at the door if it makes you feel better, and we can pretend to finish off the date. Then we can just go back to you in your bra... then out of your bra."

The lift felt a size smaller, a degree warmer.

"It would be awkward if you ignored me for twenty-four hours. I've enjoyed having someone to talk to every day – don't tell Lucy."

I wished I could've sauntered out of the lift towards the door, but the creaking of the crutch put that notion firmly to bed as I rattled down the hall whilst Ben unlocked the door.

"Thank you, for a lovely night," I said, pausing in the entrance and freeing my arm from the crutch. As our eyes met, he entrapped me with a stare, looking deep into me through his dark eyes, his glasses glinting in the hall light. A few breaths passed seamlessly between us as we waited for the next move. After weeks of being drawn to one another like magnets, against a backdrop of pain and extremity, here we were.

A man and a woman in a doorway.

"So, do you feel like a human girl now, Elle? Was that enough of a first date?"

"Something like that." My eyes darted to his lips. "Although, even my name seems out of place now... Elle."

Ben quirked his brow. "You want me to call you Maeve?"

I shook my head, gripping the door frame behind me. "No, I wouldn't. That doesn't feel right either."

"Then what does?"

I swallowed. "Honestly? Just who I am when I'm with you."

He blinked with soft surprise. "If we're being honest, I want to kiss every version of you."

I leant towards him, pausing a breath away, waiting, wanting, needing; beyond any shred of sensible control or inhibition.

Ben moved first, swiftly stepping forwards, knocking me off balance so he could catch me, the brief feeling of falling thundering in my chest. He cradled my weight easily, and it felt wildly perfect surrendering to him as he tipped me, both arms tightening around my back. I didn't smile at him, my face was totally relaxed, just moving with my breath, feeling his hand run up my spine, fingertips across my neck, interlacing with my hair. He held me in his arms and his eyes. I savoured the fleeting moment between everything changing, looking back at him, taking in every drop. My body bowed to his control as he finally pressed his lips to mine. A long, deep, passionate kiss setting parts of me instantly alive.

It was electric.

It was perfect.

My eyes closed as our lips connected, everything else melting away aside from the intense, beautiful feeling of him. He carefully walked us inside, drawing away for a moment only so he could push the door shut. The wall felt cold as his body nudged mine into it. His fingers twisted softly through my hair, tilting my head to prolong the kiss. When he eventually drew away, I tightened my hands around his neck, desperate for more. He dipped down, his hands gripping my thighs, effortlessly lifting me as our kissing became frantic. I hadn't even noticed we'd moved until I felt the sofa underneath me, him on top; bodies entwined, lips greedy, totally intoxicated with each other.

I pulled my lips away from his. "Ben, we should stop," I rasped as his knee dragged up my leg, nudging it sideways.

"You're right," he breathed, as he stole his addictive kisses away from my lips, pressing them feverishly into the crook of my neck.

I groaned, my hands pressing into his firm chest in a weak attempt to dampen things as his belt buckle caught on the material of my top.

"Ben," I gasped, arching my chin up.

He breathed me in, drawing up as his hand stroked down from my forehead through my hair, his other arm tight around my waist.

He shuddered. "Saying my name like that won't help."

"We shouldn't."

"Shouldn't what?"

My leg hooked over his as I started to move rhythmically against his body, my own limbs ignoring my rational words as they demanded more.

I pulled him closer, his heavy warmth invigorating every sense.

"You know what." I pouted.

He seized my pout, his tongue slipping between my lips, twisting with mine. "Tell me."

I gently took his lower lip in my teeth, taking back control. "We can't."

He stared into me, pressing up slightly. My lips still wanted to move with his, my body yearning to obey his touch.

"If we take off each other's clothes, Ben, I want to do it properly. I want to be able to move and relax. Not lug around a useless leg."

He danced a finger along the lace of my bra, brushing against the pink satin but not going further.

"I don't care about your cast."

"I do. Three weeks, Ben." Against my conscious control, my chin tilted in invitation, my rebellious body overpowering any self-preservation.

"Three weeks," he repeated, taking a deep breath.

I felt him hard against the inside of my leg. *God.*

"Urgh," he groaned, immediately pushing himself up. "I better get a glass of water or something, then."

I lay there for a second, not wanting to move; to cherish the lingering essence of him. I sat up when I heard him speaking, pressing my fingers to my swollen lips.

"Ever since you fell into me walking back to the cottage, I've been thinking about kissing you." His words melted through me. "It was quite the swoon."

"It was an accident, I can assure you. Although, I think I might understand why your exes are still banging on your door."

He smiled, but not how I thought he would, not ready to return a line. Instead, he looked surprised. I heaved myself up, trying to style out my hobble, heading across the strip of hall to the bedroom before pausing to reply.

"When I fell on you by the river, even in all the drama of the wet mud, I was distracted by lying on top of you."

He grinned, hungrily this time.

Retreating to the guest room, I put on my pink pyjama shorts and washed off my make-up, brushed my teeth, and headed to bed. The fabric felt particularly cool and silky against my skin as I placed my hair pins down on the dressing table.

Ben's voice trickled through the door. "Would you like company?" he asked, strolling across the room, now shirtless, placing a glass of water on the bedside table.

I leant back against the table to steady myself, and in a feeble attempt to maintain distance.

"I'd like your company, of course, but I can't, I'm sorry," I spluttered, mustering my self-control.

It was tenuous.

Bending down, he pulled back the duvet, stepping away so I could climb in.

He looked at me, more tenderly than before; less like he wanted to devour me. "Stop apologising. I get it."

"I have to build the tension anyway, with a man like you. I have to try and get that second date."

He pulled the duvet over me, tucking it firmly down at the side before he leant in to kiss me again, drawing away before I could reciprocate. "Surely you realise that's a given. Next Friday?"

Our faces were still so close as he stood over the bed that, if either of us moved, we would snap back together. He could just fall into bed and I could run my hands over his skin again. It would be easy, too easy. My body communicated my desire in every way it could think of.

"I'll think about it and get back to you in twenty-four hours."

"Funny," he replied, turning and walking away, closing the door behind him.

17

Her name?

The morning after our date, Ben had headed to the gym, leaving me alone to stare at my phone and freak out about the day before. Susan hadn't texted me, which I respected – she was obviously trying to follow Linda's warning. I didn't know if I was riding off the high of the date, or the kiss, or just trying to not think about Ben's muscles flexing downstairs, but I pressed the dial button before I could overthink it.

She answered on the second ring. "Hello?"

"Hi, Susan, um..." I was stumped instantly.

Strong start.

"Hi, Elle. How lovely that you rang, I was just thinking about you. I saw the photos of Ben on the news, was everything okay?"

Guilt rippled through me. I hadn't even considered that she might see. "Yes, sorry if you were worried. That was Sam, um, an ex of mine. Ben stepped in to help me, though. Sam tried to get photos."

"Oh, well, it's nice to see he's looking after you."

I don't understand how it happened, whether I was just giddy with ridiculous girly joy, but I started telling her about the date. We ended up having a perfectly normal conversation, for the first time.

"Well, he's very handsome." She chuckled warmly. "So, he's Lucy's brother?"

My cheeks welcomed a smile. "Yeah, she invited me to stay at Rose Cottage and he was there too. We actually didn't get on at first, but he was bound to protect his family from the dishevelled stranger. We all went for lunch one afternoon and Sophie fell in the river, so I jumped in to help her. I guess we got close after that."

We must have been chatting for another half an hour at least, as Ben came back through the door while I was still on the phone, his blue sports top gripping his back. Susan was telling me about how her and Derek had met on a fairground ride; he'd plonked himself down in her cart on the Ferris Wheel. It was a great story.

Ben stopped in the hallway and grinned easily at me. I smiled back, listening to Susan's voice in my ear.

By the time Ben reappeared after his shower, I'd finished the call, made us hot drinks, and curled up on the sofa.

I picked up the remote.

"Wait," Ben called over, moving to sit beside me. "Sam spoke to the press. If I were you, I wouldn't watch it."

The good feeling buzzing through me scattered instantly, leaving an emptiness where it had been making space. I leant forwards and gripped my mug, wrapping my hands around the warm ceramic.

Ben just watched me.

I chewed my lip. "What is he saying, exactly?"

Ben looked me directly in the eye, not faltering as he explained, with some choice words.

I looked up the headlines for myself:

Maeve White and me – what her life was like.

I loved Maeve White.

The inside story: Maeve White

"It's all lies," I spat as my eyes skimmed all the horrible stories. "He talks as if it was all lovely and perfect. Wait, *I* dumped *him*! What the hell... why, why would he do this?"

I noticed the split lip Sam had in the photo, taking marginal solace in it.

"He's just after money, or fame," Ben said with a sigh, hooking one leg over the other.

"I can't even defend myself. I can't even set things straight. The press have all these fuzzy pictures of me dodging their cameras. It makes me look awful."

Ben scratched his jaw. "There was a box in the post room. I picked it up on my way back."

"A box?"

"A box of letters and cards." He paused. "You feeling brave?"

I thumped back against the sofa; my rib hated it, but I didn't care. "No, but I guess we should just rip the plaster off."

He patted my knee and stood back up.

The ominous box was so large Ben had to carry it with both hands. It was filled with everything from cards and teddies, to letters; even some branded gifts people wanted to me wear. I took my time to read each note, becoming more and more shocked at the outpouring of grief and support. I'd spent all this time resenting the media – dodging the press and hiding – that I hadn't considered how they had actually helped me get out. People had avidly followed that cute little girl in the photo. They'd watched the documentaries and the news footage, commented on the website, and consistently searched. The cards were mostly filled with kind words about how strong I was, or how incredible it was to have me back. People didn't even seem to want anything most of the time, not even a response. They were just expressing their feelings of relief, or joy, or sadness for what happened.

There were, of course, a couple from Henworth. Some simple threats, some attempts at manipulation. Ben collected them all in an envelope for the police without even looking inside, even though some of them were aimed at him. There was one in particular that stuck in my mind, about burning down his building; it made me feel ill. Ben just shrugged. I couldn't work out if part of it was denial, or if he hadn't grasped how unhinged they were.

We ate lunch together as I packed everything else neatly back in the box.

"You don't want to put the cards up?" Ben asked as I adjusted the cardboard lid.

I shook my head. "No, I don't think so. They're addressed to Maeve, it just doesn't feel right. I do need to do something, though. I feel terrible that I've been hiding when everyone has been reaching out to me like this."

Ben leant back into the arm of the sofa. "You're allowed to hide, if that's what you want to do."

"I think I want to respond. To thank people; it would take me hours to reply to all of these. I thought people were just waiting to pull me apart."

"We could set you up an email address, or something? I saw there were a few interview requests. Although, you really shouldn't let Sam strong-arm you into doing anything you're not ready for."

I put the box on the floor, considering it. "No, I'm not ready for an interview." I did not want to sit somewhere and have a camera pointed in my face; I would definitely say the wrong thing.

"Well, if you want to set up an email address, you should probably start with a name."

"A name..."

"Maeve is legally your name. I know you see her as that little girl, but it's yours. Equally, Elle is also you. Who you've become."

"*They* chose that name," I grimaced. "They branded me with it."

"Doesn't Maeve have a middle name?" Ben asked as he put his bowl down to pick up his phone. "Ivy. Maeve Ivy White."

I tilted his phone so I could see. "Oh. I think Susan said it was her grandma's name."

ME

Hi, Susan. 'Ivy' came up in conversation as we were talking names, did you say that was your grandma's name? xx

SUSAN

Hi, how are you feeling now? Did you give any thought to tomorrow, or Monday? Yes, when you were a toddler you used to call her 'Ve'. It breaks my heart that you won't get to meet her, that her and my mum won't get to see what a beautiful woman you became. x

Oh gosh, sorry. I didn't mean to upset you. I'm okay,
thanks, I've been going through all the cards and
letters that arrived. I can't believe there were so many,
that people care so much xx

SUSAN

You haven't upset me, love. Yes, we've had a lot again
lately. People have always followed your story closely.
Me and Derek are trying to finish an ongoing puzzle
and then I'll be cooking supper. I'm best when I'm
busy. If I may say it without being too forward, it made
my day that you called. xxx

"You're pulling funny faces," Ben teased as I glanced up from my phone.

I showed him the screen, tucking my legs up on the sofa, needing to feel a bit smaller for a minute, though nothing was comfortable with the lump of plaster.

I watched his eyes flick over the texts.

"I'm so sorry," he said sadly after a minute or so.

"Sorry?"

"Yeah, she seems like she has so much love to give. It's heartbreaking that it was taken from you. You should see her on Monday, go to their house and get out of the police station."

I ran my hand through my hair, feeling it glide through my fingers. "Maybe I could cope with the name Ivy. It's not Maeve, or Elle, but it's still kind of my legal name."

"Ivy," he repeated, rolling it over his lips.

"Ivy," I said again.

Would you mind if I used the name Ivy? Maybe for a
while, I'm not sure yet. Elle doesn't feel right anymore

xx

I would love that, it would be very fitting xxx

Thank you, if the offer is still open, I'd like to come and
see you Monday xxx

"You have beautiful eyes, Ivy," Ben said softly as I looked up from
my phone.

"What are you doing?"

"Testing it out. Why do you hate compliments so much?"

I put my phone down. "Is it bad to say I prefer it when you're
grumpy?"

I watched as he ran his finger over his lips, distracting me as I
thought about how they'd felt pressing into mine. I curled a lock of
hair around my fingers, some sort of pre-programmed flirtation.

He furrowed his brow to a mock frown. "Fine. Tell me why you
hate compliments, Bambi."

I pressed my thumbnail between my teeth, feeling Ben reach for a
scar that didn't want to be exposed. "I don't."

He shifted on the sofa so that his leg pressed against my thigh,
pulling down my hand and keeping it in his. "So, if I start telling you..."
He inched closer, his eyes widening as he stared into mine, walking
two fingers up my forearm. "How stunning I think—"

I stopped him from finishing his sentence as I felt the blush rise
in my cheeks, tilting forwards and pressing my lips into his. I felt him
smile as his fingers glided up my arms, brushing past my neck and
under my ear. His warm tongue flicked over my lip, so I let him in as
my hands pressed into his lap, enjoying the feeling of his jeans pulling
tight.

"Quit winding me up," I whispered as my eyes drifted open.

Both of his hands swiped my hair gently away as he cupped my
face, softly tilting it to his lips as he kissed my cheeks, one at a time.
"So, if I wind you up, you're going to kiss me? I don't see how that will
help me stop."

My eyes shut again as his fingers gently spread to the back of my head, setting off a tingling from my scalp all the way down my back.

"Fine," I conceded, "I don't like them because I just don't believe them. I've grown up being told the opposite. No one ever found me attractive, and I learnt to accept that so it hurt less. I don't know if I can open that up again. If I want to." I bought a hand up to straighten his wonky glasses.

"They were lying, I can assure you."

"You don't know that."

"Of course I do. Think about all those cards you just read, focus on that, not them."

I wished it was that easy, but of course it wasn't. That would be like re-writing my entire brain; that would be feeling like I was safe with Ben forever, safe enough to open that part of me up. Although, it did strike a nerve as he said it, that maybe I had been focusing on all the wrong things.

I had an idea. An idea to start something new, to start a new life, Ivy's life, whoever she might turn out to be.

(O) **IvyMWhite** Thank you to everyone who sent me letters, cards, and gifts. I sat here reading them and they bought a tear to my eye. I know many of you have followed my journey, so I wanted to create this profile to respond. I'm incredibly lucky to have found Susan and Derek again and we're getting to know each other slowly. Without everyone keeping the story alive for so many years, I wouldn't be writing this; safe and starting a new life today. So thank you, all of you.

I uploaded a photo of the box with a few cards showing and put my phone down, waiting to see if anything happened. As soon as I'd made a fresh cup of tea, I sat down to see thirty comments, then over a hundred when I refreshed.

18

Visiting home

My eyes opened on Monday and I was instantly wide awake, worrying about the home visit. I pulled on my dark green dress, after trying on and rejecting nearly everything else in my small collection. I tied half of my hair up and left the rest down in the slight waves caused by my restless night.

Ben knocked quietly on the door as I dared a glance in the mirror.

"How are you feeling?" he asked, staring at the clothes scattered on the bed.

My reflection looked back at me uneasily. "Nervous. Do I look okay?"

"Now whose fishing?"

I met his smirk with a scowl.

Noting his attempt at humour had gone directly over my head, Ben walked to stand behind me as I stood grimacing at the mirror. I watched as he laced his arms around my waist and pressed his chin down into my shoulder.

"You look perfect," he whispered into my ear, brushing my cheek with a kiss. "You'll do great. Just call me if you need me, okay?"

"Thank you," I murmured, flinching as the doorbell rang. Instinctively, I reached for his hand, turning to face him. "What if they don't like me? What if, without Linda, it's too much?"

Pain flashed in his eyes, but the door buzzed again.

At first, Linda being busy had seemed easier, but suddenly it felt like a mistake.

"That's rubbish and you know it, Ivy," he insisted, pulling away to answer the door.

I heard him introducing himself formally to Derek in the doorway.

I gripped the cool, familiar plastic handle of the crutch hard and swung for the door. Derek looked at me and took a subtle, sharp inhale, prompting Ben to smile at me.

I told you so, he mouthed at me. *You're fine.*

"Sorry, I'm not used to that yet. You look really pretty," Derek said, almost with pride.

If it wasn't for the crutch, I think it might have floored me.

Ben handed him my brown satchel. "You want me to walk you down?"

"No, thank you. Have a good day at work," I replied, then hesitated, wanting a gust of wind to help get me moving.

Derek gave me a warm smile, and slowly, my legs started to move.

The car ride was slightly tense, but we found some small talk easily enough; Derek seemed nervous too. It was difficult as we pulled up to the house – I hadn't been back since the attack, and something about the small iron gate put a knot in my stomach.

"Are you okay?" he asked knowingly as we headed for the little path.

I nodded. Past the iron gate felt like a win, it felt like progress. Susan was at the door waiting, looking as if she was ready to burst into tears already, her face creased and alert. I pushed and swung forwards. The sensation of the crutch handle was grounding. I got to the green front door and she threw her arms around me, taking me by surprise. Luckily, she held me tightly, otherwise I might have fallen.

"Susan!" Derek scolded crossly from behind.

I stumbled forwards, lifting one arm, clutch hanging, and hugged her back. She squeezed me even tighter until I felt tears roll down my face. They were just there, all of a sudden, with no warning. She pulled back, her own eyes puffy.

"Thank you for coming," she said with a strained smile, before leading the way in.

Susan bought me a cup of tea, explaining that she'd added a sugar.

"This will help, tea solves all problems." She sat down next to me on the sofa, taking my hands in hers. "How are you?"

Next to the mug was a small bag of Milkybar buttons. I stared at the yellow packaging, fighting to name my swelling emotions.

I took a deep breath, drawing my eyes away. "A bit better, thanks. I'm just trying to take it all one day at a time."

Susan's fingers were cold. "Good," she replied, tentatively.

Derek sat in the armchair opposite, unzipping his blue fleece and sliding his feet into brown slippers. The house was so homely; red patterned rugs adorned with chunky oak furniture, a brown leather sofa doused in matching fleece blankets. There was a lovely pair of patio doors framing a small but well-kept garden with a rectangular, busy vegetable bed. I drank it all in.

"Do you remember?" Susan asked, too quickly.

The question cut through me. Linda had told me to be honest; she'd said that Susan would ask me difficult things, but that we had to start from a place of honesty.

"I'm sorry... I don't. It feels warm, though, cosy. You have a lovely home." I drew a shaky breath, analysing her face, waiting for her heart to break.

"It's okay, I understand, maybe you will one day?"

I let out the breath. "Hopefully."

She smiled, still clutching my hands in hers. In the corner of the room, I noticed a chunky dresser decorated with an eclectic series of photo frames. There was one of Susan and Derek on what looked like a cruise; Maeve at pre-school; Maeve on a garden swing; Derek, Susan, and Maeve smiling on a beach. It looked like that little girl was about to come bounding out of one of the rooms, teddy in hand, at any moment.

"They bought us comfort," Susan explained, following my eyes.

Derek interjected, thankfully. "How's your leg?"

"On the mend, I think. I'm back at the hospital tomorrow, hopefully to get a smaller cast. It'll make it a bit easier to get around."

"How are you managing?" Susan added.

Without Linda mediating, she was hungry.

"Okay. Ben's apartment is nice, it has a lovely view over the city." I looked to Derek to bring him into the conversation again.

"Ben seems mature; the apartment is very smart."

"I struggle with silly things, when I sit for too long, my ribs still hurt. I'm hoping soaking in the bath might be easier with less plaster."

"Is there anything we can do to help?" Derek asked.

"Not unless you have a very unusually shaped bathtub," I said lightly, smiling gratefully.

"How do you not get it wet?"

"I have a plastic stool, so I fill it a few inches and just use the showerhead. It's workable, but not ideal."

Derek stroked his beard as Susan asked more questions. I told her about the burnt lasagne, and she suggested we cook something to take back for Ben.

Together, Susan and I started a risotto. She sat me with the vegetables at a dark wooden table in the kitchen. A smoky scent filled the room as she made crispy bacon to mix in at the end, the oil crackling as it fried. The risotto would be chicken and leek flavour, but she said we needed to look after Ben and that men like protein. It was thoughtful and made me smile. Steadily, we began to bounce off each other – Susan was calmer when she was busy.

While the risotto was on the hob, she gave me another sweet tea, sitting down next to me with an old recipe book. She explained it was Ivy's and had been passed down to her. The pages were crunchy as I turned them carefully, each splattered with splodges of different meals gone by. Her family life sounded idyllic; different memories richly painted for me through the eclectic meals. She became emotional, telling me that her mum and dad had passed away in the last few years. It was a painful thought to think that I'd missed them. I tried not to show the deep root of sadness it planted; Susan didn't need that. I had to be strong for her.

On the site, there had been no grandparents. Moving away and making your own life when you married was their way of living. The thought of a grandmother cooking with Susan; plaiting hair, hiding Christmas presents... I stopped myself as I felt a tear rise. It was so much; the simplest thought or comment was like opening a door to a cascade of hurt and longing which, once opened, was always ajar. The thoughts of what had been missed, taken, stolen.

She described how her, Derek, and her brother would go round to her mum's for a roast dinner nearly every weekend. It must have been so hard for them not being able to have their daughter there; to watch her brother bring up his own family. She said her parents were totally in love until the end, joking that her dad was a strong man who spent his days agreeing with his wife and rolling his eyes. I let a picture of them take root in my mind.

When the risotto had soaked up most of the liquid, I used my crutch to come and watch her finish it off, stirring in two cheeses and mixing in the bacon. It looked creamy and delicious as I watched her spoon it into a glass container.

"It smells amazing," I said to her, the rich aroma coating the kitchen.

"Let me know what you think."

"Of course."

"Would you like me to show you around the rest of the house?"

I bit my lip. "I'm sorry, Susan, I've had a lovely time, but the idea of going upstairs feels a bit much today," I answered carefully, feeling guilty, but also petrified.

A lot of the old news coverage had been photos of Maeve's preserved, empty bedroom. Curiosity occasionally got the better of me, but the feeling of failure at the unfamiliarity quicky put it to bed.

"Of course," she said, squeezing my arm.

There was a clatter behind us as Derek came in, holding something wooden.

"Your mother had one of those bath trays that you put across the tub. I thought that, if I added some material to it, you could use it to support your leg."

I looked at the tray. Derek had cut some neat slots in the centre, with a hammock of material laid between. I looked at him, touched by his thoughtfulness.

"That's... really clever, Derek," I murmured, struggling to find volume.

I looked from one of them to the other. Everything they were doing was to be kind; they really did care. They cared about me. They wanted to help me.

Derek swung the contraption so I could see the other side. "It adjusts, see? I put some pegs in, and if you tie the material, it will lift it up and down."

"It's really great, Derek. Thank you, truly."

"Good, I hope it helps. How are you getting to the hospital tomorrow?"

"Linda said she would take me, so that Ben could work."

"We can take you!" Susan blurted.

Derek looked annoyed again, as if he was trying to control himself, and resented her impulsiveness.

"I wouldn't want to put you out."

"Don't be ridiculous, we have so much catching-up to do."

Derek shot her another look.

Susan continued, a little slower. "As and when you're ready. Derek is right, sorry, love. I'm getting swept away, I know I am."

I thought for a second, but the answer was easy. "If you don't mind, that would actually be really nice."

They both smiled.

○ **IvyMWhite** Wow, I can't believe so many of you have followed me, and thank you for all the comments on my last post! As you may have seen from the photos, I went back to Susan and Derek's for the first time today. It felt like a big step for all of us, and Susan suggested I share the photo attached. Sitting on their sofa, I found myself staring at all the memories I wish I still carried with me. I wish I could step back and remember everything, especially them, but I can't, not yet. Although, getting to see their lovely home, getting to spend more time with them, felt amazingly wholesome. I'm looking forward to spending a lot more time there.

IvyMWhite Check this risotto out. Susan is an incredible cook!

IvyMWhite This is me and Lucy – she rightly requested a mention. Lucy stopped at the side of the road when I was totally lost, considering going back, and completely broken. Her unwavering, bold kindness handed me back the first piece of something I needed. A piece that every other piece I've placed connects to. So, if you have the chance, be kind – you might just change someone's life. Thank you, Lucy #BFF

19

The Encore

My second date with Ben was a shining beacon getting me through the never-ending police interviews and sessions with Linda. Ben's assistant, Catherine, had booked us seats for a theatre performance of *The Taming of the Shrew* in an amazing raised booth, champagne included. The stage was grand, with gold accents and cascading red curtains. I let my good leg rest against Ben's, leaving my hand on his knee. He noticed, smiling at me and lacing his fingers through mine. They stayed intertwined the entire show. The costumes were spectacular. I laughed and cried, forgetting everything apart from the feeling of being there. I loved the theatre; anyone could forget their reality.

"Thank you, that was wonderful," I gushed as the final round of clapping subsided and Ben led me out, kissing the side of my head as we joined a small queue.

"You're welcome. I'm glad to have taken another first, you should write a list so we can go through them all. I was more interested in watching your reactions than the performance half the time."

We'd reached the bustling foyer when I heard a shout.

"Benji C?"

A well-dressed, broad, dark-blonde man strolled over and hugged him, taking me by surprise. They patted each other's backs in that firm, manly way.

"I didn't know you left the office these days, how've you been?" the stranger asked, with a natural exuberance and well-spoken accent.

When they stepped back, I noticed how much Ben's face had lightened.

"Good, cheers. I know, I'm sorry I missed the last quarterly. The figures look great, though. I can't wait to see some of the projects finished."

I made eye contact with the girl hovering awkwardly behind him. I noticed the bright glow she had in her cheeks, highlighted by a smattering of freckles. She was tall and pretty, very feminine, with mousy mid-length hair and a dainty, pointed nose offsetting hazel eyes. We smiled at each other, waiting for an introduction.

"You should see the library, Ben. I sketched out this middle apex that reminded me of the church in Bruges, do you remember? I'm hoping the light will have a similar effect. When it's done, I'll invite you to the opening, you should actually come this time." The mousy woman placed a tentative hand on the man's arm. "Oh, this is Paige, my fiancée," he continued, wrapping his arm around her proudly.

She seemed shy, but not displeased.

"Congratulations!" Ben smiled, pulling me softly to his side. "Jenson, Paige, this is Ivy."

"Nice to meet you both," Paige said quietly. "I've heard a few of the university stories." She smiled, seeming to relax.

"Oh, I haven't." I raised my eyebrows playfully at Ben. "Maybe you should fill me in. I just had you down as a swot."

Jenson laughed. "I like her. I saw something on the news, but I didn't realise you two were together. How are you both doing? Got time for a drink?"

He was easy to warm to, confident; like Ben, but more outgoing.

"Not tonight, mate, but I'll message you and we can catch up."

Jenson squinted at him. "Famous last words from you as always, Mr Carlson. Ladies, you've witnessed it."

⊙ **IvyMWhite** Was lucky enough to see *The Taming of the Shrew* at The Bristol Theatre today. It was my first time seeing a live performance and it was amazing. The acting was incredible, and I particularly liked the costumes. I got so lost in it that my brain's still talking in old English! I'll be adding more classics to my reading list.

Bananabookworm22 2h

You look amazing, love your post!

BristolTheatre 1h

Thank you for coming, we are glad you enjoyed it!

ClassicsbuffOXO 56m

What have you read already? Happy to recommend some good pages to follow x

Conspiracyspotters 30m

See what I mean: no collarbone mole. This isn't Maeve White.

> **BeauGInsta** 5m
>
> You're right! I thought something was off about her, my husband is a doctor and he said she wouldn't be going out like that.

Driving away in the slick Audi, the air remained easy between us.

"So, if you actually *do* have friends, what else do I need to know... Benji? I feel like Jenson just ruined your moody bachelor façade."

Ben chuckled. "I like Jenson. I have a lot of respect for him, actually. We met in our last year of uni, and although he could've gone and worked for his dad, who owns this big sportswear company, he chose to follow his passion for design and start his own architecture business. I've helped with a few bits before, but I just get too busy."

"Busy?"

"Busy."

"Come on, we're always in my head. He seems nice. Why do you shut people out?"

Ben adjusted his grip on the leather steering wheel, watching the road. "When I get close to people, it makes me uncomfortable. To feel like I need someone, or want to keep seeing someone, scares me. So I flake on them. That enough psychoanalysis for you?"

"Yes, thank you. I'll discuss it with Linda."

"Don't you dare discuss it with Linda." He laughed. "Oh, look, now we're home."

I rolled my eyes as the car swung under the barrier. Ben climbed straight out as the engine stopped whirring.

"Linda would happily do you a session, I'm sure," I teased as he opened the door for me.

He leant slowly into the car, reaching over me, lingering as he pressed the release on the seatbelt, letting the cool metal slide along the tops of my legs. He smirked as I took a sharp inhale, feeling his warmth and enjoying his cologne. Before I could think to speak, he scooped me up, lifting me effortlessly out of the deep seat.

"Ben!" I shrieked, laughing.

"You look tired," he announced playfully as I clung onto his shoulders, appreciating how solid they were as my nose grazed a shadow of stubble on his neck.

"Ever the gentleman."

"Gentleman?"

I raised an eyebrow at him. "Yes. I told you – I see you, Benji." I tapped him on the tip of his nose. "You're not as broody as you think, you know."

"Careful," he growled as he thrust me up in his arms, adjusting his grip.

I laughed. "Aww, see, so sensitive. I'm definitely texting Paige."

My feet thumped down as he practically dropped me into the corner of the lift. I went to adjust my balance but he gripped my hips, pressing me back into the cold glass, holding me there. He reached to press the button without taking his eyes off my lips, looking like he was about to devour me. The excitement sparked through my whole body, humming as he rolled his warm torso into mine, crashing his lips greedily to my mouth.

"What if I don't want to be a gentleman with you?" he rasped between kisses.

"Ben," I moaned, instantly lost to him, lurching forwards and gripping the back of his head. My heels lifted as the lift lulled to a start.

"It's too easy to get you to moan my name," he breathed. "Almost takes some of the fun out of it."

My dress rose up around my hips as his chinos ground into me, but when I reached down, he pinned both my hands above my head, snaking his fingers into mine. It did things to me. I tried to pull them away and he just gripped harder.

"My mistake, I—"

His tongue roamed over mine as I instinctively pressed my knee into his leg, trying to balance and slide it up.

"Shh." He nipped at my lip, springing backwards abruptly as the doors opened.

I was left utterly flustered, with a bunched-up dress that I was desperately trying to smooth down as he strolled out of the lift with a huge grin on his face.

"Hey!" I called after him, fumbling forwards, not missing the misted handprints on the glass.

He stood by the front door, holding it open, acting completely blasé.

"What rules do you have for second dates?" he asked, enjoying himself far too much as I walked past him and into the apartment.

I looked back, unsure what he might do next, but excited all the same.

"Not being easy," I smirked, heading for the bathroom as I heard him lock the front door.

Alone, I paused to catch my breath and shake off some of what was bubbling inside of me. I ran my own fingers over my collarbone, savouring the memory of his touch. I brushed my teeth and washed my face, before dashing on a subtle flick of new mascara. I took my time letting the cold water run over my hands, patting them against my neck. When I felt I'd composed myself, I walked back out, looking for Ben whilst pulling down the half of my hair I'd pinned up, curls falling and tickling my exposed décolletage.

"I know what you're doing," his calm, deep voice echoed from his bedroom.

I reached back and started loosening a button at the back of my dress, flicking my hair over my shoulder. "Getting water?" I suggested, as coolly as I could muster, attempting to beat him at his own game, a dangerous game, no doubt.

He stood there, waiting for me to go past, his eyes smouldering.

I burst out laughing. "Okay, you win, but only because all the tension will disappear as soon as I try to hobble a glass of water back."

He smirked. "I'll get you one, hold on."

My teeth grazed my top lip as my eyes followed him to the sink. When he walked past, he intentionally brushed himself against me, taking the glass into his bedroom.

"Er, wrong way," I said, watching him disappear round the door.

I looked around for no reason at all, trying to figure out what to do. I couldn't have sex with him, of course I couldn't. The site had taken so much from me; not this, not with him. I knew the odds were that this would happen, one way or the other; it had been brewing since Rose Cottage, whether I wanted it to or not. Against my better judgement, here we were. I wasn't going to waste it dragging around a cast. Plus, that was all this was, sexual tension. Once that was gone, it would just be us, and 'us' couldn't work. I didn't work with anyone.

"You coming?" he called through the semi-darkness.

I took a few tentative steps forwards. I hadn't really been in his room much. The oak bed was even bigger, higher, than the guest room's. It had a fluffy white duvet and pillows. There were three white walls – one dark green behind the bed's headboard. Ben was unbuttoning his shirt, steadily exposing his tanned chest. It wasn't overly muscular, but you could make out the shapes of his abdominals. He draped his shirt over the washing basket as I shamelessly watched.

Pausing, he took steady steps towards where I was stood, uncommitted, in the entrance, my hands gripping each other behind my back, one restraining the other. He leant his hand to the wall above me, leaning in, running the tip of his nose up the curve of my neck. I gasped, and my hands tried to break free, wanting to explore his chest.

I spoke softly. "If I come in, I might regret it." The control ebbed away as more parts of him touched more parts of me.

He drew back slowly, looking at my lips again. "I understand." His mouth pressed hard into my neck, sending waves rushing through me as I desperately swallowed another moan. "There are so many things I've wanted to do to you. It will make it all the more enjoyable... waiting."

He kissed me again just under my ear, the tip of his tongue flicking lightly. Ben was playing me like an instrument, toying with me, sensing my body reacting beyond my control as I let out a heavy breath. I couldn't let him, I reminded myself, for so many reasons – least of all because I couldn't be easy for him, I wouldn't be. I gripped my hands together, feigning control, repeating in my head *cold thoughts, you're in a cold bath.*

"We'll have to do it a few times, because after the first time, I don't think I'll be able to control myself," he continued, even the breath from his words caressing me sensuously.

My chin tipped up, exposing more of myself.

Iceberg, you're on an iceberg. Naked. No, not naked! Lots and lots of clothes.

My legs pressed together, twisting against each other, rubbing. "Fucking tibia," I muttered, reminding myself of my predicament.

"You realise," he whispered, "I only need the very top of your legs."

He bent down, catching me by surprise again, looping an arm under my hips and lifting me as my hands flew to grip his back, the feeling of his warm skin delicious against my palms. Pulling the duvet down with one hand, he slowly laid me onto his soft bed, pushing my dress up, gripping the top of my tights, easing them down my legs. I flinched as the elastic waistband caught on my thin knickers, nudging them down. He looked at me wickedly, slowly taking two fingers and running them along the hem, daring to breach the boundary as my skin became more and more sensitive. My hips arched up into his touch as my breathing grew heavy, the feeling of his large hands wrapped around my hip bones dizzying.

"You're sure? You're sure you don't want me to go any further? Because I would really, really like to see how you feel, see how I can make you feel."

I swallowed, rasping out a desperate reply. "Mm."

Ben ran two fingers over my arse, gripping the elastic of my knickers and pulling them higher. I felt the lace press exactly where my body wanted it to, sending my eyes rolling, my knees gripping his firm torso.

His grin was filthy. "I know you don't want to have sex, but you don't have to deny yourself completely. I could just, make you feel good?"

His fingers were firm and rough as they ignited my skin, continuing to pull down the tights; contrasting against the tender feeling of his soft lips as he began peppering my legs with kisses. His attention was so focused, so intense, like he was cherishing each new part of me.

Locked in a freezer, a gross one, a meat freezer, no sausages, I chanted to myself as I felt his tongue trail up the inside of my knee.

"Ben, I want to, I—"

"Yes?"

I took a focused breath.

Thankfully, as he carefully pulled my tights over the cumbersome cast, the awkward reality of it cooled the building heat in my thighs, as good as it felt, as desperately tempting as he was.

"You can trust me." He watched as I licked my lips. "We can stop at any time, Ivy. I will stop, you just have to say the word."

His fingers were running touches across the sensitive patches behind my knees, easing my legs apart.

"I don't trust myself, though," I admitted. "I won't want you to stop."

I released the grip I apparently had on the duvet as he tossed the tights into the basket, turning back to take my hands and pulling me up into a sitting position. I took in his brown eyes as our faces drew close, his serious expression, his flushed lips, as he lifted my dress over my head easily. My hair fluttered down, tickling the skin of my back.

"Alright," he murmured, shifting back slightly, giving me space.

"You always smell so good," I breathed as I slid my hands to his waist, unable to stop my fingers from gripping his leather belt, unfastening it.

I felt him tense underneath my touch; heard him groan as he took my hands.

"That I *can't* take," he protested, stepping back to slide off his trousers.

I felt a delicious tinge of satisfaction at seeing his shape again.

Steadily, gently, he knelt on either side of my legs, laying me down from where I was sat, gazing at me reverently. I watched as he trailed fingers over the bumps of my ribs, bending forwards slowly to kiss the ugly patches of bruising.

"Does it still hurt?" he asked in a heartbreaking tone, reminding me exactly why we couldn't do this.

He looks at me in my underwear, and that's what he thinks?

Linda's words crashed into my mind: survivor, victim, sexual assault, rape. I was suddenly cold. How could he want me like that; what did I have left to give that hadn't been taken? Sam was a distraction from it all; that was how I needed it, intimacy. When my cold reality came back, I felt dirty.

"Not really."

He threaded his arm underneath me, pulling me to where the pillow was.

"I adore this green set, it suits you," he murmured, referring to my underwear.

Laying himself behind me, he pulled up the duvet so we were cocooned together in a puff of heat. He began softly stroking my hair away from my neck, exposing it to the cooler air. But my thoughts were still raging. Ben was a drug and I kept wanting more; I wanted him to touch me and kiss me and not stop... so I didn't think. So I could keep these feelings locked up. His tenderness was shattering and I had no idea how I was ever supposed to explain that to anyone in a way that made sense.

"I've wanted you in my bed since you started staying here," he whispered, before turning to switch off the light, wrapping his arms around me.

The smell of his bed and warmth of his body enveloped me.

I couldn't find the words to respond.

"You're uncharacteristically quiet, Ivy. Are you okay?" he asked after a moment, shifting our bodies so he could see my face.

"Yeah, sorry, just tired. Thank you, for tonight, Ben. For everything," I breathed, nestling into his body.

I felt him smile as he nuzzled into my hair.

"Any time."

I woke up first as the light broke through a gap in the green curtains, white shapes dancing across my eyes. We hadn't moved; Ben's arms were still laced around me, his breathing deep and gentle. Sleeping in his arms had healed more of me than I could describe; parts I had surrendered to pain so easily before.

When I reached slowly for the glass of water on his bedside table, he instinctively pulled me back to him.

"Just a little longer," he whispered, tightening his grip.

I reached for the glass all the same and sipped the cold water, placing it back down before returning happily to the warm patch of bed.

"Will you come with me today, to meet Susan and Derek properly?"

Ben pushed himself up onto an elbow, my body rolling under him as the mattress dipped.

He looked surprised, leaning over me to drink from the water glass. "You want me to come with you?"

I smiled at him, at our closeness. "If you don't mind?"

He looked at me like I was something valuable. Like, in that moment, I meant something to him. Like I meant something at all.

"I'd love to."

20

Her Barbie

Later that morning, we came together around cups of tea on the sofa in Susan and Derek's cosy home. I enjoyed the feeling of the warm mug against my skin, sat next to Ben. They asked how I was, about the police case, and then chatted with Ben about his family. He told them calmly that his parents had both passed, stifled pain spiking his tone; another piece of the man I was slowly starting to understand exposed. It was hard to hear him say the words so bluntly. Susan sweetly offered her condolences whilst Derek seemed unsure what to say. Ben immediately redirected conversation in a way he had clearly done before, talking about his work.

I thought back to when I'd first met Ben. I'd been so vague and nonchalant about Susan and Derek. I looked over to them, sat there; Susan was even leaning forward in her armchair, she was so present and engaged; Derek always had a steady, warm energy. I swallowed, feeling a new appreciation creep in, a new understanding. It was a pleasant surprise, as if my body had released an entirely new emotion. For weeks I'd been living hour by hour, but now, I was sat next to Ben, who seemed to actually like me for me, in spite of everything, with two potential parents who just emanated love.

It was a day I hadn't thought would be momentous, but it was. A feeling I savoured deeply.

The smell of a wonderful roast dinner was filling the air as Susan excused herself to tend to it.

"Would you like any help?" I offered.

Halfway out the door, she turned to beam at me. "Of course."

I grabbed my crutch and followed her through the hall and into the kitchen.

Susan sat me down at the table like last time, handing me some napkins and cutlery, knowing I wasn't able to be particularly helpful, just pleased I was there.

"I don't remember Ben being so charming, I see why you're so taken with each other," she said, beginning to carve a perfectly steaming, herb-covered joint.

"You think he's taken with me?" I asked, suddenly desperate for her opinion.

She looked at me knowingly. "Very much so, my love."

I smiled back, feeling it. "Why... why did you keep looking, all those years?"

My life was starting to feel like an empty book that I needed to fill, like I was two thirds of the way through and needed to go back and read the first part again.

She walked over to me, placing bowls of colourful, delicious smelling food in the middle of the table. "I always knew, Ivy. I always knew you were out there. I can't explain it, and it certainly caused lots of arguments between me and your father. A mother knows. If you'd made it to the door that day, I wouldn't have needed the DNA test."

I blinked a sharpness from my eyes. "Really?"

How could she have been here, day after day, hoping for her little girl, when all I had done was survive, not questioning, not thinking about her? How could I have forgotten? How could I not have found my way home sooner?

She placed her small hand on my shoulder and tenderly curled her fingers. "We have lost a lot of years, but you sitting here, in this kitchen, chatting with me, is something I've dreamed of."

We continued the conversation as the men came to join us at the table, still deep in their own discussion. I allowed myself a second to admire them: Ben standing tall, yet perfectly engaging Derek with soft interest; Derek in his green knit jumper, taking pride in everything he was telling Ben.

Susan sat next to Derek, opposite me and Ben, before passing around serving spoons.

"Did you ever get close to finding me? I keep racking my brain, but

I don't ever remember anyone saying or suspecting anything," I asked carefully, trying to hide my guilt.

Susan looked up from the bowl of honeyed parsnips. "No, I don't think so. Especially now, knowing where you were. We thought you were in France at one point; we flew over there and put out posters." She flinched as Derek took the bowl from her. "They just swooped in and stole you away. Gone. It was like you'd vanished, there was so little to go off. Over the years so many people came forwards with information, but it was all simply cause for heartbreak. We had a few girls contact us, the police were even hopeful about of one or two."

"You thought other girls were her, me?" I choked on the words, picturing the desperate scene.

"Well, there were a few reasons to believe for each one. Sadly, as it was all so public, some people wanted to take advantage." Susan encouraged us to start eating as she spoke.

My hand shook as I bought a forkful of glistening lamb and thick gravy to my mouth.

"That's awful," Ben interjected.

I saw Susan place a hand on Derek's as his expression grew tense.

She took a deep breath before continuing. "It was, but who would have thought, after all that, you would near enough just knock on the door."

"How did you get out, in the end?" Derek asked.

He'd barely asked me any direct questions since we met in the station, usually comfortable taking a listening role and supporting his wife. I wondered what sort of answer he was looking for. Did he want to know how I got out physically, or was he asking what changed, why I had suddenly decided to leave? The latter was a question I still asked of myself.

I took a sip of water. "I took their car and ran. It was poorly planned; I just packed a bag in a rush and drove for the gate, like a crazy person." I paused to read his face. He wanted more. "I should have thought it through, planned a better route, but I think I knew that if I gave it too much thought, I wouldn't be brave enough. I never truly thought I was Maeve; I think I just needed a powerful enough reason to leave. The car got me an hour or so away and then broke down. I think you know the rest."

There was an awkward clattering of cutlery in the absence of a reply from anyone, so I instinctively continued.

"I wish I'd tried harder. I wish I'd questioned them earlier. I'm so very sorry."

Derek seemed frozen, but Susan jerked up to sit straighter, pointing a finger at me. "You do not apologise. You do not."

Ben looked at me with a half-smile. "I've told her the same."

"You're not responsible for any of it," Derek added, before looking to Susan with wide eyes. "I'm sorry. I'm sorry for the times I told you to stop." He looked back at me with new fragility.

His radiating shame drenched me with a heavy sadness, sending a lump to my throat.

"I understand," I whispered, coughing subtly to clear my throat. "The effort you two went to was more than anyone could ever hope for. I'm sor—" I stopped myself. "It's hard for me to take it in. I didn't see it, but every day, people message me, telling me how amazing you both were. That you never stopped. I googled the name; if it hadn't all been there, if your address hadn't been so easy to find, I wouldn't have come."

Susan looked to Derek with pure love in her eyes. "You tried, dear. You always tried your best. I couldn't have carried on without you." Susan wiped her eyes. "Well, Ben, I promise we aren't usually this intense."

He paused to finish his mouthful. "Don't worry about me." He looked at me and smiled reassuringly. "I imagine you all have a lot to ask each other still."

I noticed Susan's eyes drop down, a small tell of hers that I'd already picked up on.

"Susan?" I asked, sensing something left unsaid. "Was there something you wanted to know?"

She looked at me, scared, her eyes round and her lips unsteady.

"Your mum, was she—?" Susan paused, struggling for words.

My mind raced to finish them for her: what cruel detail would I need to explain? Had she heard something from the police? It was so hard to talk about the horrible things that poisonous woman had done. I'd had to survive in the moment, make it through by focusing on the next hour. I'd had to belittle the abuse in my own mind to comfort myself. When the details were aired in the cold light of day, it often felt like a whole new trauma. A whole new wound to heal.

"... was she the reason you stayed for so long?"

Susan's words struck me like daggers. Ben sensed my body flinch and he subtly placed a hand on my knee under the table. I opened my mouth, but nothing came out. My eyes darted around the room as my breath quickened. Was that what she'd been worried about? So worried that she hadn't even asked?

The horror of realisation flooded inside of me like a river bursting its banks, seeping into every inch. Ruby should have been the number one reason I left. I felt my eyes glaze over as the words started falling out, beyond my control.

"I don't remember whether she loved me at first, or how hard she tried, but she was never a mother. I couldn't fit in, and she realised it before the others. Instead of helping me, or protecting me, she was deeply and adamantly ashamed, like she had to make a show of it. I may not know what it's like to have a family, but I know that wasn't it. I know that sounds absurd. I know no one understands why I stayed for so long. I know it makes me the most stupid and pathetic person, and I hate myself for that, but I never felt like there was anything more for me. I never knew there was anyone who would care. It was all I knew." I took a deep breath as my words hung vividly in the air.

Keeping my gaze down at the plates in the middle of the table, I picked up the napkin I'd folded earlier, using it to catch a tear that fell from my eye.

Susan extended her hand across the table. I looked up at her to see she was also clutching a napkin and, holding each other's hands, we both let the tears fall.

Susan drew a deep breath, steadying her words. "I hate to see you talk about things with such pain. I'm sorry I asked."

"Don't be," I replied, shaking my head, trying to get Ruby's wrinkled, overly made-up face out of it. "I'm sorry that you ever thought that. I didn't realise."

Ben squeezed my knee again. "You lot and that 's' word."

We all laughed lightly together, grateful for the tone shift.

Once we'd finished eating, Ben stood to help collect up the plates. "That was an amazing dinner, thank you both," he said, as he headed for the dishwasher.

I'd tried to carry some crockery from the table, but had been outnumbered and told to rest.

Susan took a dish from him. "You're welcome. It was a pleasure. You can come with Ivy to see us any time."

It felt surreal seeing them interacting together; I realised how quickly I'd started to deeply care for these previously unknown strangers.

Maybe it was having Ben there; maybe it was because I already felt exposed and raw, but for the first time, a drop of curiosity had appeared in the puddle of fear in my mind.

"Susan," I stuttered. "If... if you still want to show me the rest of the house... I think I feel ready now."

Derek was the first to react, shooting me a steady look. "Are you sure?"

I nodded.

Susan led the way for the four of us as I navigated the stairs, Ben just behind me. As soon as my head bobbed above the landing, I could see the little pink name plaque labelled 'Maeve' on the door. It glittered, with fairies dotted around the golden letters. As I climbed the last step, my body paused involuntarily, freezing in place. Susan strode to the door, pushing it open without hesitation, eager in her excitement to show me the contents of the meaningful room. Ben softly leant into my back, taking some of my weight. He felt warm and familiar as he ran his hand up my arm, gently encouraging me. Derek noticed and looked back to us with fresh concern, giving me the strength to step forwards again, not wanting to disappoint Susan.

I could do this. I needed to do this. It had been a looming pressure playing on my mind throughout my visits – this way it would be over with.

They all watched me make my way through the door, nobody knowing what to expect. As I started to take in the pink walls and slatted wardrobe, something sank within me. It was like I'd never been here. It was a bizarre time capsule, preserved perfectly, with barely a fleck of dust. I ran my fingers over the cartoon dog wallpaper border, walking over to the single bed. The sheets felt soft as I sat down; it was well worn in, but not tired. It felt cold.

"You loved the pink, and the fairies," Susan explained readily as she walked to the small wardrobe, pulling it open. There were no clothes on the rail, but the small wooden shelf was covered with plastic horses, Barbies, and boxes of other toys. A tragic museum. "You would ask us to carry a different set down every weekend. For years I found Barbie shoes and Polly Pocket animals in nooks and crannies around the house. It was one of those things that I was sad about, when I realised at one point, I'd found the last one."

I looked at the cluster of teddies at the end of the bed, displayed neatly in the corner against the wall. A golden Hamley's bear, a Labrador, a small hedgehog, and a pony. I picked up the horse, stroking its soft mane.

"Did I always like horses?"

"You adored all animals, but you were very excited when Peter, your uncle, got married to Mary, who has the horse," Susan answered.

I noticed Derek at the door, quietly watching.

"I told her to pack it up years ago. I'm glad she wears the trousers," he joked awkwardly, tucking his hands into his baggy jeans.

I felt a clatter of plastic against the back of my ankle. Bending down I pulled out a brand-new Barbie in a big pink box. She had a blue, shimmering dress like Cinderella, and a collection of small animal friends. I held the box up as the lid lifted gently. She was a pretty doll, with her pink lipstick and tiny, glittery heels. My eyes narrowed as I carefully slid her out. The hairs on my arms prickled.

"You bought me this the day I was taken. I remember." I spoke slowly, as if I was talking to myself. She was still tied to her cardboard backing, the smell of the new toy filling the air. "I was sad because you said I could play with her when I got home, but I couldn't, because I wasn't there."

My fingertips stroked her silky blonde hair, neatly fastened into a spiralling bun. The memory had trickled in, but now I'd sensed it, it was like it had always been there, waiting to be seen. Susan clung onto Derek's hand. I wasn't sure what this moment meant, but I knew it was something. I smiled at them sadly, before feeling drawn back to the doll.

"I was sleepy," I started again, feeling like I'd walked through a secret door in my own mind. "For days, I was sleepy, and confused, they must have given me something." I looked around the room, searching for another memory, another connection. I noticed a small jar of sand on the drawers. Still clutching the Barbie in her cardboard, I moved to touch the little glass container. "The beach, there was a little house by the beach?" I asked, studying the different coloured granules.

Derek's voice offered a calm explanation. "My sister has a house in Devon. We all used to go down as a family. You adored the beach."

"Seahorses? Were there seahorses?" I asked, looking at him. The image felt both alien and immediately familiar.

"It's called Seahorse Cottage," Susan said, her voice wobbling.

I walked back to the bed and carefully slid the Barbie back into her box, like she was a breakable key, precious and dangerous.

"We're meeting them there for Daniel's birthday on Thursday; they wanted me to ask you to come with us, but I felt like it was too much to ask."

Derek gave his wife a warning look.

"Thursday?" I repeated, playing it over in my mind, seeing blue seahorses, hearing the sounds of the sea, recalling the smell of fresh, salty air. I could feel it. "I think... I think I'd like to meet them. I think

I should." I looked to Ben for reassurance.

He shrugged and smiled softly; it had to be my choice.

Derek stepped forwards. "There's no pressure to come. Most of the family are going, and although everyone wants to meet you, we understand it'll be a lot to deal with."

I looked to Susan, who looked like she was barely containing herself.

I nodded. "I'm not sure how it'll feel, but I think it's time to see them. It's the right thing to do now."

21

Enduring skeletons

I stewed in the bath, letting the bubbles crackle against my skin.

Maeve, I repeated in my head. *Maeve White.*

I forced the images of the day through my mind, searching for familiarity, looking for sparks or traps doors in my memory. I tipped my head back, watching the dancing steam, and came up blank. Part of being able to picture that memory had felt like bracing for an avalanche. Perhaps most infuriating of all was that I was scared of it. I hated Elle, I resented her life, but part of me wasn't ready to let her go and I couldn't figure out why.

The towel was fluffy and consuming as I rung out my hair, watching the bathwater gurgle away. Raised voices from the other side of the door caught my attention. I felt puddles gather beneath my feet as I crept over, trying to hear. My heart rate quickened. Ben was there, so I was fine, whoever it was. I nudged the door ajar to let in the conversation.

"Why have you started turning me away, what did I do Ben? I thought this was what you wanted!" a woman's voice screeched.

Ben bit back, hushed and angry, "Jessica, you're drunk. Look, you need to go, I told you not to come here."

"So calling off our engagement wasn't appropriate, but still fucking me all the time is? *That* is fucking appropriate?"

I heard her feet clatter across the floor, halting as she spotted my eyes. Redness rose to her cheeks as her body stiffened: not a blush – fury.

"Are you kidding?" she yelled, lurching towards me, pushing the bathroom door open.

I gripped tightly around the towel, feeing unbearably naked underneath.

Ben stepped over with his hand out. "I'm sorry, Ivy, she's drunk, just give us a minute."

It was the first time I'd recognised panic on his face.

"Why is she still here, Ben? I heard she was in the office, the office? What on earth was I thinking with you?"

"You're making a fool of yourself, let's go, now!" Ben asserted, attempting to herd her back out the door, firmly steadying her as she slurred more words.

She looked directly at me, her pretty face dishevelled. "Has he shown you how much of a freak he is? Has he told you what he likes? How he likes to fuck?"

I felt Ben lose it, as if he were a stick that audibly snapped. Taking her hand, he led her swiftly out of the door, not even looking at me as I stood there, in my towel, drips of water falling to the floor. My toes curled into the cold tiles.

"Get off me!" she screeched, thrashing her arms.

It was an ugly, jarring scene.

"You're leaving now, I'm getting you a taxi," he spat, bundling her out of the door and pulling it shut loudly behind him.

I stood there for a minute, recalling the words, each time hoping they would make more sense, each time feeling different emotions. When had he last slept with her? I felt sick all of a sudden, betrayed by myself.

I pulled on my pyjamas, then my cardigan, feeling exposed, when I heard Ben thump the outside of the front door and shout something before coming back in. I sat on the bed, contemplating what was appropriate to do next, tugging a brush through my wet hair. I wondered if I should get dressed. Did he want me to leave? Should I leave? Did I *want* to leave?

After ten minutes or so of feeling weird, I headed back to the living room to get a glass of water. Ben was standing at the breakfast bar when I emerged, his hands resting around a crystal glass of whisky. He looked up at me as I took a few steps towards the kitchen, quickly looking straight back down as I tentatively got a drink.

"Are you okay?" I asked carefully, hoping he would offer me an immediate explanation that would appease the deep ache in my chest.

He kept looking down, his head in his hands. "No."

My jaw tightened. I nodded, mostly to myself, and took the few steps back to the bedroom. I paused just before the door and looked at him.

He stared into his glass.

I ground my teeth together. I had nothing. There was nothing I could think to say, exhaustion weighing heavy, Jessica's voice ringing in my ears.

"I'm tired," I managed.

He said nothing in response, so I reluctantly shifted my weight to head into the bedroom.

"So that's it?" he called after me coldly.

I turned back around, forcing myself to release my tightening grip on the glass. "What do you mean?"

He swigged the golden liquid; it spiralled around the glass, catching the light. The sugary scent wafted over to me, invading my senses.

That smell. That familiar smell.

My stomach churned as my body took an instinctive step backwards, my muscles tensing reactively as jarring pictures flooded my mind.

I always avoided drinking with people on the site – it never ended well. When I'd hear the chink of bottles, it was my cue to stay busy, and stay away. Once, Gareth had gripped my head, forcing me to drink half a bottle at fourteen. When I was violently sick, they all gathered around and laughed. Another time, I'd been hiding away with Ebony in the stables, thinking they'd all just fallen into bed. When I got to my caravan door, with one step on the small metal stair, Marcus threw an empty bottle at my feet, firing glass shards into the mud. I don't know what I was thinking that day, but I marched over to him, shouting, and thumped two hands into his chest. He'd thrown me into my caravan so hard I thought I'd broken my arm. His sickly laugh still echoed through my ears.

"That's it? No questions? Nothing else to say?" Ben continued, tension building, realising I'd zoned out.

We stood facing each other a few steps apart. He must have got up. I needed a response, but I had nothing.

"*Ivy?*" he exclaimed, louder, taking another step towards me.

He wasn't angry. He was hurt.

He wasn't angry.

I took another step back, then another, avoiding eye contact. His face twisted with confusion as I edged away from him. That smell. My body flinched as Ben grew agitated. Another time at Henworth, when they were all drinking outside, I made the mistake of going back to the stable for my hoodie. Marcus thought it was funny to grab my keys and lock me out. When I wrestled him to get them back, he laughed more, pouring whisky into my hair. I had to stay out all night with that smell all over me. I'd ended up with pneumonia.

"Sorry, Ivy, look, it's complicated. Let me explain."

I felt my breathing still, amplifying the fresh pounding of my heart. I took another step back, nearly in the doorway.

No, no, no.

"Ivy!" he shouted. "For fuck's sake, talk to me!"

His height was suddenly imposing. I remembered the shivering, suddenly freezing. How my hair had stank of soured alcohol days after, like their breath... like the police officer's breath.

"I don't know what you want me to say," I said quietly, needing to escape. The more they smelt like whisky, the worse it always got. When they would get in my face to shout or worse, I would taste it in the air.

"Something!" Ben shouted and I flinched.

There was desperation in his tone, but the smell of the caravan site was stronger.

"I'm tired."

Get out, get out, get out.

He waved his arm through the air and I dipped down instinctively, even though he had turned around. "Fine," he said, exasperated, reaching for the glass once more.

Silently, I retreated into the guest bedroom, backing away one careful step at a time. Glass smashed behind me. I turned just in time to see the golden liquid forging a winding pathway along the floorboards.

I shut the door and my body crumpled as nausea rose. I stumbled to the carpet, leaning against the bed, my head in my hands, and shook.

It's Ben. Ben would never hurt me. I'm safe. It's just whisky.

Despite all the conviction I'd forced into the words, my body had slid too far down the path of panic. Why did he have to smash the glass?

My grip on myself was lost. I hugged my knees, digging in my nails, willing the pain to slow my breathing. Instead, the breaths became short gasps as my own ribcage fought against them. The tighter I gripped, the more my body tried to quiver and shake. I tried to remember the feel of the Barbie's hair, the sand in the jar. I tried to focus, but adrenaline was a potent drug raging through my body. I stayed on the floor, unable to move.

My hips ached and I realised my skin had gone cold. I clambered up, wanting to brush my teeth and climb into bed, exhausted, but it was quiet. Too quiet. I wasn't sure how long I'd sat there, but it must have been at least an hour because the carpet pile had pressed a pattern into my pyjamas.

I silently nudged the door open enough to see Ben asleep on the sofa, still in his clothes. I sighed, guilt flooding my otherwise empty shell. He'd propped his feet up, sitting back against the arm, looking peaceful, but out of place. The apartment was tidy, with no sign of glass. He'd been hurting and I'd given him nothing. I'd tumbled into myself and hadn't been able to see an out. This was what I did to people around me: corrupted them with my pain, no matter how hard I tried not to.

Using the wall, I made my way over to him, placing one hand on the arm of the sofa and the other on his round shoulder. He stirred gently.

"You fell asleep," I whispered as my hand lingered.

He rubbed his eyes under his crooked glasses before they opened, staring at me, his anger gone.

"Ivy." He rubbed his eyes again. "God, I'm so sorry. I shouldn't have shouted at you. I'm sorry, I was mad, not at you. I—"

"It's fine. I'm sorry I freaked out."

He took my hand and held it gently; he felt cooler than usual. I forced a smile for him before turning and heading to the bathroom.

"It won't happen again. I'll talk to her when she's sobered up and make myself clearer," Ben assured me as he stood up, stretching out. "She had no reason to come here. Are you okay? What she said—"

"It was the whisky that freaked me out, Ben," I explained, gripping the door, ready to shut it, needing this to be done.

I didn't want to leave him feeling guilty about Jessica. Of course, it had been bloody horrible; the thought of them alone was jarring, the thought of him sleeping with her after having broken off the engagement plain wrong, but Ben had been there for me, he hadn't judged me, he rarely asked questions. I owed him that respect, as a friend. As potentially more than a friend.

He looked at me with renewed sadness, his eyes connecting with mine even through the darkness. "The whisky?"

My body longed to walk over to him and let him hold me, to curl up in bed like the night before and let his tender touches brush away the last shreds of panic, but there was too much between us that evening. We both knew it.

I nodded, and made my exit.

22

Office politics

The next morning, I listened as Ben moved around the apartment, staying quiet, hiding in plain sight. I was awake before his alarm had started ringing and it still made me jump. Everything made me jump: the kettle clicking off, the letter box clanging, even cars moving outside. I shut my eyes, running my fingers over the duvet, imagining it was Ebony's mane, sounding her heavy heartbeat in my mind.

The animals had kept me sane. I'd found a kitten once in a hedgerow, mangy and skinny, but it had mewed so desperately that I'd loved it instantly – it had so much spirit. I'd wondered how that kitten had such a thirst for life when everything it knew had been so cold and damp. It was like the very ground of Henworth was toxic, infecting all of those treading the muddied grass. Flashes of humanity were not only fleeting, but seen as weakness. The very next week, I'd had to cover my bruises with concealer, after Marcus had held me back while his thugs set their dogs on the poor little cat.

I pushed the thought away again, unable to bear thinking about what might have become of the horses, praying Ebony held enough value to survive. I'd considered going back; breaking in and riding off with her into the night, but I knew that would only guarantee her pain.

The shower clicked on and off. I heard the tell-tale sign of keys and a bag. Was Ben really just going to leave without saying anything?

I braced myself, sitting up in bed just as the door nudged open. I felt a complicated wave of relief.

"Oh." Ben lifted the strap of his leather bag higher on his shoulder. "I thought you were still asleep."

I shook my head softly, clamping my teeth on my lower lip. "Ben, I—"

"It's my fault. Jessica. Before, things got complicated, but it's over, it has been for a while. That's what I wanted to say last night." He stood still in the doorway, running his thumb over his car key.

"You don't have to explain yourself, it's okay, I get it." I didn't, but saying it was an impulse I had to appease people; the words shot out before I could stop them.

"You get what?"

I shifted my heavy leg to sit up taller. "I know you're private, you don't have to explain. It's complicated, I get it. You have been so kind helping me," I floundered, digging a hole as he flinched with irritation.

He went to say something but stopped himself, letting out a breath before trying again with a sort of forced control. "Well, like I said. It's over, with Jessica. I'll talk to her again. She won't come back."

I nodded.

"Is Derek still coming to pick you up? Do you need a lift back?"

"No, thank you. They seem happy to help and it saves you the job, you know, with work and stuff."

"Are you alright?" He dared a step in further, his eyes rounding.

"Yeah, yeah. Don't be late for work on my account."

Ben hesitated, unsure whether to take another step. "I hope it goes okay at the station. Don't take any crap."

"Thanks."

He faltered, looking like he might speak again, before turning and walking away.

The day passed in a haze of tiredness. The police had a fresh round of questions, grilling me for every detail, bringing up yet more painful memories. Even Susan grated on me that afternoon – she was painfully excited about planning the trip, but everything felt like too much. Derek took me aside and asked if I was alright, which I appreciated, but couldn't answer.

It was silly, but I was nervous all over again waiting for Ben to come home that evening. I'd made a simple dinner and had already eaten mine by the time he texted to say he'd be late.

Catherine had offered to take me shopping the day after for a few office clothes, so that I had something more appropriate to wear whilst I worked on the VAT project. I'd mentioned to her about feeling silly compared to the other glossy women. She'd laughed, of course, but when Ben suggested we go, she'd said she would take any chance to shop during work hours. I hoped it would make me feel more confident going back in; the truth was I was regretting my brazen offer of help all together. I didn't know what I was doing. Not day-to-day, let alone anything more, anything so important.

Jessica's visit had confirmed my suspicions; I'd gone where I didn't belong.

I was looking at the telly when Ben came home, not even aware of what was playing. I turned to return his greeting, only to see him cradling a large bunch of delicately wrapped, dusty pink flowers. The fresh, invigorating smell of eucalyptus instantly filled the apartment.

I looked at him, confused; unsure what to say.

He rested the bouquet down on the worktop with a rustle. "Pink was an obvious choice. I hope you like them."

"For me?"

His keys chinked as they dropped into the bowl. "Of course."

My eyes darted around as my mind rejected the gesture. No one had ever bought me flowers before. One of the clients bought me a plant once, but it had died in the darkness of the caravan.

Ben headed into his bedroom as I wondered what to do next. I hobbled over to the counter, rubbing two fingers over a delicate petal.

ME

Thanks again for earlier. Ben bought me some flowers, they look like they're in water already, in the plastic. What do I do with them? How do I look after them? I feel silly asking, sorry xx

SUSAN

Don't thank me, we enjoyed seeing you, as always.

If they're from a supermarket, you chop a bit off the bottom of the stems and put them in a vase. There will be a packet of plant food to sprinkle in. If they are from a florist, you can just put them straight in a vase, but still add the little sachet. Does that help? xx

ME

Yes, perfect, thanks xx

I lifted the bouquet, indulging in the sweet smell, and spotted a little plastic packet underneath the thick white ribbon. I turned to open the cupboard doors, seeing what looked like a vase next to the wine cooler on the top shelf. I reached up towards it, balancing on the tip of my cast and grunting.

Hearing Ben's footsteps, I remained focused on the vase.

My shirt lifted and I gasped quietly, the worktop cold against my stomach. Ben looped his arm around me, grazing warm fingers over the exposed skin and extending his other hand easily to the shelf, lowering the vase to the worktop; pulling my body back into his.

"Your cupboards torment me," I muttered, before turning in his arms.

He huffed a laugh, not stepping back. "Need me to get you a stool? Sophie has one shaped like a giraffe."

He raised an eyebrow, smirking, so I pushed away and reached for the flowers.

"They're really beautiful, thank you."

Ben folded his arms, watching me, making me paranoid about doing it wrong.

"You're welcome."

"No one's ever bought me flowers before."

He reached for a glass to make a drink. "No one's ever made sure I got to bed before. Sleeping on the sofa gives me a crick in my neck."

I started untying the ribbon from the bouquet, tipping the old water down the sink.

We were soon chatting like normal as we moved around each other,

214

but it was different. Something was different.

When the night blanketed the sky, I headed back to the guest room again. Alone.

"Thank you, I really enjoyed that," I said to Catherine as she checked her lipstick in a small compact after our shopping trip.

The lift pinged when it reached Ben's offices. I certainly felt better about my meeting with Charlie now that I was wearing a pencil dress, although the blush lip was probably too much. Suddenly, I didn't want the doors to open, knowing there would be a sea of eyes.

No, I told myself. *You can do this.*

I was stuck between the guilt of living off Ben's generosity and the uncomfortable, imposter vibe the office gave me. I'd abandoned my CV, which, to be honest, had been a non-starter when my qualifications were one line and all my experience was, well, shady. When I got to the 'about me' section, I'd realised I had no idea what to put. So, helping Ben was the right thing to do; it made him happy, it was the least I could do. I smoothed my grey dress and brushed down the scalloped collar.

Catherine winked at me. "No problem."

Ben jolted out of his chair as she opened the door to his office, looking confused; looking for me, maybe? I was a few clumsy steps behind Catherine. I walked past her and into his office, closing the door behind me. Seeing him in his swanky office made him seem physically bigger. The businessman, both firm and fiercely intelligent, yet deceptively broken and subtly sweet. I was coming to understand Ben, the parts of him he was showing me, anyway. I knew I wanted more, needed more, and not just the parts of him that were easy to admire, but the shadows too. I resented the changing tide between us. I had no idea how to slow it down, or even if I should.

"Did you have a nice time?" he asked, looking at me, starting to get up before hesitating and returning to his big grey chair.

The glass walls were imposing.

"I did, thanks. Catherine is really great. How are you?" I asked, smiling.

His hand lay open on his desk, so I walked over and took it, propping my crutch against the wall and leaning on the wooden desk, facing him.

God, he was sexy.

"It suits you, the smart look." He licked his lips subtly, "Maybe we should fire Catherine and you could become my assistant."

I hit him playfully on the arm. "Catherine is one of a kind. Besides, I'd rather be your competition."

It felt unnatural to air the previously forbidden dream I'd dared to indulge; to think I could have my own career one day when things settled down. Forge my own path.

He sat up straight, bringing the tip of his thumb between his lips. "That's big talk." He looked at me over his glasses, half a smile breaking.

"Well, I'm starting to get the impression you may have too many people falling at your feet. I wouldn't want your head to get any bigger." I circled my finger on the desk, pausing to hold his stare defiantly. Flirting always felt like steady ground between us and I was craving something straightforward.

He rolled his chair towards me so our knees touched. "I seem to remember the first day we met you did exactly that on the verge."

I couldn't help but laugh, tilting my head back. "I told you that was an accident. I could've got back up on my own."

"If you want to be my competitor." He paused, and I felt his finger on the inside of my knee, slowly sliding up. "You're going to have to try harder than that." He gripped my thigh, making me sway towards him, the feeling of his fingers around my warm leg willing it to buckle. "Because I think I know exactly what I need to do to get you back at my feet."

"I wouldn't be so sure," I whispered, resisting the urge to fall on top of him.

His fingers gently squeezed my thigh tighter, ever so slightly pulling me closer.

"But equally…" I paused to let out a heavy breath as his hand dared to move further up my leg, the heat from it reaching the material of my new underwear. "… I don't think I'd mind."

The power started to shift as he adjusted his hips against the chair with a fresh flush of colour on his face. We made intoxicating eye contact before he swiftly pulled away from me, shaking his head.

I grinned at him, pushing my bum onto the desk to sit down. "You know what, you're right. When you've kissed me, or undone my bra, taken off my tights… you've been teasing me, calling the shots. I think you just gave away your tell. That's how you like it, isn't it?" I looked at him wickedly, dancing my fingers down my skirt, leaning towards him.

He looked up at me, entirely unimpressed. "Very clever."

I dropped my voice to a whisper to cement my victory. "I think, Ben, you would really like to tell me exactly what to do, and have me listen to each and every detail. I think you would ask me to take off my own clothes first while you watch." I saw his pupils dilate as he drank in my words. "Would you want me to take off my own underwear, or rather get a feel for that yourself? I guess we'll find out…"

"Ivy, you should stop," he breathed.

"Oh, you would want to do it, of course. Listening to me say your name as you lay me out in front of you."

I gasped as he stood up, thumping two hands onto the desk on either side of my legs with such force I nearly tipped off the back.

"Stop, before I send an email and tell everyone to take the afternoon off," he uttered, staring straight at me, daring me to continue.

I felt different eyes on us from beyond the glass. I didn't look around, I held his gaze until I shuffled off the desk, grazing my body against him as he begrudgingly moved.

"No, thanks. I'm meeting with Charlie, remember?"

He grunted through his teeth at me.

I winked. "Never underestimate the competition. I would like to point out that *I* didn't need to squeeze your thigh." My hobble out of the room was ungraceful but triumphant as I tried to hide my grin. Powerful wasn't an emotion I was familiar with, but I liked how it felt in my body. It felt decadent.

The meeting with Charlie was interesting. I walked into a room of three equally smart men sat around a shiny table with a projector gently humming. I was unsure at first, but as soon as the numbers were on the screen, I became fully invested, diving through them as we bounced ideas off one another. After forty-five minutes, we were laughing together, drawing up a proposal. I liked Charlie most, he was funny.

"That is a sexy number, Ivy," Charlie had joked.

"It is, isn't it!" I laughed.

Ben appeared behind us.

"How's it going?" he asked, sitting at the head of the table.

My mind instantly went to the image of him sending everyone home and utilising his desk.

"She's a bloody genius, this will bag those extra entities, for sure," Charlie said, proceeding to take Ben through the slides we had put together.

"Get it out, then," Ben declared, a bustle of discussion and details following.

"Will you do the same for Caroline's accounts? I know she'd appreciate it," Charlie asked me hopefully.

I'd surprised myself by enjoying the meeting, but if anything, the day had made me finally feel like I could do something, and I was coming to the clear realisation that it would have to be independently. For myself. The office was Ben's, and a lot of the women were Jessica's friends. I knew if we stood a chance at having any sort of relationship, it had to be with me on my own two feet, metaphorically and literally.

I'd guided Charlie and the others onto the right path, but corporate I was not; I'd had to ask them to explain half a dozen terms.

I opened my mouth to politely decline, but Ben beat me to it.

"Of course," he replied, answering for me.

I bit my tongue, seeing the expectant look on everyone's faces.

"Sure," I relented, feeling uneasy.

Ben walked me back to his office where Catherine was waiting with an urgent call before I could make my objections. He needed to stay a bit longer, so I took a seat on the sofa, picking up my phone and forcing a smile to reply to Susan.

ME

My day is good thanks. I've been helping Ben in the office again today. How are you both? xx

SUSAN

We're good, busy making plans for Thursday. Is 2 p.m. okay for us to pick you up? Everyone's thrilled you're coming! x

ME

Yeah, that's fine, thanks. I'm looking forward to meeting them xx

ME

Hi wino, how's your day? Agreed to that date yet?

LUCY

Ha. No. Slept with my brother yet?

I snorted, prompting Ben to glance at me from his call.

ME

And there was me trying to spare you the saucy details... but no. Touché. You should still go out with that guy that messaged you. His comment on my post was so sweet! You know I'd watch the kids.

LUCY

Yeah, yeah. What are you up to anyway? Not still kissing up to him at the office, I hope. You two are very irritating.

ME

I'm here for the spreadsheets.

LUCY

I don't know what's more gross, thinking about my moody brother making love or you getting excited about figures.

ME

You made that even weirder by saying making love. How's work?

LUCY

Busy. Some sweet old man offered to buy me dinner after I took out his catheter. So I can't commit to a date until I've weighed up my options.

Catherine walked in the door as Ben tapped away. "I can drop Ivy home, Ben? I imagine you'll want to get that done?" she suggested, looking at me to include me in the decision.

"That might not be a terrible idea." Ben turned to me "Would you mind?"

"No, not at all," I replied, stifling a pang of rejection. *It's just work. He's busy.*

"Great. I could do with hitting the gym after."

I bit my lip, hoping he just wanted to sweat out some of the tension from earlier.

Ben was gone for so long though, that when he did get home that evening, I'd already fallen asleep.

I slept awfully. There was a lot to worry about. Was it just pity with Ben? Would we have seen each other again if I'd gone to live in my own flat, as Linda had suggested? Suddenly, I wasn't so sure. I would've wanted to see him, but would he have become bored? I was so deep in thought I didn't notice him buttering toast behind me as I made a tea.

"Everything okay?" he asked casually, taking a bite.

I nodded.

He gave me a sideways glance. "You have an appointment with the police this afternoon, don't you? I was hoping Derek might be able to take you. The date for that tender is today."

I stuttered a little. "Y-yes, that's fine."

"I mean, if it's not, call me. I just figured—"

"It's fine, honestly."

"Okay."

When he left, I found myself staring out of the window, disturbed by the growl of my stomach. My phone had been buzzing all morning, so I used it as a welcome distraction.

IvyMWhite This is Maeve's bedroom. Seeing it didn't give me the rush of memories I'd hoped for, but it was a start. The memories are hidden behind locked doors in my mind, I think maybe I've always known they were there, but not had the key. I vaguely remembered a holiday home; it was like I could smell it, taste it, and hear it, even though it's like I've never been. I also remembered a Barbie I had been given the day it happened. I couldn't remember Susan buying her as such, but her hair felt familiar – she didn't feel new. I remembered a sense of longing and excitement to play with her. I'm beginning to think Maeve is a part of me that's lost; whenever I try to find her, she seems to move further out of reach. What I have found, though, is kindness, acceptance and warmth from Susan and Derek. I'm looking forward to meeting my extended family this weekend. Well, meeting them as Ivy. Thank you all for still following along.

I still had a growing collection of emails from celebrities and shows requesting interviews.

I ignored them, still clueless as to what I would say.

23

Empty threats?

Cold and punishing, the whole police station was a prison cell. Derek waited for me the entire time, which actually turned out for the best. It was a heavy meeting.

Ruby and Frank had been arrested and bailed, insisting they had no idea I'd been kidnapped, miraculously having alibis, of course. Ridiculously, due to the lack of evidence, it was likely the Crown Prosecution Service would drop the case. DS Dores and Barnes were under investigation, which was a small mercy as they were on suspension. Off the record, DS Ernest told me they'd only been able to pursue the case for so long due to the media attention. Marcus and a few of his cronies had warrants put out against them, but had avoided arrest – easily, by the sounds of it. They'd conducted some searches, finding corroborative evidence for some of the laundering, which they were following up.

If the police shut one business down, they'll build two more.

I felt frustrated by it all. It was the police who'd pushed and pushed me, frequently telling me there was hope. I should have trusted my gut all along. They seemed sure they would catch Marcus. I'd believe it when I saw it. I had a sinking feeling I would be seeing him first.

"This is unacceptable, you've just put even more of a target on her back!" Derek shouted when he heard the news.

It was the first time I'd heard him raise his voice.

"We're very sorry, Mr White. We understand your frustrations. We're trying our best and will continue to build a case where we can. We should be able to get prosecutions on Frank and Marcus," DS Ernest explained.

Derek looked to me, then frantically back at the other officer present. "And what if we bring forward a private prosecution?"

DS Ernest sighed. "That's always an option, and entirely your choice, but you will likely be working from the same evidence base, considering the case is historic."

"Derek, it's okay, let's go. I have a terrible headache," I pleaded, needing an out.

Driving back to the house for some dinner, he questioned me more. "I just can't fathom it. All these years we looked for you. It makes you want to leave the bloody country all together."

I stayed quiet, not sure what to say. My head throbbed and I felt particularly vulnerable and uneasy. He took a breath and continued with increasing frustration as his fingers gripped the steering wheel harder. His anger was carefully stifled, but somehow that simmering undertone made it take up more space.

"I'm not a violent man, Ivy, but it makes me understand why people take justice into their own hands. When the police can't even control their own."

"Derek, please don't say that," I interjected with a lump in my throat, my eyes pleading with him to change tack. The thought of him in harm's way was too painful to process.

"Sorry, love." He let out another sigh. "Maybe you should come back and live with us for a bit. Until it blows over. Now that we're retired, we're home all the time. Your mother would fuss over you non-stop." He paused. "It sounds like this is going to go on for months, maybe longer."

I nodded slowly, looking down at my stupid cast. "I can't stay with Ben forever. He's been more than kind."

"I know you two have feelings for each other. And I like Ben, he's a good man. I just think I'd feel more comfortable with you at home. Maybe I can help you with this police business. Maybe we need to apply more pressure." He looked at me kindly. "You haven't seemed like yourself today."

The thought of getting more involved with the police filled me with a heavy dread.

"I'm okay. Maybe a change of scenery wouldn't be a terrible idea."

There was a pause as I ran my nails over one another.

"Has something happened with Ben?"

"Oh, no. The more I get to know him, the more I like him, but he's been distant lately – busy with work – and I think I might be getting under his feet." The words hurt as they came out, making the sentiment more real.

"Have you spoken to him about it?"

I felt a subtle smile break over my face. It felt nice to talk to someone. I liked talking to Derek. He was just... easy.

"Not really. He's not a big talker. Not least about anything to do with feelings."

"Hm, I thought that might be the case. Dear, us men are strange; we're built differently. Plus, he's clearly had some challenges growing up. You're always welcome home, but whatever you decide, I understand. There's no pressure from us."

I smiled fully at him. "Thank you, Derek, really."

I felt on edge, but the thought of a few days with Susan and Derek was tempting; the tension with Ben was building.

I wondered if we both needed a few days to breathe.

Ben arrived home as I was nudging through the new pile of post. A white envelope with a handwritten address caught my eye. It was addressed to Chantelle and Ben. I picked it up, looking to Ben, who was headed to his bedroom to change.

I waved it towards him, considering how light it was as I turned it in my palm. "This is weird." There was something small and hard at the bottom.

I mostly got stuff online these days, but never to 'Chantelle'. The name felt alien; it didn't even feel like it was an old name – Chantelle was a different person.

Ben stopped in his tracks, walking back over to me. Seeing the name, he took it out of my fingers, ripping it open in near enough a single movement. He pulled something glossy out, before visibly stiffening, a single match falling to the worktop.

"What is it?" I asked, concerned, leaning towards him.

His eyes narrowed; his words seemed to choke him. Then, after an inhale, he handed it to me. "Just some rubbish, call your liaisons officer, they might want to fingerprint it."

He walked back to his room.

I lifted the flimsy note. As my eyes processed it, I let out a shriek, my body reacting before I could stop it. It was an article about Wayne Carlson. Ben's dad.

Brave firefighter saves baby but loses life.

I swallowed. There was a haunting photo of a charred building, barely recognisable as a house, certainly not a family home. Streaks of stomach-churning black billowed from the windows and door. At the bottom was a photograph of two happy little children, looking angelic in matching royal blue school uniforms.

Ben and Lucy.

Ben looked slender and pale, tiny in his uniform, his blue glasses perched on his nose. Lucy looked more as I would've expected, her hair not totally tamed, not sitting up straight, and with a toothy smile. I traced my fingertip over the picture, sensing the gravity of what those little faces had been through.

I looked for Ben, but he was in the shower already, so I dialled the number the police had given me, my fingers lingering softly on the silky newspaper cut-out, as if it might catch fire in my hands.

"Hi, it's Ivy White," I spoke into the phone. My voice was quiet; the words felt sad – I wanted to stifle them.

"Is everything okay?" the officer answered promptly.

"Yes, well, we've had a strange piece of post, the first in a while, but this is more... direct."

Within half an hour, an officer was at the door with a brown envelope. I hesitated to hand over the paper initially; it felt personal. It wasn't until afterwards that I allowed myself to think about what it meant, what the threat insinuated. Ben appeared briefly for a quick exchange with the officer. They said they didn't expect to find anything, but they would take it anyway. Ben did his best to seem unbothered.

"That was a strange reaction," I called gently to him.

He was watching television while I was leaned against the breakfast bar on my phone.

"I've seen it before. They can try to intimidate me all they like." He didn't turn to look at me as he replied.

The image was stained into my mind – that typical residential house melting, as if it had been made of wax. The contorted children's bike in the front garden surrounded by hauntingly scattered, coal-like debris. The image looked like death itself.

"Your dad saved a mother and a baby?" I pressed, carefully, unsure of what I was trying to ask. It was like the roles had been reversed; I didn't want to increase the distance between us by overstepping.

"Yes, he did," Ben replied dryly.

I reached for some glasses that needed drying.

ME

Hiya. We just got an article through the door about your dad. I didn't realise he saved a mother and baby, that's amazingly heartbreaking. Sorry to message you about it, but Ben's being weird and I'm not sure what to do.

LUCY

Oh shit. Is he okay?

ME

I don't know, he seems fine?

LUCY

He doesn't ever talk about it, we've all tried to get him to face what happened. I would just leave it, if I were you. If he gets himself wound up just call me and I'll talk to him. Are you okay?

I'm okay, the police took it to trace. At least they
posted it and didn't put it through the door by hand.

Thanks, I will xxx

"Do you want me to do that? Is your leg okay?" Ben asked, turning to look at me as I reached to put the glasses in the cabinet.

"No, I'm good for now."

He turned back.

"So... you don't talk about it?"

He stared at the telly. "I'm like you, I prefer to just carry on, keep busy."

"Oh." I considered my next words carefully. "But it's been, what, twenty years? Of just carrying on? Did you ever talk to a Linda?"

"I had a Linda, yes. It never helped. I hate strangers trying to get in my head; I'm a private person. I don't think there's value in talking about it." His words left a chill in the air.

"Oh," I repeated as I put away the last glass.

Ben twisted fully to look at me. "Look, if we have this conversation, it just means Marcus, or whoever sent it, gets what they want, doesn't it?"

"Okay," I replied respectfully, trying to understand.

I looked around the now spotless kitchen, light reflecting off the grey, glossy doors. I'd eaten. I'd tidied. I had no reason to stay up. Ben didn't want any company.

Sat on the edge of my bed, I felt lost. Not for me, for Ben. He was such an island, yet with me, he seemed to know exactly what I needed. When he would take my hand or gently kiss me, it was medicine. It didn't seem like Jessica would be the sort of person to encourage him to be open – her words had been shallow and cold. Maybe I couldn't judge. Maybe *he* pushed *her* away.

Pulling on my pink pyjamas, I ran my finger over the satin, thinking. Was he at all affected by the article? How much of his nonchalance was a front? I scooped my hair up, looping it with an elastic. The thought of another restless night lingered.

It stirred some courage in me.

I brushed my hands over my cold thighs and headed tentatively towards Ben's room. Drawing a deep breath, I nudged the door ajar, peering in, immediately wanting to turn back.

"Are you okay?" he asked, worried.

"Yes, sorry." I stepped closer so he could hear me better.

I stood there for a second, the silence extra stifling in the semi-darkness. The smell of his cologne wafted from the bed, the slight moonlight catching strands of his dark hair through a gap in the curtains. I couldn't find any more words, I just felt like I wanted to be with him, be close to him, feel him. I'd made it this far, so I willed my legs to take me to the side of the bed, where he sat propped up on his elbows, looking at me. I felt silly. I'd read this wrong again. This was about to be awkward.

"So?" he asked.

I thought I caught a smile in the darkness as the atmosphere shifted.

"I don't know, sorry. I'll go," I fumbled, turning to leave. I squinted my eyes shut and clenched my teeth.

As I took a step, familiar arms tugged me into the soft bed.

"I didn't say anything," he joked, pulling me into the pocket of warm air.

I wriggled to drag the cast with me.

"Thank you for making that so much more awkward for me," I mumbled as I tucked back into him, his arms snaking around my waist. I resented the instant comfort I felt.

"You make it too fun." He hesitated. "I'm sorry about earlier, I just don't talk about it. It's not you."

A few breaths passed between us as I felt myself warming up, realising how cold I'd become sitting alone.

"Why did you break-up with Jessica?" I asked, glad to be facing away from him. Being back with him in his bed, bodies connected, felt so deeply correct. It terrified me.

"Oh, straight in with the big questions."

Ben withdrew his arm from my side, tucking my ponytail away from my neck, sending a shiver down my spine. He pressed his lips into my newly exposed skin softly, then harder.

"I mean it," I protested. "Don't try and distract me, I braved walking in here."

"Braved?"

His breath was warm against my ear. I focused on trying to keep my body still, resist the desire to relax into him completely. *Not yet.*

"Yes, you can be very stern and intimidating, you know that."

"I don't mean to be, not with you," he whispered, brushing his teeth against my earlobe.

I turned around, placing a hand on his chest. "Stop it... I mean it. It's weird and I don't understand."

He sighed, rolling onto his back. I pushed up on my elbows to lean over him so I could attempt to read his expression in the dark. He rested one of his hands on the small of my back. His touch was instantly soothing; a gesture proving he wanted me there.

"She wanted to talk about the wedding, the honeymoon," he answered, sighing. "We were looking at honeymoons and all I could think about were client meetings... the office. That's when I realised how in-deep I was. I knew I shouldn't care; she should've made me not care. Everyone kept telling me that I needed to settle down, that it'd make me happy. I knew it was what Jessica wanted. My other relationships hadn't lasted because I'd always shied away from commitment, so I figured that's where I'd been going wrong; people told me everyone felt like that. But, in amongst the romance, the vow writing, I knew it wasn't right. I went away with work and thought about it a lot." He tucked a loose piece of hair behind my ear. "I tried to right it. She deserves someone who feels deeply for her. Of course, it was hard. I tried. I did. Tried to make it work. I thought it would make us both happy. Then, I tried to end it as best I could, but a few months later, she turned up drunk and it just got... messy. It was wrong. It happened a few times. I never sought her out, but at the beginning I wasn't firm enough in saying no."

"Did you love her?" I asked quietly.

"I don't know."

It struck me as an odd answer.

"What are you thinking?" he asked.

"I'm thinking that if you'd have married someone you didn't know you loved, it would have been really sad."

"Sad?"

"Sad," I repeated. I lowered myself onto his chest, resting my arm across his body.

"Did you love Sam?"

"I did." I let out a soft sigh as he stroked his hand up my arm. "Thank you for telling me," I added, appreciating that he had let me in.

"Well, you hold me to account, Ivy, more than I'm used to. I'm not sure if I like it."

We laughed.

"So, do you want me to creep into your bed another night and ask you about your mum?" I offered, looking up.

His hand paused on my arm briefly, the little hairs pricking back down. He didn't speak; I could almost feel the cogs in his mind turning over.

I twisted slowly, meeting his lips and kissing him, just gently. "I'm sorry that so many people have let you down," I whispered.

He pulled me in, hugging me tightly and kissing me back.

"Thank you." He edged back to run a hand down my cheek, gently rubbing his nose against mine. "You realise you can't leave now?"

My head tilted in his hands. "What do you mean?"

His thumb traced my jaw. "I mean, you can't leave me. You're in too deep."

"Okay." I smiled. "You have to be honest, though. No more hiding. I feel like you've been avoiding me the last few days."

He kissed the tip of my nose, then the ridge of my cheekbone. My body melted at his touch.

"I wasn't avoiding you."

I pulled my face back to shoot him a knowing look. "Honest?"

"I have no interest in avoiding you. Quite the opposite, most of the time, trust me. Things got intense with Jessica and I thought you wanted space. You said you didn't want to talk about it, then you were asleep when I got back the other night, after getting me so hot under the collar at work."

I laughed, welcoming a deep feeling of relief.

When Ben's alarm rang in the morning, it felt lovely to stretch and feel him there.

He turned to switch it off, rolling back into me.

"I'm going to miss you these next few days," he murmured, lacing his fingers through mine.

"I'll miss you too."

"Will you be okay?" he asked, analysing my expression.

"I'll be fine, I need to do it. Actually, the more time I spend with Susan and Derek, the better I feel."

"You're all like pieces of a puzzle. You have their natural kindness," Ben replied tenderly.

I smiled at him. Every time a layer peeled back, he seemed softer, but in an enticingly secret way. "Thank you. You would've hated that homely, cutesy version of me if none of it had happened."

He laughed. "I would've passed you in the street hugging a one-eyed kitten and still thought you were breathtaking; I would've still spoken to you".

"Liar."

He grinned, kissing me until his alarm went off again.

Ben had insisted I come along to his morning meeting, which I wasn't entirely comfortable about. The impressive, glass-walled boardroom held a hoard of smartly dressed people, most in their twenties and thirties. When he opened the door, they all stared at him expectantly. I followed him in, feeling like a lost puppy. My gut had been right; it was weird. The seats around the big table were taken by the higher-up members of his polished team – Head of Marketing, Sales Manager, Head of Finance – so I slowly crept to the back and stood next to Charlie.

"Hi," he whispered warmly. "Let me get you a seat."

"No, no. I just want to blend in, thanks."

Ben pulled out the large black chair at the head of the table with ease, making himself comfortable. This was his puzzle, for sure. When he spoke, he effortlessly commanded the room as people turned obediently to him. They fought to be heard and impress him.

Just as I thought I was about to get away, he called out, "As most of you know, Ivy has been with us for a few days. She's proven herself to be a huge asset to the team and has worked with Charlie on VAT reclaim for his accounts. I suggest anyone with international purchases finds her to see if there is more to be done."

Everyone looked at me expectantly, their eyes analysing. My cheeks flushed so hard they burned. Lucky for Ben, he had to rush straight into another meeting, narrowly avoiding my wrath.

Charlie walked me out. "You didn't appear to enjoy that."

I grunted. "Oh god, was it that obvious?"

He shrugged. "Maybe, but I'm not surprised he mentioned you – you were slick with the numbers."

"Thanks, but I'm hardly corporate. You're all experienced, well-educated, and well-dressed. I'm clearly out of place."

"Not at all. I'll take the compliment, I do appreciate a good suit, but when I started here it was hard for me to fit in too. It can be competitive here, but Ben is a fair boss."

"Oh, I'm not technically working here."

We were interrupted by a pristine, black-haired woman. "Hi, we've booked a meeting room at 10 a.m. Can you show us your VAT thing? Room three?"

"Um, sure," I mumbled, looking to Charlie as she walked away, red-soled shoes clacking. "Help? Who is that?"

He laughed. "Zoe. You don't need my help, but I'll sit in if you'll go to lunch with me after?"

"Deal."

I sat down nervously at the corner of the oversized table. Seriously, people only really brought a laptop with them, why did it have to be so huge? Chair wheels creaked as Charlie sat beside me, opening his MacBook.

"What perfume do you wear?" he asked, rolling his silver pen between his fingers.

"Gucci Guilty, why?"

"I like it, it's strong. It's not what I expected you to wear. I would've had you as a Marc Jacobs kind of girl... maybe Daisy. It was annoying me; I can normally identify perfume on people from across the room."

"Ben's sister Lucy insisted on buying it for me when we went out. That's a great skill though, if not particularly useful in this industry," I joked.

"No, maybe not. A perfume shop would be the dream, it's just not as lucrative."

"So, Daisy? Why?"

"You seem sweet and fluffy; Guilty is a little darker. What are you hiding?"

I laughed. I enjoyed his company. "Nothing that would interest you, I'm sure."

He grinned. I looked at the clock. 10:05 a.m.

"Basic Chanel bitches; it's a power play," Charlie stated, noticing the time.

"So, what do I do?"

"Nothing. Literally. Don't play the game. They just want Ben and you've pissed them off by making it look easy. This office is like a zoo full of territorial animals and the bitches are the worst."

I snorted my tea, laughing. "Charlie! Really? Besides, it's not like that."

"Indulge me, what is it like?" He raised an eyebrow.

"My car broke down and Lucy stopped when she saw the car, offering me a place to stay. I met Ben. His niece fell in a river one afternoon when we were having lunch." His eyes glinted as he listened intently. "I went in after her and Ben pulled me out of the water. From there we started to get to know each other. We got kind of... close."

He shook his head slowly. "Epic."

I laughed again, relaxing as I pointed at him playfully. "I saw you checking out Damien from tech in our meeting the other day. Why won't you ask him out?"

He straightened, widening his eyes. "You did *not* notice that. Have you been speaking with Catherine?" He sighed as I shook my head. "I'm not sure which team he's on."

"What? I'd always assumed that would be easy to work out when you were on said team?"

"If only it were that easy. I'm a fancy-dressing, perfume-wearing gay that is attracted to the subtle, broody, masculine gay. It's a curse; a sexy one, but an unfortunate one none the less."

At 10:11 a.m., the door opened, interrupting us and letting two smartly dressed women stroll in. There were no apologies given for their lateness.

"Charlie, are you playing babysitter?" Zoe snarked, running one pointy red nail over the back of a chair.

Charlie shifted in his seat. "Claws away, ladies, the content is there if you can get over yourselves enough to listen to her. Ivy, that's Jennifer."

My face broke into a half smile; I liked him even more.

Zoe looked to Jennifer with a flick of her shining hair. "Well, if she's such an asset to Ben..."

I swallowed. I was being baited.

Jennifer looked at me. "Go on then."

I licked my lips before running them through the process and figures carefully and simply, following Charlie's advice.

"... so you don't even need to charge, really, you can just take a percentage. An easy win," I finished.

Zoe tried to hide her irritation. "Where did you learn that? I heard you didn't even go to school."

Charlie went to speak, but I jumped in. "I learnt what I could where I could. Ben asked me to share this, so I have. Whether you choose to do anything with it or not is up to you."

Charlie clearly approved.

Jennifer laid her cold eyes on me. "What else has Ben asked you to do, though? "

"Don't credit that with a reaction, Ivy," Charlie hissed. "I hardly think our boss's personal life is something we should be discussing."

Zoe placed her hands on the table, leaning towards us. "Calm down, Charles. We're just playing."

Sensing the anger simmering in Charlie, I shut down the conversation and made an exit, lifting up the laptop Ben had loaned me.

Jennifer called after me. "Some friendly advice though, pet. Ben got bored of Jessica when they were engaged, so don't get comfortable. Wouldn't want you getting hurt."

Charlie took my hand, leading us straight out to lunch.

"Well, that was catty," he commented as we settled at a table in a nearby coffee shop.

Luckily there'd been a booth free that I could skulk in.

"Sorry, Charlie. If I'd known they would be like that I wouldn't have involved you," I said, stirring my latte. If I'd have known, I would've just gone home.

He flicked his hand. "Oh, please, it's the most interesting meeting I've been to in years. Are you okay, though?"

I prodded at the toasted sandwich in front of me. "Is that really how people see me?"

Charlie hesitated. "No, Ben is just a hard character to read. It was a surprise at first, but to be honest, I get it now, after getting to know you."

"Thanks, I think? So, what's your favourite perfume?" As I sipped my coffee, I watched the question wash over him, his eyes following someone.

I turned to see Damien ordering a coffee with two members of his team.

"Have you ever even spoken to him?" I whispered, startling him.

"Yes!"

"About something other than tech?"

"Yes. Kind of. At the Christmas party."

"Right," I said, enjoying someone else's relationship play out.

Charlie was in a trance, captivated by the tall, slender man walking to a nearby table.

"Why don't you just ask him?" I prompted, biting my sandwich.

Charlie looked at me, coming back to the moment. "Ask him what? How he feels about dick?"

I laughed. "Yes, or just to join you for coffee one day, maybe."

"It's not that easy," Charlie sighed, suddenly looking vulnerable.

Hesitating, he went on to explain how his last boyfriend hadn't come out to his family. How when they'd wanted to move in together, his parents found out, and instead of being supportive, they'd actively blamed Charlie.

"... Ben is a great boss, sure, he only cares about the work. But that's unusual, especially at this level of financial consultancy. I had an interview for a company once that told me they worked with a lot of American clients and asked whether I 'would be open about my sexuality'? I took the Pride Fundraising piece off my CV after that. So, Damien might not be comfortable being open with his sexuality, especially with a colleague – we all have horror stories."

As we walked back to the office, I turned over the morning's events in my mind.

"Where'd you go?" Ben asked, looking up from his laptop as I walked through the door to his office.

"I went for some lunch with Charlie." I smiled. "You should get to know him, he's funny, really smart too."

He glanced at an email as it popped-up. "I try not to get personal with colleagues."

"Oh, right." I fidgeted. "Well Charlie was really supportive, in the meeting."

Ben sat up, focusing on me. "Supportive?"

I nodded slowly, realising my error. "It doesn't matter."

"Did something happen?"

"No." I stopped, not wanting to cause trouble or make myself seem even more pathetic. "Not really. It was just a bit tense."

"With who?" he demanded, instantly leaning forwards.

I traced a finger over the corner of the desk, feeling the bumps of the wood. "No one specific. I just shouldn't exactly be here, should I? As your roommate, colleague, anything. People won't take me seriously."

"Who won't take you seriously?"

It was frustrating that he didn't even attempt to understand, resorting to anger so easily.

"Everyone, Ben." I leant against the desk and slipped my fingers into his, savouring the physical connection. "Being with you is like I could never have imagined. The way you make me feel, the way you're just there for me, no one has ever been any of that for me, not even close. But with everything else... it's distracting. Honestly, I'm feeling a bit... overwhelmed. I feel like since we went to the theatre, things have got complicated, and it hurts. I don't want to lose how things used to feel between us. I don't want to add more pressure... but I feel like my head is exploding by trying to put all of it together – work, living together, the police, and the mess Marcus dumped on us. Derek thought maybe I should go and live with them for a few days, so I can clear my head." I kept my gaze down, scared to read his expression.

His tone stung with the hurt I'd inflicted. "You don't want to live with me?"

Silence stilled the air in the angular room.

"It's just... a lot."

I looked up, attempting to pour into his eyes how I was feeling, willing him to make it better. He placed a hand on my hip, trying to pull me onto his lap. I resisted; the eyes behind the glass wall felt like they were burning. Zoe and Jennifer were probably out there taking bets. I hadn't meant to start this conversation in an observatory. Last night had felt like we were sharing this precious, indulgent intimacy that I wanted to protect. I didn't want us to fall out over workplace drama. I wanted to fantasise about the few parts of him I hadn't seen yet, not throttle him for dragging me into that meeting and not listening.

"I can't, Ben." I stepped back. "If you do that, no one will respect me. If you want me here, we can't. Don't you see?"

His eyes looked searchingly into mine. Even as more words came out, I knew I wasn't explaining myself properly. I could tell by the look on his face.

"I really don't care what they think, and frankly, anyone who makes you feel anything like that can pack up their desk."

"Ben!" I raised my voice, willing him to understand. "Don't you see, that's exactly it. I mean, pulling me into that meeting?" My phone started buzzing from my bag: Susan, no doubt.

"Let me walk you out," he said simply, standing up and lifting the bag I'd brought earlier.

As the lift went down, it felt painfully full of people. The desire for Ben to wrap me in his arms was overpowering; I didn't want to leave it like this. Of course, it was just my luck that there were people everywhere on the journey, even in the car park.

"I didn't realise it would make you uncomfortable," Ben mused, pausing by the waiting car.

Our hands were clasped together but both of us were tense as he pulled me to face him.

"I know, I'm sorry, I didn't want to bring it up like that." I squeezed his hand. Out of the corner of my eye, I saw Susan waving exuberantly.

He leant down to place a fleeting kiss on my forehead. "Look after yourself."

"I will, you too."

24

Family portraits

I should have drawn a diagram, preferably with sketches and colour coding. Peter was Susan's brother, Michelle his wife, and Daniel their son. Daniel was twenty-four – that's what we were celebrating – and his brother in London had the baby son. Daniel was tall, which was odd, as Michelle and Peter were a little stocky, like Susan. Mary and Paul were Derek's sister and her husband. Honestly, I tried to use their names as little as possible because it was so much to remember.

Seahorse Cottage was adorable. It was nestled on the top of a hill in a little residential town overlooking the sea. A blue seahorse adorned a silver plaque by the door. The cottages that lined the road were all of intermingling shapes and sizes; an eclectic mix of thatched roofs, elaborate weathervanes, and characterful gardens.

We were the last to make our way down the path, and even before the rustic door opened, I could sense the cosy bustle of the busy home radiating in the salty air. Susan and Derek pushed the door open with a warm familiarity as I followed closely behind. Mary looked a bit like Derek, I thought, as my eyes profiled the new faces. She was impeccably dressed; even her blush scarf was intentionally wrapped around her slender neck. Next to her, Paul looked rather eccentric, with his thin, silver-framed glasses and tufts of grey hair around his ears. He was only a little taller than she was.

Peter and Michelle made an instant move for us, pulling me in for a hug and nearly knocking me off my leg. Michelle's short curly hair tickled my nose as I focused on keeping my footing. I spotted Daniel standing in the corner, leaning more causally against the wall, holding a mug. He had a practical looking blue fleece on over faded jeans, his dark, short beard highlighting his cheekbones. He looked like Peter; a bit taller, but with a similarly long face. He waved at me and smiled, giving a nod to the friendly chaos. Although I felt overwhelmed and unsteady, the warmth of it all felt familiar somehow.

I tried my best to answer their questions as we tucked in to our food, slowly building a better picture of these new characters. I managed to sit between Daniel and Derek, who both provided a calming energy. I'd been given one of the two downstairs bedrooms because of my leg, and, thankfully, Mary tired quickly from their long drive, so I had an excuse to get an early night.

To my surprise, sleep was easy.

BEN

Good morning. How's it going? xxx

ME

Good morning, Benji. Okay, I think. It was pretty intense last night, but we're going for a walk on the beach so I'm hoping that'll be easier. They seem harmless. How's work? xxx

BEN

Busy, Bambi, I miss seeing you about. Give them time, it was always going to be a lot. Don't get too overwhelmed, take some space if you need it xxx

ME

Have you been speaking to Linda, Thumper?

BEN

Definitely not. I was thinking about what you said, though. We'll talk about it when you're back xxx

ME

Thank you. I miss you xxxx

They were all keen to show me everything, often all at once. I half expected one of them to introduce me to the sand on the beach. It scrunched under their feet as we walked down the quiet coastline, me staying on the promenade.

"They're a lot," Daniel commented, walking slower to match my pace.

A gust of wind carried the mist of a crashing wave.

"Maybe." I looked at him as we walked and smiled politely.

"You're brave," he chuckled, nudging me gently. "You should see Christmas – it's chaos."

I laughed. "I'm pleased to be able to put faces to names. I didn't want to keep putting off meeting you all. You've all been very welcoming."

He nodded as we both stepped around a group of seagulls fighting over a discarded crisp packet. "It's strange to see you, I'll be honest. I don't think any of us are entirely sure how to act. I'm really sorry; we all are, for everything that happened."

"Thank you. It's strange for me too."

I asked him about his job in tech. Each interaction became easier and more natural, each piece of information colouring the blank image of each person, although none of them came from memory.

At dinner, the questions came thick and fast again. The usual, at first: details of my upbringing, the escape, what I remembered. The word *escape* still felt wrong. The questions were respectful, but I could sense their hunger. When one person was speaking, someone else was bubbling with another thought. We spoke about the police case, about Lucy and how she'd found me; we touched on Ben and where I'd been living.

"Imagine grandchildren after all this time!" Michelle had exclaimed.

Daniel had shot me an immediate look of sympathy.

When everyone started heading in as the wind developed its evening chill, I lingered outside, needing a minute. Derek came out and settled himself in the iron chair next to me.

"You're doing very well, love. Are you alright?" he asked, having bought my wine glass out from the table.

"Yes, I'm okay," I reassured him, admiring the slip of sea above the rooftops in the distance. "Who actually owns this place?"

"We all do, a bit. Michelle was going to sell it at one point, but when you were taken, we all had a shift in priorities and came together to buy shares."

"That's such a nice thing to have done. You all seem to get on so well, both sides of the family."

"We have our moments. At first, no one knew how to deal with you being gone... when to stop living the days hour by hour. But in the end, we all came back together." He sipped his beer. "How's Ben?"

"Okay, I think."

He raised an eyebrow, encouraging me to continue in his easy way.

"When the article came through the door, I thought he might open up, but it was complicated. It's hard to know what to say. I don't want to say the wrong thing to him."

Derek took another long sip of beer, mulling over his thoughts. "I don't think someone like Ben needs you to say anything; I think he just needs you to be there. The boy grew up without a father figure, with no mother to look after him. It sounds like he parented Lucy. I don't imagine he's used to having people care about him."

It was hard to hear.

"Thank you. Those are wise words." I hesitated. "Still, I don't think he needs me to be there, as such. He seems to have a lot of people around him."

He smiled at me and raised his beer glass. "Maybe." He shrugged. "Don't tell your mother you think I'm wise, she wouldn't agree."

When we headed back inside, to my surprise, the family asked me if I would make an Instagram post. Of course, I said no, feeling that it wasn't appropriate, but they insisted. It seemed they had all been affected by the press more than I'd considered.

"People are asking me questions constantly. Have I seen you? What are you like? When am I meeting you?" Michelle explained.

"We get the same," added Mary.

I thought about how it must have been for them. How I'd been such a prominent part of their lives without even being there.

"I'm sorry, it must have been so hard for you all. I never knew anything. I wish I'd found the strength to leave sooner."

Susan, who was sat next to me on the sofa, squeezed my knee.

"No, no, sweetie, I didn't mean it like that," Michelle fumbled. "I meant that your posts are respectful; they help answer the questions people ask."

"It affected us all in different ways," Mary added. "Of course, what we felt was nothing compared to what Susan and Derek endured."

"Well, yes, we were so pleased when they got back together," Michelle stated, too calmly.

My eyes shot to Susan as she looked down.

"Mum, do you really think you need another?" Daniel cautioned as Peter obediently bought over another green bottle for his wife, filling all of our glasses.

"It's okay, Daniel." Susan looked at me, and I could sense Derek's attention from the kitchen. "Your father and I separated for five years, but we found our way back to each other."

"Hear, hear!" Paul raised a glass. "You always were a good cook; it would've been a shame to lose you."

Everyone laughed except for me. I pictured them sat all alone for all those years while I wasted away. All of us unhappy. Apart.

"So, you ride, I hear?" Mary offered, noticing my heavy expression and changing the topic.

I nodded. "I love horses. I love all animals, really, but generally, the bigger the better. Susan said you had one."

"Yes, we have a stable in our village. It keeps me busy. We have Monty at the moment." She shuffled over to show me a photo of a near black, glossy gelding.

"Oh, he's stunning," I gasped in awe. He looked shiny and excellently cared for.

"Would you like to come and see him sometime? Maybe we could go for a ride?"

"I would love that," I replied, the thought of getting back on a horse lifting my spirits. I tried not to think of Ebony.

"I remember when Daniel got dragged through the mud by one of yours, Mary," Peter added, sitting on the arm of the sofa next to Michelle.

"Alright, Dad, we know you love that story." Daniel rolled his eyes.

"Well, it was just too funny, son." He turned to me. "The horse bolted when someone shook a bin bag, but instead of letting go of the reins, Daniel clung on for dear life. He was dragged through so much mud he eventually gave up and let go; ended up sitting in a warm pile of horse crap."

Everyone laughed again.

"Mary told me not to let go!" he defended.

"Yes, your brother enjoyed that a lot," Michelle chuckled. "At least you were keen for a bath that day."

"Mum!" Daniel shouted, head in his hands.

I smiled, taking them all in. I'd been on a horse that bolted once, when I was eleven. It ran and ran, the poor thing. Dennis had fired his shotgun at a tin can. I held on and rode until it calmed, and when I dismounted, in a small woodland a few fields away from the site, darkness had started to fall. The horse was agitated and had spun around as my feet aimed for the floor, knocking the wind out of me. It had felt like shards of glass were stuck between the bones of my foot. It took me three hours to make my way back. I'd made sure I bedded the horse in before heading back to the caravan. I was freezing, with red fingers and chattering teeth, but the door was locked. I rattled it, the flimsy plastic moving and rocking, but Ruby and Frank had gone out. I knew better than to ask for help, so I went back and slept with the horses, curling up in the hay. I awoke in the morning to Frank kicking me in the side, yelling furiously about how much of a terrible child I was for not coming home on time.

"So, are you going to take our photo?" Michelle asked, snapping me back to the present.

After some organising, we took a family photo in Seahorse Cottage. Arms around one another, flushed cheeks, and full glasses. I stared at the image on my phone. I looked out of place in this wholesome, loving family.

An imposter.

[O] **IvyMWhite** Meeting the family finally. Happy Birthday
Daniel!

25

Hot baths

"That morning programme contacted me again," Susan mentioned during the drive back a few days later.

"Oh?"

"Susan," Derek grunted.

"They wanted us to go on Tuesday, did you get a message?"

"I did, but I don't think that would be a good idea."

"I have to agree," Derek added, backing me up.

"Of course, I understand. I guess... I'm just enjoying doing all these things with you. It *would* be nice to leave the press stuff on a positive note, after all the appeals we did."

I let out a steadying breath. "You're not the first person to think I should do it." Lucy and Catherine had said the same. The press were still hounding me, fighting for the first official interview. I paused, considering; it might take some of the heat off, but I had no idea what they expected of me and it was petrifying on multiple levels. "I'll give it some more thought."

"Of course, well, if you'd like, I was thinking we could get a hotel in London and see the sights on Monday. That's where your other cousin is –with little Harry. I'm sure he and his fiancé would love to have us for dinner. For men, they are both great cooks."

I laughed. "You can't say that anymore, Susan."

"She's speaking from experience," Derek muttered.

BEN
When are you due home? xxx

ME

Four-ish. There doesn't seem to be much traffic. Will you be in? xxx

Tired, I let Susan and Derek head through the apartment door first, carrying my bag. As Ben stepped aside, holding it open, Susan hugged him exuberantly. I felt myself smile as she reached on her toes and he patted her back awkwardly.

"Susan." Derek tutted, nodding a greeting to Ben.

I waited for the threshold to clear before swinging forward my crutch, bringing me next to Ben in the doorway.

"You alright?" he asked softly, eyeing me up and down.

I nodded and he smiled at me; I felt it as much as I saw it. When he shut the door, his hand came to the small of my back, his fingers curling gently. I leant into him so he pulled me tighter, the nerves of seeing him again immediately gone. Instantly, my shoulders relaxed, my body letting go of tension like it only ever did next to him.

Susan's eyes shot between us, but thankfully, as she looked like she was about to burst with joy, Derek ushered her out of the door.

I was tired, but happy, although something in my body felt odd. I tried to force a few deep breaths as Ben put the kettle on, but I noticed my hands shaking, then my arms. I looked down at my hand, willing it to steady, as my ribs started fighting my lungs, pushing the air out too quickly as the quivering moved to my teeth. I clenched my jaw and shook my head, trying to will it away. It felt like there was a ball of angst fighting its way out and all I could do was be a passenger to the growing panic. The moment I let my guard back down, my body had seized the opportunity to let out all the emotions from the week.

"Hey, hey," Ben murmured as he took my hands in his. "What's wrong?"

I fought the shake in my voice. "I'm fine. I'm happy. I don't know what my body is doing." I grunted in frustration; it felt like someone had shaken a beehive in my stomach.

"It's okay. It's a panic attack. Breathe with me."

"Ben."

"Just do it. Hold for two... one, two... out for six."

My lungs resisted as I blinked, my muscles tensing. My calf felt like it was about to cramp. "Ben, what are you—? It's not—"

He squeezed my hands. "Because you're not doing it. You need to breathe, Ivy. Shut your eyes."

"Ben."

He scowled at me, narrowing his eyes. "Quit being a pain in the arse and shut your eyes," he repeated firmly.

I shut my eyes, listening to his voice as he counted again, staring into the pink of my eyelids as even they fought me. I breathed. Then again. Then one more time until, finally, I realised my feet were back on the ground.

Still puffed out, I looked up at him. "How did you—? How did you learn that?"

Ben lifted my hands to his lips, kissing them gently. "One of my Lindas. Can I run you a bath?"

I nodded.

The warm water helped, but the panic lingered, like some emotion I couldn't see was still trying to escape. I eased into the tub, feeling the bubbles slowly crackle and burst against my skin. Hooking up my leg, thankful that the cast was getting removed on Wednesday, I slid back against the cool ceramic of the bath, letting it soothe my skin. I tried to shake the thought of Susan and Derek being apart out of my head.

I couldn't imagine Ben ever having a panic attack. Sure, he could be emotional sometimes – angry, easily frustrated – but panic? He seemed so totally in control of his life, his work, his home. Derek's words floated through my mind. Catherine had said he was lonely. She'd rattled on about how she didn't like Jessica and thought he'd only done it to spite her and all the others nagging him to settle down. But then, why me? Why open up to me? None of it made any sense.

I groaned, feeling my thoughts racing. It was like standing at the side of a motorway, feeling the rush of the cars speeding past.

I lifted my trembling hands up, willing them to calm again, splashing them back into the water after seeing that they were still shaking. I dipped my hair back, allowing the water to tease my scalp, listening to the pounding of my heart echo. A few breaths went deeper again so I sat back up, staring at the shiny grey tiles and perfectly arranged bottles.

The door eased open as Ben walked in with a mug. I glanced down, checking the bubbles weren't giving too much away, as he placed it down, the steam merging with the sweet-smelling air.

"Better?" he asked casually, as if I wasn't in the bath.

"I think so." I gripped the side of the tub, not wanting to disturb my floating blanket.

Ben loitered, his eyes running curiously over the surface of the water. He carefully sat down beside me on the floor, bending his legs and resting his arms on the rim of the tub. I could've asked him to leave, but I was relieved he wanted to spend time with me. I'd missed his company.

"I saw Lucy and the kids yesterday; they left you a present in the kitchen."

"Oh yeah, how was the cinema?" I asked, lowering my hand beneath the surface.

He leant his arm on the edge of the bath, a different kind of energy rising in me as he drew closer.

"Sophie dropped her popcorn within five minutes and Isac kicked the man in front's chair for a solid half an hour."

I laughed, jiggling the water. "Thank you for earlier, I can't imagine you ever losing yourself like that."

His eyes flicked between a few expressions as I waited for a response.

"We all have our battles."

Slowly, he rolled up the sleeves of his navy rugby shirt one at a time, exposing his forearms. I suddenly felt very naked as he took the time to fold each sleeve by his elbow. I watched him with no objection, trying to get out my next set of words, trying not to think about why he didn't want to get wet sleeves. What he was thinking about doing.

"Was it after your dad?" I asked, a little breathless, trying not to give away exactly how I was feeling; to stop picturing the vivid dream I'd been having.

He looked down to the stone tiles. "They started before Dad died. I was worried I'd lose him; then, I lost them both. The Lindas had a field day trying to reason with me on that." He looked at me and dangled a finger into the bubbles, circling a small pattern, the tip of his finger breaking the surface above my chest.

Keep it together, I told myself.

"You know, when I'm stressed," he continued, changing the subject as he dipped another finger into the bath, the ripples dancing out, "I find physical stimulation to be wonderfully distracting."

I shifted slightly in the tub.

"I'm sure you do," I replied breathily, staring at his half-submerged hand, raising an eyebrow in protest.

He was too good at derailing my train of thought when he wanted to, and I could tell he knew what he was doing. With a grin breaking over his face, Ben moved his fingers down to find the lower section of my ribs, leaning over, running his touch over them slowly, disturbing the bubbles. Each inhale pushed my bare, warm skin into his.

Sensation snapped like a flash of lightning. I lifted a hand, flicking the white fluff at him– he couldn't always have the control. It drifted through the air, catching on his face, leaving a few glimmering white speckles, one glistening in his eyebrow, another on the frame of his glasses. He withdrew his hand, leaving a small peephole in the soap.

"It's barely over a week until this comes off," I offered, as much convincing myself as him to pause, becoming more and more aware of the water gently moving against my naked body.

"That's a lot of days," he returned, leaving his hand on the side of the bath, rubbing his face into the shoulder of his shirt to dry the bubbles.

"Thanks for the tea. You can go now," I asserted, feeling proud of myself for a second.

Troublesome man that he was, he ignored me, walking two fingers along the side of the bath. "Are you always this well controlled?" he asked, the words slow, his voice a lower pitch.

"I am finding it challenging."

His smile widened, enjoying my comment, as a thin layer of mist settled on his glasses. I pulled a hand from the water, placing my fingertips on the rim of the bath and walking them towards his, water trickling down my knuckles. He moved his fingers over mine, pressing my palm down and sweeping up my arm.

Each touch rippled through me.

As his fingers passed my elbow, he flattened his hand, stroking it up to my shoulder. I tucked my chin to the side, into his soapy hand, raising my shoulder as my rogue body encouraged him. I took a deep breath, the noise seeming to fill the room. His finger purposefully drew a bubbly line across my collarbone and up my throat, teasing my senses to life. The skin was so sensitive, but it didn't tickle.

It struck me how much I trusted him, how safe I felt. I didn't feel scared that his fingers were on my throat, I felt liberated; they were there and that was okay – it could feel nice, more than nice. Giving him that permission, letting him get that close to me, when I was so vulnerable... I hadn't felt safer. My back arched just enough that my breast peeked out from the bubbles. He shot me a hungry grin as his fingers traced seductively around my lips, leaving a trail of warm water.

"Is there a part of you that's not perfect?" he asked, not looking at my face.

The bubbles crackled, swirling with my movement.

Realising I was about to hand myself to him completely, I pressed my teeth down on his fingers, dragging my tongue against the tips. His eyes darted to mine, narrowing. I eased myself slowly out of the silky bubbles to sit up further; to face him, unveiling my top half. The water trailed down me, dripping off the peaks of my chest, the little rivers of white reflecting soapy colours. He didn't hand the power back, though. Instead, he met my challenge, steadily pressing two fingers further into my mouth. I pulled my lips away as we stared at each other through a haze of delicious lust.

"We've made it this far." I leant forwards over my raised legs, having given him quite enough. "Ben, you should go."

His eyes lazily dragged across me. "No, I shouldn't. I should—"

"Ben."

We both hesitated.

His body shuddered as he pulled himself up, trying to shake off whatever was in his head.

"Fine. I'm walking away and I'm not looking back. Next time I see you, I suggest you have clothes on."

He strolled out, keeping his word. I laughed and sank back into the bubbles.

Once I was done, I dressed in my soft blue tracksuit bottoms and a t-shirt – trying to put the feeling of Ben's fingers running up my neck to the back of my mind – and wandered into the main room.

"So, you know that morning television show?"

Ben was serving up steak and asparagus at the breakfast bar as I offered up my purposely un-sexy conversation starter.

"Mm, that smells good," I added.

"The ITV one?" he asked, licking his fingers.

I wasn't sure if he was trying to be sexy, but he was.

"Yeah, you know I mentioned that I was asked about being a guest? Well, they've messaged Susan about it too, twice, actually. She wants to do it."

"Do *you* want to?" Ben asked, spooning out some new potatoes.

"I don't know... I like creating the social posts and replying to people's messages... and Susan said she wanted to end her media journey on a positive note. You know, after all the appeals? I don't want to be some kind of celebrity, and I would have to talk to the police, but I don't know. It could be good for me. Susan wants to leave tomorrow and spend the day in London, which I've never really done either. Lucy has been telling me to do more press, to take the opportunities and 'live a little'. Charlie said it might help with the volume of messages. I'm so grateful for all the support from the public, I wonder if answering some of the big questions might be the right thing to do."

He slid a neatly prepared plate in front of me as I thanked him, admiring the steaming, perfectly cooked food.

Ben sat beside me. "It could cause more trouble, increasing your profile like that. These types of shows are drawn to drama."

"I know that. But did you see there was a whole podcast discussing the comments about me not being Maeve? I'm glad Susan isn't on social media, people are brutal. I'm wondering if I come out and explain myself, show people who I am, then maybe they will be kinder?"

"You don't need to explain anything, Ivy. I told you to ignore the negative comments, or delete them." He sighed. "I'm just worried you're doing this more for everyone else than yourself."

"What do you mean?"

He looked up from his plate, fork in hand. "You talk a lot about what other people want. You say you don't want to be a celebrity, of course, but what *do* you want? I was thinking, you could easily come work with me, you know – officially, on a salary."

I tried not to choke on my mouthful. "What?"

"Why do you sound so surprised?"

"Well, because it's your business, Ben. I'm hardly qualified."

I looked down at my food, trying to distract myself as something knotted in my gut. I'd been pleased when Ben had offered to talk things through, but working with him had been too much. His office was just that: his. I needed to start forging my own path, my own person.

Between mouthfuls, he continued. "I did the numbers; Charlie says it looks like those clients will come over the line, which would make you the second top salesperson for the month."

There was a loud silence.

"Oh... I-I was just happy to help."

He was looking at me like he was delivering this fantastic news, eyes full of expectation. I felt increasingly uneasy.

"I know." He smiled. "If you truly want to go on the show, own it, go. Maybe you'll get some closure. In the meantime, I'll speak to HR and see what we can offer."

There was another long pause as he waited for the emotions he expected. As usual, mine disappointed us both.

"That's very formal. Are you going to interview me as well?" I joked, trying to lighten mood.

"It would be formal. I wouldn't want to blur the lines. I thought about what you said." His tone was serious, corporate.

Take me back to the bath. He didn't understand – blurring the lines was inevitable. Couldn't we just be together?

I tried again to brush it off. "I bet you're a brutal interviewer. Thank you so much for going to the effort with dinner, by the way. You're a good cook."

"You're welcome. I take my work very seriously; we have a low staff turnover. Everyone I take on is a certain way, always very passionate."

He hadn't clocked my attempt to move away from the pressure I felt building.

"Don't you think it might all be a bit much," I pressed cautiously, "working together and living together?"

"No. It doesn't have to be."

"I just feel like the lines blur already."

"What do you mean?"

"Well, living together, working together, sleeping together."

He sipped his wine, looking stern. "Is this from Linda again? Did she say something about the work?"

"No, but Susan and Derek did. You have to admit, it's a strange start to a relationship. Like, when did we go from friends to something more? To colleagues?"

"So, you want space?"

This conversation felt like I was running downhill too fast.

"I don't want space from you, from you and me, but sometimes the other stuff just feels like I've fallen into another role." I tried my best to articulate the uneasy feelings I'd been having, with very limited success.

"Being here is a *role*?"

"No, not exactly."

"*Not exactly*?"

Oh god.

I bought my elbow to the worktop, running my fingers through my hair, sweeping it away from my face. "It's getting complicated, that's all. I've enjoyed our dates so much, but I also feel guilty for the rest. I look around and see myself hobbling about here, arriving back from the hospital in a mess. So much has changed so quickly. If we're going to try and be together, assuming that's what you want, I just feel like we need a clean page to start from."

His eyes softened as he put his hand on mine. "You don't want to come to the office?"

"I want to finish the projects; I like helping, I like Charlie. It's just... maybe I'm not ready for anything more formal yet."

"Okay." He swallowed slowly before continuing. "Do you want to live here still?"

I clamped my teeth on my bottom lip, attempting to slow the words that wanted to tumble out. "Well, we always agreed it would be temporary. I think that's playing on my mind as well, because if *you* still think it's temporary, that makes me sad, but if it's permanent, that feels like a huge decision to make."

"Right," he said tightly.

We both ate in silence, more unsure of what to say than ever. He'd tried to offer me a job? I wondered briefly how he saw me as he looked at me, gathering up the plates.

"It's been a long day. Let me clear up and we can settle down."

My cheeks stretched with a yawn as I took his offer, curling up on the sofa.

"You sure you want a cup of tea, not another glass of wine?" Ben asked.

"Yeah, please, I'm exhausted."

He carried over the hot drink along with a bag of Minstrels, sitting beside me on the sofa. "So, Charlie told me that you two have been playing chess on an app?"

I smiled. "Yes, well, I didn't like you winning so easily."

He pulled out the board from under the side table and started arranging the pieces.

"Mary, Derek's sister, has a horse, Monty. Susan said she'd take me to ride him when I'm back on two feet."

"Does Susan ride?"

"I don't think so," I replied, moving a pawn.

He moved his own pawn. "Was her brother like her?"

I moved another piece, matching his pace. "Yeah, he was, they were both lively. Daniel seemed very on the ball too. They want me to come to all these meals and things over the next few months."

"That's a good thing, right?"

"Um... yeah, of course. It's just a lot."

He moved another pawn. "What? A lot of dates?"

I moved my knight. "A lot of expectation."

"Expectation?"

"Yeah." I paused to consider my next move, losing pace. I thought I could see a two-step check, but I was doubting myself. "I don't want to let them down, I guess."

"Why would you let them down? I thought you said they were all thrilled to meet you?"

He moved his knight, just as I'd predicted.

"Well, you saw the photo, right?"

"Yeah. It was a great picture. The comments section went mad."

"You don't think I looked out of place? Did you see someone commented a link to a whole blog where they've listed a load of reasons why they believe Sam's version of events? They think I'm lying about Henworth." I watched his fingers grip the second piece. "Wait, are you going easy on me?"

"You know that's crap." He looked up at me. "No, why?"

"Check," I said, with a swift diagonal glide of my queen and a squeak of excitement.

He grinned. "Oh. Okay. Interesting." He stroked his chin, but easily moved his king to safety. "Why would you look out of place? First of all, there's definitely a family resemblance. I mean, you're all fairly short," he joked. "It looked like a happy family photo, like you'd known each other for ages."

I moved to another position and failed to hide my grin. "Check. They're all so close, I don't know how I expected to just fit in, it's not surprising people think the same. Maeve left this hole, a very specifically-shaped hole, and I don't think... I don't think I'm the right fit anymore."

He moved to take my queen, but took my hand as I reached for the bishop. "I didn't realise you felt like that. I don't think anyone expects you to be anything. You talk about her like you're separate people. You and Maeve."

I looked at him. "They all wanted her back so badly, Ben. I just want to give her to them, you know? Instead, they have... me. Me, who stayed on the site and let myself get more and more damaged for *years*."

"Exactly, Ivy. They have *you*. Despite everything you've suffered through, they've got you back. Susan's told me how proud of you she is."

He didn't let go of my hand as I stared at the board, desperate to continue – mostly because I didn't want to talk about this, partially because I really did want to win.

"She shouldn't be, though, should she? I didn't do anything. Ben, I didn't even try when Marcus burst in here. I'm so mad at myself for being so weak. Everyone says, all the time, how proud they are of me, how happy they are, but it's all my fault. I'm broken; they'll never get that shiny, happy girl back, and I have to watch them adjust. Adjust to what I am. What I let myself become. Ugh, for god's sake, please move your piece."

He squeezed my hand before letting it go to move his rook, still holding my gaze. "It's not your fault. You're not weak."

I looked down at the board, but two of his fingers tilted my chin, convincing me to meet his eyes as he planted a gentle kiss on my lips.

"It's not your fault."

I diverted my attention back to the board. "Thanks."

"Thanks? You're not listening to me at all, are you?"

I licked my lips to swallow some of the emotions simmering. Some of the darkness. "I could've done more."

"You're being very harsh on yourself."

"You're a fine one to talk."

"Maybe, but I mean it nonetheless. You shouldn't see yourself as this broken person, or Maeve as this lost person. You are her, you're the version of her you needed to be to survive; all of us change as we grow up. You were strong enough to make it out – they're all grateful for that. *I* am grateful for that. Besides, I happen to very much like the quick-witted, headstrong, feisty woman you are."

I gave him an affectionate grin. "Are you going to move your piece or not?"

"Oh, I had checkmate a move ago."

"What! How?" I stared at the board, shocked as his queen fenced me in, using my own moves against me. "Why play with me if it's so easy?"

Ben laughed. "It's not easy, well, not *so* easy. I like seeing how your mind works. Want to play again?"

I flopped back, blowing away a strand of hair that had fallen forwards. "Not really. Let me find some more people to practice with first; I can't stand you being so smug. Do you play poker?"

"Poker? What, like Texas Hold'em?"

I reached for the bag of Minstrels, tipping them onto the table. "Yeah."

"You play poker?"

"I do, but not for too long – I need to go to bed soon."

"Okay, but I warn you, in the interest of my own smugness, me and Jenson played all through uni."

He pulled a deck of cards from the drawer and started shuffling them. I'd played and watched poker a lot on the site – I was quietly confident.

The first game was easy: I had a flush and I raised him right up to five chocolates as we attempted to feel each other out. During the next game, I figured out his tell: he had this almost sultry look in his eye when he thought I was winning, like he enjoyed the challenge. So, when he looked casual, I knew he had a good hand and folded. The next game, I let him take a few Minstrels back, setting up a small hustle on the fourth, leaving him with just two at the end of it.

He sat back and laughed. "Well, I didn't see that coming."

"I just haven't played chess before, I told you. Last game?"

"Oh, yeah, I've come back from worse. You deal."

I gathered up and shuffled the cards.

"Why didn't you fight harder with Marcus?" he asked.

He'd clearly been stewing over my earlier admission. My heart sank – the poker had distracted me.

I dealt the cards. "I don't know. I just froze."

"Like a panic attack?"

I looked at my hand. I had a three, a six, and a queen, all from different suits. A terrible hand. Ben had relaxed back, so I knew he had something better. He yawned. This was bad.

"No. I think... I think I learnt over the years that it was easier not to fight. It was like my body learnt to override my instincts. I went into stupid autopilot. On the site, whenever I fought back, it didn't end well. Acceptance was less physically painful."

I turned over the first card, the one in the middle. A king.

"Ivy." Ben's tone was heavy with pity.

"It is what it is. Call." I turned over another card, an ace.

He swallowed and adjusted his silver watch. Bollocks, he had three aces.

"Do you feel safe here... now?"

It was a tough question with an unpleasant answer, so I deflected. "Raise," I announced, sliding my entire pile of Minstrels into the middle.

"Okay, before I address that ridiculous move, answer the question. Do you feel safe?"

"Yes, I feel safe."

"Truthfully?"

I felt myself wince. "What do you want me to say?"

"I want you to be honest."

"Why are you grilling me today? I thought you hated talking about feelings?"

He raised his eyebrows at me.

I sighed. "I don't trust myself. I don't trust that I'll do better next time I see Marcus. I would run through it in my head every day, what I would do if I saw him or Dores or Barnes; what I would say. But I froze."

"You don't need to do better, you know that, right? The police have a warrant out. You don't even ever need to be here on your own if you don't want to be."

I didn't respond.

"You think it will happen again?" Ben pressed, his voice gentle, like he was trying not to spook me.

I nodded. "They don't give a shit about the police, Ben, they never have. Look how slippery they've been already. You're all underestimating them. Barnes and Dores weren't stupid, they were inside the system and will have covered their tracks. I saw the look in Marcus' eyes. Before, it was personal, but this time he was totally incensed. They won't let me get away with it; they won't give up. This won't be the end of the story. They sent that article, a match, doesn't that worry you? They're making this about you, too."

He folded his cards into his hand and pulled me into a hug. "Hey, it's okay. You don't need to worry, Ivy. I know the police have been awful, but look, I'm here, okay?"

Except you aren't.

My body held rigid. He wasn't seeing how I really felt; how it felt like everything was about to come burning down; how I refused to watch it happen. How being his work accessory would make it all so much worse. He meant well, I knew that. I knew he cared. But the comfort I used to feel with him was becoming painfully complicated.

"You're ruining my poker tactics," I grumbled, trying to diffuse the tension.

He scoffed. "You raised more than I have, so clearly, your tactics are off."

I'd known I needed to go big to hide my bluff. "If I win, I want you to insure Lucy on your car."

He cursed. "That's cruel."

We stared each other out.

"I have a good hand, you know that. This could all be a clever bluff. Oh, wait." He paused, lifting his glasses onto his head and exposing his dark eyes. "Can you see the reflection of my cards?"

I laughed freely. "You think I'd need to resort to cheating? *That's* cruel. If I'd seen your cards, I'd tell you. There's no fun in winning dirty."

"Hmm." He ran his fingers over his bottom lip.

"To be fair, chocolates aren't equivalent. Do you want to add to the wager?" I teased, fluttering my eyelashes and giving him a sultry look.

"What do you have in mind?"

Flirting with Ben felt like finally landing back on familiar ground. It was a cheap move from me, but I knew my hand was done, and I couldn't let him win this *and* chess. This was what we were best at, sexual tension. Soon, my cast would be off, and we'd hopefully have the amazing sex my body yearned for, but then what? As sad as it was, I was enjoying our time together while it lasted.

"Well, I guess my control would probably slip if you were to make me sleep naked in your bed."

It worked.

His eyes widened; the corners of his mouth twitched. "Don't be so sure that I need cards to get your clothes off."

I leant back, showing off; rolling my shoulders. His quick as ever retort had instantly distracted me with thoughts of how my body would feel naked in his sheets. About how he would feel, brushing up against me. I swallowed, hiding the heat flushing through me, not prepared to lose poker or the dangerous game we both liked to play with each other's bodies.

His eyes dragged over my torso. I raked my fingers through my hair, trailing them around my ear, slowly, then down my neck.

He tossed his cards on the table. "Alright, alright. Very clever. You win again. Show me, what did you have?"

I leant back further, laughing, and pressed my cards into my chest. "Finally!"

"Show me," he demanded as I gripped them more firmly.

I was right; he had three aces.

"Hold on," I contemplated aloud, sitting up straight. "You really did have aces. Yet you still didn't risk your car?"

He scowled at me, lunging forwards to grab my cards. We tussled as he pressed me back into the sofa. I held the cards over my head, away from him. When our eyes met, his lips were on mine instantly, compelling my body to press up into him, to connect with his warm torso and absorb the scent of his cologne. We groaned and moved together as his hand lifted my t-shirt, sliding right up to my outstretched arm to snatch my cards. The distraction worked and I didn't care one bit. His shirt felt rough against my stomach as he whipped them from me easily, drawing away his lips to look.

"No! You had nothing? How? You could've just won by calling and bluffing! Why raise?"

I looked at him above me; I felt my eyes starting to glaze over, my body yearning for his, yearning to slip out of the truth of reality, just for a night.

"Poker isn't all about the numbers. I figured out your tell."

"Oh?" He raised his eyebrow, staring down at my lips, hovering so I could feel the tickle of his breath. "What is it?"

I kissed him, sliding my tongue into his mouth and wrapping my hand around the back of his neck. As I pulled away, I dragged my lips over to his ear to whisper, "It's a secret."

I shrieked as the hand that was stroking my waist pinched my side, tickling me horribly.

"Ben! No!" I squealed. "My ribs are still sore, you animal!"

He chuckled and withdrew. "Just get into my bed already."

Sunshine poured through the curtains the next morning as my eyes slipped open before Ben's alarm. I stretched, reaching for my phone to check the time, when I noticed a message from Charlie congratulating me, telling me he how much he was looking forward to working with me.

I rubbed my eyes and sat up to make sure I was fully awake. Ben grunted next to me and I felt his hand creep up my side. His alarm sounded coarsely and he groaned.

"Have you got to go away again?" he grumbled through a yawn.

"Why is Charlie messaging me like I've taken the job we spoke about?" I asked, barely containing the panic in my voice.

Ben reached for his glass of water before pulling himself up against his pillow.

"Ben?" I urged.

He rocked towards me so I moved back. "It's a misunderstanding. I thought you'd take it. I'll put it right later."

My eyes darted around the room. How could he have been so sure I'd take it? After everything I'd said? Had he not listened at all? An overwhelming sense of being surrounded, being suffocated, enveloped me. That familiar feeling of being trapped; being controlled.

My voice cracked as I spoke. "I don't understand why you wouldn't ask me first, Ben? After what I said before I went to the coast?"

He cleared his throat. "Does it matter? I don't want us to fall out over this."

"Fall out?" *Wait, why would we fall out? Shit, he* is *mad that I didn't take it.*

"Ivy, it really isn't a big deal. They'll understand."

"I don't feel like *you're* understanding, Ben. It's a lot, all of this. It's... too much." My body felt hot. "These are decisions about things, about myself, that I'm just not sure of."

"I thought accounts was what you wanted to do?"

Frustration began simmering as I processed the hardness in his tone. "I do, probably."

"So just not with me? Not in my company, is that what you're saying?" He pushed himself up, looking down at me.

I shifted further away. "What? No. I don't know? Ben, can't we just be together? Can't you understand?"

He looked at me, his narrowed eyes slicing through me. "I don't think I do. I mean, you say you don't want any of the social media fame, but here you are, off to do more publicity, at whatever cost. You want to be with me, but not live with me. You want to do accounting, but the idea of working with me is, apparently, awful. I've tried to be so facilitating, Ivy."

I stiffened. There it was. He was *facilitating* me.

I swung my legs out of the bed. "Whatever cost? What are you talking about?"

"I just don't understand why you want to dredge through the past on television," he snapped.

"Oh?" I goaded. "Are we talking about your past, for once? Is that what this is about? Because god only knows, Ben, I've tried to understand. You know what?" I stood up. "I've been trying to talk to you about all of this and you still aren't listening. I need some consistency. This is exactly why I wanted a week or so at Susan and Derek's to clear my head. Because you're right, I don't know what I want. I never wanted you to *facilitate* anything, don't you see that?"

He scoffed. "Fine."

Fine.

It was anything but fine.

26

Messy fame

Deciding that denial was the most comfortable option, I agreed to go to London with Susan. Lucy and Charlie thought I should go. The show had called me again. I'd even asked Linda when she rang, but of course she just gave me non-committal therapist jargon. Ben didn't text me. I didn't text Ben. We just left ourselves in that horrible quiet place. Making Susan happy seemed like the least I could do, and things with Ben had been getting messy, like they were destined to; like everyone had warned me.

My mind was a maze of emotions, but London had several guiding arrows, so I followed them.

I had no idea what to wear for a breakfast show, so we went shopping and picked out outfits. Susan chose a floral dress, and I settled on a tartan skirt and an oversized turtleneck. My cousin and his husband cooked us dinner at their flat, and I got to spend time with little Harry. It was bittersweet, watching Susan fuss over him.

Once we'd finished dinner, Vince and Freddie dragged us out to a swanky London bar, leaving Harry with a babysitter. I'd been anxious about going out drinking, but it was surprisingly enjoyable – the cocktails were so fancy, all delivered in different pots and jars with smoke and props, that it felt glamorous rather than raucous.

IvyMWhite I might have to start collecting random recycling to make cocktails in, because I'm convinced it makes them taste better. Thanks Vince and Freddie for showing me London, did I mention I'd never been? What's your favourite cocktail recipe? #londontown #coolcousins

IvyMWhite You guys are getting demanding, here's a

photo of all of us. Doesn't Susan look gorgeous? Wish me luck tomorrow! @themorningshow

Arriving the next morning at the studio was intense; they re-did most of my make-up and everyone was buzzing around. We were taken to a small holding room where we were introduced to comedian Robert Jones, who was involved in the show. Fortunately for my already frayed nerves, he was really friendly and absolutely hilarious. I could see why people thought he was attractive; he had a broad jaw and well-groomed beard, brown eyes, and thick dark hair. He was rugged – manly. Even his voice was deep.

"I thought comedians hated being funny outside of shows," I joked.

"Only the shit ones." He winked. "You're more famous than me, anyway, I'm only here to gap-fill for you. I do demand a photo on your feed, though – help another lowly Instagrammer out."

"Are you mocking me?"

"Ooh, feisty. You have fifty thousand more followers than me, I counted." He slid his hand around the back of my jumper and picked up my phone to take a photo. "Can I write the caption?"

"Absolutely not."

IvyMWhite It's an honour to have been asked to share more of my story this morning on ITV @themorningshow. Thank you to everyone for welcoming me so warmly. P.S. @robertjjokes requested the photo.

Before long, we walked onto the live television set, straight past a small audience, and were invited to take a seat on a sofa next to the two hosts. It was like being in a living room that had been cut in half, surrounded by cameras, wires, people and chaos. The crowd obediently clapped in response to the giant digital cue board.

"Now, joining us on the sofa today, we have a story close to all our hearts. Maeve White, now known as Ivy, who found her way back to her family after nineteen years, joined by her mother, Susan," the female host began.

The male host smiled at us. "Thank you so much for being here today, we've had so many requests to get you on. I don't know about you all" – he gestured to the audience and the camera – "but I'm an avid follower of yours."

I blushed. "Thank you for having us, and for following my story."

"So, tell us," the female host chimed in, "did you ever suspect anything growing up? What led you to leaving after so many years?"

I took in a breath to steady my voice, but the words still came out shaky. The audience went quiet in anticipation. I stared longingly at the words scrolling on the little screens, wishing I had prompts of my own.

"Sometimes, I knew things were different on the site, more so when I was old enough to go out on my own. But whenever I suspected anything, they were ready to bury it and make me feel stupid for raising it. Over time, you get desensitised. I can see that now, living on the outside. When you see violence frequently, it stops shocking you. It becomes your normal. I can't say too much due to the current police investigation, but one day, a few too many things added up. I found the photo of Maeve after my, um, *parents* had a fight. I used the anger I felt to convince myself to drive away. It was a combination of circumstances and luck, really."

The faces in the crowd intensified. I wondered if that was on cue as well.

"What led to you thinking you might be Maeve?"

"The photo I'd found. There weren't any baby photos of me. It was like as soon as I'd opened that door, questions and doubts came easily, but I honestly never truly believed I was her. I nearly didn't get to the door."

The female host leant towards me. "And what about the famous scar?"

That got to me. They called it famous: a part of my body. I looked at Susan, who gave me a reassuring smile.

"After Lucy found me at the side of the road, I met her brother, Ben." His name hurt on my tongue, but I forced another awkward smile. "They have been so amazingly kind. I wouldn't have made it this far without them. Ben told me about the scar, but that spot on my shoulder had been burnt, twice. Once when I was young, and once as a teenager."

"Burnt?"

There was a soft gasp from the crowd, which made my jaw tighten.

"Yeah, at the time I thought it was an accident, but looking back now, I'm not so sure. Luckily, the skin has healed enough now that you can see the shape underneath."

"So, after Lucy found you, you went to find Susan and Derek," the male host prompted.

"Yes, I found their address online." I turned and smiled at Susan, before explaining briefly what happened.

The male host straightened. "So, Sam, that was an interesting story. What really happened there?"

I shifted in my seat, unnerved by the abrupt change of direction. I couldn't stop myself from checking the corridor behind the set, praying that Sam wasn't there.

He wasn't.

I took in a grounding breath. "Oh... we were together for a while. It ended before I left."

"That's not what *he's* been saying," the male host pressed, raising an eyebrow. "Come on, there are two sides to every story. This is your chance to tell us yours. I mean, he's been telling the press that the site was your community, that they were your family. You had horses there, and a job you enjoyed. How much of his story is true?"

I took a slow breath, stretching the bottom of my skirt further over my knees. "I just want to move on from my past. Leaving the horses behind was heartbreaking. They were never mine, to answer your question. The job I did suited the site's needs, but I can't say any more about it."

"You got out sometimes, right?" he continued to pry.

"Yes, on a limited basis. I never got to go to school. They signed me up to this homeschooling site and I would spend hours learning and trying to teach myself. Whenever I earned any money I'd spend it on online courses, or buy books. I could never get close to anyone; it would always end badly."

"What about the other people you got to know, other than Sam. Did no one suspect anything? Your photo was widely published, and it sounds like a very strange way to grow up."

"Like I said, I barely recognised myself in the photo. I think, looking back, they were very clever. I think that's why I wasn't allowed to get close to people. Why I was so heavily watched."

"So, Susan, what was it like when you first saw Ivy, at the hospital, was it?" the female host asked, changing the subject smoothly.

Susan swallowed, her first words too quiet. "It was at the police station. When I saw her, she was quite badly injured, but I knew she was my daughter. I felt like I knew when I heard there was someone looking for us. I can't explain it."

"And you've been catching up ever since?" the male host asked.

Susan took my hand. "Trying to. Obviously there were lots of processes to follow."

The female host looked back to me. "So, Ivy, how does it feel going back to your old home? That must be strange."

A male production member caught my eye as he pointed to his watch.

"Yes, it's all very unpredictable. Some days I feel great, and some days I struggle. I would've loved to step back into Maeve for Susan and Derek, they're such wonderful people, but it's like I'm a new person altogether. I remember the odd bit, but it's more like remembering a fleeting feeling rather than remembering being a certain person."

"Well, I think we can all agree it's been an amazing journey, thank you for being brave enough to share some of it online and with us today. What are your plans going forwards?" the female host asked, wrapping up.

I cleared my throat. "I'm taking things a day at a time. I'm focusing on helping the police as much as I can and just trying to build a life. I would like to say thank you to everyone who has followed along and for all the supportive comments. I genuinely appreciate it."

The female host smiled. "Hopefully we can get the result through the courts we all want. Thank you both so much for coming on."

The audience clapped politely as some instrumental music started fading in.

Robert strolled onto the set from behind a runner, catching the camera's just before they went to the advert break. "Right, let's get her over to *Beat the Chef*!"

Crew members stared at one another. The audience fell silent. I looked between their varying expressions. One of the directors spun his hands at the hosts.

"Well," the female host jumped in, smiling warmly at me. "If you have time Ivy, we would love to have you."

Robert winked; he had this huge energy about him that drew you in. Everyone's eyes fell on me expectantly; a camera man with a clipboard gestured aggressively for us to hurry up.

"Sure," I agreed hesitantly, as they cut to adverts.

Suddenly, people were moving us.

I turned to Robert. "Was that okay?"

"You did great, any chance you can cook?"

"Um, a bit. What exactly have I signed up for?"

"We're going to cook and try to beat the chef."

"Why rope me in to that?" I laughed nervously as hairspray filled the air.

"Because I think you'll be good, Ivy. Just loosen up, enjoy it. We'll have a laugh together, I promise."

The presenters walked past us, thanking me and Susan. Their gratitude felt so strange, but before we could finish chatting, the backstage crew were all preparing me for the next section with a flurry of words and an aggressive dash of lipstick. It was all so intense, I didn't have time to think.

We were led behind a counter with a bunch of ingredients on it:

one half was the chef's, one half me and Robert's. Before I knew it, we were off. The cameras started dancing around, people were gesturing silently to each other, and the audience were told to clap.

"Welcome back!" the male host announced. "We have a very exciting *Beat the Chef* today, with our very own Oliver Wales in the professional corner, and in the amateur corner—"

"Steady on!" Robert joked and the crowd laughed. "What makes you think I don't know my way around a cucumber?"

The audience erupted with laughter.

"Many things, Robert, many things," the male host replied. "So, we have Robert Jones and Ivy White from earlier in the show. Today's teams, you have five minutes to make... a pasta dish! Ready, steady, try and beat that chef!"

The crowd cheered.

Robert moved his hands up and down, demanding more noise. "Let's go!" he shouted, startling me as I tried to shrink behind the counter.

"Is the pasta cooked?" I asked quietly, looking at Robert. My eyes darted around the shiny tools and colourful ingredients. The stare of the crowd felt exposing; a sea of expectant faces catching in the heavy studio lights.

He grabbed a lid off a saucepan. "Yeah, it's flaccid."

Laughter rumbled again.

"So, what sauce do we make?"

"We don't have time for a planning meeting here, Chef White, grab some stuff and put it in the pan!" He frantically rooted through the different foods. "Eggs!" he shouted, grabbing the large box. "Doesn't that white Italian one use eggs?"

A laugh slipped out of me. His energy was contagious. "You mean Carbonara?"

"Yes! I knew you'd be useful. I'll do the eggs, you get the bacon."

I reached for the strips of meat; they'd set me up so I could stay mostly still, thankfully. I slid a pan onto the hob and drizzled in some oil. Robert dramatically cracked an egg in the pan.

"What are you doing?"

"Even I know the eggs need cooking!" he yelled back.

"We just need the yolks, I think." I cracked an egg and started tipping it between the shell halves to separate it.

He threw the contents of the pan into the sink dramatically. "We don't have time for this!"

He snatched the eggs from my hands, tipped them in a big bowl, and smashed them with his fists. He started pulling out the yolks and flinging them in the pan.

The audience ate it up.

"Get your hands in there, girl!"

"What're you doing? That's disgusting!"

Robert tossed them into the pan, but it was already hot and the yolks started furiously sizzling.

"They're burning!" I shouted, lunging for the pan but slipping slightly in the egg whites on the floor.

He threw a hand around my back out of nowhere as I practically slid back to the counter.

"Get a whisk, quick!" I shouted, scrambling like a cartoon character as an awful, rubbery smell filled the set.

Robert toppled the utensils jar and frantically whisked the ingredients in the pan, exaggerating every movement and elbowing half of the sauce onto the floor in the process.

"It's beautiful, *si bellisima*, smells delicious!"

I swung around to tip the barely-cooked bacon into the eggs.

"Two minutes!" the host called as we frantically danced around each other.

"What else is in a Carbonara?" Robert asked, wiping stringy egg all over a tea towel before lobbing it over his shoulder.

"I don't know, but this looks more like a bad breakfast."

Robert burst out laughing. "Yeah, Carbonara for breakfast. You wait, it'll be a new trend – hashtag breakfastcarbo."

"Oh, Christ, it's lumpy custard!" I laughed at the congealed, bubbling mess, pressing my mouth into my arm to stifle my giggles because my hands were so slimy.

"Shove some salt in, you don't get savoury custard."

"*Shove some salt in*? You can't turn pudding into dinner just by adding salt."

He tossed in a giant sprinkle of salt anyway and we plated, well, tipped it onto a plate. It looked truly disgusting. Lumpy yellow egg with pasta and bacon. I laughed so much a tear fell out. I'd never cried with laughter before; I'd always wondered where the saying came from. It felt great. Robert looked at me, wiping smears of sauce over his jeans, grinning, milking the joke with the crowd. I was out of breath as I looked around at the joyous mess.

We lost. Obviously.

They asked us to stay to try the dish Oliver had made. Luckily, we didn't have to have anything to do with preparing it.

Then, just like that, we were done.

"Well, that was epic. What a team we make! Thanks for being such a good sport," Robert enthused as we sat in the green room. "We should go for a drink, or dinner. Let me make it up to you."

"Thanks, but I can't, I'm exhausted. I didn't realise TV personalities were athletes. Thank you for the laughs, and hopefully not the salmonella."

"Ah, you should have said that on air! I prefer comedians; TV personalities are what we do when we run out of material." He reached over and typed his number into my phone. "You know, I was very much expecting you to be boring, Ivy White. It's been a very pleasant surprise. Good for you not losing your sense of humour with everything you've been through."

I dropped my phone into my small, brown satchel. "I seem to not be what most people expect. To be honest, it was good to get lost in some fun, but I am worried about the reaction online now."

He looked at me kindly, more seriously. "How so?"

I swivelled on my chair, facing the lit mirror. "I guess people think I should be fragile all the time. It's more like a constant up and down. Like, sometimes I smile at something, or laugh, like today, because life was so hard before that I appreciate these things more now. Other times, most of the time, I'm just a mess, because I'm still learning how bad things were, by allowing myself to heal and accept things. Sometimes I'm breakable, sometimes I need a distraction, and heck, sometimes I just cry."

His jovial expression dropped as I spoke, giving way to something more sincere. "That's a lot of things to feel all at once. I don't know if I'd be so brave."

"I'm not brave."

He rested a hand on the back of my chair, spinning it to face him. "You're brave, Ivy White. Don't let anyone make you feel otherwise. What you survived, other people can't imagine, so don't put any value in their opinions. You're better than that. Also, fuck 'em." He spun the chair around with a flick of his wrist.

I squeaked as my legs flew out and I gripped the handles. "*Fuck 'em?*" I repeated, dropping my feet to the floor to steady myself.

"Yep. Fuck 'em."

"Oh, they're all so lovely!" Susan announced as she burst through the door. "I met Angela, you know, who does the makeovers? She was telling me about eyebrows and showing me better shapes for my eyes."

It felt really good to see her relaxed and happy.

"What are you two chatting about?" she asked.

"How great she is," Robert answered to my surprise, embarrassing me.

Susan raised an eyebrow. "Isn't she?"

"Stop!" I mumbled, diving into my hands.

"You have wonderful eyebrows Susan," Robert added.

Me and Susan slowly made our way out, through corridors of crew – some clapping, some more emotional. One even asked for an autograph. It was surreal and I was beyond overwhelmed.

RJ

I need you to come to do more TV with me, properly, no more eggs, I promise. I enjoyed work for the first

time in ages. Let me buy you that drink. We can just talk
some more, if you'd like 😊

The thrum of the car was soothing; I rested my tired body back into
the soft seat as Susan drove. The passing cars were almost hypnotic.
What a morning we'd had.

Robert's energy had helped me gain a new perspective on things.
I could do whatever I wanted, well, within reason. I did like accounts,
but when I considered all the times I'd felt overwhelmed in the past, I
realised I always ended up with the horses. Ebony would rest his big
head on my shoulder and whinny away my troubles. Just the feeling of
bobbing up and down, trotting, was food for the soul. Even the rain
felt soothing on the back of a horse. Maybe that's what I could do, if
I could earn some more money from my story? I could take a few of
the other interview requests, the smaller, lower profile ones. Maybe I
could open stables where kids could come for therapy. That would be
an amazing job.

The car pulled sidewards into a service station. As Susan went to
pay, I dialled Ben's number. I felt ready to talk things through now
– my head was clearer. I needed to get him to understand, because I
didn't want to hurt him, I just hadn't explained myself well.

I was pleased when he answered straight away, wanting to hear his
voice.

"Hey, we're due back at four."

"Alright."

"You okay?" I asked, the tightness in his tone setting me on edge.
Disappointment flooded through me.

"Fine."

"Did you see it?" I asked nervously.

"Yes."

"So?" I probed, feeling my heart start to thump.

"So what? Look, we should probably just chat later."

My stomach knotted. "Oh, was it not good?"

"Some man was throwing egg at you. It was bit much, don't you think?"

My heart plummeted. I'd been on such a high. It was silly, I knew that, but to laugh so freely, have people laughing with me, felt electric. As the familiar feelings of shame crept in, terrible memories banged at the doors in my mind. Memories of thinking I'd done something well, only to be beaten and mocked for it.

Anger rose in me. "It was just a joke," I defended.

"Yeah, I hope so."

There was a weird pause.

"Look..." Ben's voice was cold. "I don't want to upset you, I'm just not enjoying the whole office laughing at you with another man on TV. I didn't find it funny. I thought it was all inappropriate."

"Okay." I felt confused, struggling for something else to say. "What time are you back later?"

"I don't know, I'll probably go the gym for a bit."

"Okay."

"Okay."

He hung up.

Susan climbed back into the car, tossing a bag of skittles into my lap. "I always bought you these when you were little. You and your dad used to lick all the green ones and pretend to be monsters," she reminisced, pulling the car back onto the main road.

I picked up the bag and moved around the little sweets, replaying the conversation with Ben.

"Was it stupid?" A familiar quiver rose from the pit of my stomach.

"Is that what Ben said?" she asked, glancing at me.

I nodded, biting my lip.

"No. It was hilarious." She patted my thigh. "You're allowed to have a little fun. You didn't hurt anyone. In fact, everyone else I've spoken to thought it was brilliant."

"Was it too much?"

"No!" she insisted. "It was just a part of the show. People loved seeing you be you. I think it's good to forge a new path as yourself." She patted her hand reassuringly on my knee before continuing.

"Look, we love Ben. We love you and Ben. But you're both in a bit of a boiling pot. Out of the fire and into the frying pan, and all that. If you want a relationship with him, I think you both need more space. He has a lot of sway with you, and that's developed before you truly know each other. It doesn't seem like you have much space to be you, even if he means well."

"I think you might be right." It hurt to admit so frankly, but I could sense the feelings between me and Ben slowly fraying the last week, seemingly despite both of our efforts. I wanted to cling onto every thread, grip it as it spun away, but we were both complicated. I wasn't sure how to make it work. Maybe he liked the broken, brunette Elle better. Maybe she was easier.

When Susan helped me to the lift, I thanked her. She offered to stay, but I just wanted to talk to Ben. I needed to. I'd truly had a lovely time with her; I was starting to feel like I understood her, who she was. She hadn't put any pressure on me, or even mentioned it, but I was starting to feel like calling her Mum one day.

I waited anxiously for Ben, ready to talk, but 6:30 p.m. came and went and he still hadn't come home. I moved through feeling patient, to angry, then fell into scared. I looked around the empty apartment, surveying all the memories, some good, some not so much. I looked at the fresh chips on the skirting board; the scratch in the glass coffee table.

ME

What time are you due back? I want to talk, I missed you xxx

Nothing.

I started flicking though my phone. My jaw physically dropped as I read that I now had six hundred thousand followers. Six hundred. I blinked. There were reams of comments from people saying they loved the show; some blue ticks scattered amongst them. Of course, it wasn't all positive – there were the expected comments calling me a liar, saying that me having fun on the show implied my guilt, that my life couldn't have been that bad if I was able to string a sentence together – but thankfully there were lots of comments saying it was nice to see me smiling. I was starting to realise I couldn't please everyone – please Susan, upset Ben, laugh on TV to get called real and fake, help at the office but rub people up the wrong way.

Robert had messaged me again, saying the show had been a hit, but just like that, a little resentment crept in. Ben knew this would make me feel bad – he was letting me stew on it.

BEN

I'll be back later. Don't wait up.

I sat on the sofa for another half an hour, unable to settle or get comfortable. I didn't even turn the television on, I just sat there, growing angry that all the positive comments didn't mean anything to me without his approval. Susan was right, we could do with a few days apart to clear our heads. I pushed up off the sofa and started tossing a few things in a bag. I hesitated, looking down at my black holdall. Part of me thought that if I packed slowly, he'd come back, but it was still awfully quiet. I picked up my phone and started typing another text to Ben. I deleted it. There just wasn't anything good to say.

I caught myself scanning the negative comments, trying to understand where Ben was coming from. There were hundreds, calling me everything from a slut to a liar, a manipulator and a thief. Sighing, I called Susan, not able to linger around the apartment – his apartment – a minute more. I'd only change my mind and I couldn't do this to myself again. The feeling of disappointing people was potent and threatened to entirely drag me under. This time, though, I wasn't giving in just yet; I wasn't going back there, feeling like that without a fight. So I walked away, bag in hand and heart hurting.

27

Wet shirts

I rubbed my arms as the autumn breeze wafted through my thin jumper, waiting for Derek to collect me. I needed to get a proper coat. I dropped my bag on the floor and opened my phone.

LUCY

OMG! You were frigging amazing! How was it? xxx

ME

Really good! Everyone was super nice and I didn't fall on my face. Ben didn't approve, apparently xxx

LUCY

What, why? Ignore him, he does this. What was Robert like? xxx

CHARLIE

Killed it. You killed it. *Chef's kiss*. Don't forget us little people when you're famous! Tell me everything about Robert. Speaking of sexy men... DAMIEN MESSAGED ME! FIRST! He messaged me first! x

Derek drove in his usual, quiet way. I wondered if he would confront me about it all; be as angry as Susan had been. I didn't really want to hear another rant.

"Ben is a complicated character. I don't imagine he meant to come across so brazen," Derek said eventually, breaking the peaceful silence.

I looked over at him, hoping he was right.

Two days passed slowly, with me receiving even more Instagram messages and calls with offers of work. There was nothing from Ben. I was so mad at myself when my phone pinged and my heart sank at not seeing his name. He was out of line; he hadn't turned up, he'd assumed I'd take the job. Luckily, I was wound up enough to not message him, although I did type a few angry words out a couple of times, well, fifty-odd times, before deleting them. Susan and Derek seemed pleased to have me, so I tried my best to focus on that. Guilt weighed heavy. Guilt that, when living with them should have meant everything to me, I kept thinking of Ben.

When my cast finally came off, I got another part of me back. Susan offered to take me shopping to celebrate after. Although my leg was weaker and I had to adjust my balance constantly, I felt like I glided around the shops. Picking out two-legged outfits had been a long time coming. I felt like I could finally, fully embrace the new me I was trying so hard to craft.

I was standing in the mirror that evening, trying on a few combinations, when Susan nudged the bedroom door open. Thankfully, they had a guest room – staying in the Maeve Museum would have been terrifying.

"It's so lovely to see you on two feet," she said warmly. "Would you like some dinner?"

I smoothed a crinkle out of my new black t-shirt. "I was thinking of going for a walk, actually, now that I can. Only if you don't mind, of course."

She smiled, coming over to stand next to me beside the floor-length mirror. "Of course not. What's up?"

I looked at myself stood next to her; I was slightly taller, but had her pale complexion.

"It's nothing. It's just an adjustment. My life is a constant adjustment." The words sounded more forlorn that I'd intended.

"It's Ben, isn't it? Have you two spoken yet?"

I shook my head, allowing myself to feel sad about it for just a second, before slamming the mental door firmly shut. Susan rolled her shoulders, stepping back to sit on the double bed. It was covered in lilac coloured bedding; the whole room was purple and cream, even the little teddy on the bed held a basket of dried lavender.

"You two have been through a lot. I don't agree with how he's behaving, but you need to talk."

I wondered if Ben was on his own this evening. Probably. *Hopefully*.

When I looked at Susan, my heart sank. "I'm sorry, I don't want you to feel like you and Derek aren't enough. I'm so happy to be here, I am, I just... I think I might love him."

She smiled at me. "I know."

Instinctually, my legs took me the few steps across the cream carpet to sit beside her. I dropped my arms around her waist and she warmly squeezed me back. As I dipped my head into her chest, I was hit with an emotion that overwhelmed me from nowhere. It was warm and comforting. It was new.

We sat there for a few seconds, neither of us wanting to let go. She started stoking my loose hair and I took a deep, slow inhale. Her clothes smelt of lavender fabric conditioner.

"You know," she began, "I didn't think I could love you more than I already do. But seeing the woman you've become, how you handle everything you've been dealt with such bravery, such kindness..." She adjusted one of her arms to wipe a tear from her face.

We looked at each other.

"It's a gift. *You* are a gift."

When I felt a warm tear trickle down my own cheek, Susan fumbled for some tissues on the small, wooden bedside table. As we patted at our faces, we both laughed, sharing in the moment.

"Thank you," I managed, choking on the words.

"Go for your walk, love. Take your time. I'll leave something on the stove."

"You two alright?" Derek asked, concerned to see us both crying and laughing as he hovered in the doorway.

"We are," Susan assured him. "We are."

Saturday night was pretty wild. I should have known mixing Lucy and Charlie would be chaotic, but I was happy to be dragged along for the ride.

Charlie was waiting at an elaborately converted church bar with multiple tequila shots when we found him. I smiled at his grey jeans and vibrant orange and red shirt. Funnily enough, me and Lucy had nearly matched outfits by accident. I was wearing pale blue jeans and my brand-new black corset bodysuit. I'd spotted it shopping with Susan – she'd seen me run my finger over the lace. It had felt like too much, too much of a statement, but Susan encouraged me to buy it. I'd had to ask her to fasten me into it before I left. It was nice having an occasion, and a pair of feet that could finally support some heels –the first new pair I'd ever owned. Lucy had come to Susan's to get ready, and we'd all enjoyed a glass of wine before Derek dropped us at the station.

As I pointed out Charlie, Lucy barrelled over, kissing his cheeks with such effort he nearly tipped off his stool.

We quickly settled into each other's company around a sticky table.

"So, tell me about Damien last night," I probed, sipping a wonderfully refreshing daiquiri.

Charlie shuffled on his seat excitedly. "Well, this morning—"

"*This morning*?" I repeated, giving him a high five.

"You dirty finance nerds," Lucy scoffed as we all cheered.

"Yep, I love the boy. You can both be my bridesmaids."

We laughed. "Steady on!"

"No, no, it's the gay way," he insisted. "I was going to invite him out, actually, but I didn't want to overstep."

"Do it! Ben would hate this so much; let's all have an office party," Lucy shouted, ordering more shots from a passing waitress.

I tried not to wince at his name. I'd told Lucy we needed some space, which she didn't seem to think was anything unusual, so I hadn't elaborated.

"Invite Damien," I encouraged. "What's the worst that could happen?"

We all got on so well; Damien was much calmer than Charlie, but had a wickedly dry sense of humour. He was dressed in a boldly patterned shirt as well, very different from his smart office attire. They insisted we take a photo.

"You look so hot, V, can I borrow the corset? Oh, I could get Damien to wear it for me!" Charlie joked as we posed.

The bartender took a photo of the four of us holding up our glasses, faces bright with fun.

(O) **IvyMWhite** Happy Saturday everyone! #bottomsup

A few people recognised me as the evening went on, but I didn't mind. Some bought me drinks; some I took photos with. Everyone was friendly, full of life, and merrily drunk. Charlie and Damien had a hilarious time chatting up straight men and sending them to Lucy – window shopping, they called it –and Lucy enjoyed all the extra drinks, maybe a bit too much. I took a photo of Charlie and Lucy dancing around a pole together, then another of them on a table, then another as they circled a bouncer. Me and Damien chatted and looked on, enjoying the safety of the floor.

Eventually, we piled out onto the street, looking for a taxi. I was going back to Lucy's, which was where Derek had insisted on collecting me from – we had a family meal the next day – while the guys were going back to Charlie's again.

Suddenly, Lucy broke into a stagger towards a group of lads sitting on the roadside surrounded by a smashed glass. One dramatically clasped his bloodied hand.

"I am a nurse!" Lucy yelled over the clatter of her heels.

I was impressed by how fast she moved before elaborately hitting the deck. Thank God we'd worn jeans. I darted after her as she tried to help them. They were all drunkenly shouting at each other as she tried to muscle in. Eventually, I convinced her to take the man to a local bar where they actually had first aid supplies. It wasn't until we were finally in the taxi, after haphazardly grabbing some food, that we noticed Lucy had cut her hand.

"Oh my god! You're bleeding, Lucy. She's bleeding!" Charlie shouted as I sat back in the seat.

I slid over and took her hand. She must have caught the glass.

"It's alright, Charlie, we'll sort it at home," I reassured him, taking off my blazer and using the sleeve to stem the bleeding.

"Thanks, honeybun, you should become be a nurse too," Lucy slurred happily.

I rolled my eyes and shot Damien a long-suffering look.

"Alright Lucy, just hold that, we won't be long. You okay?"

She picked up a forkful of kebab. "I am having a wonderful time." Twisting suddenly, she went to yell at Charlie, but he and Damien were passionately making out, sliding against each other with the turns in the road. She looked back up at me, suddenly serious. "Ben fucking loves you," she blurted, wielding the greasy plastic fork.

I swallowed, feeling instantly sober. At least she probably wouldn't remember this conversation. Dropping the arm of the blazer, she grabbed my face, kissing my nose. Some sticky blood printed onto me, so I wrapped her hand back around the fabric.

I was glad Charlie was pre-occupied with snogging at that moment; he had strong opinions on the situation, constantly threatening to bundle me into his car and take me to Ben's apartment to sort us out. He'd told me that Ben had been 'salty' with everyone at work, and if I didn't do it for the overdue sex, that I should do it for them. I knew Ben had been hurt when I'd told him that I didn't know what I wanted – he'd presumed I'd meant us – but the fact that he hadn't even backed down long enough to talk to me about it felt sore. Charlie said he was just jealous, but being out of the apartment made me realise how intense things had been. It made me question what any of it had meant. Whether it *had* meant anything.

Lucy waved her fork again, pulling me out of my thoughts. "You two are a fucking nightmare, but he was more annoying on his own."

I swallowed my guilt at not giving her the full story – that we hadn't spoken in days; that he had been disgusted by me.

"Thank you, bitches, for an excellent night," Charlie announced, almost spilling his can of Coke all over the taxi. "Thank you, Damien, for being such a sexy information technicality man!"

"Alright, Charlie, let's get you a coffee at home," Damien said, shooting me another look.

"Ivy finds my brother sexy!" Lucy shouted.

I laughed abruptly, feeling strange as it rippled out. I took them all in, laughing and shouting and making fools of themselves. It was the best night out I'd ever had. My toes were sticky and my clothes smelt of alcohol and I was *okay*. It was okay. It was *fun*.

"Do you need me to pay the babysitter, Lucy?" I asked as we turned down her road.

She cackled in response and I raised my eyebrows. I would have to deal with that when we got there, I supposed.

We staggered up the path through the torrential rain whilst I hooked Lucy's arm over my shoulders, trying to get her to move faster. Charlie had offered to help, insisting that he make sure we get home safe, so Damien had held the taxi and I'd handed Charlie the key I'd taken from Lucy's bag. I saw the porch light flicker on, grateful that I hadn't been left to deal with Lucy all on my own.

Lucy's heel hit a bump in the grass in the front garden and she dramatically twisted to the floor, dragging me with her as the rain tore at our faces. The grass thumped cold and wet underneath us as we collapsed in a pile of giggles.

"Oh, hello," I heard Charlie babble in the background as the door opened.

Lucy decided to completely roll on top of me in a fit of laughter, rain dripping off her hair onto me. I blinked as everything went dark and blurry.

"Oh Ivy, you are *so* sexy! Oh V, I love you!"

My body shook with laughter; I couldn't even fight her off. She was so full of drunken exuberance that we became a mess of thrashing arms and splashing water. The wet mud seeped through my jeans, sticking them to my legs.

"Lucy! It's bloody soaking wet, get off me, you drunken idiot!"

"Oh, Ivy!" she continued, grunting as she was swiftly heaved off me and over Ben's shoulder.

Ben.

I lay in the mud for a second, confused, propping myself up on my forearms and blinking away more rain. He thrust his hand out again. I watched a drip run down one of his fingers, hesitating to reach out.

"What are you two doing?" He sounded so serious compared to the rest of them.

I tentatively took his hand as he pulled me easily to my feet. In my head, I'd imagined this moment – standing before him on two legs again – but, even with heels, I felt small, physically and emotionally.

"Thanks," I mumbled.

His hand felt electric in mine as we stood in the rain and Lucy thrashed against him. I think he felt it too, because he swiftly pulled away, turning his back to me and taking her inside.

"V?" Charlie questioned, snapping me out of my trance as I stood there, curling my fingers. He looked decidedly awkward and suddenly sober.

"Thank you, I'll go make sure she's okay."

He leant in and gripped my shoulders. "Are you okay? I thought you didn't go into details with Lucy? Did she set this up?"

I shrugged. "I have no idea. I didn't know he'd be here." The rain dribbled cold down my face as I clutched my arms.

"Do you want to come back with us?" he offered kindly.

I winced as Lucy yelled something about her kebab. "I'll text Derek. It'll be fine."

"Go get inside, then, but let me know what happens. Don't take any more shit," he insisted, pulling me in for a soggy hug.

As I pushed the front door shut, I could hear Lucy shouting after me from the downstairs toilet. My breath slowed when I saw Ben rummaging under the sink unit while Lucy sat on the toilet seat, water dribbling from her flattened hair.

"Shush, you'll wake your kids," I tried, hooking a hand towel from the warmer around her shoulders.

Seeing the blood on her hand in the light, I picked up a flannel strewn by the sink and started wiping it, keeping my back to Ben. It was my fault. I should have told Lucy everything. Clearly, she thought this whole thing had been hilarious, hence the rolling around in the grass.

"Lucy, you still have a piece of glass in there, for Christ's sake," I scolded.

Ben found the first aid box as I twisted round. Looking down into the box, my heart thumped. I pulled out the tweezers. I couldn't even face the sight of his fingers on the box, the fingers that had made me feel such a spectrum of emotions.

His hands suddenly shot to my face, tilting my chin. "What happened?" he asked, alarmed, looking at my cheeks.

His fingers felt warm and firm, too familiar, as were the hints of aftershave tickling my nose; the warmth of his eyes as they bore into mine.

"I..." I choked, pausing for far too long. "It's Lucy's blood."

"*Hello*?" Lucy trilled. "Can this be about me, please, for once?"

I turned, causing Ben's fingers to drop. Thank god for Lucy, as always.

Ben shuffled out of the door, leaving us alone.

Luckily, the glass was easy to remove and the wound was fairly small. I bandaged it up and convinced her to get into bed – though wrestled might have been a more realistic word. When I pulled the door shut to her bedroom, I headed downstairs to the kitchen to get her a drink.

"Do I need to take her in?" Ben's deep voice echoed.

He was walking towards me as I opened the cupboard doors, trying to find the glasses. My mind was racing. I couldn't think. I was almost just opening and shutting the doors for the sake of it.

Casual as ever, he opened one I'd already looked in and handed me a glass.

I paused before taking it. "No, I got it out, I'm sure she'll look when she regains her senses in the morning."

We were stood barely two steps away from one another. It was too much, too tense. It was a rush of deleted text messages all over again, but this time in my head. I filled the glass and walked past him, biting down on my tongue, to take the water to Lucy. Running away.

When I'd tucked her in on her side, leaving a wastepaper bin close, I texted Derek, asking him to head over. My teeth were sugary and my vision diluted; I felt like a wounded animal, knowing this wasn't the time for a fight.

"I didn't know you'd be here," I said nervously, forced to face him again downstairs.

Ben looked different than before – somehow even more serious – as I allowed myself to look at him properly. I was used to him firing out lines and teasing. He looked... tired.

"I thought Lucy would've said."

We kept to opposing sides of the kitchen. He stood perfectly still as I shuffled across on my feet.

"No. I've texted Derek. He's on his way."

"Oh."

"She's pretty drunk, are you staying?" I asked, chewing the inside of my lip, desperately analysing his every move.

"Yeah. I'll make sure she's alright."

"Good."

There was a long, horrible, torturous pause. I sensed Ben's eyes on me.

"How's your leg?" he asked quietly.

I drew a shallow breath at the thought, wiggling my toes as they ached from wearing the heels all night; marks from the leather indented across my feet. "Fine, thanks, having the cast off is a big relief."

He nodded.

My wet clothes clung, heavy, and my skin prickled with goosebumps. "I'm going to find some dry clothes," I explained, walking away. It was a physical relief to leave the room.

My skin felt like ice when I wrenched off my jeans. I'd grabbed one of Lucy's t-shirts from a clean washing pile and found a pair of tracksuit bottoms. Reaching back to unhook my corset, I remembered how I'd needed Susan to do it up. I was trapped.

"Crap," I cursed.

I caught myself in the mirror – smudged black eyes, and a small smear of Lucy's blood on my face. I ran the time down until Derek arrived, cleaning myself up, delaying facing the six-foot something heartbreak loitering outside. I'd thought about seeing him, about what I'd say, but the reality was too much, especially when my brain was laced with tequila. I sucked in a breath and pulled the clothes on over the corset. The wet shape seeped through the material almost immediately, but I refused to ask Ben to undo my top.

I tried to stride out as confidently as I could. Ben was leaning against the worktop as I got to the landing between the stairs and the door. He immediately put his phone on the worktop and headed towards me. I saw his eyes fall to my dampened chest.

He looked up at me questioningly. "Everything okay?"

"Yep." I felt my fingernails press into my palms.

He nodded. After everything, neither of us had a thing to say to each other.

My phone buzzed. "Derek's outside," I said slowly, not moving.

"Oh," Ben replied, in the same tone as before. He almost looked... defeated?

Wincing inwardly, I walked to the door, but I couldn't turn the handle. I couldn't just walk away, not from him, not like this. I turned to find his eyes ready to lock with mine. They seemed to scream a thousand words, but I needed them from his lips. I needed something. My mouth twitched, but I scolded myself, supressing the desperate impulse to apologise for everything and nothing and just run back into his arms. I couldn't. I needed something from him in that moment, after not coming home, after what he had said. It was his move, his turn to reach out.

Come on Ben, please. Give me something. Convince me it was real.

He said nothing, so I left.

28

Burning buildings

I rolled over to check my phone. Nothing. Ben must've known he would see me. Was he not bothered? He'd looked bothered, but he hadn't said anything.

I grunted to myself as I got up, in need of a shower.

Sliding my phone into the pocket of my fresh jeans, I shoved yesterday's muddy clothes into the washing machine.

"Good morning. Can you stomach some breakfast?" Susan teased from the kitchen as I straightened up.

My mouth was a desert, and the change in position made me queasy. "Thanks, but I'm nipping to the shop quickly," I replied, walking past her for my coat.

"Well, don't be long. I want to hear all about Charlie and Lucy."

I smiled at her. "And Damien."

Susan had enjoyed the stories of the last few weeks as we'd gotten to know each other better.

"Ooh," she said, clutching a cup of tea.

I suggestively raised my eyebrows up and down.

"Grab my umbrella, it looks like it'll rain again," she added.

"Cheers, Mum," I replied easily, too easily. It just slipped out, and there was no taking it back. My lips tingled with the feeling of the word.

Mum.

I'd never thought twice when saying the word to Ruby, yet this moment felt like crashing into the cold river after Sophie. My trance was broken by Susan's movement as I stayed rooted to the spot, my pulse rocking my body. She simply raised her lavender mug and nodded. A silent acceptance. She calmly sipped her tea as I watched, transfixed, waiting for something to happen, expecting the world around me to melt, or to wake up back in my caravan in a cold sweat.

It didn't.

I didn't.

My throat was thick as I swallowed the distant taste of cherry shots, nodding slowly back and willing my legs to keep me standing. Susan's face broke into a wide, glossy, all-consuming smile and she tilted her head ever so slightly to the side. I sniffed back the breaking wave of comforting, overwhelming love – an emotion I was navigating at a terrifying pace. A feeling both liberating and imprisoning, deeply fulfilling, yet petrifying. Love hurt, because feeling it made me realise how much faster I would starve without it again.

Rain began to fall as I paced around the small street corner towards the little shop. I grimaced, not wanting to be damp again. I wondered what the surprise was as my mind calmed. It hit me that I didn't know when their birthdays were; I hoped I hadn't missed one since I'd been back. I checked my phone before lifting my head and seeing the shopfront appear.

"Chantelle."

I turned instinctively before realising why the name sounded odd.

My blood ran cold.

Marcus waved an arm at me from his chunky silver pick-up on the other side of the road.

Where was Derek?

I froze, clutching the umbrella handle. Marcus causally waved Derek's phone. I gulped. *I knew it*. I had always known he'd be back. My legs moved frantically as I sprinted towards him with rage filling my body, raising the umbrella as a weapon. I lunged for the phone, but Marcus grabbed my wrist through the open window.

"Where is he?" I hissed, feeling my bones compact under his strong grip. He pulled my face closer to his so I could feel his moist breath.

"Nice to see you again too. Let's not cause a scene this time, do as yer told, for once, and get in the truck." His voice was poison as he mocked me, tapping the passenger seat.

I wrenched my wrist from his grip, dropping the umbrella, and jogged around the bonnet, climbing into the empty passenger seat without thinking. It felt more like I was watching myself do it than anything else.

"Where is he?" I demanded, pulling the door shut with a cracking thud. "None of this is his fault, you stupid bastard." Anger possessed me violently and I welcomed it.

He pulled the truck away. "You'll see. Don't worry." He glanced at me, black hair immobile from the grease, his thin lips curling. "Put yer seatbelt on. We don't want any more attention from the pigs, do we?"

I sat back in the chair, dizzy as my heart beat in a frenzy. I'd been in this truck before. It felt like it had happened a lifetime ago. A different life. A different girl. I looked at the scratched plastic clasp of the glove box and wondered what was in there. If I could reach it, find something sharp, take us off the road...

What about Derek? A chill lifted my spine. What if Marcus just had his phone? What if I'd climbed into the truck too readily and Derek was safe in the shop all this time.

"What do you want, Marcus?" I seethed, subtly rolling my hips against the seat, feeling for my phone.

He kept looking at the road as he sped up, violently swerving around parked cars as we headed away from the village towards the countryside.

"I told you what we wanted, Miss Ivy fuckin' White, y'know what we wanted. We wanted peace. We wanted to let you go on yer merry way, not dig up shit you had no need to."

"Fuck you!" I shouted, fury and fear battling for dominance.

He wheezed a laugh. "That offer's long expired, love, but I knew you'd always come round."

"You're disgusting."

I glanced around the car; the door was still unlocked. I could jump. No. My back thrust into the seat as the truck swerved around another corner, pressing me into the door as he steered down a side road. I cursed, watching cars streak past the window in flashes of colour, my fingers digging into my palms. I moved my hips again, trying to dislodge my phone from my back pocket, easing my hand steadily to the side. The app the police had installed was two taps away.

"Touch that and they won't even find his body," Marcus stated calmly, sending a fresh chill through me.

"Why? What did I ever do to you? I taught you to read, for god's sake. I kept my promise, I never told anyone, and what? Why are you so cruel?"

He grinned, showing yellowing teeth. "Come now, yer the one that left, sweetheart."

"Why would I have stayed? How was I supposed to live like that?"

For a second, I thought I saw a crack in his grotesque façade, but my body was thrumming so hard with fear, with the image of Derek's face, with memories of atrocities I'd seen them commit, that my mind was a scramble.

"All you ever did was make life hard for yerself. Princess Chantelle: too good for us, now and always."

"What, because I wouldn't fuck you? I saw the girls, Marcus. I heard them scream."

"Don't preach to me, darlin'. We did what we needed to. You're the one insistin' on causin' trouble. I'm just cleanin' up."

I heard his foot hit the floor as we bounced down a gravelly path, crashing through potholes.

I knew where we were.

The old site was mostly abandoned. It was isolated; surrounded by trees, piles of rubbish, and rotting logs. It was at the back of an abandoned sports ground that had been shut down since they'd left it in disrepair. Even the air hurtling through the window smelt damp and sinister. I scanned the fields and scattering of trees for Derek as the brakes slammed, lurching me forwards. I desperately analysed the landscape, spotting a derelict building: *the old changing room and toilet block, they must be in there.*

As Marcus hopped out of the truck, I knew I had to act fast. I scrambled for my phone, keeping it hidden behind my leg so I could tap through to the tracking app. Then I broke open the glove box, cracking my fingernails as I frantically rifled through the contents until I found something sharp and shoved it in my back pocket. I threw the door open and ran. I ran as fast as I could through the grass, feeling my feet slide and fail to find grip. Faster and faster I pushed, step after step, strides stretching, grass whipping me. Gareth and his short, bald sidekick spun to look at me from the back of the building, sickly petrol fumes filling my throat as I gasped for breath. I slid to a stop, throwing my weight behind me.

Derek, where is he? What is this?

A shot cracked though the air, sending me cascading into the mud as my feet flew out from under me. My ears rang so loudly I couldn't think, light flashing over my eyes. I wasn't sure for a second which way was up. The pellets had bounced from the ground, sending tufts of turf flying through the air, but I couldn't stop.

I clambered up frantically, but Marcus was already there, wrenching me by my arm, pulling me to my feet as my legs thrashed. I flung an elbow back with everything I had, missing his nose and cracking it into his grey eye socket.

"Bitch!" he screamed, shaking me violently, nearly ripping my shoulder from its socket.

My muscles burned as they tried to hang on.

"Derek!" I screamed as loud as I could. "Derek!"

I fought Marcus' grip, my free arm swinging around, nails out, looking for something to hit. Other hands were soon on me, twisting it behind my back.

"Derek!"

They forced me to my knees.

A boot hit me hard in the back of the head; I flew forwards onto the floor. Unwilling to stop, I crawled through the mud, gripping it as

I crawled away. Marcus grabbed my ankle and yanked me backwards. I twisted turbulently in the mud like a possessed animal, kicking out my other leg. There was no pain, just panic; just energy. Just rage and the ringing in my ears.

"Tell me, Chantelle. Where did you see this goin'?" Marcus muttered, as the other men folded their arms, enjoying the show; circling around me like a pack of rabid dogs.

Marcus dropped my leg to the floor and I lay there for a second, panting; looking from one of them to the other, trying to catch a thought. I dragged my coat sleeve across my mouth.

"You think you're above the law, Marcus. They've got you this time. You. Will. Rot," I hissed, spitting reddened mud at his feet, tasting the blood and the dirt and the adrenaline. "I told them everything. You made me do all those books, you all treated me like a piece of shit, and thought, what? That I wouldn't try and burn you all to the fucking ground?"

I bent my knees one at a time, peeling myself up. Facing him. Stepping towards him. All those years of being beaten and undermined; all the times he'd made me feel small.

I knew I'd delivered the final blow with the evidence, one way or the other. This was my end. This was how it ended. Finally, I stood before him; finally, I felt the storm fully rumble in me again.

Before I could think about what I was doing, my arm swirled forcibly through the rain, slapping him hard across the face. Marcus was so shocked that he stumbled back, tripping in the mud, struggling to find his footing as my hand pulsated.

"You're all pathetic, weak fools," I spat, twirling around and pointing, narrowing my eyes. I was a women possessed with years of pent-up rage.

Click.

The gun cocked as Marcus snatched it from Gareth, resting the barrel over his own forearm.

"They won't get us." He crinkled his oily nose with disgust.

The stench of whisky and petrol clouded my senses.

"I wouldn't be so sure."

He curled his finger around the trigger. I watched it. I wasn't scared, just alive. In that moment, every part of me was alive.

"Show 'er in, lads," he snarled.

I barely had time to flinch as the two men grabbed my arms again, forcing them back behind me and thrusting me forwards. Marcus followed, gun pointed.

The building smelt damp and the walls were fluffy with green, the rotting structure slowly revealing itself in the gloom. We turned the corner into a changing room, heading through a small entrance hall when I saw him.

Derek.

Two wooden benches topped with hooks lined the square room. He was slumped against a big metal radiator, attached to it with a white cable tie around his wrists, silver duct tape over his mouth. My stomach churned, my eyes screaming at him, screaming pain and guilt and apology. He was my *dad*. My actual dad.

The dad who loved me.

Blue tainted Derek's face, the swelling growing, red blood and pink skin around his go-to green, v-neck jumper. They'd ruined his favourite jumper. His eyes held a sorrow so intense my knees buckled. Tears rolled out of nowhere. I felt a cable tie cut into my wrists before I was thrown onto the dirty concrete floor.

"This," Marcus's voice rang out with a sense of grotesque power, "is what happens, my darlin', when you go thinkin' yer anythin' more than a stupid, worthless slut." He gripped my hair, twisting my head to face the other corner.

Sam.

I hadn't even noticed him, bound and gagged. My body yelped. Marcus laughed as sickness rose in my stomach. Unlike Derek, Sam's eyes were closed, browning blood dripping down his face. It ran along the tape, pooling into his blue plaid shirt. I heard a noise from Derek – almost a squeak – the best he could manage, and my heart broke, parts of me cracking and falling and breaking. Sam looked dead. He looked *dead*.

Derek couldn't look like that.

"Take it all in!" Marcus crowed. "Take in what you've done. Could've kept yer ponies, and yer calculators, but no. *You* choose this. Enjoy it all, Chantelle. I know I will."

"Let him *go*! Let Derek *go*, Marcus! Kill me. Kill me now! He did *nothing*!"

He laughed, the unhinged sound bouncing off the walls. "Why would I do that? Silly, silly girl. We're leavin', cleanin' up. Tyin' up loose ends, if you will. I knew you'd like to see yer Sam, I knew you were soft, but the pain you caused our Ruby and Frank? The shame? You can watch 'em both burn for that. I hope it's real slow. I hope you burn last. I hope you burn forever."

"Please, Marcus! I'll retract my statement with the police! I'll do anything! Please!"

Derek shook his head at me frantically as Marcus laughed again, striking and throwing down a match. The whoosh of flame igniting rippled around the room as he slowly walked away.

The fire grew with such a ferocity that my eyes stung from the glare. Orange flames danced along petrol paths. It climbed the walls and swept violently over the ceiling. Immediately, dust, mould, and grit puffed and blew from the force of the greedy flames. I bent my knees, struggling to twist my hands, pulling and pulling. Writhing on my side, I slid back, one push first, then another, to the end wall, struggling up into a sitting position.

I felt something sharp between my jeans and the floor, something cool and hard as the flames glowed in Derek's wide eyes. Pulling on the cable tie I leant to my side and grasped the pliers I'd stashed, feeling around until they stabbed into my contorted palm. I shuffled back, fighting to slide one of the metal prongs between my wrists. I laughed as they caught the plastic, through a frenzied sob. With a final contortion and using the concrete to steady my palm, the plastic clicked and my arms swung apart.

I'd done it.

I lurched for Derek, immediately tearing off the tape, revealing a red rectangle over his face as my knees crashed clumsily into his.

"Ivy, get out," he rasped with his first breath.

The fire roared around us, littered with the crash of falling debris as the fragile structure started to give in – even the floor was getting warm. A smash next to us sent a whirl of dust our way, taking our sight as I felt for the cable tie on his wrists.

"No. No, I won't. I won't!"

"Ivy, look at me. Look at me!" He nuzzled at his shoulder, trying to clear the dirt from his eyes.

My thumb pulled into my jacket to quickly mop his brow. I heard another crash; I arched over him as more debris plummeted down around us and the flames danced closer.

Tears kept coming, salty warm drips sticky on my lips. "No!" I sobbed. "We're getting out. You're getting out."

I thrust the metal between Derek's swelling wrists, blinking out a tear of dirt. The angle was wrong.

"You need to go. Go for Susan. She won't survive it again. You deserve a life. I had you, Ivy, we got you back. Seeing you, meeting you, it's been the honour of my life."

I ignored him, his words burning hotter than the fire now covering each wall.

Snap.

Derek was free. He careered forcefully towards me as I fumbled to catch him, but he was heavy and we both fell to the floor.

"Come on," I pleaded with him as he tried to regain control of his battered body and stand.

I tugged his swollen arm over my shoulder and willed my legs to straighten, dragging us towards the glowing door. I knew if we burst out, there'd be a gun waiting for us.

"Wait here," I spluttered.

I felt his hand in mine.

"Ivy."

I allowed myself to pause as we cleared the first door from the changing room, just for a second. Derek tipped back heavily against the concrete wall, heaving and gulping. The flames were behind us, not yet underneath us, but I could see that the other changing room was violently ablaze, the heat clenching my skin. I could barely make out Derek's familiar face in the gloom.

"I love you," I gasped, not knowing what else to say.

"I love you too," he replied, before losing his breath to a cough. He buckled, nearly falling over.

There wasn't time to think; the building didn't have long left. Two steps back would have to be enough. I gripped my fist around the pliers, squeezing the worn rubber handle and charged, slamming into the wooden door, back into blinding daylight.

I saw Gareth turn first.

I ran. I ran into him, through him, shunting the thick metal points deep into his stomach. We fell to the grass together as time slowed. His bald friend spun on his heels, but the pliers wouldn't come free; they were stuck inside Gareth. My fingers released the handles, watching him recoil in shock and gurgle a cry. Time slowed further as I felt one foot find the earth, then the other.

Marcus came from behind me, lifting the gun once more. As the shining barrel rose, I ran with all the energy I had left. I pushed my trainers into the mud and tackled him with all my might, sending us flying through the door and back into the burning entrance. A shot fired into the air as I fell onto Marcus, both of our bodies recoiling with the force. I let myself tumble into him as we fell past Derek, smoke swirling, when the sound of another voice, another muffled cry, cut through the dense smouldering chaos.

It was Sam.

Metal slid over my shoulder. In his shock, Marcus had dropped the gun. I gripped the heavy wooden handle and lunged for Derek's hand, yanking him forward.

We ran.

As we crashed into the undergrowth, at least twenty meters from the building and finally in slight cover, Derek's legs gave way. We fell again, tumbling and twisting, legs crashing, bodies colliding, finally landing on woody undergrowth. I scrambled to prop him up against a tree and pressed a hand into his chest.

"Derek?" I cried though a new wave of tears. "Derek? Dad?"

His breathing was too fast. I crouched down, my hand on his heart, checking that it was beating. I wiped a trail of tears on my forearm as I felt it, more grateful in that moment than I'd ever been for anything.

"Derek, here, look after this," I stuttered, thrusting the cold gun into his arms, Sam's cries ringing in my ears.

Derek gasped out a plea, but I was gone. I knew if I looked at him, if I allowed him to speak, I'd lose the courage. It was crazy; I knew it was reckless, but I couldn't live with Sam's screams running through my mind. He might have been weak and ignorant, but he wasn't cruel. He deserved life. He didn't deserve to die because of me. He deserved a chance.

Marcus was staggering out of the crumbling entrance, cursing and lurching to his feet as I peered around the brambles. The entire building was glowing and crackling. My ears were still ringing, my mouth tasted of metal and soot, and my body was thrumming with adrenaline. I felt the life running through my veins. I pictured Sam's face; pictured laughing with him over a crate of puppies; his smile. I pictured the faces of his family.

Pushing off into a sprint one more time, my lungs screamed from the smoke that was now polluting even the outside air. A droplet of rain hit my forehead, cooling it, then another, and another. Cool, crisp, wet, welcome rain.

I didn't let my legs stop as I neared the door, but Marcus was too quick. He looked wild – barely human – as he bulldozed into me mid-step. Thick fingers gripped my throat before I could twist away, rushing me, one agonising step at a time, back into the burning entrance. Standing at the threshold, small flames licked around his feet, but he was too engorged with fury to care. Fearlessly, he stepped further in so he could force me against the red-hot wall. My nails snapped as I clawed desperately, choking, but he didn't flinch. He just squeezed.

My mouth desperately opened, sucking in hot, thick air that had nowhere to go. Red ribbons danced behind us, now covering the entrance. I reached my hand to his face, trying to keep fighting, but I couldn't reach. I looked him in the eyes through the dark haze. After everything, it came down to me and him. I felt him grind my body further against the wall, my feet dangling as my throat was crushed even more. The heat kept building against me, against the wall, more blazing wood toppling from the ceiling as lumps of plaster smashed to the floor. His lips pursed; he had no words, just hatred.

Both of us stood there, in the fire, hating each other.

Ending each other.

Crash.

Metal glinted in the light of the inferno, something substantial hitting Marcus on the side of his head with a glorious *thwack*. Falling, my feet hit the floor as he flew sideways. I seized my throat, my body convulsing in desperation for air, as my legs buckled. The silhouette of Marcus stumbled towards me as the glow clouded my vision.

The air was poisonous and hot. I forced my legs to take me back towards that first door, further in through the spiralling, dancing smoke. The floor was almost entirely alight due to the treacherous littering of fizzling debris. I clambered over the carnage, shaking violently with each erupting cough, until I saw him. Sam was flopped against the radiator. I was too late. He wasn't moving, the flames flickering against his jeans, my body recognising the pungent smell of burning flesh.

I felt myself scream as I dived for him, slamming my hands into his face.

"Sam!"

His head lolled to the side, his eyes open, mouth gaping. New flames hurtled towards me as the door shut in the direction I'd come from. I stumbled back over the floor, pounding my fists against it, screaming.

I was trapped.

Swerving frantically, I spotted a break in the devastation behind

Sam: a small bathroom that hadn't yet been consumed. I scrambled over the wreckage before I fell, crawling, dragging my knees. Coughs ripped my lungs and stung my throat as my breaths came slower. My airway was closing inch by inch; with each intake of air, there was even less space.

I made it to the small grey room with half a breath left, feeling the chemicals released by the fire filling my bloodstream and marring my thoughts, my body as polluted as the air. I gripped Sam's limp body, leaning back to slide him inside with the last of my strength. His cable tie must have snapped in the heat, because he moved with me.

Forcing the wooden door shut with a kick, I trapped us inside. The rims of the door glowed red as sweat dripped from my hairline. I looked around at the three stalls shrouded in black. *The sinks!* I stood up to twist the taps, but nothing came out and my hand flew back as the metal burnt my skin. Even the window was glowing as the glass cracked.

My chest moved up and down, in and out, more and more shallow, less and less movement. I felt the hot, hard floor against my cheek as a wave of quiet dizziness took the world from me slowly. Darkness spilled across my vision, the cracking and crashing fading into silence. I heard my lungs gasp a short breath, then nothing. This was truly it. Derek was out, I'd tried to save Sam. I'd tried, but I had no more to give. The fire was too hot, the smoke too thick. I was exhausted.

I could just... slip away.

My eyes fluttered open as I looked down at my feet. Curled up at an awkward angle, I saw Chantelle. Sad and broken. Alone again. Ivy had been a desperate dream – an indulgent delusion.

White light spilled from the corners of the door, growing brighter until it filled the space. A glowing figure appeared, an ethereal hand reaching out, the figure calling to me as my mind melted away.

29

His choice

Life crashed into my body unwillingly.

Tensing my eyes, I searched for the light, desperate for peace, but a huge crash thrust my body from its fiery grave.

Something freezing and wet slithered down my throat.

It felt like suffering.

Moisture soaked into my smouldering skin, my body shaking, but it wasn't *me* shaking. As the tiniest breath of air was forced back into my lungs, a bolt of electricity ignited my muscles. Messages and impulses raced as I felt my legs tense and my head roll. Arms pulled me tightly, warm against the cold wetness. My neck seized and my legs twitched as my muscles fought through throbbing agony.

A cough erupted from me and my hands found the grass as my body freely convulsed, blood and grit and dust erupting from my mouth. The coughs were violent, but they cleared space.

Wheezing, I noticed a patch of vision clearing. Hands were on me.

Ben.

Ben is here.

My heart pumped out what felt like its first ever *thump*.

I collapsed back against his bent knees; let him cradling me as I spluttered violently. His mouth moved, furiously communicating something over and over and over. All I could hear was a bitterly familiar, high-pitched ringing, his face mostly a blur. The rain splashing into the puddles on the ground was deeply soothing, like the water now trickling down my face. I welcomed the rain, letting it rinse my eyes and return my vision.

Red.

Ben had red blood dripping down his face.

My hand shook as I reached for it. My arm felt so heavy I fought to move it, barely getting a blackened fingertip to his brow. His hand flew to mine, fingers pushing my palm into the side of face. His eyes shut briefly, rainwater running through his eyelashes as the hand supporting my back gripped me tighter. I allowed my head to bow into his chest, heaving deep, laboured breaths. My fingers curled around his shirt, bunching the once-white material as his body cocooned around me, damp and warm.

I could taste blood.

I could smell burning.

But I could feel Ben.

I felt the movement of his chest against my face. *He must be talking*. I could only hear the ringing.

I spluttered another violent cough, clasping my hand to my mouth as brown blood splattered out. Other people's hands pulled at my shoulders – my body too weak to fight them – laying me back into the grass. A gloved hand bought a plastic mask that smelt of chemicals to my face, but I thrashed it away, reaching for Ben. I needed him. I needed him to keep me alive.

I watched as he waved a hand up, sensing my panic as I shielded my face. He rested his hand on my forearm, catching my gaze; asking silent permission. I slowly relented, allowing him to bring the mask over my nose. Cool mist shot into my airways.

He pulled me back into him, holding the mask in place as I breathed the artificial air.

Something popped softly in my ear. I bought my hand to it, noticing brighter, red blood. A paramedic mopped it away with something cold as sound poured into my mind – quiet and non-decipherable, like everything was underwater – but I was grateful for the return of noise that wasn't ringing. Ben's eyes were fixed on me as I realised just how surrounded we were. Hoses were releasing thundering water in the background, the field covered in vehicles. There were countless police officers and at least two ambulances.

The cool oxygen continued to fill my mouth and nose. Ben screwed his face up; he seemed to be shouting at DS Ernest, who was suddenly standing at my feet. I looked from one to the other, trying to make out the words as their lips moved consecutively.

Ben's fingers gripped me tighter again.

Derek.

"Derek!" I rasped, pulling at Ben's shirt and straining to stand.

My mind emptied, just leaving the devastating image of him slumped, black and blue against the tree, arms quivering around the gun. The oxygen cord tangled around my arm as I staggered. DS Ernest reached to help, but Ben twisted fiercely, surrounding me with his body.

Where is Derek?

Ben gripped my cheeks but it was noise and pain and burning and I screamed out again, thrashing him off, needing to see. I couldn't even hear the words, just feel my throat move; the air push through my lips. My body dipped as I fell again, my knees refusing to hold me. Ben pointed at an ambulance as I ferociously clung to him. The paramedic followed with the oxygen cylinder as Ben pulled me towards the van.

He has to be okay.

I tumbled inside to find Derek hooked up to an ECG machine, his paramedics staring at the squared paper. Fresh tears erupted and I bowed my head over his chest, holding me to him as I listened for his heart again, needing to know he was alive. In amongst the chaos, I needed to feel it.

I dragged the mask aside. "I'm so sorry. It's all my fault." My body shuddered with the sobs.

He coughed. "No, sweetheart, no. You did it, you got us out."

There was sudden movement outside the ambulance doors. Ben shouted something, waving an arm at DS Ernest, who tried to usher him away.

I staggered back to him, swiping the mask off entirely. The words cleared and I slowly made out Ben's yelling.

"I don't care about the case! *You* put her in this situation again! How incompetent do you have to be to let this happen?"

I stepped down to the grass, reaching out to Ben and steadying myself on the open door.

"We'll need a statement from you," DS Ernest explained.

I looked at Ben as the distorted words entered my consciousness in a blur. He supported me firmly, pressing my hip to his, but his body felt tense, animated.

DS Ernest continued. "Ivy, Sam is dead."

I'd known it, but hearing it aloud hit me all over again. My body collapsed into Ben's steady side as the shock took hold.

Sam was dead.

"Is that necessary right now?" Ben shouted furiously, tightening his hold. "She needs to get to hospital."

"This is a murder investigation. Processes need to be followed," DS Ernest replied sternly.

Murder. Sam was murdered.

Derek could have been murdered.

"Processes?" Ben's body shook with rage. "This is where your fucking processes have got us. Look around!"

"You need to calm down, Mr Carlson," DS Ernest commanded as something prickled in the air.

"Don't tell me to *calm down*," Ben seethed, thrusting a finger at the smouldering building. "I didn't see any of your men go in there. You would have left them all to burn!"

DS Ernest placed a hand on my arm.

I flinched.

"Don't you dare touch her," Ben snapped, pulling me to his chest and shoving DS Ernest out of the way.

Fresh chaos erupted as two police officers grabbed Ben from behind. Strong hands held me back as I tried to scream after him.

"Ben!"

30

Painful Healing

Twenty-four painful hours passed until Peter drove Derek back home from hospital. He'd suffered a minor heart attack, along with some superficial injuries, so they'd kept him in for the night. Mary and Peter stayed with us at the house. Me and Susan lay in her bed together most of the night, unable to sleep. Sam was dead, Ben was in police custody, Marcus was in and out of consciousness, Gareth was on the waitlist for a minor surgery, but I was somehow *fine*. Burnt, sore, and coughing, but not hospitalised.

My injuries were nothing compared to how I felt inside.

I was changed, fundamentally changed.

I'd realised it as I stood in Derek's hospital room the day before. A seed of hope had taken root deep inside of me. Marcus had gone too far; they'd all gone too far. This could actually stick. The third man had escaped, for now, but the police even seemed hopeful they'd catch him thanks to a host of local CCTV. Clearly, they hadn't thought anyone would survive to give statements. Clearly, we shouldn't have.

Watching Derek recover added damage to the new scar that seeing him suffer had scorched, but the feeling of it was bittersweet. The scar was there because he was not just alive, but part of my life now, like all of them were.

I stood staring at the lounge wall, trying to understand this new, unnerving feeling of a future, of a choice, of a life. I missed Ben, I knew that much. I missed living with him; I missed laughing with him; I missed him making everything feel better. I'd pleaded and cried to the police, Lucy had yelled, but we'd got nowhere. He would be out today, he had to be, but first I had to survive this emotional dissection.

"It's important to identify the emotions underneath the anger. Anger is usually a reaction to something else," Linda informed me.

I stared at the clock on Susan's mantlepiece as minute twenty-six passed since Linda's arrival that morning. I ran my hands over my jeans, rippling the material. The lounge door was shut, but I could hear Susan on the phone outside, so I couldn't concentrate. I knew Linda meant well; I understood that if I wanted to heal, I needed to do this. Her sessions always helped, eventually; usually the ones that were most uncomfortable.

But today... today I was a shell. I could still smell the smoke, my hands stung from the burns, and every time I swallowed, I was forced to remember Marcus's grip.

"Ivy, what do you think might be the triggers for your anger?" Linda pressed, tilting her worn notebook.

I sighed. "They were all in danger, because of me. I'm angry at Sam, I'm furious that it ended like that with him, and then I'm frustrated at myself for not hating him. I'm angry at the police for arresting Ben; I know you said they're just holding him for a statement, but it's wrong. I feel guilty we're sat here talking. I want to do something. *He* did something, he did the biggest something he could have done."

She nodded slowly. "Why do you feel they were in danger because of you?"

I ground my teeth, I hated when she did that, picked on the least significant detail. What did it matter? "If I hadn't reported it, if I'd kept them out of it, none of this would have happened."

"How could you have kept them out of it?"

I realised this was a circle we'd been around before: the one where I admitted that it would have been better if I'd stayed at Henworth; where she would sympathetically sigh and tell me otherwise.

"I know. We've been over this, but this proves it, doesn't it? Derek almost died; Ben ran into a fire, which is literally what killed his father; Susan was worried sick."

"Why?" she asked, staring at me.

"Why what?"

"Why did they all do those things?"

I replayed her words, slowly, confused. "Because of Marcus,

because of the police, because they had no choice."

Ironically this was just making me angrier as pressure built in my chest. Her bright yellow maxi-dress was adding to my rage – the cheerful colour seemed totally wrong.

"I think they did it because they care about you," she stated calmly. "I understand you're angry about the investigation; I expect you to feel angry about Marcus and his actions. You probably feel angry they survived; it would be perfectly reasonable. I'm just picking up on your wording around other people and their choices." She put her notebook next to her on the sofa and I swallowed, sensing she was about to say something heavy. "Since we have worked together, I've watched you grow, Ivy. I have watched you bravely face your trauma and talk about the abuse you have suffered."

I flinched.

"I know you don't like me putting it that plainly, but it's important. You escaped, you started healing, you faced it. But when Marcus came to the apartment, you told me you didn't fight. When Ben struggled to process his own feelings regarding the television appearance, you defaulted to blaming yourself. Now, you talk about anger that everyone else was there, not that this happened."

My lungs tightened as I pulled at my fingers, feeling emotions being dragged out of me like a serrated blade.

Linda went on. "Talk to me about what drove you to go back in after Sam?"

"He was trapped," I defended instantly.

"Yes, but earlier you told me you believed he had already passed; this has unofficially been confirmed by the police. I'm wondering what you were feeling, I'm wondering what value you placed on your own life when you weighed it up."

I blinked, my eyes dry. "He was trapped, he didn't deserve that, not because of me." My voice cracked as I fought to form the words.

"Did you put him in that building?"

I didn't answer, so she raised her eyebrows. I shook my head.

"Did you start the fire?"

I shook my head again.

"Did you choose to live at Henworth?"

I swallowed. "I chose to stay."

"Why?"

"We've talked about this before."

"We have. I'm wondering if you have allowed yourself to let go of any of that guilt. Guilt is a reaction we experience to prevent us doing something again. You chose to go to the police to protect people – you couldn't have known this would happen. You are the victim, they are not your responsibility; their actions are exactly that, their own. By telling the police, you handed them that responsibility, it was *their* role to keep others safe. I'm wondering, if you *had* accepted that, if you would have chosen not to go back in."

I said nothing, only the pounding of my heart sounding through my body.

"You also said you were angry that Sam passed. I want you to understand that it's okay to grieve for him, let yourself experience those feelings when you feel safe to do so. I would encourage you to write them down, then we can talk through them at our next session. I understand you are exhausted and I'm not intending to push you today, I'm trying to help you process this incredibly traumatic event. I want you to try and see yourself as Ivy White. The brave, strong young woman who stood up for what was right. Who is loved and cared for by her parents, Susan and Derek. Ivy who has a future, who has choices. Who *will* recover from this. I want you to try and see that woman – because if you can see her, it might help you to understand why Ben ran into that building; why Derek is so astounded by your fearlessness."

I bit down into my tongue.

"It's not your fault, Ivy. It's the choice of those around you to love you and care about you, not yours."

I had nothing to say, unable to process her words.

She finished by explaining that Barnes and Dores, the police officers who had been working with Henworth, had been struck off with criminal charges pending. I felt a surprising and sudden sadness.

Susan joined us then, to my instant relief. Lucy was due to bring the kids round soon, so she could head to the police station for Ben, so I mimicked Susan's more sensible emotions of relief and solace. I needed Linda to feel I was stable enough for her to leave. There was something about hearing the officers were being prosecuted for 'abuse of power'; for 'coercion' and 'fraud'; for 'rape'. The label made it real; I couldn't help wondering if it would have been easier not to live with that label. I had collected so many badges – abducted, brainwashed, neglected – giving me ample reasons to never recover. Rape victim was a bold and terrifying label to add.

Compounding all of this, as I fought the tears, was the desperate longing for Ben's comfort, the deep desire for him to reach for my hand; to hold me. I couldn't talk to Susan about how I was really feeling, I'd hurt her enough and I needed Linda to leave.

The one person I felt I could truly open up to, who didn't drown me with pity or see me as a disaster, was the one person who wasn't available.

31

The Beginning

When the doorbell chimed at midday, I was there. Sophie burst through the door mid-ramble, and Lucy followed in an obvious panic, dragging Isac past the small iron gate.

"Hi Sophie, Isac, come on in." I just about managed to maintain a cheerful tone. "This is Susan and Derek." I gestured to my parents as the three of them entered the small hallway.

Derek was sat in the lounge, but we could see him through the door, his ankle propped up on a stool.

"I made gingerbread men. I thought you could help me decorate them," Susan told Sophie and Isac excitedly.

I looked at Lucy, who was completely fraught, following her back outside so we could talk.

"So, he's out?" I fumbled as quickly as I could form the words.

She nodded. "They're releasing him now. No charges, thank god. I swear Ivy, I would've lost it. I would have actually lost my shit this time."

I agreed, nodding, hugging her tightly as she clung to me.

"I wouldn't have worked with the police on any of it, not until they released him. We would have found a way."

"I know, I know. Are you sure you'll be okay with the kids? Thank you so much for this. Thank Susan again for me."

I smiled at her as we withdrew. "Of course, Susan has baked three whole trays of biscuits; it's been the first time she's smiled in days. Just... ask him to text me or call me, will you? Or something. Just... let me know that you're both alright."

"Of course," she replied, relaxing slightly and pulling her keys out of her pocket. "It'll take just under an hour to get to Rose Cottage, he needs to go there and calm down. I spoke to Catherine and sorted it all."

"Good. How did you convince him?"

"'Convince' isn't the word I'd use. He ran into a burning building after more than twenty years of repressing his feelings about Dad, not to mention everything else. He needs time. He could have got into serious trouble."

"I know. I feel awful."

"I know, but listen..." She took my hands. "I was starting to worry he *couldn't* care anymore, you know? Yes, this is all a mess, but I don't remember ever seeing him like this. Saturday morning, he was so worked up because he hadn't spoken to you. I barely had time to sober up. He never talks to me about stuff. When Susan called, he lost it. I mean, dick move from you." She smiled, but I could tell she was only half joking. "How could you not tell me you'd fallen out like that? I know what he's like, believe me." She squeezed my fingers. "You don't keep secrets, okay, not about weird text messages, or my idiot brother. Not from me. I bloody love you, but I swear I'm going to bang both your heads together, Jesus Christ."

Some part of me deep inside clicked into place, like it had always been there.

"I love you too," I said, smiling.

I took a second to gather myself before I went back into the house. Isac was hovering by the door to the lounge, shuffling nervously.

I popped a hand on his shoulder reassuringly. "What did you bring in your backpack? Is that a spaceship on it?"

He nodded shyly. I gently took the bag and led him to the rug between the sofas. Looking through the bag, I found a new magazine with some toy cars attached to the front.

"This is Derek, my dad. He's one of the people I was looking for, remember?"

Isac nodded, still unsure.

"He loves puzzles, and when he was young, he used to fix motorbikes. In fact, he is very good at making things and fixing things."

The sound of Sophie giggling rang through the house from the kitchen. I started going through the glossy pages with Isac while Derek took the cars out of the packaging.

We were halfway through lunch when my phone finally buzzed.

LUCY

I've just dropped him off to get his car and some other stuff. I'm staying to make sure he goes. His phone is totally dead, but he's okay, I think. It's hard to tell, to be honest. Are the kids behaving? xx

ME

Oh, thank god. Of course they are. Sophie is decorated like a gingerbread man herself, I'm afraid, and Isac and Derek started sketching out some sort of racetrack to build. What did Ben say? xx

LUCY

A lot, as you would imagine. Asked about you, mostly. I've offered to stay with him, to get the kids for the weekend. I don't like the idea of him being on his own, but you know what he's like xx

ME

I agree, not after the fire. I could go, to support him. I could get the train? xx

There was a long pause. I could see her three dots bouncing up and down on the screen.

LUCY

You need to rest xx

ME

I'm fine xx

LUCY

Even if that were true, I'm not sure it's a good idea. You can't drive, you two haven't even spoken, and Ben is not in his right mind right now xx

ME

If it were you or me, he'd go. We don't need to talk
about before, but he shouldn't be on his own. I can get
the train, I know the way xx

LUCY

Susan and Derek need you, Derek needs to rest, not
worry about you xx

ME
It's Ben... xx

LUCY
Exactly xx

Another pause.

I re-read the messages. My pulse quickened at the thought. The
thought of him on his own was wrong. I was sure he'd be exhausted,
and probably not excited to see me, but he'd been there when I needed
someone so many times. I could always come back if it went badly.

LUCY
Look, he's my brother, so this is hard. I care about you
both, a lot. Go if you want to, but only if you're in love
with him like he is with you. Please. I'm worried about
him. Think about it. I'll see you when I get back xxx

The train whirred as the fields merged in a blur of green.

I'd already known the answer to Lucy's question. With each
passing station, my nerves grew. My brain played out a hundred things
he might say as he opened the door – many of them negative. Susan
and Derek hadn't disagreed with me going. In fact, Derek had said, in
front of Lucy, that I should go, because 'Ben needs people'. Then, just

as I'd thought my emotional tank was full, Isac had tapped me on the shoulder. He'd pulled out a photograph, set in a decorated cardboard frame he'd made, from Lucy's bag. It was of me and Ben at their house when we'd gone over for dinner; when I'd given Isac the camera.

I took the photo frame from my weekend bag and put it on the train table. I touched my fingertip to the glossy faces. We had been laughing, not realising anyone was watching. The way I was looking at him – eyes wide, teeth showing, the way he was looking at me – captivated... who would have known those two people had a care in the world?

The train journey was surreal, and I'd had to rush to catch it. It had been a relief that I didn't have time to stress about what to wear. I'd felt strange slipping into the green velvet underwear set I knew he liked; it felt presumptuous, and inappropriate, but I liked it, so why wouldn't I wear that, right? The dark mauve, short, belted dress had been an easier choice.

I decided I'd call a taxi at other end for the last bit of the journey: the fifteen minutes Lucy had driven in a frenzy all those months ago. I wondered, if me and Ben had met as two normal people that day, if I'd just been a neighbour, or something simpler, whether we would have been drawn together like we had been. I considered how things would have developed if we'd just had sex, if that was all this really was after all? Attraction? Maybe Ben had just been acting on his sense of duty?

The thought felt like a splinter.

Could we really know how we both felt, in amongst all the mess?

As my station was called, a missed call came through. My signal had been dipping in and out throughout the journey.

BEN

Tell me you're okay? How's Derek? I only just got my phone working. I tried to call, but it rang through xxxxx

ME

Thank god they let you out. Me and Lucy were so worried. I'm so sorry, I told them to let you go. Told

them I wouldn't co-operate, but it was no good. Are
you okay? Derek is fine, back home recovering. I'm
fine.

BEN

I was worried about you, too. I'll be following it up.
The whole thing was absurd. How are your lungs?
Derek's heart? Lucy said you had the kids, are they
alright? Are you not home? We need to talk. I need to
talk to you about everything. I meant to on Saturday. I
should have xxxxx

ME

I'm on the train x

BEN

Why are you on a train?

The brakes screeched and I made my way onto the platform at
the familiar little station. Standing there was surreal, but the taxi I'd
called was ready and waiting, so I didn't dwell on the feeling. I wasn't
exactly sure why, but I asked the driver to drop me at the top of the
road, where the verge started. Part of me was nervous about seeing
Ben, wanting to prolong the moment. A silly, sentimental part of me
wanted everything to come full circle.

The verge squelched under my feet. I paused in the dark,
remembering the awkwardness of our exchange when I'd left on foot
for the station before. I thought about how my heart had skipped a
beat when Ben followed me and reached for my arm. My phone buzzed
in my pocket again. I was committed, so I ignored it and kept walking.
I didn't want to read his text telling me not to come. I'd known that
day that I should've just walked away, yet every part of me had wanted
to stay.

The front of Rose Cottage appeared piece by piece as I slowed,
letting go of my memories and feeling the more real nerves of the
present. It was hard to make out in the dark, but the light was on

downstairs, reflecting off the silver Audi parked in exactly the same spot to the side. I rested a hand on the little gate, looking down the path I'd first walked with Lucy. Back when she had stopped. Of all the people, *she* had stopped.

I toyed with the idea of it being fate, but that would mean everything that had occurred before that pivotal moment was also meant to happen.

Getting into Ben's Audi for the first time had been nerve-wracking. I'd felt giddy and foolish, suddenly alone with him. Looking back, it made no sense for him to have been so insistent.

My feet dared to crunch down the path, heading round to the side, towards the light, but as I was drawing a deep breath, the white door swung open, the light from the house highlighting Ben. His dark hair was wet, swept away from his handsome face, his smart glasses perched on his nose, hiding his soulful eyes. He was wearing jeans; nothing else – just out of the shower, no doubt.

I stilled.

He stared.

The breeze dragged loose hair over my face. I tucked it back, forcing a smile.

He didn't smile back. He strode barefoot down the path to where I stayed rooted, sweeping me up into his arms. I let out a strained whimper as his fingers laced through my hair and he held me, wrapping his familiar body around mine. I could smell his soap; his aftershave. It was intoxicating. *He* was intoxicating.

Leaning back, he took my face in his warm hands, running his eyes all over me as we stood in the front garden, surrounded by rose bushes.

"I'm alright," I whispered instinctively, seeing the panic in his eyes.

His thumbs moved over my cheeks. "How? Why did you come?"

I felt myself smile as everything stilled in the way it always did with him, as every other thought and doubt and feeling fizzled away.

I shrugged, keeping my arms around his back. "Because."

We looked at each other for another rich, full second. Neither of us had any words. Maybe we didn't need them. I hadn't seen him this raw, this fraught, before.

Then his mouth broke into a smile, his shoulders lowering, relaxing against me. That was enough. That said it all between us somehow.

He bent down, scooping me up and easily tucking my legs around his waist. I pressed my lips to his, shutting my eyes and gripping his neck. I didn't need to know anything else in that moment; all I needed was him. His hand was pressed into my shoulder blades, keeping our chests together, stopping me from falling back.

Until I bounced steadily on top of a mattress.

The second he drew away, I pulled him closer, my body raging with an overwhelming urgency, appeased only by his frantic, breathy kisses. His tongue pushed my lips apart, sending my body arching further into his as his fingers ran all over me – up my legs, across my hips, over my face. I needed him everywhere, all over me, all at once. He dragged his lips from mine as his fingers fought the poppers of my navy coat, the layers of clothing peeling away. Each piece bought us closer, but it wasn't enough. My hands roved his bare back; my nails gripping as he swiped my dress off in one motion, immediately finding my breasts, cupping and kissing.

My head tilted back with a groan as I reached for his trousers and felt him. Felt him fully. Appreciated his hardness with my palm and tugged at his belt. He lifted his head, gasping for air as he kicked them off. I couldn't help but laugh as he hesitated while pulling my tights off. We laughed together, temporarily broken out of our lustful haze, remembering. We settled back into each other's company like we always did. It was easy. Complete.

When his nose pressed into the lace of my green underwear, my nails dug deeper into his firm shoulders. I felt every part of my body, head to toe, as his tongue slipped a long, ravenous stroke at my margins. We had touched each other tenderly, admired and caressed each other for weeks, but this was nothing like before. This was driven purely by need; a long, stifled need. His eyes shot to me as a wicked grin spread across his face. Dropping to his knees, he pulled me to the edge of the bed, fingers marking my thighs. I gasped, but he didn't stop. He slid off my underwear. After all that time, after all that tension and build up, he was finally between my legs, both of us drunk on each other and wanting more, needing more.

We were finally about to have it all.

The cool air hit my sensitive skin first as I was exposed, then I felt his warm breath and soft, slick tongue. My shoulders dipped back into the mattress as my spine flexed with pleasure. His mouth moved hungrily up the sensitive inside of my thigh; I could feel the tip of his nose and the drag of his lips. My leg tensed as he squeezed. His other hand took my breast and cupped it over the top of my lacy bra. My body was his and he knew it. My body was his and I didn't care. He knew it as my hand lunged for his and our fingers locked. All I could feel was his tongue, his hands, the increasing pace of his breath.

The tip of his tongue danced in circles before it plunged inside, releasing waves of indulgent ecstasy down my legs and all the way to my toes. I wanted him, I needed all of him. I felt my body humming with pleasure as it built and built, my core aching to be filled as he worked me into a frenzy.

I gripped his hair and pulled him away, sitting up slightly so I could run my hands up his legs, stopping to grip him briefly, before exposing everything inside his boxers: all that was left between us. He helped me to pull them down, happy to oblige, sliding a hand under my back and pressing the other on the mattress near my head, dragging me up the bed and crawling between my legs. So ready. So hard.

With a single move, his lips were on mine as my tongue danced with his. I nipped at his lip and he pressed closer against me, sending another wave of tingling pleasure, my body pleading for him, my mind wild. I felt a ping as he undid my bra and threw it to the side, pressing his chest back against me. He looked into my eyes, catching just a single rushed breath, before diving his tongue into my mouth so deeply I could feel nothing else. I moaned desperately against his lips, and it was at that exact, perfect moment that he thrust inside of me.

He groaned deliciously into my mouth, but it didn't feel like it came from his lips. It felt like it came from his entire body. His forehead came to rest against mine as the pleasure took hold, his fingers tightening on my breast, escalating everything as he thrust, deep and steady. I moaned, letting my body bow to him, to mould and clench around him. We were the perfect fit and the harder I felt him become, stretching inside me, the more I needed.

He increased his pace as I groaned with each stroke – with each sensation – until we both totally lost control. Until my body shook. I shouted his name, finally breaking through our perfect silence, and he pulsed in time with me, groaning as he sunk his teeth into my neck.

We lay there breathlessly, still connected: my pulse racing; his breaths deep and unsteady.

Shifting together, we lay silently beside one another. Ben reached for the duvet and covered us both, tucking me tightly against his hot skin. For the first time, I noticed the cosy, raised room we'd been in before. He must have carried me straight up the metal stairs; I had been so engrossed in him I hadn't paid attention to anything else. The chunky furniture and taupe walls were only lit by the light of the lounge.

Still, neither of us spoke. Ben nudged his arm under my neck so we could face each other, our bodies further intertwined. His hand stroked the tussled hair from my face. His eyes shut briefly before he planted a soft kiss on my forehead, his fingers brushing my back. My heart lurched in my chest. I realised he still had his glasses on; they were wonky against his thick eyebrows. Steadily, I guided my fingers to straighten them, to frame the eyes I was so completely lost in. I kissed the smile that broke on his face, a lingering brush of my lips on his. Ben's hand tucked my face into his neck and we slotted entirely together. Even our feet found each other as we lay there.

I didn't realise how tired I'd been until we'd found that moment of perfect peace. When I stirred from my sudden sleep, which must have been half an hour or so later, Ben was still fast asleep. The dim light highlighted the trail of clothes on the floor and I couldn't help but smile. I crept up and slipped on some of my short pyjamas, leaving him to rest. The metal steps were cold on my feet as I snuck down into the familiar kitchen.

As I moved through the cottage, I drank it all in all over again. The tartan armchair, the small sofa, the window to the garden, the fox draught excluder, all of it was as it had been. I noticed on the worktop there was an unwrapped pizza by the oven. I popped it in and made myself a drink of orange squash – the taste sweet and fresh on my tongue. It felt homely here, more than I would've thought. My shoulders lifted, a slight chill shuddering through me, so I paced across the living space to sit in the armchair whilst the oven whirred.

After I'd texted Susan and Derek, my hands rubbed some warmth into my arms. I'd reassured them; told them that Ben had been pleased to see me – which I supposed was one way of putting it.

It was funny how life worked, how many 'what ifs' came together to form most of our lives. What if the car hadn't broken down? What if Sophie hadn't fallen in the river? I stood as I heard the stairs clang, and spotted Ben stretching and walking down in his boxers, interrupting the quiet.

"Stay there," he said easily as he softly smiled at me, walking over.

My happiness made me almost delirious, like we were in a dream. It was almost too much, too easy. The feeling of just being content, of being safe. I was determined to savour every drop.

I tilted my head awkwardly, standing by the chair as I silently watched him draw closer. As if my words would shatter some sort of wonderful illusion. He ran a hand steadily over my waist and positioned himself behind me, looking out of the window at the peaceful darkness beyond. I could see our reflection, see us stood together, see his smile. He looked happy.

"What are you doing?" I asked as he traced two fingers up my arm. My neck rolled at his touch.

"Reminiscing," he answered as his palm reached my shoulder and stopped. He planted a long, soft kiss on the back of my scar.

I blinked with realisation, watching in the glass.

"I didn't have you down as the sentimental type," I joked, partially to break the tension as the emotion rose from deep inside me.

His lips kissed their way up my neck and I watched as my chest arched up in response.

"I'm not, but I remember when you showed me." He paused to brush my hair around to my other shoulder, the ends tickling my skin as the movement exposed more of my neck to him. "And even though I was shocked – guilty, because I'd been so dismissive – this tiny, terrible part of me got distracted by undressing you. Now, here we are."

"Here we are," I said, a little breathily. I turned to him. "I put the pizza in the oven. You didn't eat it."

"I had other priorities." He grinned. "I *am* hungry, but I'm hungry for other things."

We swayed closer to one another. I felt the warmth of his breath as the material of his boxers tickled my thighs.

"You should eat."

"*You* should be begging me to take you back to bed."

I swallowed as I felt my body spark. "Oh, is that so?"

He hummed, running his fingertips lazily up my thigh. I lifted myself onto my toes; our lips grew closer, but didn't touch, as we tested each other.

"Maybe you should be the one begging me, Ben? Begging for me to let you." I tried very hard to keep a straight face as his fingers teased higher; as I grew more and more sensitive.

He pulled away. "We need to talk first."

I recoiled from the sudden space. "*You* want to talk? Blimey."

"I mean it," he said more firmly. "We... I have things I need to say, should've said."

When the pizza was cooked and I'd grabbed a jumper, Ben insisted I sit down in the armchair, covering my legs with a blanket. I'd already eaten, and certainly wasn't thinking anything sensible, so I enjoyed a mug of tea as we relaxed and caught up on everything. The police had held Ben to get a statement, needing him to be calm, and not wanting us to corroborate. I mean, that wasn't exactly how he worded it, but it was the gist. Ben had needed a couple of stitches on his arm from climbing through the window to reach me.

He climbed through the window.

I'd wanted to ask more, but my throat choked at the thought. At the thought of what he'd done.

"I knew you were coming on Saturday," he admitted.

My body tensed at the change of tone. I watched his throat bob as he swallowed.

"I wanted, needed, to talk to you. About before. But I don't know, seeing you again, just you and me... You do something to my brain, I swear. It's like I can't think."

I smiled at him instantly; the last few days has cracked me open and I was done hiding my feelings, fighting my body. "You knew I was coming?"

"Of course. I'd been running over in my head what I was going to say. That wet t-shirt did not help me focus, that's why you have to stay over there." He gestured to the armchair, to the blanket covering my bare legs. "So I can get all of this out."

Of course, he'd known I was going to be there. Of course, he'd wanted to talk. Something in my chest fluttered as my eyes widened with anticipation.

He continued, taking a deep breath. "When you started saying that you wanted to leave, I panicked. I realised that you wouldn't be just mine. That you'd want to go out in the world, and I got, well, jealous. When you came to me, I should've understood, but instead, I put my own feelings first and got offended. I should've given you space. You were right."

"It's okay," I soothed, needing to reassure him, clutching the corner of the blanket.

"No, it's not. I shouldn't have said what I said about the show. For what's it's worth, you really held your own, especially with the questions about Sam, but the rest was just hard for me to watch. I knew I'd hurt you, and when I came home and you were gone, I knew I should've fixed it, but by then I thought it was too late. Then Saturday night was a mess, and then the fire..."

"I'm sorry too," I said, leaning towards him, my heart pounding.

His words were singing to me, telling me everything I'd been trying so hard to convince myself I could live without. "I knew I was hurting you, but the more I tried to explain, the worse I made it. If I'd known you were going to be upset by the way I acted on the show, I would've done things differently, it was just the heat of the moment. "

He frowned. "You have absolutely nothing to apologise for, as usual. You did nothing wrong."

"I can't believe you went into the fire, Ben. What that meant to you..."

His eyes were wide and intense as he replied, his voice breaking. "It was about what *you* mean to me, Ivy. I didn't even think, not about anything, except you. God, it petrifies me that you went back in for Sam. After everything. You're worth so much to so many people... I don't know what I would have done if I'd been too late. When I found you, for a few seconds, it was like you were dead. I... I felt like I might die as well."

His words were raw and powerful and filled me with choking emotion.

"What happened, Ben?"

He sighed, and began to fill in the gaps.

32

Ben's Chapter

2 days earlier

"I've fucked it all," I announced, sat on a very hungover Lucy's bed on Sunday morning.

I didn't know why the words had come out, but they had. I would probably regret it.

She rubbed her eyes and groaned. "Good morning, sunshine. Can you, like, get me a coffee or something before we— wait, why are you in here? Where's Ivy?"

I handed her the coffee I'd known she would need. "She's gone."

"Where did she go?" she asked, sitting up and taking the drink with her un-injured hand. "Where are the kids?"

"The kids are watching TV. I gave them breakfast while you snored."

"Hey. Be kind. Aah, it was a fun night. Charlie is fun..." She smiled to herself, reminiscing about something I doubted I wanted to know. "So, sorry, she went home? That seems odd."

"She went home last night with Derek." My throat bobbed as I swallowed.

"I'd assumed she'd have stayed when she found out you were here. I enjoyed that, by the way, thank you, that was funny. Ergh, Charlie made us do tequila shots, I can still taste it." She grabbed her phone from the side table. "I'm going to give him a piece of my mind. Wait, sorry, sorry, what have you fucked, exactly?"

"Things with Ivy, Lucy, for Christ's sake. I just... froze. It makes no sense. I've been going over and over it in my head."

She looked at me with one eye significantly more open than the other, her hair wildly tousled in different directions. "You're making no sense. Hold on. You guys had a tiff. That was all, right?"

I saw her body tense. *Shit.* "Is that what she told you?" My chest twinged. Ivy hadn't told Lucy; she'd kept it quiet. I was both sad and appreciative of yet another part of her.

"She said she moved out to get some space, but that you two were fine."

"Oh."

"*Oh*?" Lucy straightened up, nearly spilling her coffee. "Explain. Now."

I looked down, uneasy.

"Now, Ben," she repeated. "You guys are together, you had, like, that theatre date. It was all sickening and gross."

I pushed my glasses further up my nose.

"Spit it out!"

"It just got complicated, Lucy. I tried. Trust me, I tried so hard."

"Wait, did you guys break up? Did I ambush her with you? What did you do?" Lucy dropped her phone in the duvet and scrambled to find it.

"What are you doing?"

"I'm texting her to see if she's okay while you explain exactly what you did, because I'm telling you right now, Ben, I may actually kill you this time. I honestly thought this was it. The way you two looked at each other – even from that first day – I always thought you'd be alone forever, and then along came this short, sad girl who seemed to just fit with you."

"You're not helping."

She plopped her phone down and stared me out, folding her arms.

I sighed. "The dates were great, more than great. In fact, most of the time we spent together was just like this haze. Then Jessica showed up again."

"Again? Oh god, you didn't sleep with her, did you?"

"No! Of course not. We had a fight afterwards. Jessica said so many foul things. Then everything at the office escalated. Ivy was doing all this amazing work and it looked like it was making her happy, so I offered her a job."

You offered her a *job*?" Lucy shrieked at me, nearly choking on a mouthful of coffee. "Oh, good god, Ben. The girl didn't need that pressure; she needs time to explore the world, not be tied down. Why couldn't she just keep living with you for a bit?"

I tensed. "Of course she could've. It wasn't about the money. I thought that was what she wanted. It was going so well."

"She was trying to impress you! She felt guilty, so guilty, for everything, and she was trying to make it up to you. Ivy needed the opposite; she needed you to support her, not validate that she needed to work for you!"

"It wasn't like that."

How could she have thought that? I adored her. I adored having her in the apartment, having her in the office. Surely she knew? Surely she knew what she'd brought into my life? If anything, I owed her.

"So then what happened?" Lucy's phone buzzed and my eyes darted to the text. "It's Charlie, calm down."

"She told me she didn't want the job, and I didn't handle it well. I got frustrated with her and couldn't understand."

"God, Ben."

"I know. Don't you think I know? At the time it was so intense, and she pushed my buttons on purpose."

I thought back to the morning before the show; how I'd been so enraged as she stormed out of the room, looking so goddamn hot in those tiny pyjamas she wore. Everything about her had driven me mad that morning, because all I wanted to do was have every single part of her.

"I was scared, Lucy. I was losing her, I could tell. When I watched the TV show, it just confirmed it. Seeing her flirt with that prick, seeing him all over her. Seeing her laugh. She cried with laughter for him, with him. Everyone in the fucking office watched it. It was humiliating. I was so angry; I needed time to think. When I got home, she'd packed up her stuff and gone."

Lucy rolled her eyes. "I'm going to murder both of you. I mean it. I get why *you* didn't tell me, because you are so bloody emotionally illiterate, but Ivy? Oh god, she must want to kill me after last night." She groaned and threw her hand over her face, dramatically dragging her cheeks down.

I remembered it vividly, seeing them tangled in the mud. My heart had pounded the way it only did for Ivy, but she'd barely noticed me until I'd tried to help her up. Fuck, I should have just held her and not let her go.

"Please tell me you've spoken since the show." Lucy peeled back the bandage on her hand, inspecting the small cut.

"She called me and I told her I hated it. I tried not to, I did. I knew I wasn't in the right mind, but it just came out and I couldn't take it back. I said some really shitty things. I heard how much it hurt her. Lucy, I heard it in her voice, and then I didn't even come home. How the hell do we come back from that? I was jealous and embarrassed and I took it out on her."

"Okay. Okay," she repeated, leaning forwards as I felt my eyebrows furrow.

When I'd arrived home and she was gone, I should've just got in the car. *Why didn't I go after her there and then?*

"God, you have seriously fucked this up. Couldn't you have had this tantrum a bit later down the line? It's great that you are finally deciding to feel your feelings again after spending your entire adult life as a robot, but talk about picking your moments! I am way too hungover for this level of idiocy." She shook her head. "Now, Ivy is obviously on an emotional journey, with a heap of trauma to resolve, so, yes, you two having this relationship now is bad timing, but look at all you've worked through already! You shouldn't have offered her the job, she needs to feel free and independent, not like you're trapping her or expecting her to repay you for anything. Ivy only went on that show because we all wanted her to. Of course, Robert tried his luck, he was probably chasing her five minutes of fame, but I'm telling you now: she wasn't interested. He even asked her out, but all she did was mope about missing you. You have *nothing* to be jealous about."

"Lucy, I can't go on like this; I can't like her this much, it's choking me. Literally choking me. Last night..."

"Dear lord, tell me what happened last night."

"Nothing. That's the problem. I should have apologised. I intended to. I went over it in my head, again and again, but then she was there, just looking at me with that sad, sweet look on her face. My mind just went blank."

Lucy's eyes widened. "You mean she left with Derek and you said *nothing*?"

"Pretty much."

"You realise she'll now think this is what you wanted? She was insecure enough already, Ben, about the show, about her goddamn life. She must be in *bits*. How did I not see it?" Lucy ran her hands over her face again. "Okay. Right. I need a shower. This all feels like a weird dream. I will shower, you will make me toast, and we will figure this out, okay?" She looked at me sternly.

"Okay."

She leant forwards to hug me; she smelt like a pub carpet.

I wondered what Ivy was doing. Did she prefer living back home? Did it feel like her real home now? No, again, did it feel like her real home *again*? I hadn't expected her to look so beautiful last night; it was like I'd forgotten how perfect she was. She must have been freezing; I must've made her feel so uncomfortable. She didn't even want to take off her wet shirt. I didn't deserve her, what was I doing? She needed someone complete, and whole, and emotionally available. Someone who made her cry with laughter. This was always going to happen; I was always going to mess it up, and she would leave me. Why had I ever thought we could be anything more? I should never have invited her to live with me, it wasn't like me at all, but then, I couldn't have watched anyone else look after her.

"I can't tell whether my headache is from you or the alcohol," Lucy grunted as she came over to where I was sat and took a bite of toast.

"Sorry, Luce."

"Well, I'm glad you're human after all. It's fine, Ben, you're allowed to have feelings. You should talk to me about them more next time, maybe before you take them out on others." She flicked on the kettle. "What do you want to do?"

"What do you mean?" I asked, resting my forehead in my hands on the worktop.

"Well, are you going to go over there? Are you done? You should talk it out either way because she is definitely best friend material and you're not ruining that for me."

"I think she's done."

"I think we've established that you have no idea what she thinks. What I want to know is what do *you* want?" She pointed her toast at me, scattering crumbs everywhere.

"I want *her*. I want to apologise and fix it."

"Okay. You're sure?" she asked, spreading more crumbs – I questioned why I'd bothered giving her a plate.

"Of course I am, but it's gone too far. She doesn't need someone like me. She'll have plenty of men obsessed with her, Lucy. A bunch, and you know it. She should pick one that can be more supportive. She should find one that can be steady for her, that's warmer."

"Oh, Ben." Lucy reached for my hand. "When you allow yourself to be yourself, anyone would be lucky to have you. Ivy felt so lucky to have you. PTSD is complex and messy, but she doesn't strike me as the type who doesn't know her own mind. I mean, to survive what she did, to have made the life she has, it's pretty nuts when you think about it. I'd be lying if I told you that it won't be hard, she has so much to see of the world, to learn about herself; who knows what that will look like? But, I guess, that's for her to decide, not us. You need to speak to her."

"What if she *is* done, what if she needs more space?"

My phone buzzed against the side. I glanced down at the screen to see Susan's name flashing. My stomach twisted. Why was she calling me? Was it Ivy? I picked up.

"Hello, Ben?"

"Hi, is everything okay?" I asked, sensing something off in her tone.

332

"I'm probably just being paranoid, but I don't suppose you're still connected to that police app on Ivy's phone? She said she was going to the shop, but Derek never came back from taking the bin out. So, call me crazy, but I rang the shop, and she never got there. I'm sure—"

I stopped listening as I put her on speaker phone so I could bring up the app. Lucy's eyes widened as she picked up the thread of our conversation. There was an alert; she was in the middle of a field.

My breath stilled.

"Shit, Ben," Lucy gasped. "I know where she is; that's the old traveller site."

I felt a wave of nausea as I made for the door, grabbing my keys and my phone, leaving the map open. Lucy shouted something after me, but I didn't listen. This couldn't be happening again.

The car engine roared as I drove towards the flashing dot. God, if I'd just spoken to her last night. If anything happened to her, I wouldn't forgive myself. Not this time. Not again. What could she possibly be doing there?

I was ten minutes away. Ten minutes too far.

Without thinking, I followed the fresh tyre marks in the wet grass, veering off the road and over the field. There was a building and it was on fire.

Fire.

I rammed my foot down on the pedal, powering towards the collapsing structure. I threw myself out of the door before I'd completely let go of the handbrake, skidding to a stop in the muddied grass.

"Ivy!" I shouted desperately. "Ivy!"

She was inside. I knew she was inside.

I ran to the entrance but the smoke and flames made it impossible to see anything. I held my arm over my eyes, blinking. My heart thumped as the burning filled my nostrils. Marcus was there. That bastard was pinning Ivy to the wall. He had his foul hands around her perfect neck. He was killing her. Strangling her.

Instantly, I was running, swooping to grab a metal pole glinting in the embers. I didn't care that it burnt my hands as I swung it. When it struck his head and he fell, vibrations ran down the pole and into my arms, the momentum sending me skidding across the floor, barely missing a wisp of flame. Before I could reach her, Marcus was back on his feet, so I swung again, roaring through gritted teeth. I needed to get to Ivy; I needed to get her out.

Marcus threw himself at me. I would kill him, I decided. I would end his fucking life, rip it from him with my bare hands. Our feet scuffed across the burning floor as we lunged back and forth, dragging and throwing each other towards the eyewatering heat. My hate and rage fuelled me like the petrol had fuelled the fire. After all he had done to her, after the pain he'd caused, how dare he touch her. She may not want to be mine, but he would not touch her ever again.

Thrusting my elbow, I sent him flying into the back wall.

"Ivy?" I shouted, but she was gone.

I fell to my knees, wildly searching, running my hands over the sizzling debris as the smoke darkened. I made out the hunched figure of Marcus leaning against a door. I saw his fist too late as it hit my jaw. It hurt. It fucking hurt, and I wouldn't fucking take any more. There was no time. Why wouldn't he stay down? He was relentless, inhuman, evil. I thought of Ivy fighting him, all those years; all of them by herself. Never again. His nostrils flared as he clenched a fist, sweat glistening, spitting into the flames, grinning at me. I barrelled into him, gripping his shoulders and slamming them into the flames, throwing all my weight against him, riding it to the ground. Something cracked against the burning concrete so I pushed again, and again. I dug my fingers into his flesh and I slammed him down.

"Bastard!" I screamed as his body went lax. "You fucking bastard!"

His eyes rolled, but I couldn't stop. Didn't want to.

My fists pounded into his flesh. *Thump, thump, thump.* But then I remembered her touch, remembered that broken, sad look in her eyes and my fists relented, letting his body flop back.

"Ivy," I whispered, trying to stand. "Ivy!"

I screamed, but my voice was hoarse.

Flames licked at my ankles, I smacked them out, falling over the walls, searching for her. I needed her; I needed to find her. This couldn't be the end. They couldn't win. She needed to live. She deserved to live.

I slammed my hands against the door Marcus had shut, screaming, seeing movement. On the other side, crumbling wood crashed glowing to the floor.

Ivy was trapped.

I leapt for the main front door; the air was fresh and cold outside so I gulped it in. I sprinted as fast as I could around the building, desperately searching for another way in, when I found the broken, frosted window.

There she was, by a toilet block. She was on the floor. God, she was on the floor. She wasn't moving.

"Ivy!" I cried. "Hold on!"

Ramming my elbow through the remaining glass, my feet found grip in the warming stones beneath and I toppled inside.

"I'm coming!" I cried again as my legs buckled, hitting the floor.

It was an oven, a crackling, suffocating oven with red edges and torrents of smothering, gritty smoke. In two steps, I had her. My stomach lurched as she flopped in my arms. She hung, lifeless. This wasn't Ivy anymore, it was an empty body. My heart exploded as I heaved her over my shoulder. I felt it breaking and tearing open as I dived for the window, having to lower her through before clambering out. I scooped her back up, running as a small explosion echoed behind, shooting out fresh ash and rubble. Around the building, my legs gave way and I skidded down onto my knees.

"Don't leave me, Ivy. Ivy!" I cried as I knelt; as I held her.

Her face was black and grey, but tear-tracks glinted around her eyes. I wiped her golden hair away, but her head lolled as I bought her mouth to my cheek.

"Ivy. It's me. You're out." I screwed my eyes shut, feeling for breath. There was nothing.

She couldn't be gone, she couldn't. She was mine. I'd found her. She was perfect, she was totally perfect. I needed her. I needed every part of her to stay with me.

"Please!"

My voice broke as I stared into her face. She was a shell. She was a hauntingly beautiful, empty shell. Dust sat on her long eyelashes and blood smeared her full, usually pink, lips. I ran my thumb over them and a scream fell out.

"No, no, no!"

The field was filling around me but it didn't matter. Nothing mattered anymore. She was what mattered. She was all that mattered.

"Don't leave me!" I sobbed, parting her lips, pressing mine into them, blowing my air into her, my life into her.

Nothing happened.

I gave her another breath. I gave her everything I had, she could have it all.

Her head rolled, her hair sifting through my fingers as I cradled her. I stared down, holding my breath.

Her eyelids fluttered.

A flicker of life, fleeting and beautiful.

"Come on, Ivy. Please. Don't leave me," I whispered, watching for another flicker.

Her eyelids stilled again as her head became heavy in my hand, her soft cheek tipping into my palm. I screwed my eyes shut and I prayed. I crinkled up my face and begged the universe to let me have her. To give her back. I knew I'd fucked up, but I could be better, I would try again, for her. I would look after her properly, whether she wanted to be with me or not.

Life tumbled back into her as she violently rolled to the ground, coughing and rasping. I noticed rain falling from the sky; paramedics and police were standing around us.

She was breathing.

I pulled her back into my chest, cherishing her life in my arms. Savouring the feeling of her ribs rising and falling. I watched as her small, shaking hand pressed into my cheek, as her breathtaking brown eyes bore into mine.

"Don't leave me," I said one more time, just to make sure. To make sure she stayed.

A paramedic pulled at her shoulder holding an oxygen mask. I was scared to take my eyes from hers, scared if we broke the connection, she would fizzle away, but she tucked herself into my chest, quivering. She was so weak. She was barely there.

I took the mask tentatively from the paramedic, carefully offering it to her, coaxing her. The plastic was cold and firm and it smudged the blood and soot on her face. My fingers trembled as I tried to hold it steady, needing to be as gentle as I could. I felt her small body relax with each breath. She clung to me. She was so weak, but she was trusting me, to keep her safe.

And I knew instantly that I would.

33

Overdue Promises

"Oh Ben!"

I couldn't stay sat on the armchair any longer. He'd detailed everything so honestly, so brutally, almost like he was in a trance. My bare feet moved across the floor as I flung my arms around him, straddling his legs. His strong arms cradled me instantly.

I tucked my chin down over his shoulder, closing every centimetre of space between us I could. "I couldn't tell if it was real, it was all too much. I had all these feeling for you, have, but I needed time to make sure. I felt like you might pity me, or feel guilty. I didn't know if you felt the same."

I drew back to look at him as I tried to make sense of what he'd just told me.

"Ivy, I love everything about you."

My heart pounded in my chest as everything else stilled. My mind searched desperately for a response, but he shook his head, looking around the room.

"I think I knew when you dyed your hair; knew this feeling was different. I felt so protective of you in that moment, it caught me totally unaware. When we got back from our date, I was sure. I lay in bed thinking about you for hours. Thinking about talking with you, being with you, not just lust, but how I just wanted more of all of you." He smiled at me openly, embracing the words as he said them.

All those amazing, beautiful words.

"Ben, I... I had no idea you felt like that."

"I know. It's part of what makes you so captivating – the fact you don't see just how incredible you are; how easy you are to love. It makes me want to show you."

"I don't think I could've done any of this without you, Ben." I laced my fingers together behind his neck. "You've always been there for me, even when I didn't even know to ask. You gave me this life. My life. When you came back from Ireland, when you held my hand, when you chased Sam away." His name clogged my throat. "No one had ever cared for me like that before – it scared me, it didn't feel safe. But... I think I've known that, deep down, I feel the same. I've been in love with you... for a long time."

He looked at me with such adoration I had to force myself not to look away in embarrassment.

"You could have done it without me, Ivy. But I'm glad you didn't."

As I attempted to gather myself, glad he was holding me up, his hand swept up my back and his lips pressed against mine, so delicately it felt like I was floating.

"Now that's sorted," he whispered, his finger tracing my spine, "I'd better work on that begging."

He stood from the armchair, his gaze heavy with affection and desire. I knew I would be begging him to touch me again within seconds. That voice, that confidence, those lips. I wanted them all.

"You're perfect – you know that?" He picked me up effortlessly, my legs hooked round his waist as he lowered us to the rug, pulling the blanket from the chair. "Every part of you. You are beautiful Ivy, and so incredibly sexy; how you move, how your eyes shine at me, how your body responds to me. You get this little look of surprise, like your own body's reactions catch you off guard." He dragged his teeth against my ear. "No one has ever driven me so wild."

Sliding his hands down my back, Ben pressed us closer. He smiled wickedly as my head tilted back and my eyes glazed over.

"Just like that," he whispered.

* * *

Waking up nestled against Ben felt warm and cosy and exciting, but by lunchtime, we both knew we needed a break from the whims of our bodies. We needed clothes, food, and fresh air.

I pushed the lock on the bathroom door when I showered, just to make sure we made it out of the house. Now that we'd broken the sexual tension barrier, it was like there was no space between us.

We needed to be out in public, and satiate our grumbling stomachs.

After walking leisurely into the village, we ended up sitting in a secluded, rocky cove, eating paper-wrapped fish and chips. The sky was blue and we were alone apart from passing walkers and the occasional dog chasing the sea foam. We sat together, wrapped in our coats to stay warm, listening to the soothing rumbling of the glinting, multicoloured stones as each wave crashed against the shore.

"This is a beautiful beach, especially to be able to walk to," I commented, gazing out at the sea as my hunger faded.

Not receiving a reply, I looked over, to see Ben deep in thought, his eyes fixed on the horizon. I admired his face: the curve of his clean-shaven jaw, the slight furrow of his brown brows.

"We used to race to the rock pools. Me and Lucy. It was our favourite place."

"Thank you for sharing it with me."

Ben was silent again for a moment. "We scattered their ashes here. It was what she wanted, Mum."

I leaned into him as we both finished off the last of the chips. "What was she like?" I'd always found her hard to picture. "Your dad and Lucy sound similar in a lot of ways."

Ben nodded. "She was more shy, very intelligent. She'd come out with these amazing insights or points of view when you hadn't even thought she was listening. Her and my dad were two sides of a coin. While Lucy and Dad would charge around and push each other in the water, she would just stand here and stare out to sea. We would sit and talk about different fossils we'd found, or the birds we could see. Not everyone liked her immediately; she needed my dad at big gatherings, let him always lead the way. But, if she liked you, she was the best friend you could have."

With each word he said, my chest tightened. I rested my head on his shoulder, picturing them as the waves crashed. "She sounds great. I wish I could have met her; I wish you'd had her for longer."

Ben folded up the food packets, lacing an arm around my back. The birds were swooping against the clouds, the wind carrying the moisture from the churning sea.

"She'd have liked you a lot. I've always thought that. I think it even annoyed me, at the beginning."

I smiled, running a smooth stone between my fingers. "Why?"

"She would've known you were a good person, straight away. She said to me once: *Ben, make sure you find a girl who looks after you, but a strong one, one that challenges you*. Girls didn't interest me then, like most young boys, and Lucy didn't help, but my mum... she knew I needed people. I think that's why I made such a mess of things when everyone started telling me to settle down. I felt like everyone thought they knew what I wanted. I didn't want to admit Mum was right because admitting how close we were would be admitting how much it hurts now she's gone."

"That's very insightful, Ben," I said softly, hanging on to his every careful word.

"I know these things about myself, I just don't like them."

"Everyone would understand, you know, if you were a bit more open."

He turned to me and smiled. "I have no interest in everyone, just a select few. Just pretty, lost girls who look at me like they're either about to put me in my place or undress me."

I laughed easily, crunching the pebbles beneath my feet. "I'm not lost anymore. So I hope you won't go after any other projects." I paused. "The sex was too good, Ben. I knew you'd be good in bed – I could sense it – but damn."

He exhaled a little laugh. "We're well matched."

"I'll be honest, after hearing what Jessica said, I was a little intrigued. What is it you're into?" I was playing, but he looked awkward, so I filled the strange silence I'd created. "Fancy dress? I mean, I could probably live with something like that."

"It's not that. It isn't a big deal. We just, you know, played around

341

with a few things, and it just wasn't her thing."

I sat up straighter. "What was it?" I'd hoped all the sex would have sated me for a while, but the lust still felt distractingly insatiable.

He shook his head. "Why do you want to have this conversation?"

"Well, I mean, it's always fun to make you squirm a little, but I'm curious. Maybe you can... show me?" I saw his expression shift, hunger burning in his eyes, but he stifled it, adding to my intrigue.

I'd always had a thirst to experiment in the bedroom. The bad experiences never felt like sex, and they made me fearless, not embarrassed. They made me want to push my limits, in a way that *I* could choose. I had always seen a glimmer of something darkly mischievous in Ben's looks, especially the ones he didn't think I noticed.

"If I show you, and you don't like it, I don't want you to feel that I didn't adore how we were last night, or this morning... or in the shower," he recounted, running his hand up my leg with each recollection.

I kissed him, grinning. We *had* made it at least two hours clothed.

I stood up, the stones crunching around my trainers as I reached for his hand and we practically ran back up the winding path and over the verge to the cottage.

Our bodies pressed eagerly together and our lips grew ravenous as we fell through the front door for a second time. Despite my tiredness, my body cried out for him. When the door shut, he pushed me back against it. The wood was firm and the force of it stirred a deep arousal in me. He kept doing that, unlocking new feelings in my own body I didn't even know were there, new buttons to press. What I did know was that I wanted him to find them all.

His tongue slid into my mouth as I couldn't help but groan in response. I felt his lips smile against mine.

"We could just go to bed."

Oh, was it location-based, I wondered?

"Show me," I whispered, breathless, feeling his teeth against my neck.

"If you don't like it, you have—"

"Ben, I trust you."

He slowed, pausing, hovering his pink lips just away from mine, looking stern. "I'm serious, I don't know if this is a good idea. We have time, we don't have to rush things. With everything you've been through..."

I sank, instantly feeling ridiculous.

"What?" he asked as I dropped my eyes down. "Talk to me."

"I don't want you to hold back because of *them*. When I'm with you, close to you, it makes everything go so wonderfully quiet. You are so *sure*; you take control and... I don't know, it sounds silly, but that makes me feel safer than I've ever felt. Because if I can be that vulnerable with you, and you don't hurt me, if I can lay myself bare, and you still take care of me, like you always do – that makes me feel powerful. That makes me feel less damaged."

His eyes flashed with emotion before he delicately cupped my cheeks, tilting my face up to his. "Ivy."

I tipped my head down in his grip. "See, pity, it's so unsexy."

He tilted my face back up. "No, Ivy. It's love. And don't you dare make assumptions about how sexy you are to me, because you have no idea. Okay."

He looked fierce, so I nodded. "Show me what you like, please? Don't hold back. I want to know everything about you, Ben."

He swallowed, licking his lips. Where our bodies were still pressed together, I felt his jeans tighten.

"You're sure?"

I rolled my eyes and slumped back further into the door behind me. "If you're so good at reading my body, as you say, you'll know if I like it or not."

His eyes narrowed. "No, you say stop, or slow down, anything, the second you're not—"

"I can't say stop if you won't go." I pouted.

I could sense his frustration building, something in him simmering like it might explode, and I wanted it.

"Show me. I'm yours, Ben."

That unravelled him, his eyes taking on an entirely new, almost animalistic intensity. His hand wrapped roughly through my hair, pulling it back sharply, before he licked up my neck. My body was his, instantly, but he wasn't done. He kissed me hard, so intensely my mouth lost track of its own boundary.

Oh, hell yes.

My mouth fell open as he drew back and I tried to catch my breath, my chest swelling with each heavy inhale. He dragged a finger firmly over my bottom lip, pulling it down so he could trace a wet path down to my bra. I gasped as his thumb found my nipple, swirling tightly. He grinned as I made no attempt to hide my arousal, panting and flushed.

Taking my hand devilishly softly, he guided me to the table and chairs, stopping only to turn me around and pull off my leggings and underwear in one movement.

"Fuck," I breathed, realising how slick my thighs were.

I tried to gather my thoughts, but he teased his nose up the back of neck, inhaling so deeply I balled my hands into fists. I went to turn to him, to kiss him, to touch him, hell, to crawl up him, but he stopped me by gripping my hips. He was showing me he was in no hurry, and my arousal was devouring it. I heard a click, then a zip as he whipped his leather belt free, no doubt purposely snapping it against the wall behind him. My skin tingled as the anticipation became unbearable, but just as I was about to cry out, he swung a wooden chair from the table, pushing it against my knees, forcing me to sit.

He ran his hands over my arms and I tipped back into his abs, only then realising that he had already taken off his shirt. He paused by my ear, nipping at it until I squirmed.

"Enough sweetheart?" he whispered, grazing his teeth against the corner of my jaw.

I shook my head. "More."

His body jolted; I heard him inhale sharply. He softly took my hands from where they were gripping the chair, pulling them behind me.

"Good, because I want to show you exactly how well I can take care of you."

He wrapped the belt carefully around my wrists. I adjusted on the chair, the pull of the leather sending surges of pleasure to my breasts; more awareness between my legs. The small movement threatened to send me over the edge so I bit my tongue. When he thrust the chair back, tipping me upside down, I opened my mouth to scream but he swallowed it with his lips and I groaned heavily. He kissed me upside down and it was invigorating as everything moved in a different direction.

The chair clunked back down and he was in front of me, shamelessly surveying me as my whole body rose and fell with my rushed breaths.

"You're so damn sexy," I breathed as he grinned and knelt before me, firmly spreading my legs. The cool air sent my head tipping back with a yelp of lust.

Everything throbbed as he made me wait, held me there helplessly at the mercy of my own urges. Watching.

"You're the one on display," he countered. "Like a piece of art."

If I had any blood not rushing between my legs, I would've blushed. His slick, warm tongue brushed me further apart as I gasped with pleasure, licking against my legs, then exactly where I needed him.

He laughed quietly. "I'm half expecting a smartass comment," he teased, between more soft strokes.

I shuddered, searching for words. "Ben. I... what do you want me to say?"

One of his hands gripped my thigh as he slid his fingers inside of me, curving and stroking expertly whilst his tongue pressed into me, knowingly suspending me on the edge. His elbow pushed my knees even further apart as he explored me, deeper and deeper, pressing and twisting. My body responded instantly, perched on the very edge of climax, surrendering to him as he made me feel everything at once.

"What do I *want* you to say? Well, it seems I've finally got you exactly where I want you, after all."

Even his breath alone bought me closer, his lips stimulating my sensitive core.

Then he stopped.

Everything stopped.

"Get up," he commanded.

I stretched my toes, checking that it was possible, as he circled the chair. Pressing my heels down, he gripped my wrists, which was lucky because I immediately wobbled, only able to feel certain parts of my body. Before I could react, he spun me around and pressed me into the table, kicking apart my ankles and again making me wait, one hand down on my back, keeping me locked in place. The feeling of my breasts pressing into the grain washed through my body as I swallowed, cool air tickling my skin.

"Control?" I blabbered, with my face pressed sideways as I felt the heat of him standing behind me, jeans still on. "You like control?"

"I like surrender."

He grabbed my thigh as he said it, curling his fingers into the throbbing skin as I yelped again. I heard him shuffle down his trousers, finally, the tension nearing pain. I revelled in it shamelessly.

"I like that you're stood here, with your legs open, trusting me... waiting for me."

I had never known a man stir my arousal so easily without touching me; with just words. The rush was addictive, and I knew in that moment he could have me like this any time, because I had no inclination to try and stand. Instead, I did the only sensible thing I could think of, and wiggled my legs even further apart, feeling one of my knees butt up against the table leg as he pressed between my cheeks, finally reaching where I ached for him.

"I'm yours, Ben, I trust you," I breathed.

He thrust in easily.

"Ben!"

He thrust harder, deeper, pushing my hips into the wood.

"Ben," I rasped as he pressed a hand on my shoulders.

"Say my name again," he commanded.

"Ben," I gasped. "Ben... uh... Ben!"

My legs tensed as my toes curled, the table taking all of my weight as my body crumpled into a hot, pleasured haze.

His release swiftly followed, his groan of pleasure echoing spectacularly through the open space.

We caught our breath and Ben eased me back up. He carefully undid the belt without speaking, rubbing his thumb over the skin and kissing my wrists gently.

He checked over my body, tenderly turning me, running his fingers softly over my skin. Satisfied, he lifted me into his arms, walking up the stairs and gently lowering me to the bathroom floor.

When I'd used the bathroom, and he had fetched us a drink, we settled dreamily into the bed, lazily watching as our fingers played with each other and our bodies warmed.

"Ben... that was... wild," I murmured, nuzzling even closer to him.

"I nearly lost it completely when I realised how wet you were," he whispered.

I blushed. Hard.

He turned his head to look at me and laughed. "*Now* you blush?"

I turned my face away, but he rolled easily on top of me, kissing my flushed cheeks.

"I think you know full well I haven't been in control of my body since you dragged me inside yesterday," I confessed, looking into his eyes, tucking my face into his palm.

"Was I too rough? I should have checked in more. I would usually. You just seemed like you were into it, and it turned me on so bloody much."

"I was extremely into it. To give you control like that, and trust you. So much of my life has been people taking control away from me. Giving it you, of my own volition, it was empowering."

In response, he leant forward and kissed my lips delicately.

"So, what, now?" I asked.

"Well, I mean, I could probably go again, if you keep looking at me like that."

"Funny. No, I mean, what are we going to do when we go back?

My body needs a rest. Otherwise, I'll start to expect this treatment all day every day."

"All day?" he teased, his fingers slipping over my shoulder and tickling my neck.

I tilted my head in response and took his hand in mine so I could focus. "Ben," I pushed as he grinned, lifting my fingers to his lips like he had before.

"I hear you. I understand. You need some space, so I'll wait. I will wait and you just let me know whenever you feel like indulging me with your company."

"Indulging you?"

"Yes. We can go on more dates, too. I was actually thinking of taking you on holiday, I just hit a stumbling block with your lack of a passport."

"Passport? You thought this through so much you tried to get me a passport?"

"Of course, pretty much after our first date, actually."

I felt emotion rise to my eyes. He noticed, smiling gently.

"That's really sweet, Ben. Thank you... for thinking of that."

"Well, I pretty much sorted it, actually. So, you just let me know when you want to go."

"What about work?"

"What about it?"

I raised an eyebrow at him. "Ben, you *have* gone mad."

He chuckled softly. "I mean, how corny do you want me to get, here? For the record, I would take you home tomorrow, if it were my choice. The spare bed's no longer an option, of course, but like I said, no pressure."

My heart thumped at the thought of a real future with Ben.

"And what about your office, and the VAT project?"

He kissed my forehead briefly as my other hand ran up his back, tracing careless circles.

"We keep it casual. You want to come in and help out, or just plain flirt with me, you'll always be welcome. No job offers, I promise."

"So, you would just have me live with you... as your girlfriend?"

"Well..." He grinned. "I'd propose if I thought you would say yes, for real this time."

"Ben!" I shrieked and pushed both my hands against his chest. "That's not funny."

"I'm not joking... entirely. I get it now, I understand, and I mean it, I'll wait. I will. If there was any part of me that doubted you were my soulmate, you blew that out of the water on that chair earlier."

Every part of me stilled. "Ben," I whispered, not sure what else to say, some ridiculous part of me wanting to scream 'yes' and just get totally lost in him forever.

"Do you think I could make you happy?" he asked, his expression suddenly serious. "I mean it. Do you think it would be enough? You've been through so much. I'll honestly understand if you need to go and see more of the world, explore on your own."

I thought about it. I thought about building a business I was passionate about; having horses; hell, maybe even travelling. But as the possibilities floated through my mind, I knew; I knew with an exact certainty what I'd never known before.

"Ben, I don't want to do anything like that without you."

Out of nowhere, a tear rolled down my cheek, instantly embarrassing me. I wiped it away as Ben stared at me intensely, with an expression I suddenly couldn't read at all.

"What are you saying?" he asked quietly.

"Well, for starters," I sniffed as he held my cheek, ready to catch another stray tear, "I'd love to come home."

EPILOGUE

11 months later

"Why are you charging around with a pot of hummus?" Ben called from his office at the front of our house.

The Christmas after the fire, just before Susan's marvellous turkey dinner, Ben had mysteriously whisked me off to Lucy's village. We'd driven up an over-grown, dirt drive, surrounded by established trees preserving glistening, frosty shadows. When the brambles unfurled to reveal a double-fronted, characterful house, I was in awe. When Ben told me that he and Derek had been renovating it as a surprise, and that there were stables, I cried ugly, happy tears. Lucy had also cried, and we'd all sat around the table, vowing we would always spend Christmas together, as a family.

"Because this is a big deal and if Catherine has taught me anything, it's that you can't have hummus without carrots and I've lost the carrots." My eyes darted around the oak-panelled hall. "How can you lose carrots," I asked myself under my breath. "Wait, where's Clyde." I looked to Ben's feet for our brown labrador, who had a penchant for snack heists.

Ben's leather chair creaked as he glanced around. "Sweetheart, try to stay calm. You've probably already taken them to the barn. I'm not sure even *he* would go after vegetables."

I charged off into the kitchen, heading for the conservatory shouting, "Need I remind you of the time I had to take him to the vet because he ate the salsa!"

Sure enough, there was a brown tail thumping from under one of the sofas in the sunshine.

"Clyde, if you have those—" I stopped as I stepped onto the tile floor, spotting the chewed-up serving tray and trail of orange. "No!"

I dropped to my knees and despairingly gathered up a handful of mauled carrot sticks from under the sofa. Clyde scrambled to inhale as many as he could. I flopped back against the sofa, clutching them, staring up through the leaded glass at the blue sky.

Ben entered, surveying the mess. "They're not coming for the snacks, sweetheart." He reached his hand out to me, but I glared back. He was trying not to laugh and it wasn't helping.

Clyde shoved his wet nose into my cheek in apology.

"You're a bad dog," I scolded.

"Come on," Ben encouraged. "It looks like the front gate is shut, want me to go open it? Forget the carrots."

I thrust my head back against the cushions, groaning. "But then what am I going to do with the hummus? This is a sign, this was all a mistake – hosting was meant to be the easy bit."

Linda had introduced me to another psychologist, Robyn, who had become a good friend. She was doing her PhD on PTSD and wanted to host a psychodynamic, women's therapy group. Jenson, Ben's university friend turned architect, had done such a stunning job designing a large loft room for us to use above the barn, so it had seemed like a good idea to host. Now, I felt like I had just served myself up to have old wounds re-opened. Everyone spoke about me these days like I was this 'amazing role model'; told me I should be 'so proud of everything I'd achieved'. But that just wasn't how it felt.

I'd set up a small business, organising specialised, therapy-focused riding lessons, but it was as much about me as my clients. When I'd found out Marcus had been killed in prison, I'd barely spoken for three days, then lost track of time on a hack, freaking everyone out. It was like I'd flipped back to Elle and forgot everything, everyone. I'd just kept riding until a jogger spotted me and told me people were out searching. When I got back, Ben had yanked me off the horse so hard we both nearly fell, mud all up his work trousers from searching for me.

Taking the stand in the case against Barncs and Dores had felt like adding a new trauma to my list altogether. It had involved not only publicly recounting the worst experiences of my life in front of my family, in front of Ben, but also being judged by the jury on whether my story was 'believable' enough. They had been found guilty of nearly all the charges, thankfully, but I was still waiting for the relief to kick in.

Henworth was now abandoned, or closed down, depending who you spoke to. I'd been back to visit not long before the Barnes and Dores case, the private lawyer Ben had hired having suggested we go back to look for evidence to help with the prosecution. It made the news: journalists queuing at the police tape whilst we looked around. Stepping back into the mouldy shell of my old home had made me feel physically sick and emotionally numb. The entire space would have fit inside Ben's bedroom in the apartment and I could still remember looking down at how clean my trainers were against the damp carpet. It hadn't felt like a previous home, it had felt like a prison cell, and the realisation had been more confronting than anyone could have prepared me for. Ben had dropped everything and headed over as soon as I called, and I'd fallen into his arms in front of all the cameras. I wished now that he'd never had to see it, but I'd needed him perhaps more than ever in that moment.

Ben reached down and gripped Clyde's collar, walking him out of the French doors before coming back to sit on the sofa behind me. I leant my head against his knee.

"You'll be fine. Robyn is managing it, remember? You're meant to benefit from this session, and Paige will be there."

He rested his hand on my shoulder and I shut my eyes, sighing. He had always had that power: when my head was spinning, he could bring me back with just a touch.

"What if I say the wrong thing?"

His other hand pressed into my other shoulder and he ran his fingers down my arms, leaning forwards to prise the carrot remains from my clenched palm.

"This isn't an interview or a TV appearance. The only expectation is that you're there, not here clutching crudités." He dropped the carrots onto the sofa, grimacing at the dog slobber. "Come on, Mrs Carlson. We don't skip out on our therapy."

I grunted, but he wasn't having any of it, lifting me from under my arms and hoisting me to standing.

"Who knew you'd be the one preaching to me about therapy."

"Who knew," he repeated, turning me to face him.

The last year had softened him, and I admired it in his face as he offered me a gentle smile. He could have closed himself off further than ever after the fire, after everything we had suffered as we battled against the justice system. But he hadn't. He'd decided to open himself up for me, and I would be forever grateful for that.

"Thank you," I relented, lacing my fingers through his and leaning forward to kiss him.

Once I had propped the big wooden gate open, I arranged the handles of the mugs in the room above the barn three more times before the first car pulled up. I was thankful to see Paige's Corsa. She had been one of my bridesmaids alongside Lucy and Charlie, and it was nice to do this with her. I started to pour her a coffee, wondering if she would take a biscuit; if I should offer her one. Probably not, if she was feeling anything like me about all this.

Robyn was next to arrive with Harper, who was younger-looking than I'd expected, followed by Fox, who had amazingly colourful hair. Lyla was last, arriving just before we were about to take our seat, ready to begin.

AUTHOR'S NOTE

Thank you for reading Ben and Ivy's journey. As an avid reader, I was tired of seeing trauma portrayed in a softened or 'mainstream stylised' way. I hope parts of this story made you uncomfortable or made you think. I hope part of how Ivy dealt with things surprised you, because that's real life. If victims are too strong, they are often perceived as liars; if they cry too much, they are chasing sympathy. The reality is, every trauma is different because every person is different. I hope I was able to do this justice, and that you enjoyed the journey.

For anyone (and there are far too many of us) who has experienced trauma and PTSD, I am sorry for your burden and encourage you to grow and be brave in whatever way you can, whilst always being kind to yourself. There are more stories of strong, flawed, fantastic women I would love to share with you, along with more topics I think we should all be talking about more openly. Find me on my socials or my website, and sign up to my newsletter to receive all my updates first. I would love to see you there!

BookTok: @lgraceauthor
Instagram: @laurengraceauthor
Facebook: Lauren Grace Author
www.lgraceauthor.co.uk

ACKNOWLEDGEMENTS

Writing has been immensely healing, and publishing, a little dyslexic girl's dream.

Firstly, thank you to my brilliant husband, Josh; you made me feel safe enough to dive into the feelings I knew I wanted to explore. Thank you to Lauren for making me send you my ropey draft – you gave me that big, first push I never knew I needed. Thank you to all my beta readers: Sherrie, Julie, Ella-Mae and Sophie. Sherrie, your highly suspicious mind makes me laugh, but now helps me work on all my characters. Thank you to Sian for your book loans and post-it notes, they re-ignited my love of reading. Thank you to Julie, my beautiful neighbour, for always being more than a friend and cable tying me in your shed. I couldn't have done it without you all!

Contacting Cranthorpe Millner felt right from the very beginning and they have been incredible to work with. They have embraced the message and complicated characters, allowing me the creative freedom I needed to do this justice. Whenever I have worked on the book, I've felt incredibly fortunate to have gone on this journey with them.

Most importantly (of course), thank you to you, my reader. Thank you for believing in me enough to pick this up, I hope you enjoyed it. Thank you for the ongoing support I have received on social media – you didn't have to back me, but I am so glad you did. On days where I got stuck or life got in the way, you pushed me back to my laptop with every comment, like and message.

Here's to next time!